D1447408

Cotton Club Princess

Karla Diggs

Published by Waldorf Publishing
2140 Hall Johnson Road
#102-345
Grapevine, Texas 76051
www.WaldorfPublishing.com

Cotton Club Princess

ISBN: 978-1-945174-18-6
Library of Congress Control Number: 2016957001

Dedication

For my aunts Sally and Constance.

Chapter 1

Mrs. Barden loves to have her bed sheets starched and ironed, so the corners are perfectly folded. That is the only explanation I have for the lady being so stiff! My name is Nostalgia Richardson and most days I would rather be somewhere else then doing housework for the Barden family. It is 1928, and I'm a sixteen-year-old colored girl from Spivey's Grove, South Carolina! So it may seem to you I have no choice but to clean up after white folks, but I have a dream. I want to go to New York and dance at this place called the Cotton Club. I know they sell liquor and don't allow colored folks in it unless they're serving and entertaining whites, but I don't care!

My parents would kill me if they knew I lied about how much the Bardens were really paying me. I told Mama Mrs. Barden was giving me $1.00 a week. Ha! She is actually paying me $2.00 a week! I give my family $1.00 while saving the other half in a sock underneath a loose floor board in my room, until I'm ready to kick the red Spivey's Grove dust off the bottom of my shoes, and run toward my destiny! Not bad for a little girl from a backward Southern town, huh?

I live with my parents and share a room with my fourteen-year-old sister, Lily. Of the two of us, she is the good girl. She sings in the choir at the First AME Church on Water Street. She doesn't dream of anything but marrying Henry Whit, her beau of two years, and making our parents proud. I'm not saying there's anything wrong with what she wants, but there's a big world out there, and truth be told, I can't understand anyone who has no desire to see it!

One thing I do appreciate about the Bardens is they allow me to indulge in their private library, especially since colored folks aren't allowed in the Public Library downtown. In spite of finishing sixth grade four years ago I, unlike most girls my age, never stopped reading. I couldn't stop because I love it so much! All of my friends are married and raising families now. Me? I'm still free, so I can read, or go to New York just as soon as I feel I have saved enough, which may not be long!

Anyway, until I can get out of Spivey's Grove reading is how I escape. Most folks around here avoid books as soon as they stop going to school, but I read now more than I did when I was there! It really irritates my parents. I guess because they can't even read the one book they own: The Bible! For all they know they might be committing a sin by not reading it. After all, they have to rely on what Reverend Clark tells them about God. There is this one line in The Bible I do remember more than anything else: Seek ye my face! Now how can a body really "seek His face" if they can't read the instructions on how to do it? Makes no sense to me.

"Nostalgia, after you're done with the laundry you may leave for the evening!" Mrs. Barden just called to me from the hallway while I finish putting the newly starched linens on the bed.

"Yes Ma'am, Mrs. Barden!" I call back.

The one thing I don't mind about doing housework is that it's relatively peaceful. When you do exactly as the

Mrs. tells you nobody bothers you, so it gives you time to hear your own thoughts. Don't get me wrong, it is worrisome to have to clean someone else's home for money, but at my house, my name is constantly being called for one thing or another. Like last night, my mother wouldn't stop calling me to help her in the kitchen with something, and I had just gotten home! It never dawned on anybody at my house that sometimes a moment to yourself might keep you from being two straitjackets away from an insane asylum.

My mother says now that I am sixteen a woman's work is never done. Ha! Never would occur to her that this depends on the woman. I'm not ever going to live the life she's living, or the one Lily's setting up for herself. Those two are so desperate and miserable they don't even realize it. If I have my way I am going to perform at the Cotton Club, singing and dancing. Heck, I might even end up in a Broadway show like Rose McClendon! Most folks around here have never heard of Broadway, let alone seen any further than the frustrations standing in front of their faces. I know where I want to be, I have an idea of how I'm going to see it happen, and I am determined not to live my life blaming my circumstances on my color, or being a woman, or being poor.

I tucked the last corner underneath the mattress as fast as I could before spreading the quilt across the bed and fluffing the down pillows with the His and Her embroidery. The whole room is white except for the beautiful brown oak furniture.

I watch myself in the mirror over the dressing table as I get my coat out of the closet. If I'm not mistaken I'm just what they're looking for at the Cotton Club. At 5'7, 120 pounds, and skin a few shades lighter than a copper penny, I'm "Tall, Tan, and Terrific" as they say on the radio show! My nose and lips are just the right thickness, while my eyes and hair are black as untouched molasses. I don't have to work as hard as Lily to keep my hair straight, either.

I personally think I am beautiful, except for this ugly brown coat with the rip underneath the left armpit. As badly as I need another, I refuse to dip into my savings, not to mention if I did that would be a dead giveaway to my parents I've been holding out on them. Thank God winters down here are pretty easy to bear. But I've read New York winters are a lot colder. I'll wait until I get there to get me another coat. Heck, it might even be a sable!

I wish Mrs. Barden good evening as I step out onto the veranda and into the chilly night. The stars are out, so to save money I decide to go on ahead and walk toward the colored side of town instead of taking an omnibus. But before I begin my journey, I separate my wages in the darkness just above the steps. What I intend to give to my parents goes in my left pocket while what I plan to give myself goes in my underwear until I hear Lily's snoring, then I can put that with the rest of my stash.

It amazes me the way the neighborhood changes gradually as I walk down Main Street. It starts out gentile with the porches wrapping around the big houses. In the summer these same houses have white folks sitting in the rocking chairs, sipping lemonade and calling kind greetings to the neighbors that stroll by. These are the "pillars of our community" as they liked to think of themselves.

After about ten blocks the houses get smaller with the poor crackers congregating with a few coloreds here and there playing banjos and harmonicas, drinking shine, and dancing until the soles of their shoes begin to split. I admit that on some nights when I have not gotten paid, and I'm kind of in a good mood I may stop and dance a little jig, but not for too long. The last thing I need is for someone from the First AME Church to see me dancing and tell my daddy!

After another ten blocks, I find myself in my neighborhood, and closer to the house where I was raised. My side of town on a summer evening would be filled with ladies quietly fanning as they gossiped about each other, complained about their boss ladies, and waited for their husbands to come home from the sawmill, the bus station, the shrimp boats, or the fields.

The houses are even smaller than the ones the poor crackers live in, with a stoop instead of a front porch, let alone a veranda. The smell of fried pork wafts through the air no matter what time of year it is, and in the spring and summer the iceman didn't come to these parts, so just forget about sipping on a cold Royal Crown Cola unless you visit Chavis's General Mercantile when no whites are shopping. Tonight, however, is a typical winter night. No one is on the stoops because they'd rather be in their homes sidled up to the wood stove, eating shrimp gumbo or Brunswick stew.

When I walk in, I say a meek "Hello," while making a beeline for the coat stand, even before my eyesight adjusts to the brightness of the candle lights in the sitting room. It is relatively warm and well-lit in this room because we have a small fireplace, unlike most of these houses that have only a woodstove in the kitchen. Between the woodstove and the fireplace our house is fairly cozy in the winter.

I notice two figures, one sitting on the couch and the other in the easy chair when I first turn away from the coat stand. Then I realize it isn't my mother and father, but my father and another man. "Oh," I say in surprise, and give a small wave. In my attempt to pass by with as much discretion as possible, my peripheral vision makes out the second figure to be that of Noah Holdtstaff, the biggest bootlegger in town! He seems to be devouring me with his eyes as I walk by. What the ham gravy is he doing in our house, I wonder, my daddy doesn't even drink, let alone smoke reefer!

"What is that stinking bootlegger doing here?" I ask my mother as soon as I get into the kitchen, noticing she's pouring two cups of coffee and setting them on a tray to take out to the sitting room. She doesn't look up from what she's doing; in fact, she acts as though she doesn't hear me! It makes me angry! "Mama, what is he doing here?" I grab her arm to stop her so she would at least look at me, but she still manages not to when she answers in her lilting drawl,

"Mr. Holdtstaff has business with your daddy!" She takes the tray into the other room with such grace. A real lady, she is, and a real push over I might add!

My mother was sixteen when my father had her shipped here from Richmond, Virginia to be his wedded wife back in 1911. She has never discussed with me or my sister what it was like taking her first and only train ride to marry a man she didn't know, who happened to be 18 years her senior as well.

It seems daddy had gotten her picture from a deacon at the church. Apparently, she was the daughter of a relative who no longer thought it should be his responsibility to feed her anymore. After all, she was sixteen, so why wasn't she married? My father must have been pretty well satisfied with her picture because he obviously agreed to the match.

The photograph, which sits in a little frame on the mantle of the fireplace, is the only one my mother has ever taken, and she is breathtaking in it. Her hair is pinned in a chignon that wraps like a crown around her head. Her blouse is lacy and white with a high-necked collar while the long black skirt cinches in the waistline, giving character and definition to her soft rounded hips. Mama's skin is fair with a hint of sun, puffy lips, and slanted eyes. Even though she's not smiling in the picture, the delicate features of her face are somehow brought out in the way she holds her head. So modest, yet graceful. I like to think my father fell in love with her the moment he saw her, because everything between them is so practical and perfunctory. It hurts to think my mother's beauty was possibly wasted on a man who failed to appreciate it!

I get a plate from the cupboard, about to help myself to what I think is some leftovers when my mother comes back just in time to stop me. "Mr. Holdtstaff will be staying for dinner. You will have to wait to eat."

"May I ask why we're eating so late tonight?" Usually, everyone has eaten by the time I get home, and I must admit I kind of like eating by myself. It unnerves me talking about how my day went, or feeling awkward when no one is speaking at all.

"No, you may not ask! Now go get cleaned up and put on your best dress," she demands.

Put on my best dress for what?

But instead of asking the question, I run out to the back yard and manage to pump a little bit of water from the well in the biggest tin bowl we have that happens to be clean. The water is cold, but it revives me as I splash it on certain parts of my body and my face while standing on the back porch in the dark. I think I might nearly freeze to death between bathing in the frigid water, braving the frosty night air, and my bare feet grazing the pine splinters of the porch.

I empty the bowl out into the yard when I'm done, scampering through the back screen door, crossing the short breezeway, and into the bedroom I share with my younger sister, Lily. She's dressed in her best dress too, seated on the bed, embroidering some new work of art. Probably something else she intends to add to her hope chest for when she finally marries Henry. Instead of being cordial she looks like she wants to say something, but doesn't know what. Why is everybody acting so peculiar, and I still don't know what the ham gravy that damn bootlegger is doing in our house!

Finally, she asks me how I'm doing. "Fine. I'll be even better when that man is gone! Up there salivating at me like I might be a bowl full of chitlins!" I manage to laugh at my own joke. When I look up, she has tears in her eyes! "Lily, what's the matter?" She can't seem to look at me either, much the same way Mama had done in the kitchen. "Lily, talk to me! What's going on?"

She breathes hard, shooting an exasperated glance at the door before answering in a hushed tone. "Daddy brought that man here to marry you, Nostalgia." She breaks into full blown sobs upon this revelation.

I sink to the bed as her words anchor my spirit to bottomless depths. It begins to make sense. I'm the same age as Mama when she came here from Richmond, and I'm still not married! For them, sixteen marks the transition from being a girl sheltered by her parents, to becoming a woman subservient to her husband! They are struggling, so they have to get me out of the house, and though Daddy doesn't much like him, Noah Holdtstaff has money! Our houseguest may be a greasy, racketeering bootlegger, but Daddy sees provision for me, his oldest daughter.

It made perfect sense! Getting dressed up, waiting for me to come home before they ate, and him! Black and tan shoes, and felt fedoras don't hide that he's seventeen years older than Mama, one year younger than Daddy, fat, sweating, and stinking like a mess of fourteen-day-old pigs' feet!

I begin to cry too, in spite of myself, but I couldn't cast off the thought of the life of drudgery that would be mine if I go through with the marriage! Lily walks over to the bed to try to comfort me. We must have hugged each other in tears for a good ten minutes before we are summoned by our father's baritone. "Be out directly," I shout back, trying to sound as cheerful as possible.

Lily helps me put my dress on and fix my hair. This must have been what it was like when those queens locked in the London Tower prepared for their executions. Getting all dolled up, being fussed over, only to die. Marrying a man you don't want is not a death of the body, but of the spirit.

At least my daddy was handsome in those pictures I saw of him when he was younger, heck he still is now, but this man… oh dear God, could this really be happening? Panic races through my brain like a squirrel being flushed out by a pack of beagles trying to please a hunter! Now, my mama might have put up with this mess, but I certainly couldn't see myself doing it. Hell, I couldn't see a period with all the tears blurring my vision. I can't tell if I'm mad, sad, or what, but I do know I have got to get out of this!

Lily and I walk into the dining area hand in hand to try to keep the tears from spilling out onto our cheeks. I try my best to smile. We take our places at the table with Daddy at the head, Ma next to him on his right side, while Lily takes the seat to the right of her. Across from them, I'm on Daddy's left side with Noah seated to my left, and boy does he smell! His yellow teeth smiled back at me like he's doing me a favor. Ha! I'd rather eat nails boiled in the liquid fire.

Dinner lasts a good two or three hours with the men exchanging nonsense while we ladies look on with our heads hanging down demurely, like daffodils on the first day of spring. Now, I don't know what Ma and Lily are thinking about, but by the time dinner's over, I know exactly how I'm getting out of this mess!

* * * *

The next morning, I get up bright and early for work. I make sure Lily is out of the room, so she doesn't see me put a few extra things in my purse: a pair of fresh underwear, a cake of lye soap wrapped in a washcloth, and a photograph of her and me as little girls. I had taken the stash out of my hiding place the night before after I'd heard her snoring, and put it in my underwear. I usually don't wear underwear to bed, but this is a different occasion.

I put my ratty coat on and look around the room one last time. I hold back my tears with all my strength, lest my family will get suspicious. I walk out the bedroom and down to the kitchen, dead set on not changing my mind. I stand at the door for a few moments listening to the clank of the silverware against the dishes. As usual, they ate in silence. "Pass the butter, please, Lily," said my daddy in that deep rich voice I love so much. A tear escapes my eye when I realize this might be the last time I hear the sweetness of it. I had to get myself together, or else I would get found out. If I didn't do it now, I would be stuck here to marry that weasel!

I quickly brush the tears off my face before sticking my head in the door, "I'm gone on to work!" I yell.

"Nostalgia, come in here for a minute." My father's voice always stopped me, as I knew it would. "You get on home as soon as you can tonight. I got some things I've got to discuss with you."

I seize my composure before lying to my father. "Yes, Daddy. I'll be home directly."

* * * *

I left for work that morning with a heavy heart at the thought I may never see them again. I already missed the stoic, quietness of my mother as she floated like a magic carpet around the house doing woman's work, my sister's sweet soprano singing voice resting in my ears, my father's manly gait as he walked anywhere, commanding respect. The strength of his presence shocked white folks whenever they showed up in the yard to collect a debt.

Now that I thought about it I'd never been scared of anything… until now. Oh, my, God… I was leaving. All along I talked to myself about it, but now the time had come! Did I dream about it so long I began to think all I would ever do was dream about it? I was prepared for it situation-wise, I mean, I had the money, and it wouldn't be anything for me to go down to the station and pick up a ticket… but was my mind and my heart prepared to probably never see my family again? The people I'd lived with every day since I was born… was I really ready for this…?

"Nostalgia! Do you hear me speaking to you?" Mrs. Barden's gentile southern speech had taken on an edge at the suggestion the hired help was ignoring her. I didn't remember walking to work, much less getting here.

I must have been in a daze since I stepped off the stoop in front of my parents' house. "No, Ma'am! You were saying?"

"I was saying I needed you to dust the chair legs and baseboards today in addition to your regular dusting." The furrow in her brow seemed to ask if I had dropped my brain somewhere down the street. Mrs. Barden tried not to get too personal with the hired help. However, that didn't stop me from thinking I might be able to use her in the future.

"Yes, Ma'am, Mrs. Barden!" I chirped as a recovery. I didn't feel much like doing any housework, but maybe it would keep me from crying. It's funny how you didn't want to do anything when your heart was heavy. I felt like a circus elephant was tap dancing on my chest!

Instead of using the feather duster I decided to fill a bucket full of hot water and Murphy's Oil Soap since it would be the last time I dust the beautiful oak and maple furniture in this grand house. I also had to place all the books I borrowed back in the private library. I was right in the middle of *Vindication of Women's Rights* by Mary Wollstonecraft. I guess I'd gotten all I needed from that book since I was in the process of vindicating myself from the circumstance of being forced to marry… Goodness! I was really leaving…

"Nostalgia! What is the matter with you today?" Mrs. Barden's lips were pursed together now!

"I…" but before I could conjure a flimsy excuse the tears gushed from my eyes.

"Oh, dear! I knew something was wrong by the way you came in without saying good morning to me! Take a deep breath and tell me what's wrong."

I took several before I could speak so Mrs. Barden could understand what I was saying. Before I knew it, I had spilled the beans and everything else! I told her about going home last night and finding Noah Holdtstaff talking to my daddy. I told her what Lily had said to me and how I had been planning to run away anyway, but because of my daddy's plans to marry me off, I had to go through with it sooner than I wanted to. She hugged me, listening with a sympathetic ear.

The whole time I had been working here, she and I had an unspoken rule not to get any closer than employer/ help relations. It was bad enough her snooty, fake friends knew I borrowed books from her, and they were right in suspecting I always used the indoor toilet like she and Mr. Barden.

One day when she was having a luncheon for the Ladies Aid Society and I was serving, I heard one of them say when they thought I was out of earshot "… and I told her to stop hiring those pretty light-skinned colored gals! It might give Thomas some ideas, not to mention the help."

Ha! As if I could be interested in her bald-headed, pot-bellied husband! He's always gotten here when I was on my way home anyway. In fact, the most he has ever said to me was, "Evening, Nostalgia."

"Mrs. Barden, I need a favor from you," I asked.

"Anything, Dear." Thank God she didn't hesitate!

"If I sent Lily's letters to your address would you see that she got them?"

"Absolutely I would! Do you have everything you need? It's very cold up there. Let me let you have one of my coats. I've been meaning to give it to you ever since I noticed that rip in the left underarm of yours."

"That would be lovely!"

Instead of cleaning I spent the rest of the morning choosing select pieces from Mrs. Barden's extensive wardrobe. She and I were about the same size. She gave me four flapper-style dresses she had bought on a shopping trip to New York, insisting they were just "vacation clothes" and she didn't have anywhere to wear them around here anyway. She also gave me two pairs of high heel shoes, a wool coat with silk lining, a fur collar and cuffs, a matching fur hat, and an old suitcase, which was new to me because I'd never had the pleasure of owning one, or anything she'd given me, for that matter! This made the leaving a little more bearable.

"Now you look like a real New Yorker!" Mrs. Barden beamed. "Now don't smile at anyone, always look like you know where you're going, especially if you don't, be wary of strangers, and don't give any beggars your money… Money? Do you have enough?"

"I have $375.00," I said.

Mrs. Barden was deep in thought for a moment, then with finality she said, "I'm going to run down to the bank, and while I'm out I'll check the bus schedule. We have to get you on the next one well before your parents know you've gone… or maybe…" Her eyes lit up, "We should leave now so I can take you to the station in the next town. Everybody knows you here, and word is bound to get back

to your folks!" I will admit I hadn't thought of that!
Somebody would tell Daddy and Ma they saw me there,
wouldn't they?

I placed everything she had given me, except the coat
of course, neatly into the suitcase. I also transferred my
extra underwear, the lye soap, and the picture of Lily and
me from my purse into the suitcase as well. It was heavy,
but I managed to carry it.

I put some of the money in my purse, left some in my
underwear, and the rest got stored in various secret pockets
in the lining of the coat. Mrs. Barden also allowed me to
keep the copy of *World's Best Fairy Tales* by Hans
Christian Andersen because she knew Cinderella was my
favorite. It seemed appropriate since she'd taken on the role
of my Fairy God Mother! Today would have been grand
under happier circumstances.

I put on the coat and gathered the suitcase she had
given me before following her out to the garage. Mrs.
Barden pulled the top up on the Chevrolet and told me to
get in the back seat with my suitcase and scoot down as far
as I could. First, she was going to stop at the bank, then she
was taking me to the bus station in Yemassee.

That back seat was so uncomfortable with lugging the
suitcase and wearing that heavy coat, and it was already
small to begin with! I was in no position to argue, though.
She had helped me so much that morning.

While Mrs. Barden was in the bank, I could not stop
wondering when my family would figure out I wasn't
coming home that evening, or what they would do when it
finally sunk in for them. It probably wouldn't become real

to me until I got on the bus! I never imagined I would be leaving like this, but how else would it have been? Would my father have allowed me to go up north for no other reason except I wanted to be there? The more I thought about it, I came to the conclusion I would have had to sneak off anyway!

I also wondered why Mrs. Barden was so eager to help me, and how she knew exactly what I needed to do! I mean, it would not have dawned on me to leave from a station other than the one in town until after I'd bought my ticket, and by that time it might have been too late! It was morning, if the bus was coming in the afternoon, somebody who knew my parents would have told them before it came. My escape would have been intercepted before my foot hit the platform!

When she got back into the car I had to ask her, "Mrs. Barden, have you ever…"

"Ever what, Dear?" She had that same lilting drawl as my mama.

"Have you ever had to… leave in a hurry?"

"As a matter of fact, I have. You see, my daddy wanted to marry me off to someone too, but I was in love with Mr. Barden, and I was determined to marry for love. So we ran off and eloped. I stayed away for about a year, but I managed to keep contact with Mama. Eventually, Daddy got used to the idea that I married who I wanted, and he forgave me."

"Somehow I doubt mine will forgive me for leaving."

"Well you never know. I think it's a good idea you plan on keeping in touch with Lily. You do remember my phone number and address, or should I write it down for you?"

"No, ma'am, that won't be necessary. I've got a memory like an elephant!" She kind of chuckled when I said this.

She gave me some greenbacks stuffed into a small bankroll before we got out of the car at the Yemassee Bus Station. "I know I gave you your wages last evening, so consider this a parting bonus for being such a diligent employee for the past four years."

Once we were out of the car, we stood there like a couple of sentimental old friends looking at each other for what may have been the last time, and now that I think about it, that's exactly what we were, we just didn't know until that moment we had so much in common. My suitcase was heavy and pulling down my left shoulder while the wool and fur coat hung over my right forearm.

She finally broke the silence with a quiver in her voice and a shiny film covering her blue eyes. "Pardon me, but I wasn't expecting to see you leave today. Well, I wish you all the best… and you be careful up there." She took something else out of her pocket as if she could give me anything else! I looked at the little slip of paper, and it was her phone number and address after all. "You know memories can play tricks on us. Keep it somewhere safe and use it anytime you see fit, okay?"

"Yes, Ma'am." We hugged for a little longer than we should have before I broke the embrace and crossed the street to the bus station.

* * * *

Karla Diggs   Cotton Club Princess

    When I got inside, I bought my ticket and read the bus
schedule. The bus for Penn Station in New York City
would be leaving in about 25 minutes, with major stops in
Charleston, Charlotte, Raleigh, Richmond, and Washington
for a one-hour layover. The next major stop after the
layover would be in Delaware, followed by Philadelphia,
New Jersey, then finally, New York! It was now 7:00 am!
According to the schedule, I wouldn't see New York City
until, 9:30 pm! I'd never been on a bus longer than a few
minutes at a time traveling around Spivey's Grove. This
certainly would be an adventure!

    I figured I'd better use those 25 minutes to relieve
myself. I found the colored only restroom and luckily there
was no one in there, so I sat in a stall, and had a good cry.
My last cry, I decided, before I left South Carolina to begin
my new life.

    Once I was out of the stall, I washed my hands,
checked my hair, and made sure all my tears were dried.
The atmosphere had changed when I ventured back into the
waiting area! This time it was a bustle of activity with
women fussing over whining babies and men talking about
starting a game of craps or Three Card Monty. Some folks
were standing in a listless daze while others were sitting on
their luggage if they had the luxury of owning some sort of
satchel. I was one of those lucky few thanks to Mrs.
Barden.

    When I got in line, I noticed there would be two
omnibuses, one for whites and one for coloreds. They
checked our tickets, herding us onto the bus like cattle. As
soon as I snagged a window seat, the lady right behind me

was on my heels claiming the seat nearest the aisle. She smelled of cold chicken grease and whiskey. I knew then it would be a long ride.

Chapter 2

I woke to a new seat mate and some argument between a mother and child over the last pork chop. It had not occurred to me to pack anything to eat as the smells of different foods wafted up my nose. I was so hungry, and I really needed a bathroom.

The bus driver stopped at the side of the road several times for coloreds to use the woods because most of the small stations didn't have restroom accommodations for us. Thankfully I was no stranger to using the great outdoors, let alone distinguishing between poisonous and non-poisonous leaves to fold for makeshift toilet paper. Northerners on their way down and back from visiting family down here were another story! One little boy complained, crying he was itching down there after going outside. That could only mean one thing: his mama had folded the wrong kind of leaf! That poor thing would surely be suffering for the rest of the journey.

As I grew hungrier, I began to wonder what Mama would be cooking for dinner tonight, and when they might guess I knew the plan and had no intention of returning home. I would not allow myself to shed another tear over how they were going to attempt to be rid of me—and to a bootlegger at that! It made me kind of mad the more I thought about it. I was supposed just to sit there and let them tell me how to live. Just because you gave me life does not mean my life belongs to you. I might have been sad and lonely, but I was free. I might have been hungry, but I was in control of my destiny. I might have been a lamb among lions, but I was the judge and jury of my limits. For the first time since realizing I may never see my parents or sister again, the tears rolling down my cheeks were of joy and relief!

As soon as we got to Washington, D.C., I got off the bus and used a good and proper bathroom! Even though it was for coloreds, it had stalls, toilet paper, and running water. I splashed the water on my face, dampened my washcloth and lye soap, and wiped under my arms. Mrs. Barden let me take some mint from out of her garden before I left, so I chewed on a sprig of it then swished more water around in my mouth to kind of freshen my breath.

I found a vendor selling cups of vegetable soup and soda crackers. Even though there was no meat in the soup itself, I could taste chicken stock in the base. Yummy and satisfying!

I figured I'd better hurry back to the bus as soon as I finished eating so I could hopefully reclaim my seat. I could have left my belongings on the bus and just showed the new driver my re-boarding ticket, but I trusted no one. I was alone. As a result, I felt I had no choice but to keep my satchel and coat with me.

"How much longer before we get to New York?" I asked the driver.

He took his time inspecting my ticket before stamping it and giving it back, "Eight hours."

Eight hours. Eight hours before I could shake the dust of this grueling trip off my body and mind, and longer than that before I could stretch out in a good bed. I wanted this so I couldn't complain.

Once I got settled into wherever I ended up I knew the first thing I would have to do was write my sister a letter. Goodness, she must be upset with me. I left her to her own devices with Daddy and Ma. But I'm sure now that I was gone they would probably let her go on ahead and marry Henry. The plan always had been to get me out of the house first, and she'd be gone soon after that. I didn't think it mattered I made the move of my own volition, just as long as I was gone.

The bus moved again, and I got another seat mate, a young man about my age. I thought nothing of it, closing my eyes as my brain drifted in and out of nowhere special. One moment I was home listening to Lily's coloratura soprano voice hitting unmitigated heights, and savoring Mama's buttery cornbread. Another moment I was watching myself dance on a stage with my tap shoes keeping time with some Jelly Roll Morton masterpiece. All the time no matter where my visions ended up, I could feel a hand moving up my thigh and a hot whisper in my ear…WAIT A MINUTE! GET YOUR MONKEY HANDS OFF OF ME, FOOL! I was on my feet in an instant, swatting him upside his head, once I realized I was being taken advantage of!

"Oh, I, I was jest…"

"No, you were about to lose some damn fingers, fool!" I kind of patted the lining of my coat and my person to make sure he hadn't taken any of my money while I slept. As I pulled my satchel from between him and me, I got back into the aisle, slapping him square across the face!

An older lady sitting closer to the front behind the driver slid over onto the window seat to make room for me as I sat down next to her. "Well that was quite a show, and I can't say that I blame you. My name is Mrs. Evelyn Spears. What's your name, dear?"

"Nostalgia, Ma'am."

"Nostalgia! That's different. How far are you going?"

"All the way to New York. I want to go to Harlem."

"Is that right? Well, I declare! I'm coming from my sister's funeral in Raleigh, N.C. I've lived in Harlem since I was in my 20s."

"You have? Wow! What made you leave North Carolina?"

"Oh, my husband just couldn't stand living there. I'm sure I don't have to tell you the south is a hard place to live for colored folks, especially men. He found a job as a Pullman porter on the Reading Railroad, and of course Penn Station New York was one of the regular visits. He told me to start packing and that he would send for me as soon as he found a place to live. Well, luckily I listened. I was on a New York-bound train within a month of him starting the job!" She chuckled as she continued reliving the memory, "We lived on 145th Street and St. Nicholas Avenue. He made enough so I didn't have to work. I enjoyed taking care of my house for once. I didn't particularly like him being gone four nights out of the week, but it was a good living. You know, a man loves to be able to take care of his wife on his own without her help."

I could attest to that. My father would never allow my mother to work outside of our house, or to cook for any other man but him.

Mrs. Spears went on to explain her husband died some years back and she was living on his pension from the railroad. I asked her why she had taken the bus instead of the train, "Oh, trains remind me so much of Daniel. We used to take trips together all the time. I don't travel as much anymore. Now that I'm older and widowed, it just isn't as much fun. So what has given you the courage to come this way by yourself?"

"Well, I'm from Spivey's Grove, South Carolina, born and raised, and I found out my daddy was planning on marrying me off to a man I couldn't bear the thought of calling 'husband', so I left. I guess they've figured out by now I'm gone."

"Oh, you poor dear! So you've been riding since early this morning?"

"Yes, Ma'am!"

"Well, what do you plan to do in New York?"

I decided I'd better get to know her before I go telling her all my business, "Oh, I'm not quite sure just yet."

"Well, you're welcome to stay with me if you like. I own a boarding house, and I happen to have a room available. We can discuss payment arrangements after you've seen the place and decided whether or not you want to stay there."

"That would be lovely!" I was so relieved!

* * * *

From Pennsylvania Station we took a cab to upper
Manhattan, otherwise known as Harlem. Once we'd
stepped out into the street underneath the electric street
lamp, Mrs. Spears didn't allow me to stand and look at my
new surroundings as much as I wanted to. "You must look
as though you're from here to avoid getting mugged. Don't
look up at any buildings, and whatever you do PLEASE,
don't smile at anyone. You're so pretty, you'll have strange
men following us back to my house!"

But it was so hard not to smile because I kept thinking
to myself "I'm here, I'm here! I made it!" That feeling of
seeing a dream you've wanted all your life finally fulfilled
washed over me every five minutes it seemed! With every
new step I took on that concrete I smelled different foods
and heard different languages, or it was English but still
spoken in strange tongues, and it was nighttime!

It was well after 10:00 in the evening and people were
out and about as though it was the middle of the day! It was
cold, but I didn't feel it. Partly because of the coat Mrs.
Barden had given to me, some because my blood was warm
from the activity of moving so rapidly while carrying my
suitcase, but mostly because of the excitement of
experiencing new surroundings! This place called Harlem
did exist, and now I was a part of it. If I didn't stop thinking
I just knew I would faint. I wasn't even hungry anymore, I
was so excited!

We walked up a small flight of stairs to a brick
building… A BROWNSTONE! I'VE READ ABOUT
THESE! While Mrs. Spears had her back turned to me to

unlock the door, I stole that moment to look up, down, and around me. Nothing but concrete, brick perfection.

"Nostalgia, Dear, please hurry inside," Mrs. Spears insisted.

I hadn't realized she had unlocked the door and was standing inside the foyer waiting for me to follow. Once I stepped into the building's delicious warmth, she locked the door behind me, glided past me to open yet another door, leading to a room, and switched on a light.

When I followed her inside, I gasped, amazed at the beauty of it all. It may have been ordinary to her, but it was breathtaking to me! The carpet was thick, tan, substantial, while the sofa, chairs, and tete-a-tete, were all burgundy, suede, luxurious. There were paintings on the wall of Louis XIV in all his foppery, and Marie Antoinette sporting a blue dress and white powder wig. The tables, desk, and settee were all a black wood I had never seen before, while Queen Anne was well represented on the feet of the chairs and sofa, and each in a fussy lace doily on their high backs.

"I can look at you and tell you are too fascinated to be tired. Let me make you a spot of tea," said Mrs. Spears as she placed her coat on the coat stand in the corner of the room. "Rest your coat." She left the room with gazelle-like grace, heading toward the kitchen.

I finally took my coat off to lay it over my satchel. I wouldn't be placing mine on that rack until I'd taken all the money out of the lining and put it in a bank account somewhere safe.

The room was so warm. I looked around for the fireplace, but instead found a metal contraption that hissed, spit, whispered, and smelled odd. The sweat running off of it reminded me of Noah Holdtstaff. Ha! He was no longer my problem!

Mrs. Spears returned carrying a tea set made of fine china. She set it on the coffee table and asked me how many lumps. I said I didn't know. "Well, we'll start with two." She dropped in two sugar cubes, offering it to me. I took it and waited for her because I didn't know what exactly to do with it. I mean I'd seen Mrs. Barden and her fancy friends have tea parties, Lord knows I'd even made the food for those occasions, but I had no idea how to conduct myself with such highfalutin fare! I watched, imitating Mrs. Spears as she daintily stirred the lumps into the hot liquid. Once the lumps dissolved, she added milk until the tea was about the color of her complexion.

I noticed then that she'd taken off her hat. Her hair was silky, gray, and pulled back into a tight bun at the base of her neck. Her eyes were brown and bright. She was quite attractive. She smiled, as she dipped a tea biscuit in her tea, "would you like one?"

I nodded my head. The sweetness of the two together was like a welcoming committee to my taste buds. I'd never had hot tea before, let alone these tasty little cookies. As much as I'd seen Mrs. Barden serve them at her parties, I never had the courage to try to sneak them from her kitchen for fear of being found out.

"So have you thought about what you'd like to do first?"

"What do you mean, Mrs. Spears?" I asked.

"Well, you need to find a job to survive here, even if you brought money with you. How do you intend to make a living? Somehow I don't see you cleaning up after anyone except maybe yourself."

"I don't know. I'm sure I'll find something."

"Well, you should start looking soon. You don't have to start tomorrow. But you should just start thinking about it. In the meantime, finish your tea so I can show you to your room."

* * * *

I woke to the smell of hot buttered biscuits, bacon, and eggs! It smelled so much like home I almost forgot I never intended to go back! I sat up on the bed as I took time examining my new surroundings in the daylight, remembering the night before. I recalled arriving in Penn Station, the cab ride to Mrs. Spears' brownstone, the tea party, and finally coming up to this beautiful room to settle into this cushy four-poster feather bed.

I looked at myself in the mirror of the vanity table from across the room and smiled. I looked and felt rested. I hadn't decided to stay here right away, but Mrs. Spears took the liberty of telling me that should I stay, my room and board would be $5.00 per week to be paid on Fridays. I was allowed no overnight guests. Any guest of the opposite sex could not come upstairs and had to be off the premises by 10:00 pm. The bathroom I was to use was two doors down the hall, and I was to share it with two other young ladies who were about my age. Their rooms were also on this floor, in fact, we three were the only tenants living on this particular level. There were four more residents on the top floor. I would share the kitchen, dining room, and sitting room with the rest of the house.

It was clean, it was affordable. Where else would I go? "Well, I'll be! I've already found a place to live!"

* * * *

Breakfast was in full swing when I came into the dining room. Mrs. Spears was placing a biscuit onto a gentleman's plate who looked to be about her age, or maybe a little older. "Good morning," she said. "Everyone this is Nostalgia. Nostalgia this is Mr. Greer, that's Mr. and Mrs. Collins, and on the other side of the table is Mr. and Mrs. Irving. The other two who share the second floor with you are asleep because they work nights. You'll meet them later. Have a seat, and I'll come back with your plate."

"Thank you, ma'am," I said, taking the seat next to Mr. Greer. Everyone looked at me and smiled. I guess they didn't know what to make of me.

"Nostalgia? That's an interesting name. Where are you from?" asked Mr. Greer.

"I'm from Spivey's Grove, South Carolina."

"South Cackalcky! What brings you here?" I blushed because I didn't know how I should answer him. The Cotton Club had a clandestine reputation down south, and I didn't know what anyone would think of me once I revealed why I chose to come north.

One of the married ladies inquired, "How did you meet Mrs. Spears?"

"We met on the bus yesterday. I told her I was on my way here to Harlem and she offered me the room."

"Well, you better take it! It's the best place in town to be," said one of the husbands.

His wife quipped, "And it's safe too! This city is a dangerous place for a girl living by herself."

The first wife looked at me with interest. "What do you plan to do for work? New York is an expensive place. You might want to think about that."

"I've already mentioned that to her, Cicely. Hey, are they hiring at the beauty parlor where you ladies work?" Mrs. Spears set a plate of eggs and bacon in front of me as she gestured for me to help myself to the biscuits on the table.

"That's what I was thinking!" said Cicely.

"Well, y'all better get going if you want to keep your jobs," said Mr. Greer. He began taking up the used plates as the two couples got up from the table. Each husband helped his wife with her coat, and the wives said they would inquire about a job on my behalf. Their husbands bid the rest of us a respectful good day before leaving.

"You never answered my question! What brings you here?" Mr. Greer asked again. I lowered my head as he and Mrs. Spears sat, waiting for my response.

Finally, I spoke, "I came here to be a dancer at the Cotton Club!" There! I said it.

They looked at me, then at each other. Then the strangest thing happened: they laughed. I mean they doubled over as if I had told them the funniest joke they'd ever heard! Finally, after what seemed like forever and 50-11 days, they stopped.

Mrs. Spears caught her breath, assuring me, "Honey, we're not laughing at you. We're just ecstatic because you came to the right place!"

Chapter 3

They refused to tell me exactly what they meant by that, but insisted I would find out soon enough. Rather than sit there and continue to be the butt of their inside joke, I asked Mrs. Spears if she had any stationary and a pen I could borrow. She told me I would find them in the desk in the parlor. I sat at the beautiful black wood desk to write Lily a letter.

February 16, 1928, Thursday
My Dearest Lily,
I am truly sorry for leaving like I did but I couldn't bear the thought of marrying that awful man! But it's best for you, isn't it? Now that I'm out of the house Daddy and Mama will allow you to marry Henry!

I'm just writing to let you know I am fine. I'm in New York and living in Harlem of all places! I had been saving money from my job at Mrs. Barden's for some time, and I have always wanted to live here! When you told me of Daddy's plan to marry me off, I knew then it was time for me to leave. I just wish it hadn't been so quickly. I wanted to tell you, but I knew you would tell them before I could get away. Daddy and Mama must be very angry with me, especially Daddy. I didn't mean to hurt anyone I just had my own dreams.

Mrs. Barden should be giving you this letter within a day of its arrival to her house. She told me to tell you, and yes she knows all about it, to come to her house at least every two weeks to pick up letters from me. Who knows, she might even offer you my old job! If she does, you should take it. She pays really well. Quite a bit more than I let on, I might add.

I'm living in a tenement house owned by a lady I met on the bus. She moved here from Raleigh with her husband when she was much younger. He's dead now, and she owns this beautiful home with three floors, and carpet, and THREE bathrooms! Yes, she has indoor plumbing! I haven't met all the tenants yet, but the ones I have seem nice. Two of the ladies have offered to inquire to their bosses about giving me a job! I think they work at a beauty parlor, so I might be doing hair instead of cleaning up after white folks.

Speaking of white folks, I haven't seen any since we left the bus station yesterday evening! When we got to Harlem, I saw only coloreds!

I haven't been out of the house today, but I hear so much noise coming from the street. I hear cars running, children playing, vendors calling whatever their selling. I miss you, though. Please write me back and let me know how you, Ma, and Daddy are doing. And please, don't be mad at me for leaving, I just couldn't see myself married to a bootlegger and happy.

I love you,
Nostalgia

I couldn't fold it and put it in the envelope just yet because I had to let my teardrops dry. I didn't realize I missed my family until I started writing. I bet they must be so worried, especially my mama.

She'd probably never understand why I left, considering she graduated from being a child in her parents' house to wife in her husband's. The way I see it, Mama spent the whole of her life shivering in a shade of second class citizenship. I'll bet she'd give birth to a small Angus cow at the thought of living by herself, not to mention for herself. I hoped Lily would reassure her I'm fine.

I didn't see my sister actually admitting she knew where I was. If she did, I could see Daddy beating her until she gave up my whereabouts! The image of him busting in here, dragging me by my hair back down there was so fresh I could smell it! Or he could do just the opposite and decide I wasn't worth the trouble, disowning me altogether. Either way, he'd be dealing with his own hurt pride at my actions.

"Are you finding everything you need?" Mr. Greer came into the parlor carrying a toolbox. I guess he was on his way to fix a toilet or do some other odd job. "Yes, Sir… could you tell me where I would find a post office and a bank?"

"Sure can! The post office is downtown, but the policy bank is right around the corner. Just tell Mrs. Spears. She'll be glad to go with you."

I folded the letter and placed it in the envelope then wrote Mrs. Barden's address on the front. Then I remembered I didn't know what to put for a return address. I went to the dining room where Mrs. Spears was sitting, having a cup of coffee. "Mrs. Spears what's the address here?"

"2225 139th Street, New York, New York. Is that a letter to someone back home?"

"Yes, Ma'am. My sister."

"Oh! Older or younger?"

"Younger," I said.

I could tell Mrs. Spears wanted to inquire further, but thought it might not be appropriate at the time, so I asked if she would take me to the bank and the post office.

We got our coats, hats, and purses and met at the bottom of the staircase in the foyer just outside of the parlor. My first outing in New York City and how excited I was! When we got onto the street, it was sunny and freezing. At least down south there was warmth on a cold day in the sunshine, but not here. Mrs. Spears explained that cold air from as far up as Maine and Canada blew off the Hudson River. On days even colder than this, miniature glaciers could be seen floating downstream toward lower Manhattan! "We'll see the Hudson on another day. Right now we have to run your errands. So you wanted to buy some stamps to send the letter, and go to the bank, did you say?"

"Yes, Ma'am." I'd never opened a bank account before, but I knew I had to protect my money. By some standards what I had wasn't much, but it was all I had in this world. I couldn't risk anyone stealing it because I left it in my coat, or underneath a mattress.

Mrs. Spears raised her hand to hail a cab. "Ma'am, Mr. Greer said the post office was downtown, but the bank was around the corner. Can't we just walk to the bank first?"

Mrs. Spears kind of cocked an eyebrow when I said this, "Really? And what kind of 'bank' did Mr. Greer say was around the corner?"

"Well, I don't know. I think he said The Policy Bank." Mrs. Spears shook her head at my answer, "That's not the kind of bank where a lady keeps her money. I'm taking you to The Empire Savings and Loan of New York, which happens to be closer to the post office."

* * * *

The Empire Savings and Loan of New York was a tall building made of cinder bricks and windows occupying the entire block of 48 Wall Street.

I looked up, even though Mrs. Spears told me not to, and saw two men sitting on what looked like a ledge, washing windows. It frightened me so much I wondered if anyone had ever fallen and died from keeping windows clean!

The huge double doors of the bank were brass and heavy. It took Mrs. Spears and me to pull one of them open. Luckily a man standing inside the bank dressed in a policeman's uniform saw us scuffling and helped us.

I looked around, and it was all tall red oak tables with little lamps so folks could see what to write on banking receipts. It was dark in there except for those lamps! In spite of there being so many people, it was quiet too.

Off to the side, there was a waiting area with fancy, red velvet chairs. Mrs. Spears took a seat! She looked at me, smiling, and told me that it was alright for us to sit there. "You're up North now; there's no Jim Crow here. Oh, white folks still think they're better than coloreds, it's just not as blatant."

I allowed the plushness of the chair to envelope itself around my body. I'd never sat anywhere more comfortable! A white woman glanced at us as she took a seat across from us, but she said nothing.

After about 15 minutes a balding white man in a dark suit came out of his glass office, "Who's next?" The white woman looked at us in expectation as I stared back at her.

By this time Mrs. Spears was already on her feet, "Come, dear." She didn't even acknowledge the white woman! Was this normal? If this had happened in South Carolina, we'd both be dangling from a sycamore tree, if not finding a burning cross in our yard that evening!

The white man asked no questions as he led us to his glass office. Again, Mrs. Spears didn't ask if she could sit down. She sat, gesturing for me to do the same, "Close your mouth, dear." I didn't realize it was open, I'd just never seen a colored person act so uppity around white folks and get away with it!

"What can I do for you ladies today?" I looked at the plaque on his desk that had his name on it: Rubin Goldfarb. Too preoccupied with the banker's name to realize Mrs. Spears and the man were waiting for me, I didn't cease to mull over the strange moniker.

Mrs. Spears, somewhat annoyed with my naiveté, took it upon herself to speak on my behalf. "This young lady would like to open an account."

"Alright. What kind of account, checking or savings?" He insisted on looking to me for answers, but Mrs. Spears knew what to say.

"She'd like to open both."

"How much money do you have, Miss?" He called me "Miss." A white man has never called me that!

"Uh, close to $400. I didn't count it before we came in."

"May I count it for you?" he asked.

I looked at Mrs. Spears, "Well give the man your money, dear. He'll count right here in front of us."

Ironically, I must have looked like a bootlegger's wife because I took money out of both pockets of the coat, as well as the inside pockets and the lining before taking it out of my purse! This Mr. Goldfarb showed a range of different emotions, from shock to happiness as he took each wad of cash, straightening the bills into several neat little piles. Finally, he said, "Miss…?"

"Richardson, Nostalgia Richardson."

"Miss Richardson this is $525."

"What! Are you sure?" I knew when I left that morning I counted $375, and I spent some on the way up here for food… and then I remembered Mrs. Barden went to the bank to get my parting bonus. When she handed it to me, I never took the time see how much it was. Well, I'll be! She gave me quite a small fortune, didn't she?

"How would you like to divide this up?" Mr. Goldfarb asked.

"Divide?" I was so confused.

Mrs. Spears explained, "How much did you want to put in your checking account and how much did you want in your savings account."

"Exactly," said Mr. Goldfarb.

Well, I didn't rightly know what to say, so I said to Mrs. Spears, "What do you suggest, Ma'am?"

"Well, you could put $50 in your checking and the remainder in your savings."

"I think that is an excellent idea," said Mr. Goldfarb, separating the money.

We looked on while he prepared some sort of paperwork, then he asked for my signature in what seemed like a million different places. "I've put $50 in your checking account. Is there any you would like to take with you before I put the rest in your savings?"

"Yes. She'll take $20 for now!"

"I will?"

"Yes, dear, you will," and at Mrs. Spears' suggestion, Mr. Goldfarb gave me $20 in 1's and 5's.

I was stupefied. "Thank you, sir."

He chuckled, "Don't thank me, it's your own money! Will there be anything else?"

I looked at Mrs. Spears, and she said, "No, thanks! That'll be all for now."

"Well, Miss Richardson here are your receipts for your checking account, and for your savings account. If you have any questions, please feel free to ask."

"Well, actually I do have one. What is the difference between a checking and a savings account?" After I had said this, it was Mr. Goldfarb's turn to look at Mrs. Spears.

Mrs. Spears said to him, "I'll explain it to her on the way out. Thank you, sir."

"And thank you."

* * * *

When we got back out into the street and began walking toward the post office, Mrs. Spears explained to me that the difference between a checking account and a savings account is that you use the money from a checking account on a regular basis, and the money from a savings account sits in the bank drawing interest until it is needed.

"What's interest?" At that moment all things banking was fascinating to me!

Mrs. Spears explained patiently, "That's money the bank pays you over time for keeping your money with them. When people take a loan from the bank, they pay interest on what they borrow. The bank uses that money to pay you for your savings account. Do you understand?"

"A little bit."

"Now when you start making wages from the Cotton Club, you'll put 10% in church, 10% in your savings account, and the rest you will put in your checking account to pay for your daily necessities and me for your rent. Don't worry, you're off to a very good start!"

"Yes, Ma'am. Ma'am, how do you know I'll get hired at the Cotton Club?"

She gave me a sly grin, "Let's just say you have a couple of secret weapons that are sure to work in your favor!"

By this time, we stopped in front of another tall brick building that had an American flag hopelessly waving at the mercy of that cold breeze. The doors were brass but not as heavy, in fact, they were kind of funny looking because people would get in this little space that led you inside, while people across from you on the other side were going back out doors. I didn't realize until I was in the little space and on the back of Mrs. Spears' heels that I was supposed to wait until she got in the little space and moved ahead of me. Then I would get in another little one behind her before I would get inside the post office. When we managed to get out, we must have looked like a sight from a Buster Keaton picture, because everybody stopped to look and stifle a laugh!

Mrs. Spears was somewhat flustered with me, but still patient, "Don't tell me. You've never been inside of a revolving door before now?"

"Is that what that is?"

"Yes, Nostalgia. It's a revolving door, and only one person goes in at a time!"

"Yes, Ma'am."

The post office had the same kind of tall tables as the bank, but we went right to the line and waited our turn. "You've already put the address on your letter, so all you have to do is get some stamps. Do you intend to write your sister regularly?"

"Yes, I do."

"Well, then you need to get at least… $.50 in stamps. That way you won't need to come down here but every so often. Now today after you put the stamp on the letter you'll drop it in that slot over there. After that, you'll just give your letters to the mail carrier from my house."

"Yes, Ma'am."

I looked around, and there was a white man behind us who did not even seem to notice he was standing behind two colored women. Wait until I tell Lily about this! Another thing that amazed me was, like in the bank, it was quiet. In spite of the number of people in this place, and the different types at that, it was quiet in here… Until the clerk yelled "Next," impatiently.

Of course it was directed at me because I stood there trying to take it all in, the various and sundry skin colors, languages, and RICHES, if not the lack thereof! I mean it was nothing to see unrefined working stiffs standing next to socialites wearing fur coats and patent leather shoes! There were all kinds of souls, and no one was outwardly claiming to be better than anybody else.

I've been astonished since I set foot on the pavement outside of Penn Station last night. If Mrs. Spears hadn't been there anybody could have taken advantage of me. I truly thanked God for her.

After I had purchased the stamps, and dropped Lily's letter in the box marked "Out of Town Mail", Mrs. Spears said to me as we stepped back into the street, "Dear, you haven't eaten since breakfast. You must be hungry." It had not occurred to me, but she was right: I could have eaten a hippopotamus and his mama! "Before we get back to Harlem, let me treat you to lunch."

We stepped into a drug store, and there, again, were all kinds of folks sitting at the counter, even coloreds were sitting and eating next to whites!

We seated ourselves at a table before an old white man wearing black and white with this funny looking little hat gave us these sheets of paper… oh, these must be menus! I've read about these. I looked, and there was quite a selection, none of which I recognized. "Are you ready to order Dear, or should I order for you?" Mrs. Spears was getting used to the idea that this was all new to me.

"Please."

When the man came back, he had a notepad and a pencil and asked us what we wanted. He talked funny as if he had a mouth full of marbles!

Mrs. Spears ordered for us. "We'll start with two bowls of matzo-ball soup, two chicken salad sandwiches on toasted rye with kosher pickles, and to drink we'll have iced grape juice." After he had read it back to us, Mrs. Spears confirmed the order, and he shouted something at the kitchen that sounded like… like I honestly didn't know what!

He came back in less than two minutes with two bowls of soup that had these balls in the middle of this thick yellow stock. The stock tasted like chicken and the ball in the middle had the consistency of wet cornmeal. It was good, filling, and perfect for a cold day!

When we had warmed up some, we removed our coats. I realized we'd been wearing them since we left Harlem. The restaurant was the first bit of real warmth I'd felt all day! By this time our chicken salad sandwiches arrived. They were on this brownish bread that had these little black seeds. "Nostalgia have you ever had rye bread before?"

"No Ma'am, but I'll try anything new!" I bit into the sandwich… mmm, I had never tasted such spices! The chicken salad was tangy, peppery, and sweet while the bread was pungent. Even the lettuce on the sandwich was different. It was greener and crispier than the kind Daddy grew in our garden back home. The pickle was cut into a long wedge and left on the side of the sandwich instead of between the bread. It tasted bitter. I wouldn't be picking that up again!

Except for the pickle, it was a satisfying meal. I thought it was a little too cold for iced grape juice, but it tasted so good.

"I know the grape juice is cold, but you need to drink it to ward off pneumonia. You've never experienced winters like these! It's going to be this cold until well into April, so you need to build up your immune system." Mrs. Spears was a wealth of advice! I began to wonder if she had any daughters. She could not have taken better care of me if she was my own mother.

Speaking of my mother, what was she thinking now? If she could read I would have had Mrs. Barden take her a letter on my behalf, but I'm sure she would have mentioned it to my father…

"Nostalgia, are you okay?"

"Yes, Ma'am. You were saying?"

"I was asking if you were ready to go back home?"

"Yes, Ma'am." I was starting to get cold again, and I wanted a nap. I looked forward to getting back to my new room in the brownstone and laying across that feather bed for a refreshing slumber.

I waited by the front door while Mrs. Spears paid at the counter. When the cashier gave her the change, she smiled at him, and they both said this funny word. I decided to ask her about it when we got outside. "Mrs. Spears, what was that word you and the cashier said when you got your change?"

"Mazel Tov?"

"Yes."

"That's a Yiddish word, it means 'Good Luck'."

"Oh." Yiddish? I was sleepy from walking all morning, and eating a late lunch. I figured I might ask her more about that when I was more rested.

That feather bed was the best thing that ever could have happened to me that afternoon! You would think with all the chores I used to do around Mrs. Barden's house and the harder physical labor I did around my parents' home that just walking would be nothing. However, that was not the case at all. I don't know if it was the coldness of the air or the hardness of the pavement under my feet, but I don't ever remember feeling so tired in my life! Or maybe it was walking on pavement in those high-heeled shoes. Now that I thought about it, my feet and legs did hurt a tremendous lot.

I suddenly got worried. If my feet and legs couldn't handle walking on pavement in high heels then how would I become a showgirl at the Cotton Club? Oh, dear! I better learn to get used to my new surroundings. I was too far into my new life to turn around and go back to what was familiar.

"Nostalgia, are you awake?"

"Yes, Mrs. Spears!"

"Well come downstairs. I want you to have dinner now!"

"I'll be out directly," I wondered what time it was? It felt a little too early to have dinner.

I stretched, yawned, and looked at myself in the mirror. The crusty leftovers of my languid slumber had settled into the corners of both of my eyes. I figured I had better run to the bathroom to splash my face and swish my mouth. I still had a mint sprig left in my purse from the bus ride. I wondered where I could find some more.

When I got downstairs to the dining room the company was far different from that of the morning. Mr. Greer and the married couples were nowhere to be seen. They were replaced by two of the most beautiful young ladies I had ever seen in my life! They looked at me too, then the one with the fairest skin said, "You must be Nostalgia! I'm Tessie Jefferson."

"And I'm Mitzi Daniels," said the other, who had hair the color of obsidian and skin about my complexion.

"I see you three have met!" Mrs. Spears brought in three dinner plates with meatloaf, steamed potatoes, and cabbage. "Have a seat Nostalgia."

I sat next to Tessie. The fairness of her skin brought special attention to the redness of her hair and green eyes. You could tell she was colored only by the way the hair at her temples needed to be freshly straightened, otherwise, she looked like a white girl!

Both Mitzi and Tessie had very short hair finger-styled into Marcelle waves. The irony of their appearance was that neither wore make-up, but they still looked glamorous.

I happened to take a look at the grandfather clock in the corner. Why, it was only 5:00. I knew it was early yet! "Mrs. Spears, is it normal to eat dinner this early up north? Back home folks usually eat around 6:30."

"Well, Mr. Greer and the couples do eat around that time. I told you these ladies work nights and I like to make sure they have a good meal before they leave for the evening."

"Oh, where do you two work?"

They said in unison, "The Cotton Club!"

I nearly choked on my meatloaf!

Chapter 4

So these were the secret weapons I had "working in my favor"! That Mrs. Spears was something else! I couldn't believe this was happening to me! Was it my feeble imagination or was my life falling into place before my eyes, exactly as I wanted it to happen, and all for the asking.

"Nostalgia, are you alright?" Mrs. Spears asked. All I could do was nod my head.

"How old are you, Nostalgia?" asked Mitzi.

"Uh, 16."

"Well that's a little young, but you could easily pass for 18," said Tessie.

Mitzi seemed to be examining me. "You know what the first thing to go has to be?" and the three of them said in almost perfect harmony: "The hair!" My hand flew to the top of my head and stroked my long tresses. I knew they were right. Everyone who looked anything close to chic had short hair.

I think the four of us were all too excited to eat. I just sat there and listened while the three fates planned my future. Sometime this week Cicely and Mavis would have to do my hair and get me some make-up. I would also need tap shoes, character shoes, modern dance slippers… "Tessie," said Mitzi, "didn't the schedule say the next auditions would be in two weeks?"

"I believe you're right Mitzi! Nostalgia do you have any idea of a piece of music you could do a dance to?"

"Um, no I don't rightly know of anything off the top of my head."

"Well, who's your favorite singer?" asked Mrs. Spears.

Then I got an idea, "I could do a dance to Black Bottom Stomp by Jelly Roll Morton!"

"No, honey, that's juke joint music. They play big band jazz at the Cotton Club. You know, Jimmie Lunceford, Duke Ellington, Cab Calloway." Mitzi's eyes lit up like fireflies, "Tessie, I know what she's going to dance to: Black and Tan Fantasy by Duke Ellington!"

"Why not the rendition by Jimmie Lunceford?"

"Well, The Duke wrote it."

"But Jimmie's has more substance."

"Oh, please. It's not any different! You're still carrying a torch for him, aren't you?" At Mitzi's revelation, Tessie's cheeks blushed even brighter. Then they both laughed at themselves for their feigned bickering. I was still too shocked at my good fortune to make any yay or nay comments about the direction to which these ladies were pointing my fate.

"It's five-thirty. You three can make your plans tomorrow. Nostalgia will be here. Have a safe night at work. No joy juice, no reefer, and come home as soon as you can after your last gig!" said Mrs. Spears.

"Yes, Ma'am," the ladies chirped as they put on their coats, which were very similar to the one Mrs. Barden had given me.

"What time do they usually get back?" I asked.

Mrs. Spears puckered her lips, granting me a lively response, "Late. So don't try to wait up. You'll be keeping the same hours soon enough."

* * * *

I was awakened bright and early the next morning by Mitzi knocking at my bedroom door. "Get up, so we can take you to the beauty parlor. Mavis is one of the best. If we get there too late, we'll be stuck in a line waiting for her. Cicely wants to do your make-up colors today too!"

I hardly recognized myself by the end of that day! Mavis had cut my lengthy tresses into a stylish bob. I looked like a colored Clara Bow. Cicely plucked my eyebrows into catlike arches. The sting reminded me of the yellow jackets back home, but it made my cheekbones look higher while giving my face a feline slimness. She also plucked the hair from my top lip and chin, which was even more painful than my brows.

Next, Cicely chose colors for my make-up. My lips were bright red, my cheeks were pink, and my eyelids were blue. "And don't worry about having to maintain your look. Since we all live in the same tenement house, Mavis and Cicely give us touch-ups and trims at home," said Mitzi.

In the following two weeks, Mitzi and Tessie took me downtown to the Theatrical district to buy make-up, various types of dance shoes, rehearsal clothes, sheet music, and records. We took a cab downtown almost every day to the corner of 42nd Street and Broadway. There were big theaters with marquees, bright lights, and velvet ropes out front of the box offices to guide the crowds when buying tickets. There were smaller theaters with actors out front practicing their lines, and panhandlers standing next to them in hopes of getting a dime at least. One old colored man was holding a cup and doing a bit of hoofin'. If you stopped to listen, you could distinguish each little tap. I was amazed at how clean his performance was despite being at the mercy of the sounds of the street.

"That reminds me. We've got to get started on your dance, Nostalgia," and Mitzi nodded in agreement with Tessie's statement.

That afternoon when we went back to Harlem the girls told me to put on one of my new rehearsal outfits, and bring all of my new dance shoes to the cellar.

"What's a cellar," I asked.

Tessie explained that it was the very bottom floor of a house. Back in South Carolina we'd call that a basement. "That door off to the side in the foyer leads to the cellar. If you get there before we do just switch on the light and go on down the stairs. We'll be there directly."

I did get there first, and it was dank and dusty as all outside after a hard, hot rain when the sun comes back too quick. If it wasn't for that dim light, it would have been completely dark too. I almost went back upstairs when I heard a rattling noise that sounded to me like a rodent settling into a nest. Then Mitzi and Tessie came downstairs before I could cut into a run. They were carrying all of the records we bought, while Mr. Greer followed them lugging a RCA Victrola.

"First we need to listen to the records and let you decide on a song you like, then we'll start the choreography," said Mitzi.

"The what?" They laughed at me. They must have thought I was green as the palmettos back home.

"Choreography is the dance steps," Tessie explained.

"Oh!" I learned something new every day since I'd been here.

We listened to all of those records, but I came to the conclusion Tessie was right: Black and Tan Fantasy by Jimmie Lunceford was the best. There was a rift in the clarinet solo that was absent in the Ellington rendition, since there was no piano solo. Plus, the trumpet in the Lunceford rendition was the dominant instrument.

"Well, I just hope you never tell the Duke that when you meet him!" Mitzi teased me. The thought of meeting Duke Ellington made me blush!

"Now should the choreography be on the one, or on the two?" asked Tessie. She and Mitzi looked at me expecting me to answer.

I had no idea what they meant, "Huh?"

They looked at each other, making the decision for me in their own unique unison, "The two!"

* * * *

Tomorrow would be the audition, and I was so nervous! Mitzi and Tessie assured me I looked beautiful, and that I danced like a seasoned professional. I was to tell the judges I was 18 when they asked my age. I was also supposed to wear the green leotard and white tights Tessie picked out for me the day before. "Why green?" I asked.

"Because everybody wears black leotards, you won't stand out otherwise." Tessie was adamant in her theory.

Mitzi added, "Not to mention green is Mr. O'Neil's favorite color! That'll give you another advantage over the other girls!"

"Mr. O'Neil?"

"He's the owner," Mitzi explained.

As of right now, though, Mitzi and Tessie are upstairs still asleep, so I'm going to use this final morning to go downstairs to the cellar to practice my dance. My plans are put on hold when I hear Mrs. Spears call me into the parlor.

"I thought that was you coming down the stairs. You have a letter from South Carolina. Is Lily your sister?"

"Yes, Ma'am," and as she handed me the envelope I resisted the urge to tear into it like a thirsty Bedouin fighting for the last droplet of water! I thanked her for it and ran back upstairs to my room, forcing myself to sit down. Taking a deep breath, I opened the missive calmly without destroying its valuable contents:

February 27, 1928, Monday

Well, look who was good enough to write little old me a letter! Nostalgia Richardson, I can't believe you did this to us! I can't believe you did this to me! You've got a lot of nerve, you know that? Daddy and Ma are beside themselves with worry over you, you highfalutin heifer! I admitted to them I told you about the marriage. Daddy back-handed me so hard he busted my lip! You must have been planning to leave for a while, otherwise you couldn't have left so quickly.

And no, Daddy still won't let me marry Henry, the love of my life! I'd like for you to know I have to marry

Noah Holdtstaff now that you've gone! I didn't tell you
everything that night. You really think that bootlegger was
just going to marry you because Daddy asked him to? Ha!
NOAH HOLDTSTAFF PAID DADDY FOR YOU! Now
Daddy refuses to give him back the money. I don't know
how much, but it was enough for Daddy to quit his job at
the sawmill, and buy a house, some land, two chickens, two
pigs, and a cow! He and Mama have moved to an eight-
room farmhouse outside of town.

All you had to do was wait. That night when we were
all sitting at dinner, I was coming up with a plan to have
you out of that marriage in at least two years, at best five! I
was going to tell you about it that night when you got back
from work, but you never came home. But don't you worry
none, I'll use it for myself.

There was one little part of it I didn't know exactly
what to do about, but that's where your little Mrs. Barden
will come in real handy. If she was brave enough to come
to this part of town by herself to deliver a letter on your
sorry behalf, then I know she'll help me. She's smart! She
told them she came to "inquire as to Nostalgia's
whereabouts" because you hadn't been to work. When
Daddy told her you had gone, she asked to speak to me in
private. I thought she was going to offer me your old job,
but instead, she gave me your letter, telling me to come to
her house every so often to see if you had written.

So you're living in Harlem? I can believe that. You,
working in a beauty parlor doing hair? Ha! And I'll be a
blue pig singing soprano on Sunday! You went to work at
that Cotton Club, didn't you? You couldn't find a juke joint

in Louisiana, could you? Jelly Roll Morton would have made you one of his showgirls the minute he saw you, but you're too uppity for that, I see.

Well, I've got to wind this letter up. Mama's going to take me to town to get my dress for the upcoming nuptials. I would invite you, but your sorry self is living the high life in New York City!

Your Beloved Sister,

Lily

PS

I'm just mad right now. Please don't stop writing me. Once I've gotten away from Noah, Henry and I will come up there to see you directly. I miss you.

Wow! I had to read Lily's letter a few more times to let the contents of it settle in my brain... Noah Holdtstaff gave Daddy money to marry me? My own father was going to sell me to a bootlegger to get himself out of debt? Well, why wouldn't he? He paid to marry my mama. Of course, he'd sell his daughter to a potential husband. Talk about not letting the circle be unbroken.

Oh, Lily, I am so sorry. And Henry! Oh, I never thought that much of him. I mean he's skinny and quiet and doesn't do anything but sit there and smile, but he loves my sister. He opens the door for her, jumps whenever she asks him to do the littlest things, takes her to church every Sunday, and just stares in awe when he hears her sing.

My sister was right. I am selfish. It just never came to mind my leaving would ruin anybody else's life.

And Lily had a mind of her own after all! Where was this spunky girl when we were growing up? All this time I thought she was a spineless pawn of my parents. She had an opinion! And a plan? I almost wished I had of stayed just for the pleasure of hearing how she would get me out of that mess, not to mention getting to know this person who had been under my nose all those years, but had no reason to step forward until real trouble showed up.

Mrs. Barden was smart, and Lily had no idea how smart… wait a minute. Just how elaborate was this plan that she would need Mrs. Barden to help? In reading that letter, I suddenly felt like I was missing out on all the fun! I decided dance practice could wait for a little while at least. I ran back downstairs to the parlor, sat at the Mahogany desk, and I commenced to answering Lily's sour words.

March 6, 1928, Tuesday
Oh, Lily!
I didn't mean to put you in such a fix! Why didn't you tell me about the money? Why did you have to tell them you told me about the arrangement? Or maybe I should have expected there was money involved considering our parents' history. Daddy bought his wife, why wouldn't he sell his daughter? I really don't know what to say to you about this, except that I feel awful.

But I am curious about this plan you have. Lily, you are 14 years old. How the ham gravy are you planning to go toe-to-toe with a 49-year-old man? Not just any man either: a bootlegger! You can't drive, and I don't see how you could have any money of your own since you've never had a job outside of our parents' house!

Did you even ask Mrs. Barden if she would consider giving you my old job? That way you could do what I did. Tell Noah you're making less than what you actually are, give him that amount every week, then you keep the rest somewhere safe until you're ready to use it.

I'm almost afraid to ask, but what does Henry have to say about all this? I'm sure he's not speechless now. If anything he's calling me everything but a child of God for making you have to marry that wretched skunk.

Oh, my God, Lily, can you ever forgive me for this? Are you sure you don't want me to send you some money so you can buy a ticket and come up here and stay with me? I'm sure Mrs. Barden wouldn't mind driving you to the bus station if you really want out of this bind. Once we get you settled, you can send for Henry. Tell me you'll at least think about it.

Your sister,

Nostalgia

PS

You're right about the Cotton Club. My audition is tomorrow.

* * * *

I stood outside of that waiting room looking at all those other girls with the same hopes and dreams as myself. We all could have passed for cousins if not sisters. All of us no darker than a paper bag, all of us no shorter than five-foot-seven inches, all of us no heavier than 120 pounds, all of us with hair no longer than our earlobes, and all of us desperate to be "Tall, Tan, Terrific" showgirls at the Cotton Club. I will admit Tessie and Mitzi were right: if it wasn't for my green leotard I would have looked like everybody else!

Tessie and Mitzi further explained to me I would have to perform the dance they choreographed for me, and if I made the first cut, I would get a call back to come in the next day to learn a portion of a dance that was in the company's repertoire. If I make the second cut I would get a call back for the day after tomorrow, and I'd have to learn another company dance, but if I could make that third cut, it would mean I was one of five girls who were new members of the company!

"Nostalgia Richardson!" I jumped slightly at the sound of my name and followed a white lady onto the dance floor of the World Famous Cotton Club! It was a parquet floor with dining tables all around it. The orchestra pit wasn't in a pit at all but on a raised platform behind the dance floor. I looked out in front of me. Despite the bright lighting, I could still see there was a table with three white men, smoking cigarettes and drinking coffee out in the audience.

"Name," one of them shouted.

"Nostalgia Richardson." I wasn't quite sure, but I think I heard one of them mutter "What kind of name is that"?

I know for sure I heard, "Age?"

"18 years old," I said. No one seemed to think this was peculiar so I figured I looked old enough.

"Alright, Nostalgia, what are you dancing to?"

"Black and Tan Fantasy by Jimmie Lunceford."

I heard them whispering amongst themselves as I walked over to a colored man seated in the corner of the stage next to a Victrola and gave him my record. He smiled as if to wish me good luck. I went back to the center of the stage and took a deep breath. I took a moment to look at the Victrola man and nod my head. I was ready to dance.

It took all of two minutes for the routine to be over, but I felt in the very texture of my existence that every kick was high enough, every turn was full circle, every toe tap had a musicality all its own. I not only danced, but I also performed!

Then a scratchy voice with trenchant Irish accent cut through the cigarette smoke, hitting me right between the eyes, "And what made you choose to wear green instead of black?"

I looked over in the direction of the voice, and I stated calmly, "Because it's my favorite color!" I knew then I would be back tomorrow.

Chapter 5

The next couple of days we learned dances for Creole
Love Call which was also by Duke Ellington and a George
Gershwin tune called Naughty Baby. By 'we' I mean the
other girls who made the first, second, and third cuts. For
all I knew they all could have been professional dancers,
but Mitzi and Tessie certainly made up for my lack of
classical dance training.

The day I made that first cut I went home immediately
as they'd told me to do. They didn't waste a minute
celebrating my first minor victory.

"Don't even bother going upstairs to take off that
leotard! It's not over yet. You've got to learn the
choreography for Creole Love Call by tomorrow!" said
Tessie.

"And when you do take off that leotard you've got to
wash it out, and let it line dry in the alley so you can wear
again tomorrow!" added Mitzi.

I was so sore by the afternoon I didn't even eat until
Mrs. Spears woke me up at 8:00 pm from what was only
supposed to be my late day nap. And of all the things to eat
for dinner, she'd made me bacon and eggs! "You've never
worked your muscles like this before. You need as much
protein as possible!"

I must say she was right about my muscles never
working so hard before. While I have always been active,
I've never moved like this on a regular basis. I've ducked
into movie houses and watched those little vignettes
between the pictures. I've seen Martha Graham, Ruth St.

Dennis, and Ted Shawn, and Bill Bo Jangles Robinson and others dancing. I'd go home and try practicing their moves, but intense study escaped me until now.

High heels, walking on pavement, frigid temperatures, and now dancing on a daily basis for hours at a time; I know my body couldn't make sense of it all!

Creole Love Call was a relatively slow number, so I had no problem learning the dance and making the second cut. As I'd done the day before I went home immediately to learn the Naughty Baby routine, which was a faster tune. This one did not come to me as quickly.

I was up until the wee hours of the morning practicing. I took two breaks: one to wash my green leotard and change into one of my black ones, and the other at the insistence of Mrs. Spears that I eat another bacon and eggs dinner.

When Mitzi and Tessie came home and found me still practicing down in the cellar, they made me go to bed.

If it had not been for Mrs. Spears, I would have overslept that last morning! I shoved my oatmeal down my throat in a rush to get to 142nd St. and Lenox Ave., as quickly as I could. I barely made role call!

The choreographer taught all of us the routine to Naughty Baby, or rather taught all of them the routine, for me it was just a memory refresher.

We were then divided up into five groups of five, with me being in the first one. Each group of five performed the dance twice before the next was called to the floor.

The same three men watched us the whole time. One man, in particular, looked specifically at me. When we were told to "Take five", I asked the choreographer who the man was in the green tie. She told me, "Oh, that's Arnie O'Neil. He owns the club!"

Two hours later when my legs felt like spaghetti and I was sick to death of hearing Naughty Baby, the choreographer announced the judges had made their final decision: "Clara Sloane, Margaret Bates, Sally Woods, Eugenia Pyle, and Nostalgia Richardson! Congratulations Ladies. Be here tomorrow morning at eight am to learn other dances in our repertoire and get fitted for your costumes. To the rest of you, thank you for participating, and good luck in your future endeavors!"

I walked home in a daze. I wanted to shout to the world "I'm a Cotton Club Showgirl! I am officially Tall, Tan, and Terrific!" But I remembered what Mitzi said about celebrating too early and making sure you'd actually won. As soon as I stepped into the house, I found Mrs. Spears, Mitzi, and Tessie waiting for me in the parlor.

"Well, don't just stand there looking at us! Did they call your name or not?" Wow! Even Mrs. Spears was anxious.

"Yes, Ma'am, they called me. I'm a Cotton Club Dancer!" I looked at Mitzi, "Can we celebrate now?"

"Yes." They all embraced me at once. It was the happiest I'd been in weeks!

March 17, 1928, Saturday
Nostalgia!
I couldn't leave even if I wanted to! Once you take a bootlegger's money, he has his meat hooks sunk too deep

in your flesh. If I left, that would put Mama and Daddy in danger. Daddy has to give him the goods, which happens to be me now, because he's already spent the money on the house and the farm. If not that, he would have to give Noah any profits he made from selling what he grew on the farm, to the point he'd have nothing to sustain himself and Mama. I don't have a choice but to stay. Besides, where I am now, I can at least see Henry, even if it is from a distance. Henry's going to be alright. He's a little melancholy, but we're going to be fine. He's more patient than you'll ever be, thank God!

Well, I know you got the job at the Cotton Club. I just don't understand why you would trade one Jim Crow for another. As I understand it, the Cotton Club is one of the only places in New York where colored folks serve and entertain a whites-only crowd. You went all the way up north to work at one of the few places that keep Jim Crow laws active. If you were going to do the Jim Crow Shuffle you might as well have stayed down south.

Now I figure being a showgirl for Jelly Roll Morton on the juke joint circuit doesn't pay as much, but he travels as far north as Canada and as far west as California. The last I heard they were performing in Chicago. You could have been in a different city probably every week, and you would have been entertaining colored folks. What's wrong with that? But oh well, I'm glad you're happy.

Your sister,

Lily

PS

Mama and Daddy are fine considering. Daddy refuses to say your name. Mama is trying to act normal, but every now and then you see a tear in her eye if you stop to notice. By the by, my wedding is this afternoon.

My heart sank when I read that last line. Oh my God. My 14-year-old sister was married to a 49-year-old bootlegger and it's all my fault! To think of my cute little sister at the mercy of that disgusting man made me want to throw up. I'd been walking on a cloud for days since the audition, and now this. She never told me the details of her plan. I wondered if there was any way I could help her carry it out sooner so she could marry Henry.

This time I didn't feel like writing her back right away. Honestly, what do you say to someone after you are responsible for ruining their life? How do you make this up to anyone? When you ruin a dress or a rug you buy them a new one no matter what the cost, but life can't be bought back or replaced. When a life is ruined, apologies aren't worth anything. Truthfully you might as well keep an apology to yourself in an instance such as this, because you can't say a thing that's going to make them feel any better. In reality, I hadn't ruined one life, I'd ruined two. Henry didn't love anybody except my sister, and she was settling up a debt I was supposed to pay. Lord, have mercy on my soul!

* * * *

"Are you nervous," asked Tessie as I applied the remnants of burnt matches to my eyebrows. Of course, I was! I couldn't believe it had been almost a month since the audition and I'd learned an entire repertoire of dances. After rehearsal six days a week for three weeks I would finally be setting foot on The Cotton Club stage for my first performance!

"Yes. What if I fall off the stage?"

"Then you'll keep dancing like it was part of the performance. Professionals keep going, even if they miss a step or fall," said Mitzi.

"There are five changes in all tonight ladies. Make sure you check to see that your costumes are on the rack. If you notice any wardrobe malfunctions let us know immediately so we can have them fixed before you get on stage," said Esther, the company's head costume mistress.

I looked at myself in the lighted mirrors and decided I was satisfied with my make-up and hair. One of the other costume mistresses helped me squeeze into my first outfit. The bodice was so tight I could hardly breathe, plus it had a feathered bustle around the derriere that was heavy! She asked me to turn around so she could look at me from behind. "The seams in your stockings aren't straight. Bend over." Starting from my right ankle she pulled them upward and shifted them to the right all the way up to my thigh, then she repeated the action on the left leg. While she was finishing my stockings, another costume mistress was applying my leg dressings. They were feathers that started at my ankles and seemed to grow upward over my calf, then cascade downward. Honestly, it looked like I had two upside-down feather dusters on my legs. "Okay put on your shoes now," she ordered. The last thing to put on was the wide feather headdress that matched the leg dressings and the bustle.

"Ten minutes to places," warned Eddie, our stage manager.

"Thank you 10 minutes," Mitzi shouted in reply.

"You ready?" asked Tessie.

"No. But the show must go on, right?" She and Mitzi smiled at me, and the three of us hugged, before leaving the dressing room to head upstairs to the stage.

Once the stage lights went up, I made the mistake of looking out into the audience. The sight of all those white folks looking at us made me forget my footing, and I had no choice but to take Mitzi's advice and just keep moving. I realized no one could hear me tapping specifically out of all the girls, and they certainly couldn't detect my mistake over the orchestra. I continued to smile and do the upper body movements until I remembered what my feet were supposed to be doing. No one knew I'd messed up. I relaxed upon this revelation and the choreography never left my brain the rest of the night. It was exhilarating to be up there! And then suddenly that number was over, and we were rushed back downstairs to get ready for the next number.

The costume mistresses were there waiting to help us with quick changes, freshen our make-up and hair, give us ice water and moral support. One of the other new girls, Sally I think, broke the zipper on her costume during the second change, she was so nervous! Her costume mistress hooked a hairpin in the grooves and zipped it right up like it was nothing, then told her, "Now when you take it off tonight, make sure your name is on it and put it in the pile labeled 'repairs'. We'll have it ready for you tomorrow night!"

The dressing rooms and the backstage were so organized. No matter what happened, or didn't happen, nothing stopped moving. When Eugenia, another new girl, complained about a cramp in her leg, she was given a banana and cup of water. "Eat, drink, and walk around. It should be gone by the time you get back on stage!" Sure enough, she was ready by the time our next number was called to places.

It was almost magical the way the night moved. It was like nothing could go wrong, or if it did it could be fixed in a matter of minutes. My cheeks hurt from smiling so much. My teeth felt tacky from all the petroleum jelly I'd smeared on them. Each costume made me hot, itchy, breathless, and I would not have had it any other way. I had never been happier than I was tonight!

At the end of the evening, Tessie told me to only take off the face make-up and leave the eye makeup and lipstick on. When I asked why, I was told that in the event we'd met anyone who was in the audience tonight, we'd still look glamorous to them. Even when we were not performing there was an image a Cotton Club Showgirl was always expected to project.

"But we're not going home right away," said Mitzi, "I told Mrs. Spears there was going to be a small party at The Basement to welcome the new girls to the club."

The Basement was across the street from The Cotton Club at 646 Lenox Ave. It was owned by the establishment as a meeting place for the performers. They may go there during a performance to get a bite to eat between sets or, as in this case, to meet up with fellow entertainers after hours when the show was done.

As far as I could tell the party was not small by any means. The Duke had gone home, but some of the members of the orchestra were there hob-knobbing with the dancers. The kitchen staff had brought over some of the food from the evening. Roast beef, baked potatoes, asparagus, and petit fours were on a long table with a white tablecloth. There was alcohol too. I wasn't even curious to try it and neither were Mitzi and Tessie.

Tessie and I sat at one of the tables in the dining area while Mitzi danced The Charleston with a short, brown-skinned gentleman wearing the orchestra's signature suit and a pair of black and tan shoes. They were quite a charismatic pair! "That's Bunky. He plays trombone," explained Tessie.

It felt kind of strange to be sitting instead of dancing. I knew I was only getting a small taste of what the white patrons had been looking at all night. I watched as my new cohorts entertained each other. I was mesmerized as two gentlemen had a tap-dance-off. They looked like they might have been twins to me, so in my mind there was no way one could best the other.

"Those are the Nichols Brothers! Aren't they something?" said Tessie. I nodded in agreement.

Some of the men from the orchestra had brought over their instruments and were playing old Negro spirituals, but with big-band jazz accents. One of the girls, it might have been Clara, sang *Blessed Assurance* in a way I'd never heard it before! I saw beauty and talent in that room that was enthralling, as well as intimidating.

"Hello," said a deep voice from behind me. I turned around and looked up into a pair of big brown eyes with long curly lashes. His black hair was slicked down close to his head with pomade. The whiteness of his teeth was a startling contrast to the blackness of his skin. The smell of Knize Ten cologne trickled into my nostrils because I could only breathe slowly at the magnificent sight of him.

"Nostalgia, this is Josiah James. He's one of the alto saxophonists for the orchestra," said Tessie.

"Nostalgia? That's a different name. It's nice to meet you."

I gave him my hand but said nothing.

"Hi, Josiah," said a breathless Mitzi as she plunked down at the table.

Bunky came up behind her, slapping a low five with Josiah, "Ladies, you want something to eat?"

"Sounds good to me," said Mitzi.

"I know it sounds good to you. My baby can eat a whale," said Bunky as he tickled Mitzi until she let out a squeal. "C'mon man, let's go get these dolls some eats!" He and Josiah walked toward the food table leaving the three of us alone.

Mitzi gave me a sly grin, "well, well! I know Josiah ain't here to see Tessie!"

"And what makes you think he ain't?" I teased.

"Because we come here every week and he's never bothered to talk to us until you showed up!"

"Uh, huh," said Tessie, confirming Mitzi's statement.

I didn't know what to make of Josiah. I mean, I didn't have any gentleman callers when I lived back home. I snuck out the house once late at night to kiss Bernard Jackson underneath a china berry tree when I was twelve, but Lily's big mouth put an end to any hope of hush-hush meetings real quick. When I stepped back into the house, the lights came on, and there was Daddy sitting in his chair. Boy did he ever beat my hide! I lost all interest in sneaking out with boys after that.

Miss goody two-shoes Lily never snuck out the house. Henry always came by to visit her at a decent hour, and they sat in the sitting room until about nine or nine-thirty every evening. Those two are so perfect for each other… or at least they were…

"This one's for you." This time that deep voice was accompanied by a plate of eats coming down over my right shoulder.

"Still playing the waiter. Man you kill me with that," said Bunky. "Y' see this man got a job here as a waiter back in 1925 when he was nothing but sixteen. Man, he came to rehearsals and auditions for two years! But when The Duke heard him play last year, oh, his waitering days were over. Don't be modest, tell her man!" Bunky bragged to me on Josiah's behalf, but he didn't have to. I was already impressed.

I thought he looked a little younger than the other band members. Josiah had a smile that put the sun to shame. In all my nervousness I still couldn't speak. He was only 19. I wondered if it was safe to tell him my age, or where I was from. Certainly, I couldn't divulge how I came to be here just yet.

"Tessie! There's someone outside who wants to talk to you." The look on Esther's face when she came over to our table was a cross between shock and apprehension.

"I know. Tell him I'll be out directly," Tessie took another bite of her roast beef while the others of us waited for some explanation to which she did not offer. "Mitzi, Nostalgia, I'll see you two tomorrow morning. Good evening, gentlemen," and with that Tessie gathered her purse and coat, and was gone.

Chapter 6

We stayed an hour longer at The Basement after Tessie left so abruptly. The four of us went riding around Harlem and the Upper West Side of Manhattan in Bunky's Cadillac before the boys dropped us home to Mrs. Spears'.

I was sitting at my dressing table wrapping my hair in a silk scarf the way Mavis taught me to do every night to keep my hair flat when there was a quiet knock at my door. "Come in."

Mitzi came in looking somewhat afraid, "Tessie's not in her room. Did she say anything to you while I was dancing with Bunky?"

"Anything like what?"

"Did she mention anybody's name, or that she was planning to go out?"

I shook my head 'no'.

Mitzi sat on my bed deep in thought, "Y'know, Mrs. Spears doesn't like for us to separate at night, and Tessie knows this."

"Well, what did Esther say when you spoke to her?"

"Nothing! Apparently, she's been sworn to secrecy."

"Well if she thought something was wrong she'd speak up, wouldn't she?"

"I guess you're right. I still don't like the way she left tonight, and she's going to get a big chunk of my brain when I see her tomorrow." Mitzi sat thinking for another minute before changing the subject, "So, Miss Lady, what do you think of Josiah James?"

"I think he's too good to be true. What is a man that handsome doing all by himself in this city?"

"Well, you're by yourself except for us."

"That's different. I just got here. He's been here at least since 1925. That's three years. What woman is going to let that alone for so long?"

"You heard Bunky. He was 16 years old when he became a waiter, and he did it for his first two years at the club. Believe me, Cotton Club Showgirls don't date waiters, especially not young ones. Both of you are not strangers to lying about your age to wiggle your way in. You two make a handsome couple, and both of you carry yourselves older than you actually are."

"Wait a minute. Who said anything about being a couple? I think I need to get to know him a little better before I go that far."

"A lot of it has to do with life experience. A 16-year-old and a 19-year-old who lied about their ages to work in one of the most popular jazz clubs in the world? Trust me, you two are made for each other. On that note, I'm going to my room to listen out for Tessie. G'night."

"G'night."

* * * *

On Sunday morning Mitzi and I sat in a pew at The Abyssinian Baptist Church watching Tessie nod, struggling to stay awake while the honorable Reverend Adam Clayton Powell, Sr. preached. Luckily Mrs. Spears and Mr. Greer didn't seem to notice.

I wanted to ask Mitzi if she had gotten a chance to talk to her, but my mouth was trained long ago to never open in church unless I was whispering a prayer or shouting a praise. Every time Tessie's head did that involuntary bounce at the neck Mitzi's shoulder nudged her fully awake. I'd been warned by the girls for weeks, even after we visited The Basement after the Saturday night gig, Mrs. Spears expected us to be at church bright and early on Sunday morning before we went to work for the Sunday Matinee performance at the club.

As performers, our "weekend" was Sunday evening, all day Monday, and Tuesday until 6:00 pm, instead of all day Saturday and all day Sunday like everybody else.

My mind kept wandering back to Tessie. After Mitzi had left I went right to sleep as soon as I hit the mattress, so I didn't hear her come in. Mitzi's room is right next to hers and closest to the staircase, so she would have been the one to hear her unless she was tired too. I don't see where she got the energy to cut the rug with Bunky all night at The Basement after performing anyway!

After Reverend Powell said the benediction we stood and waited for the people in front of us, and then Mr. Greer and Mrs. Spears, to get out into the aisle.

"You certainly kept some late hours, Miss Lady! Where'd you run off to last night?" Mitzi was not one to bite her tongue.

Tessie smiled, "I had some previously made plans."

"Well, who with?"

"No one you know. The aisle is free. Let's go." She turned and walked away before Mitzi could ask further questions.

"Did you even hear her come in last night, or this morning rather," I asked.

"No. We're all going to the Savoy tonight. I'll ask if she wants to come. Then maybe she'll bring whoever it was she ran off to meet."

"Who's we?"

"You, me, George and Cicely, Jude and Mavis, Bunky, and Josiah," her slanted eyes danced with mischief as she smiled coyly.

This was the first I had heard of this. "Fess up! How long have you and Bunky been planning this outing?"

She sighed, "For about two weeks. Bunky said Josiah saw you at rehearsal that first day and couldn't stop talking about you, and you're the first girl he's ever showed any interest in. And I figured I'd better get as many people as possible in on this because you know Mrs. Spears isn't going to let just Bunky and me take you out, so I invited George and Cicely, and Jude and Mavis too. Girl, it'll be fun, you'll see!"

* * * *

And fun it was! It was so nice to see Mavis and Cicely and their husbands dressed up instead of in work uniforms. All the skills those ladies use on everybody else at the beauty parlor did not go to waste. They each had hair in a feather cut layered close to the skull and wispy around the ears. As for their make-up, the emphasis on their lips and eyes made their brown skin tones look even more flawless. Cicely was a little taller than Mavis by about three inches. George and Jude looked handsome in their zoot suits and black and white shoes.

I originally had no intention of going anywhere tonight. I thought I would go back to Mrs. Spears' house, have a quiet dinner, and go to bed. After a full week of practicing, quick changes, putting on and taking off make-up, wearing high heels, and dancing, I figured I was entitled to a night and a day of sleep. Tessie apparently thought the same as me because she didn't come out with us.

After Mitzi had made Mrs. Spears aware of our plans for the evening, she insisted Bunky bring Josiah to have dinner at her house since all of us were going to the same place. I think Mitzi was right when she said the only reason Mrs. Spears was so persistent about feeding them too was she was curious about Josiah. All during dinner, she asked him so many questions, it was a wonder he even finished his meal. Seemed like every time he put the fork up to those full dark lips she would ask him something.

"Where are your people from?"

"Biloxi Mississippi."

"How long have you lived in the city?"

"Three years."

"What brought you all this way away from your family?"

"I wanted to be a horn player, Ma'am."

"Do you live by yourself?"

"No, Ma'am! I have a room on 125th and Lenox at Mrs. Forrester's."

Mrs. Spears seemed pretty well satisfied with his responses. Mr. Greer just smiled and shook his head.

Tessie yawned, bidding us all good night before excusing herself from the table and heading upstairs. Mitzi said not only did Tessie not say who she was out with the night before, but didn't bother to mention what time she actually got in. I just hoped Mrs. Spears didn't find out. She'd taken great pains to making sure the three of us were safe.

When we got out onto the street me, Mitzi, Josiah, and Bunky all piled into the Cadillac while the other four got into Jude's Ford. All eight of us ventured toward the world famous Savoy Ballroom!

Before we got out of the car 596 Lenox Ave. was already in our ears. We had to park one street over on 7th Ave. and walk another block over to Lenox.

Mrs. Spears was right, an evening in April felt a lot different in New York than in South Carolina. We were still wearing our hats, coats, and gloves. The night was clear though. After two months I was still getting used to the stars not being as visible because of the streetlamps. The chill in the air nipped my nose, but it somehow added to the anticipation of my first evening as a night club patron instead of an entertainer.

The Savoy Ballroom first opened its doors sometime in March of 1926 as one of the few night club venues catering to whites and people of color. With the owner being a Jew, Moe Gale, and the operator being colored, Charles Buchanan, why wouldn't it be so?

After Josiah had paid the $.85 entry fee for the both of us, I walked in feeling like I did that first evening when I saw the inside of Mrs. Spears' brownstone: I'd never seen such luxury! The walls were pink and seemed to match what everyone was wearing. The floors were solid wood, which was perfect for dancing. The chandelier just above the marble staircase looked like it might lead you to Heaven.

Earlier that evening while helping me decide what to wear, Mitzi explained to me Sunday evening was Glamour Night, and all the performers would be there, from the Cotton Club to Broadway and everywhere in between because it was the beginning of our weekend.

The hostess sat us, and I saw The Duke having dinner with his wife at a table across the room, Langston Hughes walked past our table on his way up the marble staircase, while Rose McClendon sauntered by on the arm of some handsome escort!

There were two bandstands instead of one. Josiah said that was to keep the music non-stop all night. The house band was Fess Walker who was playing in the room where our table was, while the guest band for the evening was Benny Goodman. I heard them playing *Heaven* which was one of my favorite songs.

"Did you want to dance, Nostalgia?" asked Josiah.

I nodded, and he led me into the next room.

He was a gentleman. I didn't really speak to him last night at The Basement or at dinner this evening because I was still in awe of him. His gaze asked permission to put his hand on my waist. Once again I nodded.

"Are you ever going to speak to me," he asked in earnest.

I bobbed my head up and down to avoid saying something childish and stupid.

He laughed, rubbing his cheek against mine. He smelled good and felt even better.

The next song was *A Wink and A Smile*, and I heard a soft shoe melody being tapped out on some distant plain. The ballroom had dancers on duty to do the Lindy Hop, which was what The Savoy was famous for, and to teach various dances to the patrons. Someone must have been getting a tap lesson.

"Nostalgia. You never told me how you came to be named that," he inquired as he looked me in the eye. The thick curly lashes were complemented by substantial black eyebrows. I would have been happy looking into his eyes for the rest of my life, if not forever.

"Huh? Oh, um…"

"What? She speaks," he laughed.

I felt the heat rising off my face. I took a deep breath before speaking. "Sometime before I was born my daddy said he was walking down the street in my hometown behind two old white men who were talking about a wedding reception. Of course, all the hired help was colored. Then one of the old white men went on to say that the way they were serving the white guests gave him a bit of nostalgia for the 'old days' when he was a little boy. When daddy heard the word, he said he liked the sound of it. Daddy named me, and my mama named my sister Lily after her grandmother."

"So you have a sister," he asked.

I only nodded this time because I found myself getting a little melancholy at the thought of her.

"Well, what is she like? Is she as beautiful and talented as you?"

"She…." I couldn't hold it any longer. "Where is the ladies room?"

"Up the marble stairs, but…"

I wriggled from out of his embrace, rushing away through the first room, up the stairs.

* * * *

When we came in that night, we found Mr. Greer sitting in the parlor with a skein of yarn wrapped around both of his hands while Mrs. Spears sat across from him rolling it into a ball.

"Well how was the evening," he asked.

"I had a good time, but I am so tired!" I said.

"I don't see how you could be tired! All you and Josiah did was dance cheek-to-cheek on two songs. Otherwise, you two sat at the table the rest of the night! Y'all didn't even get up on the fast dances. But George and Cicely, and Jude and Mavis, really cut up the rug! I didn't know they had it in them," said Mitzi as she plopped down on the couch.

The married couples had come back early because they all had to work tomorrow.

"I'm going to the kitchen to make some tea. Will you two be joining us," asked Mrs. Spears.

"Please," I said.

"Me too," chimed Mitzi.

Tea would be just the thing to tone us down after the excitement of the evening. Being in such close proximity with all the talented elite gave my head a feeling of lightness!

On her way to the kitchen, Mrs. Spears stopped as if she'd suddenly remembered something. "Where is Tessie?" she asked.

Mitzi looked puzzled, "What do you mean? She ate dinner and went back upstairs before we left the house."

Mrs. Spears replied, "she came back downstairs an hour later saying she'd changed her mind and asked Mason if he would hail her cab to take her to The Savoy."

"Yep, that's what I told the man," confirmed Mr. Greer.

"We haven't seen her since we left," I said.

"Mason, you don't think she…" Mrs. Spears began, but Mr. Greer cut off the thought.

"Stop, Evelyn! I don't wanna hear it!"

The four of us sat in silence for a few minutes before Mrs. Spears said, "well, since we'll be up later than anticipated I guess I better make that tea mighty strong." She got back up again, and walked to the kitchen.

When we were sure we heard her rattling around, Mitzi asked pointedly, "What was she going to say before you stopped her, Mr. Greer?"

He looked at both of us then rolled his eyes and sighed as if he didn't feel like going into a long story, but would make the sacrifice for us.

* * * *

Geraldine Crocker stayed in the boarding house while working as a Cotton Club Showgirl from 1923-1925, and she was gorgeous. Mr. Greer didn't rightly know what part of South Carolina she was from, but the indigo plantations were never far behind her. Unlike most of the dancers, she was one of the few that were hired in spite of not passing the paper bag test. She was the right height and the right weight, while green eyes and silky hair offset the dusky darkness of her reddish-brown skin. Plus, she was quite a dancer.

She told them her mother's family was slaves turned sharecroppers on an indigo plantation, while her father's family was full-blooded Seminole Indians.

Arnie "the killer" O'Neil had labeled her his personal Hottentot Venus. He'd bought the Cotton Club while doing time for murder in Sing Sing prison in Ossining NY. Whenever he went back to prison, sometimes on charges, other times to parlay, keeping a low profile while there was a raid at one of his clubs, he would have some of the showgirls come visit him for conjugal purposes. Geraldine was his favorite. This went on for the entire time she danced at the club.

Wanting not to be a busybody and mind her own business, Evelyn Spears never spoke to Geraldine about her unseemly activities. Geraldine never offered her any information. Long nights often turned into early mornings and sleeping all day until it was time to go to the club to perform. Then it would start all over again the next day.

Evelyn never insisted Geraldine go to church, or whomever she went out with be properly introduced because she kept the rules. She stayed out all night, but she never had overnight visitors, and the rent was always on time.

One night there was a knock at the front door so loud that Mrs. Spears and Mr. Greer thought someone was trying to break in. When asked who it was there was no answer, just a weak moaning. When they opened the door a lifeless, apathetic, Geraldine fell over the threshold black and blue all over while a black car sped off into the night. Geraldine never talked about what happened that evening, or who was responsible for beating her, and again Mrs. Spears did not ask.

It took two weeks for the bruises, the two black eyes, and the split lip to go away. The shaking and the needle tracks in her arms lasted much longer, especially since Mrs. Spears and Mr. Greer ignored her pleas for a fix, choosing instead to hold on to her tightly through the quakes and the sweats.

In the meantime, those lost weeks were enough time for Arnie O'Neil to replace her with another dancer who was younger, not to mention lighter. On top of being a junkie she'd just turned 21 anyway, what did he care? Geraldine was devastated at having lost her job. She auditioned for several other venues, but Arnie monopolized most of the speakeasies and clubs in the city.

The final straw was when Mrs. Spears heard her go into the second-floor bathroom and turn on the tub one night. The water ran a long time. Mrs. Spears knocked on the door, asking if she was alright. She didn't answer the knock. When Mrs. Spears went in the tub was full of red water, Geraldine's once vibrant green eyes were open with no signs of life, and a blood-stained straight razor lay on the floor.

* * * *

By the time Mr. Greer finished retelling the story, my heart had descended to my stomach. In the corner of my eye, I thought I saw Mitzi let out an involuntary shudder at the thought of what Mrs. Spears witnessed three years earlier in the bathroom Mitzi, Tessie and I now shared.

"What happened after that," I asked.

Mr. Greer shrugged his shoulders. "Geraldine never got any letters from home and other than what I told you we never knew anything about her, not even what town she was from. With no way to find her people, Evelyn had her buried in a little grave in one of the cemeteries here in Harlem."

Mitzi stayed quiet, deep in thought a long time, then she spoke, "Did I hear you call him Arnie "The Killer" O'Neil?"

"Sure did," said Mr. Greer.

"What did you mean by that?"

"I meant what I said. In addition to bootlegging and racketeering, your boss is a murderer! He went to jail for killing a man for looking at some woman he was out with. In fact, that's why he was doing time in Sing Sing when he bought the Cotton Club from that boxer, Jack Johnson. Other than that one time, he's always managed to get out of murder charges."

"Which means he has the police, and God knows who else on his payroll," added Mrs. Spears, coming into the room with a tray of tea and biscuits. "It seems to me that right before someone with associations to him dies or one of his clubs is raided, he ends up having to go to Ossining and spending some time in jail. I think it's a little too convenient," said Mrs. Spears.

"Did you say she died in 1925?" Mitzi seemed to be putting something together.

"Yes, that's the year it happened," confirmed Mrs. Spears.

"I remember reading in the newspapers that the club closed for two months back in 1925. Was that about the time she died?"

Mrs. Spears nodded her head at Mitzi's revelation. "The news of her suicide was in newspapers all over Harlem, and maybe even a few in lower Manhattan. The club closed, and he happened to be in Sing Sing on some unrelated charges, of course, during that time. When the story became old news and everyone lost interest, the club reopened, and he was back out on the street. Ladies, I know you love working at the club, and I am not even going to suggest you quit. Just be careful to look out for each other."

We were all quiet again, sipping our tea, thinking about Geraldine when Mrs. Spears decided to go upstairs to check Tessie's room. "I know it's far from likely, but maybe we're wrong. Maybe she's been up there all night." When she came back five minutes later frowning, we knew Tessie was still not in the house.

* * * *

Mitzi and I tip-toed down the hall the next morning to Tessie's room to see if she was back. If she was really tired, you could sometimes hear her snoring through her bedroom door. When we got to the door, we heard something, but it wasn't snoring.

"I thought I told you to be back in this house before they came back from the Savoy," someone whispered. "And I thought you said y'all would be in bed by 9:00! If you hadn't been up, nobody would have known I wasn't here."

"Well from now on you need to be back here when you say you gonna be back. And I ain't helpin' you come up with whatever lie you gonna have to tell to get them three off your back! They worried sick about you."

"You just better keep your mouth shut, or else I'm telling everybody what I know."

"Oh, look out now, 'cause that can go both ways." When we heard footsteps coming toward the door, we managed to duck back into Mitzi's room just in time to see Mr. Greer sneak back down the stairs.

* * * *

Sometime before breakfast that morning, the mailman arrived, and I received this letter from Lily.

April 10, 1928, Tuesday
Nostalgia,
I thought you would have written me back by now, but I see I'm just gonna have to chase you down. Please don't stop writing to me. I really need to hear from you! Did you think I wouldn't want to talk to you because you left? I know you didn't know about the deal Daddy made with Noah. I told you I have a plan to get out of this. I'm going

to be alright it's just going take time. I can't tell you exactly when it would be, but I think it might be sooner than two years.

Just because I'm only 14 Noah thinks he's going to be able to control me. You know I had to tighten my coochie by making a woman's wash out of alum and bathing in it for two weeks! I knew the reception would be a pig picking, so I had Henry collect some of the blood in a tiny glass bottle. On that first night after Noah got up to use the bathroom, I poured the hog blood on the sheets and between my legs. He really thinks he slept with a virgin! I had to do it. If it had gotten back to Daddy that I wasn't a virgin who knows what would have happened! My being 'unhandled' had to have been a major factor in the bride price. If it got found out that Henry and I were having relations, Noah would have had his men kill him!

I've already lost you so I can't lose him too. Noah's so much older than me that it's always quick. Then he goes to the bathroom, comes back, and goes to sleep. Other than that he doesn't touch me. He doesn't talk to me but to tell me what he wants for dinner. He does talk to everybody else though, and all I have to do is wait and listen. While I'm waiting and listening I need to be hearing from my sister.

Daddy and Mama seem fine. Daddy has really taken to working for himself as a farmer. Since both of us are out the house the extra work of being a farmer's wife seems to agree with Ma, but I can't really tell because she's never been one to complain. I have never been able to tell if she is happy or sad about how her life with Daddy turned out. Now that I am a wife too maybe she'll talk to me.

I have to go make Noah dinner. He likes pigs' feet.

Your Beloved Sister,

Lily

PS

Noah has allowed me to go to Mrs. Barden's house to work a few days a week! Little does he know it happens to be on the mornings that Henry delivers the milk! It's not ideal, but it's all we have for now. Henry's not mad at you, he's just sad about losing me. He knows we'll be back together soon. I miss you.

Lily wasn't a virgin when she married!? My little sister had lost her virginity, and I STILL hadn't lost mine? Well, why else would Henry, an 18-year-old man, have a relationship with a 14-year-old girl? When did they ever find the time to… to… OH MY GOODNESS! I didn't want to think about it, but I couldn't stop! My little sister wasn't a little girl anymore, and apparently hadn't been one for quite some time.

Alum and hog's blood? Where did she get that idea? And she had to be right in her assessment: the chance to mold and control a virgin would be priceless to a louse like Noah Holdtstaff, or any man for that matter. At 14 years old my little sister, Lily Richardson Holdtstaff, was a woman, and a resourceful one too! She was right. It had been too long since I'd written her, so I took the time to do it right then.

April 16, 1928, Monday

Lily!

I was not prepared to hear how you feigned virginity on your wedding night, let alone that you weren't a virgin when you married! When did you and Henry ever find the time to be alone long enough to… engage in such activities?

What is this plan you have to get out of the marriage? Exactly what are you watching and waiting for?

I see how you're using Mrs. Barden. How is she anyhow? I guess her high-class friends are pretty satisfied with you being the hired help since you're darker than me. They always insisted that I was so light-skinned that I'd give her husband 'ideas'!

I wasn't ignoring your last letter it just hurt me to think of what you were going through at my expense, and at the hand of our father's actions.

So Noah never touches you unless he's satisfying his desires, and he never talks to you except to tell you what he wants for dinner. How that must make you feel! I am truly sorry, Lily. Now that you're a wife maybe Mama will talk to you instead of just floating around the house as if nothing is wrong.

The more I think about it, the more I wish you had come up here like I asked. I understand why you stayed, but the truth is Daddy created that situation for himself, and getting out of it should very well be his problem! You still could come up here and get a job singing in one of the clubs. I really wish you would reconsider.

I went out last night to The Savoy Ballroom of all places, and it was the bee's knees! Duke Ellington was there, as was Langston Hughes, and Rose McClendon. The inside of it looks like Heaven on Earth.

Believe it or not, I think about you all the time having to live with that monster. Please be careful. What if he found out you were meeting Henry at Mrs. Barden's house? Lord knows what he might do to you both!

Your Beloved Sister,
Nostalgia

Chapter 7

"Good morning, everyone," said Tessie as she sat down to breakfast. After the conversation we heard between she and Mr. Greer, Mitzi and I could find nothing normal to say. But it made no difference because Mrs. Spears pounced like a lioness, "Where were you last night, young miss? Nostalgia and Mitzi didn't see you at The Savoy." I'd never seen Mrs. Spears' lips pursed so tightly in annoyance, but she kept her composure.

"It was so crowded I changed my mind about going in, so I went to Esther's. We talked most of the night. I didn't mean to get in so late, but I just forgot about the time. Y'know that Esther really is a hoot!" Tessie laughed.

"Esther? A hoot? Since when is that dud any fun? And furthermore…"

"Stop it, Mitzi," I pleaded, but she ran over me like I was a rat in the street.

"… just what were you and Mr. Greer talking about this morning when he came out of your room?"

"I beg your pardon?" Mrs. Spears directed this question at Mr. Greer more so than Mitzi, who calmly continued spreading butter on his toast.

Mitzi continued, "Nostalgia and I heard those two talking about telling some secrets on each other! And I don't know about anybody else, but I'm ready to know what they are."

"I think that's a very good idea, Mitzi," said Mrs. Spears still looking at Mr. Greer who had yet to look up from his breakfast, but chewed slowly on his toast.

Tessie looked at Mr. Greer too, as if she were pleading for help.

Finally, he looked at Tessie, then at Mrs. Spears who looked like she wanted to box his ears. "Tessie, we can't hide this anymore. Go ahead and tell them."

"I will not. You go first."

"Well somebody had better go first before they're looking for a new place to live!" Mrs. Spears would decide to be the landlady at this moment.

Mr. Greer looked at her in earnest, "About two weeks ago I found Tessie coming home late…"

"As he was coming out of your bedroom, Mrs. Spears," added Tessie.

Mrs. Spears' cheeks turned crimson.

"Oh, please! And who don't know that?" Mitzi stifled her giggles. "You call each other by your first names all the time. Just last night you were helping her roll a skein of yarn. A man doesn't help you roll up a skein of yarn unless he's getting something in return." Mitzi laughed so hard she about fell under the table.

"Alright, Mason and I have been…" but rather than confirming any of her own naughtiness, the blushing, discombobulated Mrs. Spears briskly changed the subject. "Well… that still doesn't tell us anything about what Tessie has been up to!"

"Very true," agreed Mitzi.

When the looks on the faces of Mrs. Spears and Mitzi demanded an answer as to her whereabouts last evening, Tessie skulked like the kitten that had purloined the last bite of tuna. "Mitzi do you remember a few weeks back when The Duke had the band practice late on Saturday night…"

"Uh huh…"

"… and since nobody would be at The Basement, Bunky told us to wait for him at The Savoy?"

"Yeah I remember. What about it?"

"Well, do you remember a waiter brought us some drinks and said the person who bought them wished to remain anonymous?"

Mitzi thought a minute before answering Tessie, "Yeah, I do remember that!"

"Well, let's just say I found out who sent us those drinks."

"Was it Arnie O'Neil?" asked Mrs. Spears.

"What? Of course it wasn't," Tessie insisted.

"Well, in that case, your new beau will be joining us for dinner tonight, and I am not taking no for an answer. Tell him dinner is served promptly at six-thirty. If he can't show up to meet you here, then Tessie, you don't need to be taking time with this person! And that goes for you two as well," and with that Mrs. Spears took her plate to the kitchen. She must have set it down and turned right around because she came straight back out empty-handed with a continuation of her thoughts. "And as for you, Mr. Greer," she put special emphasis on the 'Mr.', "how dare you allow the three of us to sit up all night worrying over this, talking about Geraldine, when you knew right well Tessie was in no danger at all!"

"Who's Geraldine," asked Tessie.

"We'll explain it to you later," I whispered.

Mr. Greer turned so red I would have sworn he'd spent a day out in a cotton field. "Evelyn…"

"Don't you Evelyn me! You sat here all night letting me think I'd lost another girl to that jackal." She started to leave the room for a second time, then turned around and said to him calmly, "you can sleep in your own room until further notice." She went back into the kitchen.

Mr. Greer got up from the table, threw his napkin in his plate while glaring at Tessie, and walked in the direction of the parlor.

* * * *

"You mean Mrs. Spears found this Geraldine in our bathroom?" Tessie's green eyes were wide with wonder.

"And she thinks Arnie is the one who beat her," added Mitzi to the already gruesome details.

A sense of anxiety washed over me afresh at hearing the story all over again. Truthfully I hadn't stopped thinking about it since I'd heard it. I didn't sleep well at all.

"Y'all know what this means, don't you," said Mitzi. "Means we can't ever leave the club alone. Not just for the sake of Mrs. Spears, but for each other. If we're going anywhere without the other two, then we've got to let somebody know."

"Yeah," I said.

"No, you just got here," Mitzi continued, "You don't get it. Did you know once you turn 21 you can no longer be a Cotton Club Showgirl?"

I suddenly remembered Mr. Greer mentioning Geraldine had turned 21.

"Ever since I've been here, and Tessie, you can vouch for it because you've been doing this longer than us, the girls just suddenly disappear when they turn 21, or when they make too many mistakes in the routines."

Tessie nodded in agreement with Mitzi.

"There's never a farewell party or anything like that. Up until last evening, I'd heard the girls were sometimes taken up to Ossining to see him in jail, but the folks who said it were always club patrons or entertainers. Mrs. Spears and Mr. Greer have first-hand knowledge it actually happened. All this time I thought it was just talk. Since we've been there, Tessie, think about all the girls who just didn't show up to perform. Did you ever stop to think Arnie may have had anything to do with it?"

I didn't know where Mitzi was going with this, so I asked, "well, do we tell the other girls about this?"

"Nope. People with big mouths have a way of disappearing too," added Tessie.

"What do we do?"

"Throw everyone else a hint that they should look for another gig if we know for a fact they're about to turn 21," Mitzi stated with conviction, "as for the three of us, we leave with Bunky, Josiah, or have one of the other band members hail us a cab."

"And to be safe, I'm leaving all together when I turn 20," said Tessie.

"Can we change the subject, because quite frankly, this is making me sick," I said. They both agreed to my proposal.

"I'm sick of talking about it myself... So what's his name?" Mitzi smiled at Tessie.

Tessie shook her head, rolling her eyes because she knew the interrogation was coming, "I refuse to say."

"Well, what does he look like?" I chimed in.

Tessie looked at me, shaking her head no.

"Okay, can you tell us exactly what happened that night at The Savoy," begged Mitzi.

Tessie walked over to the coat stand to get her coat. Then she sat back down with it in her lap before beginning the story. "After the waiter sat the drinks down you never stopped talking, Mitzi. I, on the other hand, sat back in my chair and looked calmly all around the ballroom. Then I spotted a man gazing at us. I suddenly realized he was just gazing at me!"

Tessie continued after letting out a whimsical sigh. "He slowly raised his glass. You didn't even notice, Mitzi, but I raised my glass too... and we sipped our drinks at the same time. That's when I knew who bought the drinks. Then Bunky showed up, and it was like you both forgot about me. I didn't mind though, because I went up the marble staircase. I don't know how I knew it... I just felt he'd be there. I looked over the balcony watching you two Lindy Hop... and I waited... a few moments later I felt warmth on my back and a whisper "hello" in my ear... I turned around and there he was..." Tessie's eyes had glazed over as she relived the moment.

She'd forgotten she was talking to us. Mitzi and I were looking at her, in awe of the tale.

"We leaned in close to each other, and began dancing to a music no one heard but us. I stayed with him on the balcony all night, sometimes watching you and Bunky dance, other times staring into his eyes. Before I knew it, you two were back at the table looking around for me. Apparently, you were ready to go and waiting for me. When I was about to bid him good night, he asked me to meet him the next night at Washington Square Park. We met there for the next two nights…"

Mitzi shook her head, cutting Tessie off, "Wait a minute… Washington Square Park? Tessie, is he…?"

This time she cut Mitzi off, "I have to go to Western Union to send him a telegram about dinner!" she said as she pulled on her coat, rushing out the door.

I was confused, "What was that about?"

Mitzi looked at me evenly, "You'll find out tonight at dinner."

* * * *

With all the excitement of the morning, I thought I might be able to sneak in an afternoon nap so I could be somewhat fresh for dinner when I heard a knock at the door.

"Nostalgia, dear, you have a phone call. It sounds like that nice young man who went out with you all last night. Invite him to dinner." Mrs. Spears sounded like she was in much better spirits, so to stay in her good graces, I decided I would.

I knew Bunky was coming, and Tessie was supposed to introduce her mystery man, so I thought why not. "Hello?"

"Hello, there! It's good to hear your voice. How is your day?" The timbre of Josiah's voice made me fluttery all over on the inside. I wondered if he could sing.

"Interesting... I know this is short notice, but we're going to have some folks over for dinner tonight, and I was wondering if you'd like to join us."

I could hear him smiling through the phone! "That's one reason why I called. Bunky insisted. Apparently, he spoke to Mitzi earlier about it, and I guess I'm letting you know I'll be there."

"Well, then I look forward to it! You said you had another reason for calling?"

"Yes. When you came back from upstairs last night, you barely spoke to me the rest of the evening. What did I say that was wrong?"

"Nothing, I just really miss my sister. I didn't mean to offend you."

"You didn't. I understand missing family. I can't take the place of your sister, so can I just keep you company in the meantime?"

"I appreciate that. I'll see you tonight."

"I'm looking forward to it... and you."

I placed the phone back on the receiver. Wow! Someone's looking forward to me. I ran back upstairs to find the perfect dress for dinner.

* * * *

"Blue is really your color," said Mitzi as she finished helping me put on my dress. She looked beautiful in her pink chiffon number. It was relatively form-fitting to show her shape. The pale pink orchid behind her left ear matched her dress and gave her an exotic aura. I was wearing one of the dresses Mrs. Barden had given me before I left.

Mitzi helped me bind down my chest, so the lines remained straight until there was a flirtatious ruffle around my derriere, which gave the dress, and my silhouette, a subtle accent.

We left my room and knocked on Tessie's door, but she said she wasn't ready. We headed on downstairs.

Bunky and Josiah were waiting for us in the parlor with Mr. Greer and the married couples. I sat next to Josiah on the settee, Bunky and Mitzi shared the tete-a-tete sofa in the corner, while the married couples sat jumbled together on the couch. Mr. Greer was in the arm chair, and if you listened closely you could hear Mrs. Spears moving between the kitchen and the dining room.

The ladies were all gussied up for the evening in perfect hair, make-up, and dress. All the men looked just as handsome as they did uncomfortable in their zoot suits and two-toned shoes. I must say I didn't mind getting all dolled up two nights in a row. The men would probably have begged to differ.

As soon as the doorbell rang the race between Tessie's footsteps coming down from upstairs while Mrs. Spears was coming into the parlor from the dining room began. Being younger and more anxious than everyone else gave Tessie the competitive edge. There was a small whispered exchange between the two of them in the foyer at the base of the staircase in which Tessie insisted Mrs. Spears go back into the parlor with the rest of us and wait for her and her mystery man to enter together.

Mrs. Spears acquiesced reluctantly, coming back into the room with us. Mr. Greer shot out of the armchair like a poppet to make room for Mrs. Spears to sit down. She sat as regal as a queen without giving him a glance. We all waited.

The door creaked open as Tessie peeked inside the parlor to see if we were all there. She stepped inside followed by the most handsome white man I had ever seen in my life!

Chapter 8

"Everyone, this is Peder Skaagens. Peder, this is everyone," said Tessie.

No one moved. Everyone looked surprised except Mitzi, and of course, Mr. Greer. So this was what she meant when she said I would find out at dinner!

The tension in the room developed its personality, tugging at the corners of some lips while the tongues in between remained immobile, raising some eyebrows while others were furrowed, all the while we anticipated… somebody had to speak, now who among us would play the sacrificial lamb….

"Mitzi, Bunky, I feel as if I know you just from watching you Lindy Hop every Saturday night." His voice was so deep. It almost reminded me of my daddy's! "You must be Nostalgia. Tessie really enjoyed helping you get ready for your auditions, and she is so impressed with the way you have adjusted to life in the city." His eyes were so blue, his smile was so perfect. He turned from me to Josiah, "Saxophone, huh? I've got to come hear you play one night," he stuck out his hand as a baffled Josiah shook it. He turned to the couples next. "You must be Mavis! One of the things I first noticed about Tessie was her hair. She said the style was all your idea." Mavis giggled in spite of herself. "Jude, right?" Somehow Jude mustered a speechless, open-mouthed nod, shaking hands with Peder, "Good to know you. Cicely, make-up artist extraordinaire! George… how's it goin'?" The half-smile on George's lips complimented Mavis's giggle.

I realized that he had been holding a pink cake box the whole time, giving it to Mrs. Spears and Mr. Greer, stating in earnest, "Your home is lovely! Thank you for letting me come."

Taking the cake box, Mrs. Spears' lips were pursed so tightly together she looked at Mr. Greer who answered for them both. "We appreciate you coming."

* * * *

"Skaagens... I don't recognize the origin of your name," Mrs. Spears sat down and began her line of questioning as soon as she was sure everyone's plate had been served.

"Danish, Ma'am," Peder said between bites of roast beef.

"Mmmm," she replied. "How many generations?"

"Three. My grandfather moved here in the mid-1800's."

"Ah, the famine!"

"Yes, Ma'am," Peder confirmed.

"Most people of your... descent moved to the Midwest. Why did your family stay?" Well her name wasn't Mrs. Spears for nothing. She was sharp!

"Does she treat everybody's new beau like this?" I leaned over and asked Mitzi, who looked at me out of the corner of her eye, nodding silently as she ate.

Peder smiled, "My grandfather was a stonemason who couldn't find work in his trade. A Jewish gentleman inquired about a job on his behalf. When my grandfather got the job, he had my grandmother make the gentleman and his family a batch of Danish pastries as a way of saying thanks. The Jew and his family were so impressed with the pastries that he offered to give my grandfather the financial backing needed to open his own pastry shop at the rate of 20% of the profits for ten years."

Mrs. Spears was thoughtful for a moment before her eyes widened, "Skaagens' Danish Pastries?"

"Yes, Ma'am," said Peder.

Mrs. Spears smiled for the first time that evening.

* * * *

The pink box filled with Danish pastries served as a satisfying dessert after our meal. When everyone finished eating the men sat at the table while we ladies helped Mrs. Spears clean up the kitchen. Every now and then we heard hearty laughter at some joke Bunky was telling.

"Man, you and Josiah had it easy! The first time I came here to see Mitzi, she roasted me on a spit!"

When everything was put away, we went back into the parlor where the men moved the furniture. Tessie, Mitzi, and I got our records from upstairs to play on the RCA Victor. All the couples cut up the rug while Mrs. Spears and Mr. Greer sat and watched.

The evening ended when George reminded Cicely, and Jude and Mavis, of the time. Bidding everyone goodnight, the married couples went upstairs. Our gentleman callers kissed our cheeks and whispered fond farewells in our ears before leaving at 10:00. We three stepped back into the parlor to find Mrs. Spears and Mr. Greer smiling, walking hand-in-hand in the direction of Mrs. Spears' bedroom.

* * * *

And all the warmth in the house that night, what with the two new love affairs and the rekindling of the old ones, ushered in the warm days of spring and summer! Cold weather may have lasted longer up north than down south, but the days seemed hotter. Mrs. Spears explained it was because so many people were all in one place, plus the cars, and subway system all required some sort of heat to function.

On that first really hot day I heard laughter, giggles, and water running in the street. When I rushed to the window in the parlor to see what was happening outside, I saw children of all ages, shapes, sizes, and shades running around an open fire hydrant! The playfulness of it all looked like such fun I wanted to get barefoot and jump in it myself. Later that night I mentioned it to Josiah, and he said we might be able to satisfy that desire. I decided to be patient and see how he would impress me.

That following Monday morning he and Bunky picked up Mitzi and me for what I thought was the longest car ride of my life. Just as I was about to complain about being cramped in the enclosed backseat, the air changed, and for the better! I smelled salt water wafting on a breeze. Sea gulls screamed at each other for no other reason than to hear their own voices, and the clouds rolled around the pale blue sky giving the sun's rays an obstacle course to run. Finally, Bunky parked in front of the boardwalk on Coney Island! I'd never seen a beach before with such yellow sands.

I wriggled out the backseat of Bunky's car, ran across the wooden planks, nearly knocking over some man with side curls and a yamaka. He acknowledged my "Excuse me," with a shake of his head and a wave of his hand. I ran on the sand dunes toward the ocean until I lost my footing, falling forward on my face. A mouthful of sand didn't stop me. Josiah, Bunky, and everybody else possibly seeing the knots in my thigh-high stockings didn't stop me. I was desperate to feel the cool ocean on my hot legs and feet. I got up and ran toward that blue-green water again, and this time I made it!

* * * *

"So why do they call it Coney Island?" I asked as I licked the mixture of ketchup and mustard off my fingers. I'd never had a grilled hotdog before either. We always boiled or fried them back home.

Nathan's at Surf Avenue was crowded so we wormed our way through the masses. I didn't know where Bunky and Mitzi were.

"Well, I heard that a Coney is a rabbit, and since everybody hops from the beach to the boardwalk, to the carousel, why wouldn't it be called 'Coney Island'?" I decided Josiah's explanation made just as good sense as anything else I might hear, so I accepted it.

As par for the New York course, there were all kinds of people speaking different languages and accents. Old World Jews wearing dull colors, while Indians and Arabs wore bright ones. White folks and coloreds near each other, but not really acknowledging one another, and everybody sucking down hot dogs, cotton candy, popcorn, and Royal Crown Cola! It amazed me how food always brought folks together. I guess it's because we all get hungry.

We saw Mitzi and Bunky coming toward us from the direction of the carousel. She was carrying a giant Raggedy Ann doll, and I could tell from the strut in his walk and the swell in his chest Bunky acquired it by some manner of showing off.

"Did you get on any rides yet?" he asked me.

My mouth was full so Josiah answered for me, "Not yet. I don't think we should, I mean you are eating…"

"No please take me, please," I begged. He took me to the carousel, which would be the only ride my busting stomach would allow on that first visit.

Chapter 9

My first spring and summer in New York consisted of evening walks through the Morningside Park, kisses beside the Seligman Fountain after performing at The Cotton Club, stompin' and Lindy Hopping at The Savoy on Sunday nights, trips to Coney Island on Mondays during the day, dinner at the house and dessert with Skaagens' Danish Pastries on Monday evenings, days of sleeping as late as 9:00 am, and vague letters from Lily.

That summer Noah taught my sister how to shoot a handgun and a rifle, and how to drive a car! She insisted her mysterious plan was working better than she anticipated, and she just couldn't tell me the particulars because she didn't want to get her own hopes up, let alone mine.

She still managed to see Henry on those milk-man mornings when Mrs. Barden would turn a counterfeit blind eye to the shenanigans of the hired help. In the hindmost corners of my mind, I wondered how long it would last, but I would no sooner remind myself Lily's letters were upbeat and happy. Why should I worry? However, every Sunday morning at the Abyssinian Baptist Church, as well as every day in between, I prayed those missives remained so.

Early fall showed up just as suddenly as the spring and summer. The kiddies went back to school. No one smoked cigarettes on their stoops anymore because of the frigid air. Thick stockings felt good hugging my legs once again, and the chic coat and hat Mrs. Barden gave me were still en vogue according to Harper's Bazaar.

True to her word, when she turned twenty, Tessie began auditioning for other venues. Not two weeks after her birthday, Tessie became a Lindy Hopper at The Savoy Ballroom. No more Cotton Club for her!

Sometime during the middle of October when the leaves began to change, and dew was ever so slightly frozen on the windows in the mornings, Bunky let Josiah borrow his car one Sunday evening. He told me to pack a bag.

I asked, "Why?"

He said it was a surprise.

When we got to Cape May, New Jersey I smelled the ocean but didn't see it. Partly because the beaches were abandoned and it was too cold to explore them, partly because we were colored, thus making it harder for us to find a hotel with a view of the shore. It didn't matter. The room was cold with dingy walls, one window facing a brick building, and a bed with lumps in the mattress… perfect. The first time, when it's with the right person, was always perfect.

* * * *

"But Josiah my teeth are chattering," I said as we were walking toward the Seligman Fountain in Morningside Park. It was so cold the city had cut off the water in the fountain weeks ago to keep it from freezing over.

Josiah insisted we come out here after dinner on this particular Sunday night because he wanted to be alone. Before we said goodbye to everyone and left for the evening, he told me to get a wool blanket from my room.

After we had gotten out of the cab, we got two hot chocolates from a dime store. Now we were walking in the cold, late fall evening breeze.

"I told you, every time your teeth get to chattering just say it as fast as you can, and they'll stop." He insisted it worked for him ever since he moved up here from Mississippi three years ago.

"Alright, I'm going to try it. M- I- crooked letter, crooked letter, I- hump back, hump back, I!"

Josiah laughed at me, "Naw, Baby, you missed three letters. Lemme show you. M- I- crooked letter, crooked letter, I- crooked letter, crooked letter, I- hump back, hump back, I! You want to try it again?"

"No, I want to go where it's warm," I said.

"C'mere and have a seat then," he said.

We sat down on our bench. I held the hot chocolate while he spread the blanket over us. He took his chocolate then pulled me closer into the crook of his arm. Suddenly it was so warm! It was as if we were on our own little cozy island while the rest of the world shivered outside.

"Did you come up with that way to spell your home state?"

"I wish. That's how the teachers taught us to spell it when we were in school," he said as he blew on his chocolate.

We were silent a minute, taking in the nighttime sounds of the park, watching other people pass by. An older couple was walking their dog. When they saw us, they smiled politely.

"You think that might be us one day," he asked.

"If not them then Mrs. Spears and Mr. Greer." We looked each other in the eye when I said this, then we both burst into laughter.

"Why don't they just get married," he said.

"Lord knows he never sleeps in his room," I added.

We were quiet again. I asked him, "How did you end up coming here three years ago?"

"If I tell you that will you admit to me why your sister is such a sore subject," he replied.

Touché! "You got a deal," I acquiesced.

He pulled me even closer before he began, "I don't know what happened to my parents, but I was raised by my grandmother. We lived on what used to be a cotton plantation because she was born a slave. The cotton plantation, of course, turned into shareropping, and she'd been there so long and was so old the 'Massa's merciful grandson' let her live there for free until her death. I was 16 when she died and wanted no parts of what they offered me to stay on the land. So I left."

"You don't have any more family down there?" He chuckled at my question.

"I do, but they have this mind everybody who stays down south seems to get. Makes you just settle for what your parents and grandparents had, or what the white folks are willing to let you have. I wanted something else. I had three cousins I used to run with, Snake, Boo Boo, and Gizzard. I don't even know their real names if you want the truth. We all used to go to this juke joint called the Bucket of Blood Saloon."

The look on my face at hearing the moniker made him stop a minute to explain. "The place got its name from all the knife fights they used to have. Just a backwoods kind of place. Moonshine ran like a river. You could smell cigarette smoke for miles down the road after you left it. Fast women. I think Boo Boo lost his virginity to one of those strumpets. And music… loud, loud music. The four of us were outside of it every weekend. They were there for the usual stuff: the women, the booze, and the cigarettes. I was there for the music. Every weekend they had a new band. And there was something about that alto sax." He was on his feet now, pretending he was playing one. He was animated and passionate about his instrument.

"One Saturday we went there a little early, and we saw the band setting up for the evening. The alto sax was just sitting there as the band members were taking in the equipment. I picked it up, and I held it just like this… and I know I shouldn't have, but I couldn't help it… I put my mouth on it. You know what makes the alto sax so special?"

I could only shake my head in answer to his question. I was so moved by what he was telling me.

"When you hold it close to you, it feels like a woman, and sounds like one who's getting loved on the right way." He moved with the imaginary sax for a few more moments. "The next thing I hear is 'what the hell are you doing with my woman, fool?' I looked up, and there he was coming at me like he was going to kill me! I dropped it and ran. I came back later that night to apologize to the owner. He laughed and told me I couldn't have his, so I better get my own girlfriend. I asked him how. He said I needed to save some money for one and get some lessons. Then he told me he could look at the way I was holding it and tell I was a natural. I asked if I could hold it again. He looked at me, and he said, 'see if you can make some sound come out.' I blew on it the first time, nothing. I blew on it the second time, nothing. I blew on it that third time… she sounded like you the other night." He laughed at his own joke.

I must have looked a little embarrassed because he sat back down, taking me back into his arms before continuing, "He looked at me with his eyes all bugged out, and he said, 'Dang, Baby! You better go get yourself some lessons!' Grandma died a little bit after that. Every time I was in town folks would be listening to the jazz station on the radio, and it was always 'Live from the Cotton Club in Harlem NY'. I knew one day I had to be here. So here I am." He concluded his tale with a smile on his lips, squeezing me even tighter.

"Alright, your turn," he said, reminding me of our pact.

I really didn't know how or where to start my story, so I picked up from where he left off.

"A few years back I started working as a housekeeper for a white woman who always listened to the same jazz station, and that's how I heard about the Cotton Club myself. I managed to save a lot of the money I made by lying to my parents about what I actually made. I gave them what they thought was all of my wages and kept the rest in a sock in the floor board of the bedroom I shared with my sister." I could tell he noticed the tears in my eyes by the way he rubbed my back as I told my tale.

I took in a deep breath then continued, "One day when I came home the biggest bootlegger in town was sitting in the sitting room with my daddy. Lily told me later that Daddy had brought him to the house to marry me. He was 49 years old! So the next day I took my money from the hiding place, and I went to work like I always do. I ended up telling Mrs. Barden, the lady I worked for, what happened. She helped me get a ticket on a New York bound bus. I met Mrs. Spears on the way up. She offered me the room, and here I am."

"But that still doesn't explain why you're so sore about your sister."

I could see he was not going to let this thing go, so I fessed up in a hurry. "The bootlegger paid my daddy for me, so when I left Daddy made Lily marry him!" I said through tears.

He stared at me with his mouth opened, shocked for a few moments, then he asked me like he was trying to piece it all together, "He's 49? How old is your sister?"

I was crying so hard it sounded surreal, even to me, when I said it, "14 when the wedding happened. She turned 15 late in the summer."

"That pig!" shot out from his lips like he had spit.

"She didn't tell me there was money involved until she wrote me back after I had moved here. Otherwise, I never would have come. I would never have put her in a fix like that."

He held me as I cried. "Have you asked her to move here with you? You could send her the bus fare or Bunky would let us borrow the car…"

I shook my head no at his suggestions. "She said if she left, Noah, that's his name, would probably kill our father, or make him pay dearly from whatever he grew on the farm that he bought with the money. I know she's right. Plus she has this beau she was supposed to marry. She and Henry had been keeping company for two years when I left. She manages to sneak away and see him on the sly a couple times a week. She's not leaving him for anything in this world." My face was burning from feeling the mixture of cold wind and hot tears. Josiah gave me his handkerchief to wipe my runny nose.

I was so embarrassed carrying on like that, but I couldn't help it. "She says she has some sort of plan to get out of it, but she hasn't said what it was, just that it's 'going better than she thought possible.' Oh Lily, I am sorry I let this happen to you."

"I don't know what you're sorry about. It's that daddy of yours who's at fault. I know he is your father, and I don't rightly know the man, but I know the difference between right and wrong. Making your 14-year-old daughter marry a 49-year-old man to settle your debts is wrong. And that reminds me, Nostalgia how old are you?"

My eyes widened at his question, but I knew that soon it would come up, so I chose not to avoid it, "I'll be 17 come January."

He crinkled his brow, shook his head, and shrugged his shoulders, "Okay. I realize we should have had this talk before we went down to Cape May and spent the night together. Are we moving too fast for you?"

"No. We're fine." I said quickly to reassure him. He smiled, covering us again with the blanket.

We stayed there cuddled together until the moon had risen above the tree tops.

Later, when he walked me to the front door of Mrs. Spears' brownstone to kiss me good night, he whispered in my ear, "If anything about us doesn't feel right to you, promise me you'll let me know."

"I promise," I said.

We kissed once more before I opened the door and went inside for the evening.

Chapter 10

October 29, 1928, Monday
Dear Lily,

It's been some time since your last letter, I hope all is well. I wanted to let you know that I have a beau! His name is Josiah James, he comes from Biloxi, Mississippi, and he plays the alto saxophone for The Duke Ellington Orchestra. We met the first weekend I performed at the club, and we have been spending a lot of time together ever since. He's tall, dark, handsome, talented, and a gentleman.

Before our first date to The Savoy Ballroom Mrs. Spears picked him over with a fine tooth comb. I found out later that she treats all of our gentleman callers like that.

I guess what I really want to tell you is I am no longer a virgin! He took me to a place called Cape May, New Jersey, back in the early part of the month. It's a beach town. We got a room at a hotel, after what seemed to take forever because we were colored, and spent the night. You could have at least warned me that it hurt.

Anyway, Tessie is no longer a Cotton Club Girl. She got a gig as a Lindy Hopper at The Savoy Ballroom. She does the Lindy Hop, of course, and she gives dance lessons to the patrons at the club. It's odd not having her around at the Cotton Club anymore, but she still lives here, and we see her on Saturday nights after we're done performing. She works every other Sunday evening at The Savoy. On those Sundays when she's working, Peder, the white man I told you she was seeing who brings the Danish pastries, still eats with us here at the house, then he heads over there to spend the rest of the evening with her. They seem happy.

Fall in New York feels like the dead of winter in South Carolina. The change in the weather is coming, and I'm feeling a bit melancholy.

This past spring I didn't miss getting up early to work in the garden before going to Mrs. Barden's house. This summer I didn't miss getting up early to pick black-eyed peas and dig for potatoes. Now it's getting cold again. It will be my first Thanksgiving, Christmas, and birthday without my family. This is the beginning of my favorite time of the year, and there's no Indian summer either! You're somebody's wife now, so I guess you're too busy to notice the difference. My relationship with Josiah could not have happened at a better time.

Well, I have to go, but I wish you would write me back soon. I miss you so much.

Your Sister,

Nostalgia

PS

How are Mama and Daddy?

* * * *

On top of fewer letters from my sister and there being no Indian summer, it had been raining for what seemed like endless stretches of time. The combination of fall rain, gusty wind blowing colored leaves around, and a lack of sunshine made it get colder quicker. I had never seen my breath during the fall down south! I happened to let out a sigh as I was waiting for a cab to take me downtown to the bank one Monday morning close to Thanksgiving. The little puff of freezing smoke surprised me as it escaped my lips. Then I felt a rush of cold air plunge down the back of my throat. As my defense, I pulled my hat down over my ears and my scarf tighter around my neck.

I began to regret not waiting for Mr. Greer to come back upstairs from the cellar. He had promised Mrs. Spears he would bring up the Christmas decorations by that evening so we could start dressing the house after Thanksgiving Dinner this Thursday. He would have gladly hailed me a cab, but I was so anxious to see how much money I had saved in my Christmas Club account so I could start shopping for gifts.

So far my first Holiday season was not as lonesome as I thought it would be. Josiah had been taking such good care to make sure my doldrums over not being in familiar surroundings would not ruin the season for me. "48 Wall Street, please," I said to the driver as I got into the cab.

I found Mrs. Spears had given me sound advice in the way of saving money. I made $27 a week at the Cotton Club, thus, I put $2.70 a week in the collection plate at church, and $2.70 a week in my regular savings account which left me quite a bit even after I paid her $5 for rent. Mr. Goldfarb suggested I open a Christmas Club account to avoid last minute scuffling trying to come up with money for Christmas gifts.

My Christmas list was longer than it had ever been before! Used to be just Mama, Daddy, and Lily. Now it's Mrs. Spears, Mr. Greer, Mitzi, Tessie, Mavis, Cicely, all the girls in the troupe, my main costume mistresses, and Josiah. I figured I could send something to Mrs. Barden and

Lily as New Year's gifts so I wouldn't have to struggle with the postal service on top of all I would have to deal with during Christmas week.

By the time I arrived at The Empire Savings and Loan of New York the security guard had just opened the doors from the inside to let in a line of patrons who had been waiting. Most of them went to sit in the red velvet chairs to wait for Mr. Goldfarb or some other banker to speak to. I stood in line behind two others waiting for the teller.

When my turn came, I went to the far left corner. "And how might I help you today, Miss," said the lady. I was still trying to get used to white folks calling me "Miss"!

"I need to know how much is in my Christmas Club account, please."

"Certainly. Your name?"

"Nostalgia Richardson."

"Account number?"

"CC 58201." I watched as she flipped through the cards before coming to mine.

"Alright, Miss Richardson, is it?"

"Yes, Ma'am."

"As of today, you have $53.47. Will you be taking any out to begin your shopping this weekend?"

"Not yet, I just wanted to get an idea of what I had so I could plan how to spend it."

"Well, that is an excellent idea. Here is your receipt, and you have a nice day."

"Thank you. You too." I left the bank in a happy daze. I'd never had so much money at Christmas time in all my life. I actually had enough money to buy everyone exactly what I wanted them to have. My first Holiday season in New York and I could afford to shop!

* * * *

On Thanksgiving morning Mitzi and I had to wake up early to go over to the Cotton Club to prepare for the Macy's Christmas Parade, which started at 145th Street and ended at 34th Street in front of Macy's Department Store. It was so cold! Mitzi promised me once we started dancing we would feel warmer, and that the route didn't feel as strenuous as it sounded.

The day was cold, clear, and cloudless. We were to perform Black and Tan Fantasy, but instead of all the feathers, we would be wearing Santa Suits. The dresses were just above our knees, red velvet with black sashes and white cotton fringes at the hem, cuffs, and collar. We had to pin our matching Santa hats on our heads to keep the wind from blowing them into the street. The band would be behind us playing on a double-tiered float. The Duke, of course, would be on the top tier playing his grand piano, while the orchestra would be surrounding him on the bottom.

We were warned every so often he would stop playing to take a minute to wave at the crowd. To avoid letting it distract us, we were to listen closely to the band playing, as opposed to the piano rifts to keep our dance movements in time with the music.

I was so nervous because I had never performed in a parade before, let alone a parade in New York City! The other girls reassured me that after we started dancing, I would forget about the crowd, and it would be fun, and all such as that. However, it was hard to believe at that moment.

On either side of the street, there were all types of onlookers, mainly immigrants, sitting, standing, and holding little children on their shoulders so they could get a better look at us, the performers. Benny Goodman was there, as well as Bill Bo Jangles Robinson, Shirley Temple, and others. Mayor James 'Jimmy' Walker sat on a float and waved. The Felix the Cat balloon looked like he was about to swallow you whole, and if he did he certainly had room enough to hold you in the pit of that big stomach.

A few times I got a glimpse of Josiah looking at me instead of his sheet music. His smile still could brighten any day for me.

When we finally reached 34th Street, we were told we could try to go home if we liked, or we could stay for the grand finale to see Santa and watch the balloons. Since Bunky had gotten up extra early to park on 30th street and take an omnibus back uptown, we decided to go on ahead and leave. We figured by the time we take all those alternate streets back uptown to Mrs. Spears' house it would be time for the grand dinner.

And grand it was! Turkey, ham, dressing, cranberry sauce, mashed white potatoes, mashed sweet potatoes, cabbage, collards, cornbread, and string beans were the menu, and for dessert, I volunteered to make a pumpkin pie and a cherry pie the night before.

All got their fill. Before we could think about going into the parlor or up to our rooms to sneak in an after-supper nap, Mrs. Spears reminded us all we were not just there for dinner, but to dress up the house as well. I'd never seen a bought Christmas tree, but it was beautiful and fragrant. Mrs. Spears told me it was a fir tree. When we finished dinner back home on this day, Lily and I would go to the woods with Daddy and his ax to chop down a pine. However, a pine looked mighty sparse in comparison with a fir. There were fronds on top of fronds.

Mr. Greer trimmed the stray branches to make garnishes for the windows. Mrs. Spears placed a fake holly wreath on the front door and delegated decorating responsibilities to the rest of us. Josiah and Bunky were assigned to help Mr. Greer with the windows. Tessie and Peder hung mistletoe and holly boughs. Mitzi and I made a garland out of popcorn. George and Cicely, and Jude and Mavis sifted through ornaments to find the ones that hadn't been broken since last Christmas, and everybody helped decorate the tree. By 7:00 George, the tallest male, placed the angel on top of the highest bough. By the time the brownstone was ready for Christmas, we were all ready to eat again!

* * * *

November 30, 1928, Friday
Nostalgia,

I am so sorry for taking so long to write you back, but today is the first day I've had to myself in the longest! I'd no idea what our mother had to deal with until I had a house and a husband of my own, not to mention a job outside the house! Thanksgiving was held here, and Mama and Daddy, Cousin Ruby, Minnie Mae Funderburke, The Tuckers, Reverend and Mrs. Clark and their little ones,

Uncle Chester, Cousin Reese and her husband, and five of Noah's hirelings showed up for dinner. I thought it was just going to be Mama, Daddy, me, and Noah. I found out differently three days ago!

I had to help Mrs. Barden get her house ready for Thanksgiving and Christmas, and get my own house ready for Thanksgiving. And no I didn't set foot in the woods to help Daddy try to find a Christmas tree this year. I was too blame tired! I made turkey; Mama brought a honey ham and a sweet potato pie. I made potato salad, chitins at Noah's request, corn muffins, and mustard greens. String beans, pig's feet, candied yams, cranberry sauce, red velvet cake, peach cobbler, and pecan pie all made it here, too. I just don't remember who brought what.

There were so many people in the house I could barely keep up.

After dinner, the men went out in the yard to do a little bit of target practice, and do you know what Noah did? He called me to the backyard and had me shooting with them. The gun AND the rifle! Then he bragged that he taught me everything I know, which is actually true, but I didn't know he thought I was that good with a gun. You remember how Daddy used to never let us, or Mama, touch guns? But now, every time I pick one up I feel like Annie Oakley, or Carry Nation. Knowing how to use a weapon of some sort, be it a gun or a hatchet, makes you feel like you can conquer the world! I try to remember though, that Reverend Clark says if we live by the sword we die by the sword. I'm sure that applies to guns as well.

I also have to remember the only reason Noah taught me to shoot was in the event somebody tried to break into the house when he wasn't around, so I can defend myself, or whatever he might be hiding in a stash. He thinks I don't know he keeps stuff here, but I do. I just don't know where. I don't rightly know why he taught me how to drive a car, but that's okay. It's bound to come in handy one way or another.

The only folks missing from yesterday were you and Henry. He's fine. He realizes our new situation is only temporary. I'll see him Monday morning when he delivers milk to Mrs. Barden. She told me to tell you hello and to call her directly if you needed anything.

Your Beloved Sister,

Lily

PS

Please tell me how your Thanksgiving was! Surely Josiah is keeping you good company up there. I didn't tell you it hurt because I thought maybe you had already… well, you know… I'm happy for you! I know he'll take good care of you until I see you again.

Well, it was nice to know Lily had a good day on Thanksgiving, even if she was married to a pig, and didn't go with Daddy to the woods to pick out a tree. I couldn't help not thinking about last year when it was just the five of us: Mama, Daddy, me, Lily, and Henry, and most years to tell the truth…

Wait a minute! Wonder what was that nosy old biddy Minnie Mae Funderburke doing at my sister's house? It amazed me I wasn't the least bit homesick until I read Lily's letter! I hadn't thought about the twins, Cousin Ruby and Cousin Reese since I saw them last Christmas. I could almost see their father, Uncle Chester, smoking his pipe and Mama looking at him out the corner of her eye because he was stinking up the place. Reverend and Mrs. Clark with their little army must have made a big noise, and an even bigger mess before they left for the evening, I'm sure. She was six months pregnant with their fifth child when I left. Wow! Wonder if it was a boy or a girl?

Henry. What did he do all day long on holiday without my sister? I know he has a family of his own, but blood relations don't take the place of who you choose to lay your heart and your bones next to every day of your life. That's why I was so satisfied being with Josiah that day despite it being my first Thanksgiving away from all I'd known my whole life. After spending the last two Thanksgiving days with Lily and my family, how did Henry bide his time that day?

I started feeling bad all over again, so much so I didn't write her back right away. I decided when I did I would send a card that had a Santa on it or something that would be cheerful and not so serious.

In the meantime, I lay there curled up on my bed listening to the sounds of the street. Vendors hawking their wares, kiddies playing stickball, cabs, and omnibuses whizzing by, neighbors greeting each other, strangers walking by themselves to no place in particular, or to some place that meant everything. Time was moving, feelings were changing, thoughts were rampant, while I lay still, holding my sister's letter to my chest. Everything seemed to be passing through on its way to somewhere, or somebody, else. That was when I realized holidays for me would never be the same again.

Chapter 11

New York was truly a magical place at Christmas time, so magical it proved to be what I needed to take my mind off my guilt over Lily and Henry. The lighting of the Christmas trees all around the city, and even the one in Mrs. Spears' house seemed to say 'all is forgiven', 'everything's going be alright', 'look forward to the future'. The city was constantly baptized in a gentle snowfall that reflected the lights and seemed to confirm the purity of everyone's heart.

Happy Chanukah! I'd learned my first bit of Yiddish. For the first time in my life, I put folding money into the Salvation Army collection bucket as opposed to loose change. It felt so good to have money at Christmas and feel loved. Josiah and I were two expatriates from down south who'd created love and adoration for each other up north, yet had stumbled upon familial affection through Mrs. Spears' brownstone. There were no blood relations in that dwelling whatsoever, but it made no matter. We were a family.

I realized it the weekend after Thanksgiving when Peder took Tessie to meet his family. At the mere mention, she was once a Cotton Club Showgirl, there was no doubt she was colored. Tessie said the congenial attitudes of the evening changed after that, however, Peder did not. He continued to take her places like Chinatown, Williamsburg, Brooklyn, even Astoria, Queens, and any other place where her being colored was never really an issue. And of course, there were always dinners at Mrs. Spears' brownstone.

Even though he was white Peder was welcomed. Not because he happened to bring the best pastries in all New York City, but because he was Peder.

George, Cicely, and Bunky all had blood relations in the other boroughs. Jude and Mavis were from Virgilina, a little border town that couldn't decide whether it was in North Carolina or Virginia. I was from South Carolina, Mrs. Spears and Mr. Greer were both from North Carolina, Mitzi was from Georgia, Tessie was from Washington D.C., and Josiah was from Mississippi. All of us, despite our various and sundry upbringings, had created our little family in a brownstone in Harlem. Some things can only happen in New York City!

* * * *

I found a nice card with a Russian Santa standing in a snow drift with Christmas trees behind him in a small grove. I was in much better spirits, thus I began my letter to my sister:

December 4, 1928, Tuesday
My Dearest Lily!
I am so happy you seemed to enjoy your Thanksgiving. You sounded like quite the hostess! Mine was good too. I made pumpkin and cherry pies, as I always do. Mrs. Spears made turkey, ham, dressing, cranberry sauce, string beans, collards, mashed white and mashed sweet potatoes, and cornbread. Everybody was there I've told you about, Mr. Greer, the married couples- Jude and Mavis, and, George and Cicely, Mitzi and Bunky, Tessie and Peder, and me and Josiah. We ate until we were about

to bust, and instead of taking naps Mrs. Spears had us all dressing up the house for Christmas. She and Mr. Greer bought the tree a few days before, and it was beautiful. Much thicker than any pine we could have found out in the woods with Daddy.

When we finished dressing up the house we were all hungry again, so we ate our second dinner. Then Mrs. Spears made hot chocolate, and we sat around the tree singing carols. It turned out to be a full day. Not only did I not take a nap after dinner, but the Cotton Club Showgirls, along with The Duke Ellington Orchestra, also had to perform in the Macy's Christmas Parade that morning.

When I finally got to bed, I declare I was asleep before my head hit the pillow, I was so tired! Even through all the excitement, I thought about you, Henry, Ma, and Daddy, and the last two years when it was just the five of us on Thanksgiving. My how things have changed.

Well, I have to wrap this note up so I can go out and do some shopping. Tell Mrs. Barden I said Merry Christmas.

Your Beloved Sister,

Nostalgia

* * * *

I went down to 37th Street and 5th Ave. to begin my shopping at Tiffany & Co. The first gift on my agenda was to get Mrs. Spears one of those lamps. I decided to get her gift first because she was the first person I met here, not to mention, it happened to be the most expensive of all the gifts. From there I walked over to Bergdorf Goodman and got four Balenciaga scarves for Mitzi, Tessie, Mavis, and Cicely. I got twelve 1.2 ounce bottles of Chanel No. 5 for the girls in the troupe and my main costume mistresses. A pair of canvas work gloves for Mr. Greer. And finally, I spent my last two dollars on a felt derby for Josiah.

I was so excited! I had never spent so much money on such extravagant gifts in all my life. Furthermore, this was the first Christmas time I have ever had the pleasure of having my own room, so I could hide them in there without worrying about anyone sneaking in and looking for their gift. Lily was the worst for that. I don't think I ever really surprised her at Christmas, certainly not birthdays. She always figured out where I hid her gifts no matter where they were. I knew she'd be surprised this year, though. First of all, I'd be sending hers as a New Year's gift. Secondly she's not familiar with the stores up north, so there was no chance Mama would get her the same thing. Mrs. Spears told me to wait until the day after Christmas to shop for the folks back home, that way I could take advantage of all the sales they had at Macy's.

By the time I got back to Harlem and stashed everything away, it was almost time for me to get ready to meet Tessie and Mitzi for dinner. Even though she didn't work at the Cotton Club anymore, Tessie still worked the same hours except every other Sunday night.

"Well, Nostalgia, how was your shopping trip?" asked Mrs. Spears as she set a plate of smothered chicken and mashed potatoes in front of me. "It was hard deciding what I wanted to get for y'all just because I could afford it, not because I couldn't. That Christmas Club account is the bee's knees!"

"I know," said Mitzi. "I didn't know there was such a thing until I moved up north."

"So what did you get Josiah?" asked Tessie.

"I got him a felt derby."

"Wow!" said Mrs. Spears.

"Yeah, and he better wear it too. It cost me enough."

"I don't know what to get Bunky, God bless him. I ask him if there was anything he wants or needs and he keeps saying, 'Just you Baby, just you'." We all laughed at Mitzi's rough imitation of her honeybun. Tessie seemed deep in thought.

"Tessie, is everything okay?" asked Mrs. Spears.

"Yes, it's just that in the past if I didn't know what to get a beau, I would ask one of his sisters or his mother what would be good for him. This time I don't have that option. It's just strange that's all."

None of us knew what to say because we couldn't imagine having such a problem, but we knew what she meant. Peder's mother and sisters practically ignored her the rest of dinner that evening after he had mentioned she was once a Cotton Club Showgirl, while Peder's father and brothers tried to be nice but it was a perfunctory nice, and all made it a point not to touch her hand when she left.

Before being a customer in some of the stores, the bank, and the post office downtown, I had never been near white folks unless I was working for them. Other than Peder, I had never sat down at a dinner table with them, let alone a sitting room to have after dinner tea and biscuits to try to have a conversation. What do you say to them? Do they talk about the same things as us? Peder was different because he didn't seem to notice or care we were colored. He even said once that Harlem reminded him of his own people because it was settled by the Danish, and the major areas still had Danish names.

One day Josiah and I walked outside on our way to Morningside Park and overheard Peder having a conversation with his driver, Avery, about what to get his wife for her birthday, of all things! He made suggestions about places to take her and gifts to buy her like he was talking to an old friend. In a lot of ways I supposed Avery was an old friend, because he had been driving for the Skaagens' family since he was in his teens. It made no matter, people were just people to Peder. It was a shame all white folks didn't feel that way.

"Well, my first Christmas with Mason I got him a pair of cufflinks from Tiffany & Co. I'm sure Peder would like that, especially coming from you," suggested Mrs. Spears.

"That's not a bad idea," said Tessie.

Mrs. Spears glanced at the grandfather clock, "You three had better head on over to Lenox. You don't want to be late."

* * * *

The two weeks before Christmas flew by, and with each passing day the number of gifts under the tree in the sitting room grew until they took up half the room! Thanks to the decorations we hadn't moved the furniture to dance in a while. The RCA Victor played Christmas music constantly. It snowed just enough to enhance the scenery, but it was never to the point of bothersome. Mrs. Spears told me the big snow drifts wouldn't happen until well into

January. The whole city smelled of pine and sweet cakes. Everybody was happy and giving. The children stopped their snowball fights just long enough to allow strangers to pass as they were carrying gifts home. Mrs. Spears also commented that was only because they knew Santa was coming and he was surely watching. After January 5, the official final day of Christmas, everybody would once again be a target.

Jude and Mavis were planning to go back down to Virgilina until right before the New Year, so they wouldn't be here on Christmas Day. George and Cicely would probably go to Brooklyn to visit their families. Mitzi said she and Bunky would be going to visit his family in Yonkers sometime after dinner that day as well.

Either way, the house would still be full. Mrs. Spears had planned to cook enough to last the entire week. After shopping, cooking, cleaning the house between the holiday trimmings, getting the gifts ready, and sending the cards she said she wouldn't find any time to rest otherwise.

In between all the fussing around I wondered about Lily and the folks at home. I'm sure I would have heard if something was wrong. Mrs. Barden might not live directly in my old neighborhood, but Spivey's Grove was still small enough for her to be an effective extra pair of eyes and ears.

On the last night that we all performed at the club before it closed for the Holidays, Arnie O'Neil announced that everyone was to step into the dining room before heading over to The Basement for the Cotton Club Christmas dinner. He gave each of us an envelope and said

"Merry Christmas," in that Irish accent he refused to get rid of. Mitzi and I each opened our envelopes and found a card with a Santa saying 'Merry Christmas' and a $50 bonus! This season was getting sweeter and sweeter all the time.

* * * *

"Josiah James, get from underneath that Christmas tree this instant," warned Mrs. Spears as she came into the sitting room from the kitchen carrying a tray of hot cinnamon cider. It was 2:00 in the afternoon on Christmas Day and we had yet to have dinner or open our gifts because she insisted we all wait for Bunky and Peder.

The knock at the door had a musical beat so we knew that could only be Bunky. "I'll get it," Mitzi was on the other side of the parlor in an instant! Anticipation does wonders for the blood stream. When she reentered the room from the foyer, Bunky and Peder followed carrying more gifts to add to what was already under the tree. As usual, Peder handed Mr. Greer a pink cake box filled with all our favorite Danishes. Since Jude and Mavis were down south, I didn't have to share the raspberry ones with anyone. "Alright, I hope you all brought your stomachs. Let's go into the dining room and eat!" Apparently, Mrs. Spears was hungry too.

Compared to Thanksgiving the menu was relatively small, yet satisfying and plentiful. Turkey, mashed potatoes and giblet gravy, biscuits, cranberry sauce, and green beans were for dinner. For dessert, I made a coconut custard and carrot cake, and of course, Peder brought the Danishes.

Mrs. Spears insisted we all sing Christmas hymns around the tree before opening the gifts in order to acknowledge the birth of the Baby Jesus was the real reason for the season. Bunky then put on his red and white Santa hat and began passing out gifts with Josiah, acting like an elf, assisting him. Aside from leaving the gifts that were for Jude and Mavis under the tree, we were able to see the floor once again!

Mrs. Spears loved the Tiffany lamp. However, she loved the sapphire earbobs Mr. Greer got her even more. Among the other gifts she received a glass cake dish, a set of handkerchiefs with flowers and her initials embroidered on them, a box of Whitman's Chocolates, and lastly, Josiah gave her a 1.2 ounce bottle of perfume by Van Cleef and Arpels. "If I had children of my own they could not have treated me better," she said!

George gave Cicely a gold band implanted with a diamond stud. The underside was engraved 'All My Love'. Cicely gave him a pair of suspenders with matching sock garters. Bunky gave Mitzi a sterling silver bracelet from Tiffany & Co, while she gave him a silk bow tie, with matching cummerbund and pocket handkerchief. Josiah loved his felt derby, while I got a sterling silver lavaliere with a garnet surrounded by diamonds! Was it just me or had every man in the room visited Tiffany & Co?

Well not quite! Peder was the exception. His gift to Tessie was the biggest box under the tree. When Tessie opened it a brown mink coat with gray lining, and her initials sewn into the collar spilled out! Tessie was flustered, speechless, happy. As if to compliment her joy,

Peder took off the cuff links he was already wearing to replace them with the ones she'd bought him. Family, be it blood or adopted, a filling dinner, lavish gifts, and being in the presence of the one you love most, has all the makings for an unforgettable, all be it perfect, Christmas!

* * * *

On New Year's Eve, we all sat around the parlor sipping egg nog, eating another carrot cake I made, and listening to the radio for the ball to drop at the One Times Square building. For dinner, George and Jude managed to get their hands on some catfish from the Gansevoort Market, and boy did Mrs. Spears fry it to perfection! It was so good it reminded me of my mama's. We also had collard greens, black-eye peas, and cornbread. Delicious. I wasn't expecting to ring in the New Year in Harlem with real southern food, but I was not about to complain.

I remembered last New Year's Eve at home with my folks, Lily, and Henry. There was no egg nog or staying up late. Henry left at 10:00, the latest he ever stayed at the house on any night, and we all went to bed so we could get up and take the decorations down before January 5th.

"They starting the countdown!" said Bunky as Mrs. Spears turned up the radio. We all began counting with the radio announcer, "… 10, 9, 8, 7…" Josiah pulled me closer to him in preparation for his midnight kiss, my first time ever kissing a man at midnight, "… 6, 5, 4, 3, 2, 1, HAPPY NEW YEAR!" With the exception of an instrumental rendition of Auld Lang Sine playing on the radio, the room was quiet for at least one minute because we were all kissing our beaus and husbands. We all clinked glasses, drank egg nog, and wished each other Happy New Year personally.

No one had to go to work the next day, so we all stayed up, even Mrs. Spears and Mr. Greer. This was the first time guests were allowed to stay later than 10:00. Mrs. Spears warmed up second helpings of the dinner. My carrot cake was eaten down to the last crumb. Bellies were full, eyelids were droopy, thoughts were pleasant, and all of us were ready for bed. The married couples eased up the stairs while we each kissed our company good evening and Happy New Year under the watchful eyes of Mrs. Spears and Mr. Greer once more before parting. I went to sleep humming Auld Lang Sine. 1929 was off to a great start!

Chapter 12
1929 & 1930

January 2, 1929, Wednesday

Lily,

HAPPY NEW YEAR! How was your holiday? I hope it was fine. Mine was nothing to complain about whatsoever! I have to get down to the business of shedding these pounds I've gained from all those holiday dinners. Esther, the costume mistress for the troupe, will not be happy with me on January 6th when I go back to work.

What did you get for Christmas? Josiah got me a sterling silver lavaliere from Tiffany & Co., this fancy jewelry and novelty shop in midtown New York City. It has a garnet stone surrounded by diamonds in the center. It is so beautiful. I hope one day you'll see it. I got a few other gifts too. A $50 Christmas bonus from my boss at the club, a box of chocolates, a pair of black satin gloves, a pair of silk stockings with seams, and a few other things.

I hope you like the gift I got you. One thing I did not miss about you this Christmas is that you were not around to go snooping and looking for your gift. I picked it out especially for you, I just wish I could see the look on your face when you open the box. Make sure you give Mrs. Barden credit for your present if Ma, Dad, or Noah ask where you got it, okay? Speaking of Mrs. Barden, let me know how she likes her gift too.

How did Ma and Daddy fare this Christmas? Did you and Noah get them a collective gift? Who all showed up at the house this year? Was Christmas at your house too or

did you go somewhere else? Lastly, what are your plans for
the year 1929? I sincerely hope you have it set in stone to
get out of that marriage and come up here and live with me.
Please let me know.

I miss you so much,

Nostalgia.

* * * *

I realized when they sang Happy Birthday to me that
I'd never heard so many people sing it to me all at one
time. I'd expected it would be a quiet night with just me
and Josiah maybe going down to Cape May for some time
alone. I'm glad about how it turned out, however. The gang
was all there: Mrs. Spears, Mr. Greer, Jude and Mavis,
George and Cicely, Mitzi and Bunky, Tessie and Peder, and
of course, Josiah.

Mrs. Spears made my favorite dinner: smothered pork
chops, string beans, mashed potatoes and gravy, and
biscuits. The cake was a Neiman Marcus. White cake,
white icing, topped with 17 candles! I'd never heard of a
department store having a cake named after it, but that
didn't stop me from making several wishes before blowing
out those candles.

Josiah got me a pair of dangling pearl ear bobs from
our old friend Tiffany & Co. I also got a Max Factor make-
up set, 1.2 ounces of Cartier Perfume, and a batch of
raspberry Danishes.

I still thought about my family, though. I know they
were thinking about me and wondering what I was doing. I
hope Lily reassured our mama I was okay. I got a letter
from her this morning, but I thought I would wait until I got

in the bed that night to read it. I so wished she was here in Harlem with me.

I wondered after she got away from Noah if she would consider moving up here. If she moved, I know Henry would follow. If they got married, I was sure they might be able to live in Mr. Greer's room since he never uses it. I could always hope.

"What did you wish for?" asked Mrs. Spears.

I just smiled because I knew none of my wishes would come true if I revealed them. "I can't say what I wished for, but I will say this, I would love for these moments to last forever."

"Wouldn't we all!" said Mitzi.

"Let's have a toast to that sentiment," suggested Peder. We raised our glasses of hot cider in the request that these times of friendship and prosperity would linger in this house forever.

* * * *

January 11, 1929, Friday

Nostalgia,

If I have done my figuring right, you should get this letter on your birthday... So HAPPY 17TH BIRTHDAY! By the time you begin reading this, I will have been thinking about you all day long! I know you've had a great one, I just wish I could be there!

Before I continue, I want to say that I have never owned a pair of cashmere gloves with a matching hat before. I don't think I have ever seen anything like it in Spivey's Grove! It came just in time too for those frosty days. I get so many compliments on them, and since I have been telling everybody they were a gift from Mrs. Barden, her friends are so jealous. She thinks it is so funny. She thanks you for the gift you got her too. You can't ever go wrong giving any woman Chanel No. 5!

We went to Mama and Daddy's new house for Christmas dinner, and all the same folks from Thanksgiving showed up with a few more new faces. I'm just waiting for old biddy Funderburke to start some rumor about what did or did not happen at the house that day. On Thanksgiving Day I supposedly had a dry turkey and not enough food. Ha! Do you know she brought a container from her house and filled it before she left? I invited her here because I don't like for anybody to be alone on the holidays. Looks like I done started a tradition, so I can't un-invite her next year. Oh, well.

I don't know how they did it, but Ma and Daddy had a gift for everybody under the tree that came to the house. Even for Reverend and Mrs. Clark's chaps. Most of those folks were curious to see what a real farmhouse looked like. It was a good one, I just missed you and Henry.

So what did Josiah get you for your birthday? What did you do all day long without us? I remember last year I got you that copy of Uncle Tom's Cabin and accidently burnt your cake to a crisp! I should have known better than to try to bake a cake for a dessert maker like you, but I just thought for once you shouldn't have to bake your own cake. I should have bought it like Mama said.

Speaking of Mama, she told me something quite interesting! She told me to let her know if anything went "amiss" in my house. Now, why would she do that? I mean she is our mother, but she has never seemed to take much interest in anything outside of what our father demands her to do. I'm floored! She actually wants to know what goes on in my house. To tell you the truth I have nothing to tell her. It's the same as it was when we first married.

He is, however, starting to get a little lax about his business like I knew he would. Like he left some papers from some of his dealings on the chest of drawers one evening! He just took them out of his pocket, laid them up there and went to the bathroom then got in the bed. When he started snoring, I snuck out the bed and looked at them. Nothing of real importance. They looked like prices, but I don't know what the product might have been. Or it could have been a list of payroll amounts without the names to keep the people secret.

It's only a matter of time before he leaves something that I can use. Because I'm so young, and a girl, he thinks I won't understand what he does. He'll slip up soon enough, I just have to wait. He's the head of a big operation. All you have to do with the head of any snake is cut it off to make the kill.

Well, I have to go to work. Henry is expecting me!
Your Beloved Sister,
Lily

Mama is starting to talk to Lily. Noah is starting to get lax. Henry is still waiting. I didn't know what to make of the letter. I was glad she still sounded happy, considering. I just wish I could see, actually see, that she was for myself. What could she be looking for Noah to leave unattended? If she managed to get any information what could she do with it? I don't claim to know what Noah sells, who buys it, or who works for him, but one thing is for sure: Lily better be careful. The last thing I need is to lose my little sister. My conscience would be done for at the thought of her finding out something that would make Noah or his henchman want to kill her. I don't think I'd be able to live with that for the rest of my life.

January 18, 1929, Friday

Lily,

You were absolutely right on time! I got your letter the morning of my birthday and saved it to read that evening when I was in my bed. I am so glad you enjoyed yourself at Mama's house. I just wish I could see it. You said it had eight rooms? Wow, all that on the inside, then the chickens, the pigs, and the cow on the outside. And I know she has flowers in a little garden somewhere around there.

What do you think she meant by 'amiss'? Did you ask her if she thought you should be looking for anything in particular? 'Amiss' could mean anything from dust on a chair leg to whatever it was you'd hoped to find in the papers he left on the chest of drawers.

You're waiting for him to leave some evidence of his questionable dealings is what I'm guessing. Lily, stop looking because it ain't bound to happen. He's been doing whatever it is he's been doing to make money longer than you or I have ever been alive. He knows how to cover his tracks. I don't ever remember hearing about him getting caught, let alone going to jail.

If your plan A does not seem to be working by the middle of the year and you don't have a plan B, I will gladly be your plan C. Mrs. Barden will drive you to the bus station. Henry would be up here a day later I bet if you asked him. Just be careful. Are you going to say anything to Mama about this? You trying to blackmail a bootlegger might be her idea of something 'amiss.'

Well, I better go. We're learning some new dance routines, and I wanted to get a little bit of rest before I go to work. Take care and write me back sooner than you've been writing.

Nostalgia

PS

For my birthday we all had dinner and Josiah got me a pair of dangling pearl ear bobs! Maybe you'll be here for my birthday next year. I hope so.

Chapter 13

Mavis was so tiny Jude could just throw her around like a ball when they did the Lindy Hop! Our Sunday night dinner routine was to have a little dance contest in the living room to work off the heavy dinner Mrs. Spears always made. Tonight, though, Tessie and Peder decided to go out to dinner since it was her first Sunday night off from The Savoy since the New Year began. The music from the RCA Victor was loud, and the joint was jumpin' until I thought I heard something that sounded like a knocking on the window. I said something to Josiah, and he stepped out into the foyer to see if there might be someone at the front door. Sure enough, he heard someone knocking and told Mrs. Spears. When she lowered the volume on the Victor, we all heard desperation pounding on the door! The frantic sound sent Mrs. Spears, Mr. Greer, and practically the whole house into a run for the foyer. Mr. Greer opened the door to find Avery, Peder's driver, holding up a crying and frightened Tessie. Peder was nowhere to be seen.

"What happened?" demanded Mrs. Spears.

Avery looked devastated himself. "Mr. Skaagens had me drive them to Perth Amboy for dinner at a restaurant. One of the owners must have figured out Miss Jefferson was colored because he walked up to her and spit on her."

"Dear God!" said Mrs. Spears, taking Tessie into her arms and leading her into the parlor. We all followed them inside where Avery continued to tell the story.

"Mr. Skaagens stood up so quick he almost flipped the table over! Then he punched the man square in the jaw.

Before anybody could stop it, the fight was on. It took three police officers to get Mr. Skaagens off the man. As they were hauling him into the paddy wagon, he shouted to me to bring her back here."

Tessie's big audible sobs sounded so pitiful I think all of us ladies were about to join her lamentation. The men just listened to Avery, shaking their heads and getting angrier with every detail.

"Man, I hope he busted him good!" said Bunky through clenched teeth as he struck his palm with his fist.

"Bunky, PLEASE!" said Mitzi.

"Sorry, Ma'am," he said apologetically to Mrs. Spears.

We were all quiet a minute before Bunky said, "We gotta go see about this!" in mid stride toward the coat stand.

Josiah looked at me before saying, "Yeah," and following suit.

"I'm comin' too," said George.

"You and I gotta stay here with these ladies in case some fool followed Avery back here," said Mr. Greer to Jude, who nodded.

"I'm going down to Washington Square to tell his family, so they can bail him out. I'll be back," said Avery.

They were all gone on their assignments, leaving us ladies, and Mr. Greer and Jude, to console an overwrought Tessie.

* * * *

Avery came back first with the most depressing news I'd heard since Daddy made Lily marry Noah. "They disowned him and refused to post the bail money. He gotta stay there."

"Well surely he has money of his own," reasoned Mrs. Spears.

"Yes, Ma'am, but he can't get to it," said Avery as he shook his head, taking off his hat.

After hearing this exchange, Tessie wailed like a March wind anticipating a month of April rain. Her eyes and nose were so red she used every handkerchief in the house to the point of exhaustion it seemed.

Mrs. Spears looked at Mr. Greer. He nodded wordlessly and they went back to her bedroom. We all eyed at each other, wondering what that communication could have been. When they came back, Mrs. Spears asked Avery, "How much?"

He looked at her wide-eyed, "For the bail?"

"Yeah, man! How much?" confirmed Mr. Greer, annoyed.

"$500," Avery sighed.

They looked at each other, then nodded wordlessly again before Mrs. Spears conceded, "We're getting up early to run down to 48 Wall Street first thing tomorrow morning. Cicely, Mavis, you two will be responsible for making breakfast for the house."

"Yes, Ma'am," said Cicely.

Just then George came into the parlor followed by Josiah with Bunky's arm across his shoulder while holding a bloody handkerchief to his face. Mitzi let out a cry. Josiah led him over to the couch as Mitzi hovered closely.

"Baby I'm alright! Dang cop hit me with a Billy club. All I did was ask if we could see Peder before they treat me like some kind of criminal! Talking about 'does he know any of his kind of people', and then gonna git to laughin'… stupid cops!"

By this time Mavis had brought out a cold towel to give to Mitzi who placed it on Bunky's face. I walked over and hugged Josiah when I noticed a scratch above his eye.

"Don't worry. Bunky did it when George and I pulled him into the car to keep the situation from getting any worse."

Mrs. Spears left the room to get cotton balls and alcohol, giving them to me. Josiah winced but sat still as I doctored on him the best I could.

When Mrs. Spears was sure all the blood, tears, and bad feelings caused by the night's events had been stanched, if not completely stopped from flowing in the house at least for this particular evening, she reminded everyone it was well past 10:00.

As he was leaving with Josiah and Avery, Bunky promised to come back the next morning to take Mrs. Spears and Mr. Greer downtown to The Empire Savings and Loan of New York, and then to Perth Amboy.

* * * *

"They wouldn't even let us post the bail money let alone see him," said an obviously flustered Mrs. Spears as she, Mr. Greer, and Bunky came into the parlor in the early afternoon. They had been gone since 7:30 that morning after what had been a sleepless night for all of us.

"Did Tessie come down at all today," asked Mr. Greer as he took Mrs. Spears' coat from around her shoulders, and walked over to the coat stand.

"She came down, had two bites of her eggs, then started whimpering. She went back upstairs, and hasn't been back down here since," said Mitzi, who came in from the kitchen with a tray of hot cider, sitting it down on the coffee table.

Right before she sat down next to him on the settee, she looked at Bunky, shaking her head at the bruise across the bridge of his nose and the two black eyes making him look like Brer Raccoon. "What is The Duke gonna say when he sees you tomorrow night?"

"I don't know, Baby. I'll figure out a way to sneak in when he has his back turned or something," he reassured her.

That suddenly reminded me, "Should one of us call The Savoy? I don't see Tessie going to work for at least a couple of days."

"I'll be alright by tomorrow night. Working will take my mind off this whole mess," Tessie's voice startled us all. She came in dressed, but looking like Peder had walked through her dreams. I felt so bad for her. She sighed, looking at Mrs. Spears, "He's still in there isn't he?"

Mrs. Spears nodded.

"They refused to let you see him or let you pay the bail because you're colored?"

Mrs. Spears nodded again at Tessie's revelation.

Tessie sat down, leaning her head on the back of the sofa like she was about to start crying again. None of us knew what to say to her, or to each other for that matter.

Bunky left, saying he wanted to get some rest, try to doctor on his face a little bit before tomorrow night, and figure out how he would conceal the evidence of the fray from The Duke for the next few days.

I can't say I knew what anyone else was thinking, but I wondered how these events would affect the family we had created. Not only had we enjoyed a beautiful holiday season, but we've been eating dinner together on Sunday and Monday evenings since last April. In the past few months, Peder had been here just as much as Bunky and Josiah, not to mention sitting at The Savoy during Tessie's shifts. Courtship makes any man an important part of a woman's house and family. It felt like we were losing a part of our family.

* * * *

The upstairs of the Middlesex County Courthouse was sweltering even in the winter. The heat from every radiator in the building seemed to rise to that one spot where only coloreds were allowed to watch trials. The only consolation of it was that we were looking down on all the white folks. It was me, Josiah, Mitzi, Bunky, Mrs. Spears, and Mr. Greer sitting at the front row of the balcony. When I looked behind us, there was a sea of colored faces, all shades, and all there to support some relative or friend who had the unfortunate circumstance of being caught up in a justice system that tended not to show us justice at all.

Avery picked Tessie up at the house earlier to drive her here. She had just arrived. Tessie was so fair she managed to sneak downstairs and sit among the white folks. If we didn't know any better, we would barely have been able to make her out. Mavis put a texturizer on her temples to keep them from turning back kinky, but just to be safe Mrs. Spears insisted she wore one of her turbans pinned at the forehead with a rhinestone broach a la Gloria Swanson, a pair of dark glasses, and the mink Peder had given her for Christmas. She looked like a movie star! Those crazy ofays probably thought she was.

An officer opened the door for her as she walked in, then another man got up from his seat and allowed her to sit on the inside of the bench. Another lady smiled and moved over to give Tessie more room to sit. We all watched, laughing. If they only knew.

Just then one of the doors from further inside the courtroom opened, and I thought it would be the judge, but instead it was Peder. He was wearing what he had on the last time we saw him when he picked Tessie up from the house a week ago, but it was wrinkled. There was also a rip in one of the sleeves. Then I noticed the hand cuffs and leg shackles. I let out a small cry, burying my face in Josiah's shoulder. He answered by holding me tightly. "I know Baby, I know," he said.

Peder looked tired and disheveled like he hadn't had any sleep, which probably was the truth. He had a black eye, a bruise along his jawline, and a band aid across the bridge of his nose. He was not the same Peder. The officers escorting him on either side led him to a table where a tall skinny man in a gray flannel suit sat with a briefcase and started whispering something to him. "That must be the public defender," said Bunky.

After a while, I noticed Peder seemed to be looking around the room. His gaze seemed to stop in Tessie's direction. I'm pretty sure I saw her give him a small nod.

"All rise for the Honorable Judge Kenneth H. Mark," said the bailiff. We all stood up as an older white man with a balding head and gray on the sides entered, taking his place at the bench. He was so short! If he wasn't sitting so high up you wouldn't have been able to tell.

"You may be seated. Case number 167-09, The State of New Jersey versus Peder Skaagens is now in session," smacking the gavel on the desk to confirm the announcement. The bailiff walked over to the judge, handing him a file. He took his time looking it over while the whole courtroom, colored and white, held a collective breath. "Counselors you may approach the bench," said the judge.

I hadn't noticed the other gentleman, who was somewhat heavyset. His suit was black and seated next to him was another man. The heavyset man approached the bench at the same time as Peder's lawyer.

"He must be the prosecuting attorney, and the other man must own the restaurant," whispered Mrs. Spears.

"Well why is there no jury?" asked Mitzi, and I must admit I hadn't thought of that.

"Probably because it's not a matter of if he did it, it's a matter of sentencing," Bunky rolled his eyes when he said this. Apparently, he'd had a little experience in legal matters.

"Either way it's still a bunch of white men out to get the sympathizer," Josiah said in disgust.

"Yep," agreed Mr. Greer, shaking his head.

The lawyers went back to their seats, each whispering something to the men they represented. Peder listened to what his lawyer had to say, suddenly looked surprised, then angrily shook his head as though he would not hear of what the lawyer suggested.

"Peder Skaagens please rise," said the judge. "On the charge of assault and battery, how do you plead?"

"Guilty as charged, Your Honor," Peder held his head up high.

"There is now a matter of you bringing a Negress into a white's only establishment. Apparently, your escort for that evening was so fair she could easily pass for a white woman. If you agree that you unwittingly brought this woman into the establishment, not knowing she was colored, then the state of New Jersey will drop the charge. Mr. Skaagens, how do you plead?"

"Guilty, your honor," Peder said with pride.

The courtroom got loud! I heard everything from "Oh, no he didn't", to "Nigger lover"! Comments were coming from all directions. Every kind of opinion that could be had on the subject was present, even on our bench, "Atta boy, Peder!"

"Bunky, please." Mitzi begged.

I looked at Tessie who remained still, not shifting her gaze from Peder's stance of brave stoicism, awaiting his fate.

"Order in this courtroom… I said… Order in this courtroom," demanded his honor as he repeatedly tapped the gavel. He stared at Peder incredulously before leaning forward, stating, "Young man, do you understand the ramifications that may follow what you just said?"

"I am aware, Your Honor." Peder seemed to stand straighter, more dignified as he answered.

His Honor sat back shaking his head before continuing, "I'm going to give you one more chance to understand exactly what I am telling you: if you consent to not having known your company for that evening was colored, this charge will be dropped, otherwise you will be punished to the fullest extent of the law!"

"I am aware your honor. I plead guilty to that charge as well," Peder was immovable. It made me proud, as well as sad.

"Peder Skaagens by the power vested in me by way of the state of New Jersey I do hereby sentence you to six months in the county jail without bail."

The courtroom got loud again, but as the officers were collecting him, Peder shouted at the top of his lungs, "Learn to speak French. Go see your family. I will come get you when I'm out!" Tessie had her instructions.

Chapter 14

"Learn to Speak French", "Go See Your Family", and "I Will Come Get You When I'm Out" were all splayed across The New York Daily News, The New York Post, and The Amsterdam News as headlines respectively. Underneath each headline was a picture of Peder standing before the judge. The news of the liaison between the New York socialite and heir to the Danish pastry throne, and Tessie was all over the news in New York and New Jersey for at least two weeks. Everyone knew all three statements were commands given to "the negress" as she had been called because Peder refused to disclose her name.

"Apparently when he is released he has plans to take the Negress to France..." said one paper. "...Danish socialite Peder Skaagens has since been disowned by his family, the Skaagens' of Skaagens Danish Pastries, who refuse to comment on the recent turn of events that has placed their oldest son in the spotlight..." said another. When the headline "The Mystery Negress" graced the Daily News sometime during the second week, Tessie was long since on a train to Washington, D.C., and no one at The Cotton Club or The Savoy who knew the particulars had opened their mouths in a show of solidarity.

We missed Tessie and Peder so much. Avery brought his wife by for dinner one Sunday night. He had said that the family would allow him to keep his job but he was to have no further dealings with Peder, whom he drove for mainly.

Avery went on to say because Peder was disowned by the family he would no longer have any right to go visit him in the jail. The last time he went, on the pretense he was relaying a message from the second oldest brother, Kroyer, he was told Peder was taken to solitary confinement because he had gotten into a fight with another prisoner who had made fun of him because of the negative publicity. Avery looked so sad. Apparently, after being his driver for so many years, there was an attachment that could not be replaced by Kroyer, or any other member of the Skaagens family.

* * * *

February 20, 1929, Wednesday

Nostalgia,

I am so sorry to hear about what happened to Tessie and her beau. You remember when we were younger and we used to think the north was a place where everybody had money, and all the races got along? I guess that just ain't the case nowhere. I still can't get over that your landlady wasn't allowed to post the bail just because she was colored! The only color that should mean anything is green, just as sure as Noah will sell booze and reefer to white folks AND coloreds.

Speaking of Noah. I was taking a walk around his land the other day, and I saw something growing that I didn't recognize. It was a plant with a long stalk and leaves with five points. So I took a sprig of it to show to Henry to see if it might be what I thought it was. You better believe it was REEFER! I've found Noah's reefer patch! And where there is reefer there is a whiskey still. It's just a matter of time before I find it. But don't you worry none. I won't get ahead of myself. I'll just work with what I got.

I won't go into any great detail, so I'll just say this: I'm gonna put a new ingredient in the chitlins and see how well he likes it. Oh, this is just the beginning.

Now that I think about it, it was about this time last year that you left! Can you believe it has been one year since you and I have seen each other face to face? I know this is gonna sound crazy, but if you hadn't left like you did I don't believe you and me would have ever gotten so close. I know you better now than I ever did. In that regard, I'm glad you went away. Your leaving also tested Henry's loyalty to me. I really know now for sure he loves me. I still miss you, though.

Your Beloved Sister,

Lily

PS

Mama and Daddy are alright. Speaking of the only color that should matter is green, I think Daddy's gonna try to sell some of what he's growing to Chavis's General Mercantile. Let's see if they buy from a colored man.

In the case of Noah, I felt Lily was getting a little too bold, so I wrote her back almost immediately!

February 27, 1929, Wednesday

Lily,

You stay as far away from that reefer patch as you can, you hear me? That's one of Noah's main commodities! I just bet he has it fixed so that if anybody stole from it, they'd get found out. Girl, you are just too much for me some times! I gathered from your last letter that you're planning on putting reefer in his food, but why? I never heard of reefer killing anybody, or do you know something that I don't?

I learned from this past year of exchanging nothing but letters with you that you are wise in ways I had never thought about. On that note I must ask you again: what is the point of putting reefer in his food? You just be careful. I don't care if you are his wife. He's still a bootlegger, and he'll just as soon kill you as look at you if he thinks you've crossed him!

So Daddy has so much land and crops he is going to try his hand at selling. That would be a good thing if Mr. Chavis bought from him. If he doesn't that should not stop Daddy from selling to the colored folks in town. I tell you, it sure was annoying to have to wait to go into that store when white folks weren't shopping. If Daddy sells to them, they won't have to wait anymore. I agree with you, when it comes to exchanging money for goods and services the only color that should matter is green.

I also agree these letters have brought us closer together, I just wish you could come up here so I can SEE how you're doing!

Everybody here is fine except we all miss Tessie and Peder. We haven't heard from him so I guess they don't send his letters, or he hasn't bothered to write because he knows they'll be opened before they even leave New Jersey. Mrs. Spears hears from Tessie every couple of weeks.

Well, I have to get some things done before it's time
for me to head to the club this evening.

I love you,

Nostalgia

PS

Tell Mrs. Barden I said "Hello!"

* * * *

Mrs. Spears told me later that Peder was allowed to
send one letter a month, and of course, that one letter went
to Washington. She heard from Tessie that Peder kept
getting into fights with other prisoners who knew about his
situation. The final straw was when he heard another
inmate refer to Tessie as a piece of 'pun tang!' Calling him
a "pretty-boy-Floyd" was one thing, talking junk about her
was quite another. Apparently, he beat the man so badly
they put him with the colored prisoners for the duration of
his time. He has not been back to solitary confinement ever
since.

Bunky was tickled to death, "Woo wee! Peder kickin'
ass and takin' names," which warranted the proverbial
"Bunky, PLEASE!" from Mitzi.

Tessie started teaching private dance lessons in the
D.C. area. I know it wasn't the same as what she was used
to, but at least her mind was occupied. She said her family
was getting used to the idea she'd be moving to France in a
few months. I couldn't begin to know what it would take to
prepare for such a journey. I guess that in addition to
learning to speak French and bidding her family farewell,
she must be getting her passport and all such as that.

Some folks might think it's too much just to leave blood and family relations, but if I've said it once I have said it too many times, no one is happy unless they're laying their body in the same place where their heart is.

My heart has been here in Harlem since I was 12 years old when I first heard about the Cotton Club while listening to the radio and cleaning Mrs. Barden's house. My body left South Carolina because it knew my heart would never be happy marrying with Noah Holdtstaff. Now my heart won't rest until I know my sister has gotten away from that louse!

Chapter 15

"Nostalgia, a telegram has just arrived for you!" Mrs.
Spears knocked on my door, interrupting my afternoon nap.
I dragged myself to the door. When I opened it she looked
pensive, like she wanted to stay there to see what it may be.
I'd never received a telegram before, so I was more than
curious. I took it from her but left my room door open
knowing she would follow me inside out of curiosity if
nothing else. I opened it:

Nostalgia stop

I regret to inform you that Lily has been beaten very
badly by her husband stop

She is under doctor's care and told me to tell you not
to worry stop

Call me when you get this stop

Mrs. Barden stop

I couldn't breathe... that man had beaten my sister!
My bed caught me just in time when my knees buckled. It
wouldn't stop going off in my head like a siren wailing,
THAT MAN BEAT MY SISTER!

"Nostalgia?" Somewhere in the background, I heard
Mrs. Spears say my name, but my mouth wouldn't allow
me to answer back. She gently took the notice from me and
read it herself. "Dear God! You never said your sister was
married. How old is she?"

When I tried to answer Mrs. Spears' question, my
breathing got shallow and jagged.

I heard her rush out into the hallway and holler
something down the stairs to Mr. Greer. When she came

back, she spoke gently, but I couldn't hear what she said. I couldn't breathe, but my heart was pulsating in my ears. My mouth got dry when I tried to speak.

Mr. Greer came in and gave her a glass of water to give to me. I took it. I drank it so fast I spilled it down the front of myself. It was like the wetness of it on my tongue facilitated tears in my eyes, then eventually big audible sobs, heaving sighs, and I couldn't stop thinking my worst fear had happened: the only thing that could make Noah beat Lily is he'd caught her with Henry! Oh dear God, had he killed Henry too? My brain was all over the place worrying about my sister and Henry.

Mrs. Spears and Mr. Greer stayed with me in my room waiting for me to regain my composure. When I told them Lily was 15 and married to a 50-year-old bootlegger, they quoted Josiah, "That pig!" When I told them I ran away and came here to avoid being married to him myself, they did not judge.

"Do you know why he would do such a thing?" asked Mrs. Spears.

Before I knew it, I was telling them about Henry and how they had been keeping company since Lily was 12, and still seeing each other even though she was married.

"If this man found out, that would make him angry enough to hurt her. I am so sorry, Nostalgia!" Mr. Greer shook his head, giving me his handkerchief.

I didn't mean to blow my nose right in front of them but I couldn't help it. I was a mess. I most certainly didn't feel like going to the club tonight.

"Well, do you have this Mrs. Barden's number? She asked you to call her. Talking to her might make you feel a little better."

At Mrs. Spears' suggestion, I made the call.

"Barden's residence!"

"Hello, Ma'am. It's Nostalgia."

"I see you got my telegram. I'm so sorry you had to find out like that. I hope you weren't alone when you read it."

"No ma'am I wasn't. Have you seen her?"

"No, he allowed her to call me…"

"They have a phone?"

"Yes, but she didn't want you knowing that because she knew you'd try to call her. Plus she loves getting letters from you. You should see her face light up whenever she checks the mail."

"When she called what did she say?"

"She just said that she wouldn't be in for a few days. Then when I asked if anything was wrong, she started crying and told me that he had beaten her. She's not bedridden or anything like that. She just wanted to stay in long enough for the bruises to heal." Mrs. Barden paused a minute before adding, "He hit her in the face…"

My heart stopped when she said it. Then I asked slowly, "How is Henry?"

"As far as I know Henry's fine. He delivered the milk this morning like he always does. Nostalgia, I'm under the impression the beating had nothing to do with him."

I was confused. "Well, then why else would Noah beat her?"

"I don't know dear. But she couldn't go into any great detail with me because he was in the next room when we were talking. I'll have her call you when she comes back to work."

"Please do, and Mrs. Barden?"

"Yes, Nostalgia?"

"Thank you for looking out for her. It really does mean a lot."

"Of course! I'll have her call you." We hung up.

Mrs. Spears was right. I did feel better knowing she wasn't in the hospital, and that Henry was alright, but I wondered. What could make him want to hit my sister otherwise? And in the face at that? He must have found out she'd been putting reefer in his food. That was the only other thing I could think of that would make him want to lay hands on her, and there was no doubt in my mind he hit my poor defenseless sister in the face with a closed fist!

* * * *

The next few days were like sitting on a porcupine. I wanted to talk to my sister, and nothing comforted me. Not piano riffs in the Ellington songs, not the taps on the bottoms of my shoes meeting the parquet floor of the stage, not even the thought that spring would be here soon if I was patient.

Josiah never said a word. He just offered handkerchiefs and held me in his arms while I cried. He didn't tell me everything would be alright because he didn't want to get my hopes up. I appreciated that. Sometimes it's best just to be there when somebody is hurting. He understood.

On the fifth day after receiving that awful telegram I woke to Mrs. Spears knocking on my door saying I needed to come quick, I had a long distance call! I almost bruised my knees stumbling out of bed. I pulled on my robe as I ran down the stairs to the parlor. Mrs. Spears was holding the receiver in her hand waiting for me. She looked as anxious as I felt.

"Hello?"

"Nostalgia it is so good to hear your voice," said Lily.

"It is so good to hear from you period! What happened… did he find out about you and Henry? Are you still doctoring up his food?" When I asked this Mrs. Spears whole body shook, and her eyes got wide, but she remained quiet.

"No, he still doesn't know about Henry. And he says I make the best chitlins he ever tasted, so he doesn't suspect I been doctoring up his food…"

"Well, why'd he do it?" The line was quiet a long time until she finally said, "I can't tell you that now…"

"What do you mean you can't tell me that now? Don't you hand me that nonsense…"

"Nostalgia I just called to let you know that I'm fine, that Henry is fine, in fact, he just got through, ahem, delivering the milk!" She laughed, but I didn't see a blame thing funny! She continued, "My plan is working…"

"Well, it ain't working for me! What is the point of putting…? "

"Nostalgia, stop it! Everything is fine…"

"The hell it is…"

"I'll write you a letter tonight," and she hung up! She didn't say goodbye or nothing. She hung up on me. She hung up on me, and I still don't know why that fool husband of hers beat her?

"Nostalgia let me make you some pancakes…" I walked right past Mrs. Spears' efforts to calm me down. I went from being angry at Noah to being livid with my sister. How dare she hang up on me! It was the first time in over a year that I had even heard her voice, and she hangs up.

I marched right upstairs to my room and found my personal stationery, lavender paper with my initials at the top in cursive. I went directly back down to the parlor, sat down at the desk, and I did not mince words:

March 19, 1929, Tuesday

Lily,

How dare you hang up on me after I get that horrible telegram from Mrs. Barden and finally hear from you after another week! I have been worried sick about you all this time, and I demand to know why Noah beat you. So he still has no idea about you and Henry, and he still doesn't know you been putting reefer in his food. What else are you not telling me in addition to that elaborate plan you been hinting at for over a year? Did you tell him how bad he smelled or give him some other back talk? I really need to know, because quite frankly, waiting for you and your plan has gotten old!

You and Henry should have been here with me long before now, if not you by yourself. I don't know how much more of this I can take, Lily. Maybe it's just my guilt talking because I do admit you wouldn't have had to deal with all of this had I gone on ahead and stayed. I'm tired of wondering if I'll ever see you again. Promise me you'll forget about this plan and just come on up here if he beats you again!

Your Beloved Sister,

Nostalgia

PS

And what do you mean by not telling me that you have a phone? You could have been calling me all along. Mrs. Barden gave you my number, and I demand you use it! I'm serious Lily, you better call me!

She obviously wrote and sent her letter back to me the very same day, because I received this letter exactly one week later. It was nice to know she and I were on one accord in some aspect.

March 19, 1929, Tuesday

Nostalgia!

I know I just made you mad by hanging up on you, but there are some things you need to realize. I can't go into great detail over the phone because this is a small town and any operator can hear all of our conversations. Mrs. Barden told me she told you I have a phone, well on top of the operator listening on the line, Noah would be listening in the house and wondering who I'm talking to! In short, there are EARS of corn in the field!

I don't think I have to worry about Noah caring even if he did find out Henry and I was having relations. He beat me because I caught him cheating on me! He thought I was following him I guess. I found them in the woods when I was on my way to the reefer patch. Instead of going to that patch I'm just going to find a seed and plant it somewhere he won't find it. I'll keep that one to put in his food, so he won't catch me out there again.

I walked up on them, and I was so surprised all I could do was stare. Apparently, I made some sound when I was looking because they stopped kissing. Next thing I knew Noah ran over to me, slapped me across the face, called me a nosy little bitch, grabbed me by my hair, and started beating me like I stole something. I don't see him ending the affair because I caught them. Ha! I bet he goes back for more, which is fine with me because that means I ain't got to lay underneath his stinkin' self no more.

It explains why he started sleeping in another room a few weeks ago, too. I'm surprised at myself for not suspecting it before. I mean why else would he sleep in another room? I guess I was so glad he didn't seem to want me anymore I didn't even stop to wonder. I just wish it had happened sooner because now I ain't got to worry about him bothering me.

Well, let me go. Mrs. Barden wants me to dust the chair legs and baseboards.

I miss you,
Lily

I must have read that letter a good fifteen or maybe even twenty times to make sure I read what I thought I read. Noah was cheating on my sister. I didn't know if I was angry or relieved. No matter the circumstances it's only natural to get angry at the thought of any man cheating on his wife, but then again he found someone else to satisfy his desires so he won't be climbing on top of her no more.

Then, of course, I looked again and again to make sure she didn't leave a name for the hussy. Who in the world would want that stinking bootlegger? So what if he had money. He smelled like a mink cuddling with a skunk on a rainy night! Who in my hometown would be so stupid they wouldn't care a man was married and stinking as long as he had money... Sarah Deets! It had to be. That woman was the biggest tramp in Spivey's Grove. She made it a point to go after married men because she didn't like to be tied down. "Sarah Deets with the Big Ol' Teats" was fooling around with Noah Holdtstaff. Now ain't that a whole lotta nothing? I couldn't leave go of this, so I wrote her back immediately.

March 27, 1929, Wednesday
Lily,
Are you serious? I don't know if I am happy or angry about this bit of news. You caught him in the woods with another woman? I know it's Sarah Deets, that heifer. That woman just ain't interested in finding a man of her own. No matter the circumstances surrounding the marriage it's always a shame when any man cheats on his wife, but at least he won't be going to your bed for a while. I must say

I'm relieved. I just don't want you to get over-confident. I mean, he might not be interested in you right now, but that doesn't mean he wouldn't do something drastic if he ever did find out about you and Henry. Noah is just the type of man to show the whole blame town his manhood at your expense for the sake of himself not looking like a sucker.

Has Daddy or Mama said anything to you about this? Or are they just staying out of the business of your house? I hope Minnie Mae Funderburke hasn't heard anything about him beating you up, or the fling with Sarah. You invited her to your house for Thanksgiving. I still can't get over that one. It took you inviting her to your house to figure out why no one else has invited her to theirs!

By the by, I am still not fully understanding why you insist on putting reefer in his food. Please explain that to me in your next letter, which should be coming here soon, I trust!

I have to go to rehearsal. We're learning a new dance today.

I love you,
Nostalgia
PS
I promise to never call you on the phone. I now understand why you didn't tell me you had one. Call me from Mrs. Barden's house if she'll let you.

Once again, Lily did write me back in a timely fashion.

April 4, 1929, Thursday
Nostalgia,

Thank you for understanding why I originally had no intention of you ever finding out I had a phone.

I must tell you that was quite a good guess about who I found Noah with in the woods. I'm just mad I got beat up because of it. I don't care that he's dealing with someone else. He can tell the whole town as long as I get to see my Henry three times a week like we've been doing. I do realize he would start a row if he ever found out about us. Men always have to have the last word in everything! I think the secret is always to let them think they have it while you just don't complain and keep whatever you do quiet.

You know right well our father didn't bat an eyelash at me getting beat up. Our mother surprised me, however! She sent word by Reverend Clark's oldest son that she wanted me to come by the house the first chance I got. Well, I thought she wanted to get rid of some jars of pickle or chow chow, because it's almost time for Daddy to start planting again, which means she's going to be canning vegetables soon.

I go over there a couple of days later, and she asked me how I was doing. I said fine, and she says, "That ain't what I heard." I asked what she meant, and sure enough, Minnie Mae Funderburke told her she happened to see Dr. Banks come to the house! I do declare, why would a bootlegger live so close to the biggest gossip in town? Anyway, I insisted I was indeed fine, and she says, "Are you sure nothing is amiss?" I'm starting to hate that word! Well, she said she didn't believe me, and told me if I needed anything to let her know.

I thought I had kept the scuttlebutt under wraps, considering I went directly into the house after the beating through the back door, and I didn't come out the front entrance until a few days later when my whole face had healed. Just SEEING Dr. Banks' car in the yard was enough for Minnie Mae Funderburke to say something to my mama? Now don't that just take the rag off the bush?

Well, I've got to wind this letter up. On days when I don't see Mrs. Barden's house, I've got to clean my own.

I love you,

Lily

PS

The reason I put reefer in Noah's food is to make him mellow and mess up his concentration. He's going to get so comfortable he's bound to slip up and leave something lying around that I can use. Just the other day he emptied his pockets on the kitchen table then went to bed. He ain't ever done that before! I looked at the contents and found a small bankroll, a piece of crumbled up paper with a list of names, and lastly, a seed. I kept the seed because I just ran out of what I'd found in the patch the last time I was there before he hit me. Now I can start growing my own. I wrote down that list of names in a book I been keeping since we got married. Now I can start doing some research!

Chapter 16

I didn't have time to write her back so quickly this time. I had two new dances to learn, I needed Mavis to give me a trim, and I needed some new make-up. Eugenia got pink eye the other week, and the doctor wouldn't let her dance for a few days. As a result, we had to alter the dance numbers to accommodate nine of us instead of ten. I had no interest in missing an evening of work. On top of not getting paid you run the risk of being replaced the longer you stay out! Luckily I hadn't gotten sick or missed any days.

Speaking of replaced, Helen suddenly disappeared from the troupe and then comes Constance. She even looked like Helen to make it so strange! The same tinted complexion with yellowish undertones, brownish-black hair, unusually long legs. They really could have passed for twins. Mitzi had said she heard Helen was turning 21 and was on the look-out to see if she suddenly didn't show up. As expected, Helen most certainly didn't, but what was really odd was that there was no talk of auditions this time, either, just one girl replacing another.

Something else I committed to memory was that all of this was happening while Arnie hadn't been around! Josiah told me one of the clubs, I think it might have been The Paradise Club, was raided by the police two weeks back, so it seems Arnie went to Sing Sing just before the raid to create an alibi for himself. The things troublemakers do to keep themselves out of trouble makes me wonder if it's really worth it. I mean so what if he was nowhere around when the raid happened, by just being in the joint he made his rap sheet that much longer.

Furthermore, Helen disappearing while Arnie was in Sing Sing made me wonder if she had been giving him conjugal visits. And if she was, did he just suddenly tire of her enough to give her job away without having auditions? If that was the case, it certainly enforced that Arnie considered us expendable at any time.

* * * *

Sunday nights at The Savoy weren't the same without Tessie and Peder, but life and living were always going to move no matter what. I remembered one thing Peder used to say about The Savoy: the most beautiful thing about The Savoy Ballroom is that when the music's playing we're all the same color. How right he was about that. Just as sure as the pink walls, the marble staircase, and the crystal chandelier complimented every skin tone in the place, the music satisfied our ears.

Cab Calloway was the guest band tonight playing against Fess Walker. I had to admit Cab was a dynamic performer! When he sang, he included the entire band as well as the audience, not to mention he danced to the music while waving the baton. I wondered how his band did not get distracted by his antics. His dancing was just as charismatic as the Nichols Brothers, and it was just him by himself.

"Uh, oh, Cab's in the house!" said Bunky as he helped Mitzi take off her coat.

"C'mon Bunky. I'm ready to do my own Jump n' Jive!" said Mitzi as they sashayed to the dance floor.

Josiah helped me with my coat and my chair before he sat down. He took my hand as we watched Cab jump, jive, and hi-de-ho. "I think Fess done lost the battle of the bands tonight."

"Sure looks like it," I said.

We listened to the music for a time, then he said to me, "you been distant, Baby. What's on your mind?" He was always so genuinely concerned about me.

"I'm just thinking about Lily."

"Henry or no Henry, if that fool husband of hers hits her again we gotta go down there and get her," he affirmed.

"No, it's nothing like that. It's just that she is getting into some things I think she should leave alone."

"What do you mean?"

"I told you she was putting reefer in his food to make him lazy with his business dealings. Just as she hoped would happen, he's not as careful or discreet anymore about his activities."

"What did he do, leave a bankroll on the table," Josiah chuckled.

"That's exactly what he did! He left a bankroll and a list of names in plain sight. She says she wrote the list of names in a book she's been keeping, and now she's going to do some research. I guess she's going to try to find out if the people on the list are clients or hirelings on his payroll, but how would she begin to do that without getting caught?"

"I must admit your little sis is resourceful. I hope I get to meet her one day," Josiah said earnestly.

"I hope you do too."

We were quiet again before he said, "If I were you I'd be grateful for that Sarah Deets woman. She's keeping that pig off your sister, and as long as Lily doesn't seem to be following him outright, he's not gonna pay her any mind."

I sighed, "I guess you're right. Plus as long as Sarah has his nose open he won't even suspect Lily and Henry are seeing each other on the sly."

Cab took a bow and walked off the stage waving and glad-handing the crowd. Some of the band members went out into the audience to say hello to folks they knew.

One man I noticed worked the room, making his way to our table. He was a little shorter than Josiah, with curly black hair, dark brown skin, and hazel eyes, "Hey, hey, Josiah James! Man, I heard you stopped slinging that hash, and started playing that sax!"

"Charles Sherman this is Nostalgia Richardson. Nostalgia, this is Charles Sherman. He plays the trumpet for Cab's band," said Josiah.

Charles squeezed my hand, looking deeply into my eyes, "I like your name. It's different."

No one had ever told me they liked my name before. I smiled, feeling the heat rise from my chest all the way up to my cheeks.

"No need to blush. It's a beautiful name for an even more beautiful lady."

"A beautiful lady who is very much taken!" I couldn't tell if Josiah said that as a warning to Charles, or as a reminder to me. Whatever the case it seemed to surprise Charles, who said a quick but cordial goodbye without even acknowledging me. What an abrupt exit!

"That was a strange first impression," I said.

"Charles is a piece of work." The way Josiah said this made me want to ask some questions, but I thought better of it. Charles' mysterious behavior was not worth making Josiah jealous.

* * * *

Apart from Lily's escapades, the thing I remember most about the spring of 1929 was that it was almost 90-degree heat in the early part of April, then it dropped back down to the 40s, maybe even the 30s. I never seemed to know what I would need in the way of clothes, but my big coat with the fur collar and cuffs stayed at the ready on the coat stand in the parlor at the advice of Mrs. Spears.

Eventually, the weather gave all the way in by the beginning of May to milder days and blue skies. Josiah and I were able to walk once again to the Seligman Fountain and sit on our bench. It was only a matter of time before the city would cut the water back on, allowing the whispering whir and tiny cool splashes to calm our spirits after a night of stompin', hoofin', and entertaining at the Cotton Club!

Josiah finally got a chance to take me to the Rialto Theater to see *The Broadway Melody of 1929* one evening, and I loved it! When I told him the character Francis Zanfield had to have been patterned after Florenz Ziegfeld he was apt to agree with my observation.

We enjoyed each other so much sometimes it made me wonder about my parents. I never saw them having any kind of fun while I was growing up. They never smiled just because they were happy. It makes me wonder if they ever were at all. Everything seemed to be about survival. How we were going to eat from one day to the next, what bill collector came to the door that day, was it planting season or harvest time?

The way Lily was talking, they made her marry Noah for nothing as far as I could see. They had a good sized farm now and a big house, but was life any easier for them? Had anything changed? I'll bet they were talking about the same things in that new eight room house as they talked about in the shack my sister and I were raised in! I knew it had never occurred to them to go somewhere to see it just because they wanted to be there. Their lives had no imagination other than what went on in Spivey's Grove, South Carolina.

Marrying for circumstance instead of love was normal for them, so naturally they would expect the same of Lily and me. From where I sat it didn't look much like anyone could ever be happy doing such a thing. I'm glad it occurred to my baby sister to marry for love. I didn't know quite what she was doing down there now, and I was still remorseful that I put her in that mess, but I was proud of her for letting her love for Henry fuel her desire to be out of that dreadful situation!

June 17, 1929, Monday
Nostalgia,
You will never guess what I found out! You remember that paper with the names on it I told you that Noah left lying on the table before he went to bed a few letters back, like maybe back in April? I didn't tell you this, but I asked Mrs. Barden if whenever I found anything that looked

suspicious would she give it to her husband. She said yes! I also asked her about some of the names on that list. She recognized the names of men on the police force! I knew he had some of those fools on his payroll. This is just the beginning. I knew my plan would work. Well, why wouldn't it? I mean let's face it. Any bootlegger that chooses to live in a house down the road from the nosiest old biddy in town, and allows his wife to become the maid for the District Attorney's residence can't be the most solid cube in the icebox!

Plus I knew I'd be able to use Mrs. Barden. All I have to do now is continue to find anything that looks suspect, keep track of it in my book, compile it all, and give it to Mrs. Barden to give to her husband when the time is right! Soon enough Noah's gonna lead me to wherever he keeps the money in the house. Right now though I need to find out who else in town, other than cops, is on his payroll.

A couple of days ago he had some men over here playing bid whist, and he got some hooch into him. They all did. They got a little loose in the lips too, talking about who bought what and how much it cost. I stayed in the sitting room the whole time working on some embroidery unless they wanted me to run to the kitchen and make them some eats. I memorized and wrote down so much of what they said!

The next card playing night they have here, watch what I tell you. They are bound to give up the whereabouts of the still before it's all over with. If I didn't need it to be so, I would be outdone at how simple this man thinks I am! If I just played dumb, I knew this would happen. Henry and

I might be up there to see you by Christmas at the rate this thing is going now.

Well, I got some things I need to do around the house this morning. Mama wanted me to take her to the mercantile later on. Oh, I didn't tell you, Noah gave me his old Ford because he just got a new Buick! It might be a few years old, but its mine. I might take you for a ride in it one day sooner than you think.

Your Beloved Sister,

Lily

PS

Daddy pitched to Mr. Chavis at the mercantile, and he offered him half as much on the dollar as the white farmers. I guess it's a start.

So that was how she planned to use Mrs. Barden to get away from Noah: Mrs. Barden's husband is the District Attorney! Of course. It all began making sense to me now. Why didn't I think of all this myself? Well, the answer to my question was real simple: I didn't think of it because I didn't have the patience to sit and wait. Thank God my sister did, though. Now I knew what she meant when she said in a previous letter, cut off the head and the rest of the snake would die. She was planning back then to pull down the whole operation starting with her trifling husband!

Chapter 17

July's hazy heat sat around the house like an unwanted guest that did nothing but suck the life out of you. In the middle of my second summer in New York I realized I could walk on the sand at Coney Island, or sit by the Seligman Fountain all I wanted to, but in the end I would never get used to heat if the smell of fresh cut grass and the taste of sun-ripened strawberries didn't accompany it.

I couldn't tell if I really missed home, or if I was anxious over that last letter Lily sent me. I wish she wrote more to keep me posted on her progress. I was all into the small town trifles myself, in spite of wanting to be as far away from Spivey's Grove as possible. I still worried one day Noah would be onto her by finally tasting the reefer in the food, missing things that she had taken as evidence of his racketeering and whatnot, or worse yet, finding that book of notes she'd been keeping about the goings on in his business.

I wondered what Mrs. Barden thought of my sister being the little spy, and finding out about Noah's shenanigans. It took everything inside of me not to swallow my pride, go back down there and face my daddy and everything else I left behind just to satiate my own curiosity.

My thoughts were interrupted by a weak knocking on the window. "Go around to the front door," I shouted to whoever it was. I got up and stood in the foyer for a few extra minutes to see if I would hear the knocker on the front door. It seemed to take a while. I almost thought it was one of the kids playing a prank because summer vacation was way too long, then I heard the door knocker. It was so weak... "Who is there?" I asked impatiently.

A hoarse voice said, "It's me!"

I got a little scared. "Just a minute." I ran back through the house and found Mrs. Spears and Mr. Greer shining silverware in the dining room.

"Are y'all expecting anybody," I asked, "There's someone at the door."

They looked at each other puzzled then got up from the table. Mrs. Spears and I both got behind Mr. Greer as he led the way back to the foyer. "Who is it?" he asked in a tone that made certain whoever it was, knew there was a male presence.

"It's Peder, Sir!"

Mr. Greer was so excited he fumbled with the indoor lock for what seemed like an eternity. When he finally opened it, we found Peder so skinny we would not have recognized him if we didn't remember the suit he was wearing when he picked Tessie up for what would be their last date for quite some time. His eyes were sunken in their sockets, he needed a bath, he needed a meal, he needed a nap, he needed us. Peder especially needed Tessie.

"I don't have any Danishes this time, Ma'am. May I still come in?" he said weakly.

Mrs. Spears with tears in her eyes and a smile gracing her lips nodded. He fell into her arms like a flower wilting in the desert that had finally felt a droplet of rain.

Mrs. Spears immediately began delegating authority after she and Mr. Greer led him to the couch in the sitting

room. He was supposed to draw Peder a hot bath and find
him a decent change in clothes. Mitzi was told to run down
to Western Union and send Tessie a telegram letting her
know he was out. Bunky and Josiah were to go to
Skaagens' Manor and find Avery, under the pretense that
they were his long lost cousins. I was to find Dr. Gaddison
and inquire as to how soon he could make a house call.
Mrs. Spears put fresh linens on Mr. Greer's bed, as if they
needed to be changed, and made a big dinner. Peder's
homecoming was the breath of fresh air that finally made
the laborious July heat move.

* * * *

"Well, he's exhausted and malnourished, but he'll live
to tell about it," conceded Dr. Gaddison as he, Mrs. Spears,
and Mr. Greer walked out of the bedroom Peder was using.
Apparently, he owed Mrs. Spears a favor from some time
before and charged her nothing for a visit.

"Well, how long before he can travel? You know he's
planning to go to France, but he has to get to Washington
D.C. first."

"Traveling? He needs to be concentrating on getting
back his strength." Dr. Gaddison sighed, rubbing his head
while he was thinking, "Alright. I'll come back in a week
and check in on him. If anything changes in the next few
days, give me a call. He does not leave this house for any
reason! All he does is eat and sleep until further notice."

"If we have to chain him to the bed consider it done,"
said Mr. Greer.

Tessie's not here, I thought, so we might have to do
exactly that.

On that note, Dr. Gaddison bid us all good evening as Mrs. Spears led him to the foyer. When she got back, she asked if anyone had heard from Bunky and Josiah.

"Not yet," said Mitzi who was clearly worried, "They haven't called or sent a telegram. You don't think that uppity family of Peder's put them in jail for trespassing or loitering, do you?"

"If they're in jail, don't you think Avery would have sent us word by now?" I said.

Just then there was a musical beat on the window that could only belong to Bunky. It sounded upbeat enough so the news must have been good. Mitzi and I both ran to the foyer before Mrs. Spears could tell us to calm down. When we opened the door, Bunky and Josiah had brought an ecstatic Avery with them. Apparently, the Skaagens family believed the fib. He didn't even say hello, he just asked if he could see Peder.

"He's asleep right now, but why don't you stay for dinner, Avery, and see if he wakes up," suggested Mrs. Spears.

Since she was quite the cook, she didn't have to twist his arm. Mrs. Spears made Peder's favorite: fried chicken, potato salad, collard greens, pickled beets, and corn bread. He had really taken to southern cooking when he first got here.

After everyone had eaten their fill Mrs. Spears went to Mr. Greer's room to see if Peder might be awake. She came back frantic, "He's gone," she said.

"Evelyn, what are you talking about?" asked Mr. Greer.

She shouted back in distress, "I mean he's not in there Mason! Oh dear, Jesus where could he be?" She was almost in tears.

Mr. Greer looked in his room. When he came back he was perplexed, "I don't guess he had the energy to climb out the window."

Mrs. Spears walked past him to check the kitchen and the bathroom, but there was still no sign of Peder. I knew we should have chained him to that bed.

"He might be upstairs," suggested Josiah.

"I'll go look," said Mitzi. Sure enough, he was fast asleep in Tessie's room.

"Well how in the world did he find his way up there without us seeing him?" asked Bunky.

"Apparently he found the back staircase. Just like Tessie used to do when she'd sneak into the house from seeing him late at night," said Mr. Greer.

"No doubt she told him about it when she called earlier this evening. Otherwise he couldn't have found it," added Mrs. Spears.

"Wait a minute? There's another staircase that leads to the upstairs part of the house?" I asked.

Mitzi had a revelation, "So that's how she always got back to her room without me hearing her before she told us about Peder!"

"Yes," said Mrs. Spears, "and don't even think about using it! I made the mistake of telling Geraldine about it and look what happened to her."

"Who's Geraldine?" asked Josiah.

"I'll tell you later," I said.

"I don't know how Tessie found it, but she confirmed the main reason why I've never told any of you girls about it. Whenever she came in at an ungodly hour, she used it. Furthermore, I better not catch either one of you using it," she said, looking squarely at Mitzi and me.

"Yes, Ma'am!" said Mitzi.

I simply nodded.

Mr. Greer tried to change the subject, "Evelyn, I know it's against the rules, but you're not going to make him come back downstairs, are you? He's been through so much and Tessie ain't even here right now."

I suppose the looks on all of our faces made Mrs. Spears reconsider her position on guests of the opposite sex. "I guess it's alright for me to make an exception this one time considering, but otherwise, no unmarried men are to ever come up those stairs. Do I make myself clear?" this time she looked squarely at Josiah and Bunky.

"Yes, Ma'am," they said in unison.

* * * *

"So let me get this thing straight: Mrs. Spears found Geraldine in the bathroom that y'all use?" asked Josiah after I'd rehashed the saga of Geraldine Crocker.

I nodded.

Josiah sat thinking for a time. "You know what? I got hired right after The Cotton Club opened back up in 1925 and this is the first I've heard of this. Man that is scary! I hate that Mrs. Spears had to see that!"

"I do too," I said. We sat on our bench in Morningside Park next to the fountain. Avery had dropped us off at the dime store on his way back downtown. We got two ice cold Royal Crown Colas and walked over to our spot.

The clear, balmy night was perfect refreshment from the day's sweltering heat. I sat barefoot with my legs across Josiah's lap as he massaged my ankles and played with my toes. Cicely insisted at the beginning of the summer I get my toes painted regularly. It made no sense to me until one evening at the beginning of the cycle of hot days when Josiah asked me to start wearing shoes that showed my toes. Then he insisted one night at this very fountain I take them off so he could massage my feet. I've been most grateful to Cicely ever since!

Now that he knew about Geraldine, I remembered something I'd been meaning to ask, "Had you heard anything about Helen…"

"About Helen doing what?"

"Paying Arnie visits while he was in Ossining?"

"No. Why?"

"After what I just told you don't you think it's strange that Constance just popped up without there being any kind of audition?"

"Well, Helen was 21, so it was time for her to go," Josiah shrugged.

I pressed on, "Since you've been here had you heard of anyone going to see him for… you know… conjugal purposes?"

"Anyone like who? The showgirls?"

"Yes."

"No. I just always thought it was convenient that he seemed to be in Sing Sing every time there happened to be a bust at one of his clubs. Obviously, some flatfoot tipped him off in time for him to drop out of sight. 'If he's not there how could he know about the activities that go on there,' even if it is his club," he used his voice to imitate a lawyer presenting a case.

"I know he killed some man for looking at one of his girlfriends a few years back. In fact, that was why he was doing time when that boxer sold him the club in 1923." After Josiah had said this, I remembered hearing Mr. Greer say Arnie had bought the club from Jack Johnson while in jail for murder, thus prompting the moniker Arnie 'the killer' O'Neil.

The name alone said so much that Josiah voiced my thoughts with conviction, "That's one dangerous man we work for, Baby. Which is why we entertain the white folks, then go home. Other than that, we don't do nothing else at The Cotton Club."

I was ready to move on to a happier note, so I changed the subject, "Speaking of white folks, Peder's back!"

"Praise God! He's tough. Any white man that can survive colored jail gets props from me."

"Can you believe what those cops did to him once he got to colored prisoners jail?" I added.

Josiah shook his head, "Back home every time I turned around my cousin Snake was in lockup, but he never said anything about the cops standing in a circle with him in the middle of it and, giving him a pee shower."

"And every day those fools did that to him! No wonder he smelled so bad when we let him in. Just a regular beating should have been enough," I took a sip of my soda.

"No, that would have left too many marks. Disowned or not his last name is still Skaagens. You know they wouldn't leave any evidence of a real beat down. Plus if he wrote Tessie about it those letters wouldn't have left New Jersey anyway," Josiah conceded.

"I guess you're right. Well, I'm just glad he made it back to Mrs. Spears' house," I said with a sigh.

Josiah burped before adding, "And went upstairs on top of it! I don't know exactly what she did to him, but one thing is for sure: Tessie slipped that man a mickey," he giggled.

"Would you sneak upstairs for me?" I asked flirtatiously.

"Sure... once we're married. I can't have Evelyn Spears looking at me out the corner of her eye."

I was taken aback by this comment! He's actually surmised that we might get married one day. Wow! I'd dreamed about it with my eyes wide open, and sometimes when I was asleep, but to hear him say it made it all seem within reach... and I wanted it badly.

"When do you think that would be?" I had to test the waters before I got my hopes up.

"When I feel like you're ready, because it won't be tomorrow. Trust me on this." He was the one who started talking about marriage, so I figured I had better let him have the last word in any conversation we had about it. He's certainly not running from me. For this reason alone I took his advice, and trusted him.

Chapter 18

I never felt comfortable just opening the door to Mrs. Spears' home when I heard a knock unless I knew for sure it was Josiah or Bunky. I was sitting in the parlor at the desk about to begin a letter to Lily when I heard a tap on the window. I found Mrs. Spears in the kitchen about to start dinner when I asked her if she was expecting anyone. She dried her hands on her apron as she followed me into the parlor.

We arrived just in time to hear a second knock. In response, Mrs. Spears asked whoever it was to go to the front door. I followed her into the foyer, as she asked, "Who is it?"

It took a minute, but Avery answered, "It's me."

When Mrs. Spears opened the door, Avery was there, standing sheepishly behind a younger version of Peder.

"I'm Kroyer Skaagens. Where is my brother?"

Mrs. Spears answered him with pursed lips and narrowed eyes, "Young sir, you can stand out there on the porch all night until you learn you will not disrespect me or my home!"

He blushed so red his blue eyes turned purple, "Forgive me, Ma'am. May I please see my brother?"

"That's better. In answer to your question I don't know. After being disowned he very well might not have any desire to see you at all."

"That was my parents doing, I had nothing to do with that," Kroyer said in his defense.

Mrs. Spears looked him straight in the eye for another moment. "You may stand here in the foyer and wait while I inquire on your behalf."

"Thank you, Ma'am," he said as he stepped inside.

"Nostalgia, don't take your eyes off of him. I don't trust him," with that Mrs. Spears went back in to find Peder.

Kroyer and I looked at each other awkwardly before he asked, "Is she always like that?"

"Yes. She's very protective of everyone who stays here. Especially if they've been in jail for sixth months and didn't deserve it!" I didn't mean to snap, but I couldn't stop myself.

He blushed again and didn't try to start anymore small talk at that time. It must have been apparent we had adopted Peder, and we were not about to let him get hurt again if we could help it.

Suddenly I refused to bridle my tongue any longer, "Do you know what he went through in that godforsaken place? Why didn't you at least post the bail?"

"Because I don't have half the courage of my brother to stand up to our parents," he snapped back, then admitted quietly, "or the money." He looked at me like he wanted to cry. I left him alone, and we just stood there, waiting for Mrs. Spears to come back.

When she did, all she said was, "Come in. Peder will be here directly."

He entered the parlor, taking in all of the space. His eyes lit up in surprise as if he was not expecting such beautiful surroundings. He took his time surveying the quality of the furniture, the height of the ceiling, the thickness of the carpet, before letting his eyes rest for a few moments on the Tiffany lamp. It made me angry!

Mrs. Spears must have shared my sentiments because when he made his way over to the sofa and was about to bend his knees, she said, "I gave you no permission to sit," reminding him she by no means considered him a guest. He blushed for a third time, stopping mid squat. This time I felt sorry for him.

I think she did too, "Have a seat, young sir."

"Thank you, Ma'am. And Ma'am, thank you for taking care of my brother."

Mrs. Spears nodded curtly as she left the room, "Nostalgia, when Peder arrives, you may leave them alone."

Another awkward silence in which he tried to make small talk yet again. "This is a lovely home," he said.

"Well, what did you expect? Did you think we lived like apes?"

"I suppose I didn't know what to expect because I've never…"

"… been in such close proximity to colored people? On second thought wait a minute, you were there that night when he introduced your family to Tessie. Did she seem like some sort of animal to you? She told us you folks didn't even touch her hand when she left! I just want to know one thing: is Tessie's being colored worth losing your brother? Over circumstances beyond my control, I may never see my sister again…"

"Nostalgia," Peder's voice stopped me. I heard Kroyer let out a breath followed by a small sound at the sight of his brother. When I looked, there were tears in his eyes. "I'll be okay," Peder reassured me.

I took another look at Kroyer Skaagens before leaving the room.

I left the dining room door ajar just enough to hear the conversation. It didn't surprise me to find Mrs. Spears was waiting on the other side, looking at me with wide eyes, her forefinger crossing her lips. We listened…

"Those are two formidable myrmidons standing at your guard," said Kroyer with a small laugh.

"If Bunky had been here you'd really be impressed," replied Peder.

"I beg your pardon?"

"Nothing. So how's the family?"

"Everyone's fine. You know the debutante ball is in September. A. A. Busch II, is coming all the way from St. Louis to take Inger."

"August Anheuser Busch II, is taking our little sister to the debutante ball? I guess that is something," said Peder before continuing, "and who will you be escorting?"

"Doris Merrill."

"And what do you plan to do after you take her home? Go to Mott Street."

The reply to Peder's question came slowly, "I don't know what you're talking about…"

"No? I'm talking about February of last year when I suggested we take a drive through Chinatown for the Chinese New Year celebration. You were reluctant, even standoffish, until that pretty little Chinese girl with the braid down her back sold us those roasted lychee nuts." I could barely see, but it looked like Kroyer was biting his lip as Peder continued. "I ask Mother and Father the next night at dinner where you were. They seemed to think you'd gone out for billiards and cognac with your fellows. I let them think that. Later on, I asked Avery where he'd driven you that night. He told me he'd taken you back to Mott Street."

"Good old Avery!" Kroyer shook his head.

Peder waited for Kroyer to respond to his revelation but he said nothing else, so Peder continued, "So what are your plans for the rest of your life? Placate the wife for the sake of consolidating family fortunes and then having Avery drive you over to Chinatown…"

"It's not like that…"

"Then how is it Kroyer? Charles Merrill is the biggest womanizer in this city, it would only be appropriate for his daughter to marry someone who won't stay faithful."

"Who said I was going to marry Doris Merrill?"

"You're escorting her to a debutante ball! It's what both families are going to expect!"

"You know what? I just came here to give you these," because we were behind the door in the dining room Mrs. Spears and I couldn't really see what Kroyer had given Peder, but it looked like one of those leather binding envelopes that held important paperwork. "I volunteered to clean out your room…"

"Well thanks a damn lot, Brother!"

"Don't use that sarcastic tone with me! If anyone else had done it, they would have thrown everything out!"

"I suppose I should thank you," Peder readjusted his attitude.

"Yes, you should. I came here not knowing what I was going to get or how I would be treated."

"So Avery admitted he'd been coming here to see me since I've been out?"

"Of course he did. The man doesn't know how to tell a lie," they both snickered as if remembering some sort of trouble they'd gotten into as teenagers and Avery had told their parents. It was good to hear them laughing.

"If you look you'll find my private post office box address in those papers," said Kroyer.

"I thought it might be," said Peder, before inquiring, "So, what are you going to do about her?"

"Mai Ling, or Doris?"

"Which one do you love?" Kroyer didn't answer Peder's question right away, then we heard a sigh, "For all I know Mai Ling and I might end up in France with you and Tessie."

"It's that serious?"

"It's that serious."

"Find a way out of going to that ball, save your money, and put it in a Swiss account. I'll be in touch." There was silence. I got bold and peeked into the parlor. They were shaking hands, then Kroyer grabbed Peder into a hug. I think Mrs. Spears and I were both crying by this time.

They broke the embrace, "Use my address as soon as you get settled in France."

"I will." Peder showed Kroyer the way out. When he came back inside the parlor, he shouted to me and Mrs. Spears, "You two can come out now!"

* * * *

"Well I certainly recognize the name Anheuser Busch, however I'm not familiar with Merrill," Mrs. Spears set the serving tray on the coffee table. She figured ice cold lemonade would be just the treat after the heated exchange between the brothers.

"Securities and financial services. Merrill, Lynch & Co.?" said Peder.

Mrs. Spears' eyes widened when the connection was realized.

"So these people used to be your friends?" I asked. Quite frankly I still didn't know who Merrill was.

"If they were friends, it was of the fair-weather sort, I assure you," said Peder.

The phone rang, and his eyes lit up. Tessie always called at 6:30 on the dot so Mrs. Spears let him answer it. "Hello… hello, Sugar-dumpling… I'm better just hearing your voice… Oh, the day was quiet, but I've had quite the evening! Guess who just left?"

* * * *

As it turns out Peder's brother had given him the key to his safety deposit box at The Empire Savings and Loan of New York, some paperwork concerning his Swiss bank account, his passport, and his post office box address. Thanks to Kroyer, Peder had everything he would need to relocate to France. There was nothing left for him to do now but get better, and get Tessie.

It was quite interesting to hear a conversation between a pair of brothers, and white ones at that, who were experiencing something similar to what I was going through with Lily. Our parents' decided, or attempted to decide, our fates, without regard to our input or feelings. The two older siblings, me and Peder, fought back and as a result were left to our own devices. The two younger ones, Lily and Kroyer, were left to clean up the debacle. Peder and I had both saved our money, me because I'd been planning to leave for years anyway, he because he just happened to be resourceful.

Both younger siblings had loves of their own that would be deeply affected by our parents' wishes. Lily was forced to leave Henry to marry a bootlegger to get our parents out of debt, and Kroyer might soon have to decide to do what is expected and marry for financial security, or follow in the footsteps of Peder and marry for love.

I would like to think our parents were acting in our best interests because they'd struggled in the past and didn't want us to. However, the more I thought about it, the more convinced I was that our parents, Peder's and Kroyer's too, were selfish and unhappy because they could not fathom marriage that didn't in some way have a price tag attached. It disturbed me greatly because I felt badly that both the younger siblings had already found places and people to lay their hearts next to, while Peder and I both just happened to make crash landings in Harlem, finding Tessie and Josiah in the perpetual heap. I'd always heard love was blind. Whoever said it forgot to add it was also complicated.

Chapter 19

August 17, 1929, Saturday
My Dearest Lily!
Happy 16th Birthday to you! I wonder what you are doing today and how you intend to celebrate. I wish I was there to make your favorite cake. So in your honor, I'm making one for the folks I live with now. Please tell me what you got as gifts. If Noah gave you his car, he may very well have gotten you something decent, or did he know it was your birthday in the first place?

Nothing really exciting going on other than Peder's brother showed up to see him. He looks so much like Peder did when we first met him. He was just as stuck-up as I thought he might be but Mrs. Spears put him in his place. He brought everything Peder would need to go get Tessie and move to France. All Peder has to do now is get his strength back, which according to Dr. Gaddison may not be too long. After he gets better, he plans to go to Washington and meet Tessie's family, and they're going to sail from there. I am so going to miss having him here, but I am sure one day we'll all see each other again.

Summer is still hot! If it wasn't for the Seligman Fountain, Coney Island, and Cape May I'd be in dire straits for fresh air and open spaces. I'm happy, but I still miss home sometimes.

How is the investigating going? Have you found anything new? You might find some surprises as to who in the community has associations with Noah. If you do let me know.

Tell Mrs. Barden I said Hello.
Your Beloved Sister,
Nostalgia

* * * *

Dr. Gaddison decided at the top of September that
Peder was healthy enough to travel, and he wasted no time!
He and Jude were about the same size, so instead of going
shopping Peder bought two outfits from Jude and called
himself packed. Kroyer paid Avery to drive Peder down to
Washington to avoid a long ride on a train or bus.

Tessie was so excited she almost couldn't stand the
wait! She told her parents and her brothers Peder was
indeed white, she was indeed going with him to France, and
if they didn't like it, she would just go back to New York
and leave from Pier 72. Her family saw her seriousness and
decided to adjust to the idea.

It made me somewhat jealous, but I was still happy for
them both. I wondered what it was like to have your parents
trust your own judgment about what you wanted for your
life. Her parents were going to let her move to France and
marry a white man, while mine wouldn't begin to
understand why I wouldn't want to live the life of a
bootlegger's wife just to get them out of debt. To say my
parents lacked imagination was an understatement. If your
child had the chance to live a life better than you why
wouldn't you let them?

I began thinking about Lily all over again willingly
forging ahead into the marriage with Noah, patiently
waiting for the right moment to escape, all for the want of
marrying Henry. No one should have to go through

anything so tedious for love, or anything else for that matter.

Like Tessie's parents, Mitzi's mother and father were also supportive of her leaving the south to pursue a career as a dancer. Both Mitzi's and Tessie's families allowed them to move to New York and study ballet with Adolph Bolm, who was one of the few instructors who took colored students. Once they graduated they each auditioned for the Cotton Club.

It's strange what we all have to go through to get to the same place. My journey to New York and The Cotton Club was a series of jumps in which each time I leaped a net happened to open. My first leap of faith was merely deciding to leave Spivey's Grove. From there everyone I needed was in the right place, starting with Mrs. Barden, then Mrs. Spears, who led me to Tessie and Mitzi, The Cotton Club, and finally, Josiah. When I think about it, the transitions I made were quite smooth. Mrs. Spears says my guardian angels were faithful to me. I hoped they continued to be.

I hoped Tessie's and Peder's angels followed them as well. Peder promised to send us a telegram when he and Avery made it to Washington, and then a postcard after he and Tessie got off the boat in France. Bon Voyage, Mon Amis!

Chapter 20

"Nostalgia, wake up! We have to go to the bank! Hurry up!" Mrs. Spears had never rushed me like that before. She was knocking on my door so hard I thought she might bruise her knuckles.

I pulled on my robe in mid-stride to the door. When I opened it she looked better than exasperated. "Mrs. Spears what's wrong? I was just at the bank yesterday."

"The financial markets have dropped, and we have to get our money now!" With that she went down the stairs. Rather than ask any questions I went down the hall to the bathroom to splash some water on my face and swish my mouth.

By the time I got there Mitzi was coming out, "I'll meet y'all downstairs," she said as she passed me on the way back to her bedroom.

I didn't understand what was happening, but I figured they would explain it all to me once we were in the cab. I hurriedly cleaned up and found any old thing to put on, which happened to be a pair of Josiah's pants that I wear when I help Mrs. Spears clean the house. The way she was acting, I somehow didn't think she'd care if I wore them outside.

As I was making my way down the stairs, I noticed Mrs. Spears on her way up to shout at me again to come down. Mitzi was running out the front door at that moment. When she saw me she said, "Hurry, I have your coat!"

Mr. Greer had the cab ready for the three of us. I got in, still not registering what the rush could be about.

"48 Wall Street, and step on it!" Mrs. Spears had never spoken to a cabby like that.

"But Ma'am…" he was about to protest.

"Please!" she said, giving him money. He began driving toward downtown after that.

Finally I asked, "What's all the fuss about," as I struggled to get my coat on.

"Remember the first day I took you to the bank, and I explained to you how interest works on the savings account?"

"Yes, Ma'am."

"Well, some of those that borrow money from banks are large corporations. The markets have plummeted, preventing them from paying the banks interest on their loans! Our money is wrapped up in those investments, so we have to get it out now." I had never heard Mrs. Spears talk so fast, so loud. Mitzi and I just looked at each other. I don't think she understood it either, but it was apparent the situation was dire.

As we got closer to Wall Street, the traffic got even more congested. When we got to 35th Street we were moving at a snail's pace. By 24th Street, we had all but stopped. People were getting out of their cars and running toward the downtown area. Mrs. Spears gave me both of her account numbers, ordering Mitzi and me to get out of the cab and run as fast as we could to Wall Street! We both happened to be wearing pants and house shoes, so we did as we were told.

We got out, running and weaving between the cars. We were pushed and shoved by other people, so we pushed and shoved them back. I was sweaty, my gut felt strained from running in the cold, polluted air, my calf muscles tightened as if they were ropes being tied into knots.

Mitzi and I made it to 48 Wall Street, but there was a mob of civilians in front of the door with police officers arguing with them, refusing to let them into the bank! The panic and pandemonium scared me.

"Mitzi what's happening?" I asked.

She looked dazed, but she answered, "I think we've lost all of our money," her eyes were wide with confusion. I'd never seen her look so scared.

We tried to get closer, but the coppers were starting to beat some people, both men and women, with Billy Clubs, throwing them into paddy wagons as if they were taking out the trash! I'd never seen women, and white ones at that, treated in such a shoddy manner. This was serious.

"I'm not going any farther," said Mitzi.

I forged ahead, demanding to know why I couldn't get my money back! The money I'd worked so hard for since I was twelve years old sweating and slaving to keep Mrs. Barden's house spotless, and later entertaining ofays who considered me inferior to them! Even before I was twelve, every cent my daddy told me to take to Chavis's General Mercantile to buy myself a treat for my birthday, Christmas, Easter, Tooth Fairy, what-have-you, got socked away in the floor board of my childhood home until I took it out to sneak up here. That was my nest egg, and I was losing it on account of some stock market? That didn't make any sense to me.

Determination, as well as my anger at the thought of it, pushed unfortunate souls out of my path. I might have trampled some of them in my attempt to storm the front door.

From some outer realm a man with an accent I couldn't place, probably Yiddish, pulled me out of the line of fire, falling on top of me, "Girl are you crazy? Those cops will kill you!"

I lay there on my face, feeling the weight of his gut on my back, hardly breathing. I didn't notice the gunshots until I saw people succumbing to their deaths right in front of me, all because they too demanded to know where their money was, and when or if they'd get it back.

He got up, pulled me to my feet, pushing me in the direction of uptown, "Run, now, run!" he shouted at me while disappearing as miraculously as he had arrived.

I muscled my way back to 24th street to the Flat Iron building where I'd last seen Mrs. Spears. She and Mitzi were so relieved to see me, "I almost made Mitzi go back there and find you. I didn't mean for you two to separate." She sighed, looking around at the chaos, "Well I guess we better make our way back home." The cabby managed to make an illegal U-turn going back uptown. We went to Harlem, without our money.

* * * *

That strange day, October 29, 1929, otherwise hallowed as Black Tuesday, segued into a strange night! It was like no one had spoken all day. We went back to the house in complete silence at what we'd just witnessed. We ate our dinner in silence before going to the club. We prepared for the night's performance with tight lips. We danced and pranced to an almost empty house.

I'd never seen The Cotton Club audience so sparse. I didn't need this tonight. Usually no matter what happened to me during a day, preparing to entertain and getting on stage seemed to be the panacea for the blues, frustrations, doldrums I'd felt for the past year and a half.

Tonight was different. The cloud of disappointment I'd been walking on all day followed me to my sanctuary. No one laughed at the minstrel show or marveled at how deep and high Adelaide Hall's voice was, or made goo-goo eyes at the 'Tall, Tan, and Terrific' Cotton Club Showgirls. The performance hall was vast tonight and those that did come out more than likely had their minds on the events of the morning and afternoon.

I still had no idea what happened today, but whatever it was, it wasn't just going to go away after a good night's sleep, or a week's worth of newspaper speculation. I couldn't shake the foreboding fear from my gut that my life was about to change for the worse.

Even Bunky was speechless when he and Josiah drove us back to the brownstone. We kissed them quickly and bid them good night.

When we got in we heard Mrs. Spears and Mr. Greer conversing in the sitting room. "Oh, Mason what are we going to do? This is all my fault!"

"What? That those fools let the stock market tank?"

"No! I encouraged everyone in this house to have bank accounts. George and Jude put off owning their own houses and starting families so Cicely and Mavis could open their own beauty parlor. Those ladies have been so diligent about saving their money and growing a clientele. They were all set to do it next year, and now this!"

"First of all, if they did have their own houses they'd be worried about property tax right now, second to that, all of them are under 25. They got plenty of time to open businesses, own houses, and have chaps. Stop blaming yourself for this."

"Property tax. I hadn't even thought of that! How am I going to pay the property tax if I can't get my money? Who knows when or if they'll open the bank again?"

Mr. Greer was quiet a moment before saying, "I'll be back." We were about to run up the stairs when we realized his footfalls were going back toward his room, which he never uses anyway. We heard him reenter the parlor. "Here," he said.

We heard paper rustling for a minute. "Mason, what is this?" Mrs. Spears asked.

"That's all the back rent you refused to take from me since I been here. You know I never trusted any bank."

"But Mason you shouldn't have to do this."

"Evelyn it's the only way right now! Between what I just gave you, and Jude and George working at the meat packing plant we gonna be alright. We've seen a lot of depressions, and we got through them. We gonna be alright."

"I don't know Mason. This one is different. You should have seen how they were acting downtown today."

"Evelyn, I ain't ever had nothin' to do with downtown because everything I've ever needed since I been living in

New York has been right here in Harlem. We gonna be just fine. I put that money away because I knew that bank would end up flimflamming you sooner or later. Jude and George still working in the meat packing place, and I got several jumpers down in the cellar…"

"Jumpers? Mason…"

"Evelyn we gotta do what we gotta do. Let's go to bed before the girls get home. If they see that we up they gonna be worried."

"Mason, how did you come by this money?"

"Evelyn, you ain't gettin' on my nerves no mo' tonight, now. Let's go to bed." We heard the lights switch off after that, as the two of them headed toward the bedroom.

While Mitzi and I tiptoed up the stairs, I couldn't help but ask, "Mitzi, what are jumpers?"

She shook her head, "I don't know, but we'll find out sooner than later."

Chapter 21

It seemed Mr. Greer had several talents. Among them, working with gas and electricity. He used the jumper cables to control the power surges and gas all of us used during the course of the day and evening, that coupled with designated times in which we could take baths, cook, and have lights on, thus creating a lower electric bill.

Word of Mr. Greer's gas and electricity tampering talents got out all over Striver's Row and beyond, so he lent his services out for money or goods. If the New York Edison Company found out he would surely go to jail!

George and Jude had always brought home extra meat from their jobs at the Gansevoort Market, now they brought home more to sell or barter with the neighbors who were also struggling. To maintain the lifestyle we ladies had so grown accustomed to every man in the house had taken on some sort of illegal activity.

Mr. Greer's other talent was playing the numbers, and Mrs. Spears was none too happy with him about it. She seemed to jump out of her skin every time there was a knock at the door. It's a wonder the top of her head didn't graze the ceiling!

She still received checks for Mr. Spears' pension, but with the banks being closed there was no way to cash them, and if she tried they might bounce. With all of the uncertainty there was no other way for her to get money but to let Mr. Greer continue to pay visits to the policy bank at 409 Edgecombe Avenue, the residence of Madame Stephanie St. Clair.

Madame Stephanie, or Queenie as she was called in Harlem, was a marvel to me! I knew she was into some shady dealings, and came by her riches in ways unbecoming of a lady, but it made no difference. There was no denying she was uniquely her own woman, w/hat I aspired to be minus the path she'd taken to gain her notoriety.

Stephanie St. Clair moved to Harlem in 1912 by way of the Caribbean Island of Martinique. Her first association with the seedy underworld of organized crime was with the 40 Thieves Gang, a group of Irish immigrants that originated in the five points area of lower Manhattan. By 1922 St. Clair moved uptown to Harlem, where she spent $10,000 of her money to set up one of the most successful numbers rackets in all of New York City. With her bodyguard and possible lover, Bumpy Johnson, Madame Stephanie had the world of Harlem at her feet.

The numbers Mr. Greer played so faithfully every week, were now Mrs. Spears' primary source of income, as much as she hated to admit it. Mitzi and I suspected Bunky and Josiah played the numbers as well, but they'd never own up to it because they didn't want to scare us.

Despite losing honorable jobs, or getting laid off downtown, the numbers racket was one hustle that kept many residents of uptown from losing all they held dear in these trying financial times. Madame St. Clair was our queen because she gave us colored folks a fighting chance to survive.

Chapter 22

The remainder of the year 1929 left the Spears household eager to see positive change. The Empire Savings and Loan of New York stayed closed until November, but when it did open back up the risk of seeing checks bounce was still too great. We cashed our checks and took the money back home to hide in our rooms if we were fortunate enough to see a dime. Eventually, Arnie began paying the showgirls in cash, and miraculously, he never missed a week. The club slowed down quite a bit, but our wages stayed the same. We asked no questions, instead, we were grateful.

The good news was that Tessie got married after Peder officially changed the spelling of his name, not the pronunciation, from Peder Skaagens to Peter Scoggins, thus ending his association with his immediate family in the United States. However, Peter would not be completely devoid of familial ties. He established a relationship with some long lost cousins in the Netherlands, and they could have cared less that Tessie was colored. In fact, they attended the wedding with enthusiasm! Tessie said the only things she missed were her father giving her away and having all of us there.

We received word of the nuptials right before Thanksgiving, which gave us something to feed on because the turkey was not an option. But George and Jude managed to get Mrs. Spears five Cornish hens, one for each couple to share. In addition to the poultry we had white potatoes, cabbage, and corn muffins. No cranberry sauce was to be found, and the five sweet potatoes had to be used to make pies, otherwise I would have no dessert to make.

The tree was sparse and shorter than last Christmas, but the smell of pine filled the sitting room, nonetheless. Mrs. Spears couldn't find mistletoe this year to hang in the various corners of the house, so she knitted miniature wreaths to put in its place. It was decided there would be no popcorn garland because we might need it for food. As a result, Mitzi and I drew and cut a garland of paper dolls to the wind around the tree.

"I tell you," said Mr. Greer, "not having a whole lot sure can make you creative!"

By God's grace we found the ornaments and lights still intact from last year. This time the tree was so small Jude was able to place the star on the top. After we had lighted the lights, Mrs. Spears said we could eat the rest of the leftovers, which were only the cabbage and the corn muffins. Instead of complaining we each decided it was a gracious plenty.

* * * *

Without Christmas Club accounts this year, our gifts were nowhere near as elaborate as Christmas of 1928. The previous year had spoiled me because once again I was putting loose change instead of folding money in the Salvation Army bucket. Mrs. Spears said I'd better be grateful I was still able to donate as opposed to having to depend on their services. I decided she was right, and I donated something every time I heard one of those officers ringing the bell.

Mrs. Spears continued to remind us the season should not be only bout gifts, but first and foremost about God allowing us to make it through another 365 days without losing a life, a limb, a family member, or sanity!

To save money on gifts we drew names, and at Mrs. Spears' insistence, the item we chose was not to be over $.50. I got George's name, and when I asked Cicely what she suggested she said a pair of socks would be sufficient. I understood Mrs. Spears demanding we be thrifty this year, but I couldn't help it. I went down to Macy's just to have a look-see as to what I could maybe get for her and Josiah, but most of everything was out of my budget. I wanted to cry. Despite our wages at the club remaining the same the price of everything from food to toiletries, to novelties had gone up! I couldn't stand the thought of not getting those two a little something at least.

I ended up knitting Josiah a scarf and making Mrs. Spears a small decorative pillow she could place on her bed. I managed to find George a small pocket knife. Josiah got me a brass hair clip to keep my bangs out of my face. When I wore it, it looked like a daisy resting on my temple. I thought it was beautiful.

Dinner was small again with a bony roasted chicken George and Jude managed to purloin from the Gansevoort Market. Mrs. Spears made stuffing this time and had string beans with pearl onions for the vegetable. She allowed me to use all the flour to make a chocolate cake, so there were no biscuits, but we didn't miss them anyway.

Tessie and Peter sent a card filled with best wishes for the season. Jude and Mavis, due to lack of funds, remained here with us this year instead of visiting family in Virgilina. Bunky took Mitzi to Yonkers to his brother's house directly after dinner and the opening of gifts.

A week later we rang in the New Year eating tuna salad sandwiches on sourdough bread, instead of catfish and cornbread, raw lettuce with tomato slices drizzled with olive oil, instead of ham hock-seasoned collard greens and pickled beets, and heated apple juice, as opposed to heated apple cider. Out of love for my carrot cake, Mr. Greer did manage to find some carrots, raisins, brown sugar, and flour. Much to everyone's surprise it still tasted good without the frosting.

We listened to the radio broadcast of the ball dropping between 11:30 pm and midnight with hopes and dreams that the year 1930 would bring an end to The Great Depression.

* * * *

Happy Days are Here Again by Benny Mereoff just happened to be the #1 song in the country in 1930, and for some it may have been true. Rodger's and Hart's *Simple Simon* premiered on Broadway, astronomer Clyde Tombaugh discovered a small planet he named Pluto, and Babe Ruth signed a $160,000 contract to play for the NY Yankees. However, little of that prosperity was witnessed in Harlem. What we did see was breadlines, soup kitchens, and unemployment.

Mavis and Cicely left the beauty parlor thanks to a significant drop in clientele, so Mrs. Spears allowed them to take patrons in the cellar of the brownstone. There was already a sink down there. All Mavis needed to do was set up a few chairs, hot combs and curlers, while Cicely asked Mr. Greer to hook up the circuit breakers to put lights around some mirrors so she could do make-up and manicures. They bartered or charged very little for their services, while Mrs. Spears did not make them pay extra for using the space. Instead, she made them promise to sock away whatever money they made so they could eventually afford their own store front.

George and Jude managed to keep their jobs at the Gansevoort Market, but the number of days a week was cut back from five to three. The other two days they spent in the neighborhood helping Mr. Greer cut back gas and electricity in exchange for funds, goods, and services. Mr. Greer's luck playing the numbers never seemed to run out, granting him the means to pay them a little folding money for the extra help.

The unreliability of the pension checks from the Reading Railroad caused Mrs. Spears to continue turning a blind eye to Mr. Greer's illegal survival methods.

Lily had informed me in one of her letters that a group of white sharecroppers started a shanty town, otherwise known as a Hoover Ville, just down the road from the house she shared with Noah. For protection Noah bought two more pistols and a double-barreled shotgun just for Lily to keep the house safe! Unfortunately, there was an incident in which she pulled out one of the pistols when she heard a sound on the back porch like someone rummaging through the vegetables Daddy was able to give her off his farm.

Lily further explained in her letter how she had tip-toed to the back of the house, gun at the ready, only to find a beat down white woman and her little girl stuffing potatoes in their clothes! They stopped when they saw Lily, begging her not to shoot. Lily gave them a couple of chicken hobo pies, let them keep whatever they had in their pockets, and sent them away before Noah got home, hoping Minnie May Funderburke would keep her big mouth shut! The last thing my sister needed was Noah getting angry at her for not shooting them, or worse, her conscience eating at her for not feeding them!

The radio constantly talked about how the lack of rain created dustbowls out in the mid-west, otherwise destroying corn, potatoes, soybeans, and other cash crops farmers depended on for the livelihood of their families. While some families gave up on living off the land all together, choosing to venture into big cities like Chicago, Detroit, and Los Angeles to try their luck at finding industrial jobs. Thus the ears of the entire nation, north, south, east, and west, hung on every placating word of President Herbert Hoover. However, the year 1930 ended with no promises from the gentleman's mouth coming to fruition.

Chapter 23
1931

The things I remembered most about the year 1931 were that the *Star Spangled Banner* became the official US National Anthem. The #1 Big Band Jazz tune in America was *Minnie the Moocher* by Cab Calloway. On May 1, the Empire State Building opened on 34th street in New York City. I had never seen a building so tall that I just about broke my neck looking up at it, and still couldn't see the top because the sun had gotten into my eyes. Joe McCarthy was named manager of the New York Yankees.

I got a terrible stomach ache one late spring afternoon when Josiah took me to Coney Island. Mrs. Spears ran down to the five and dime store and brought back these chalky tablets I'd never seen before. She dropped two of them in a glass of water, making this fizzy sound. I drank the unfamiliar concoction that tasted salty, caused me to burp loudly, and made my tongue feel tingly. I found out later this strange medicine was called Alka-Seltzer, and after the way it cured me so quickly, Mrs. Spears made it a point to keep some in the house at all times.

Hoover Flags still swung aimlessly outside of folks' pockets to show The Great Depression gave no signs of going away. Industries suffered in Northern cities while cash crops felt the pinch in rural areas like Spivey's Grove.

Lily wrote me another letter saying Chavis's General Mercantile had reneged on the deal they made with Daddy. Instead of giving him the original .50 for every dollar the white farmers made, Daddy, the only colored farmer Mr.

Chavis dealt with, would only be making .25! I was outraged, but not surprised by the change. Daddy would have been better off selling only to colored folks, and letting Mr. Chavis and all those other white folks have their mercantile. We spent money in that place like everyone else, so why should we have to wait to enter when there were no white patrons?

The most significant event of 1931, however, was that the Duke announced at the beginning of June he had booked a long engagement with a club in Paris, France. As a result, his time at The Cotton Club would come to a close at the end of the month!

To keep the cost of the trip within his budget, he would be taking only seven Cotton Club Showgirls instead of all ten of us. We would have to have auditions to determine which of us would be going with him and the band to France. It broke my heart to think I would be competing against Mitzi, the one who taught me everything I knew, for this opportunity.

Constance automatically disqualified herself, saying she'd just gotten back to the states from touring with another dance company and had no interest in going back to Europe any time soon. That didn't cushion the blow because it still left eight other dancers for me to compete against, not to mention I was the only one who had no formal dance training.

On the morning we were to compete it didn't matter what color leotard I wore because Arnie wasn't making the final decision, The Duke was. He knew all of us, which made me think he already had his cast in mind, but for the sake of being fair, he wanted to watch all of us before officially making a final cut.

There were nine of us, so we were divided into one group of five and one group of four. We performed five songs from our repertoire, with each group dancing twice on each song. It only lasted an hour before we were told to take a ten-minute break.

During the break, we went to the water cooler. I heard so many conversations speculating who made it and who didn't, which reminded me of why I hated auditions! It was one big popularity contest, and if you weren't careful you could walk away feeling lower than the belly of a snake. You had to constantly talk yourself into loving yourself no matter the outcome.

"It's time to go back in, Nostalgia," said Mitzi. She smiled nervously because she knew how I felt.

We walked gracefully onto the Cotton Club stage, stood in our places with such poise and smiles held together with a mountain of Vaseline. We each waited, hoping to hear our names called. Out of respect for Esther as she made the announcement no one spoke until all the names had been called.

I heard Mitzi's name called first, and I never heard mine called before Esther said: "Congratulations to all of you who were chosen. To those of you who will be staying here, you'll be learning a new repertoire for the new house band, The Cab Calloway Orchestra, otherwise known as *The Brown Sugar Revue*. Auditions will be held next week to fill the other seven spots. Have a good morning, Ladies. We will see you tonight!"

I congratulated Mitzi and the other girls who made the cut. Then I walked over to Loretta, the other girl who hadn't made it, and we hugged. I really didn't know what she was feeling, but I was struggling to smile through my tears.

* * * *

Later in the month when Mitzi told Mrs. Spears she and Bunky planned to get married downtown at the magistrate's office, Mrs. Spears told her she wouldn't hear of it! "The wedding will be held here. Just decide on a date, and we'll have the house ready in time."

"But…" Mitzi tried to protest, but Mrs. Spears insisted the wedding would be held in the parlor and the reception in the dining room.

True to her word we were all there for the nuptials. Josiah and I served as best man and maid of honor respectively. Jude and George greeted all the guests at the door, Mavis and Cicely did our hair and make-up. Mr. Greer stood in to give Mitzi away since her father had died some years earlier, and Mrs. Spears cooked a grand dinner, thus adding wedding planner to her long list of talents. The three-tiered cake appropriately came from The Sugar Hill Bakery.

The guests included Bunky's parents and three younger brothers, plus Mitzi's mama and older sister came up from Georgia. All the girls in the troupe sat with Mitzi's family, while the boys in the band sat with Bunky's. Tessie and Peter weren't there, but they sent a wire transfer all the way to Downers Grove, Illinois to the FTD Florist, thus paying for the flowers. Reverend Worley, a member of the pastoral staff at the Abyssinian Baptist Church was the officiating minister for the auspicious occasion.

"Do you, Stanley Buchannan, take this woman to be your lawfully wedded wife…"

"Stanley?" said Josiah.

"What," answered Bunky, "you didn't think I had a real name?"

"Bunky, please!" whined Mitzi.

"Sorry, Baby! G'head, Pastor," Bunky apologized.

"…to have and to hold from this day forward," continued Reverend Worley.

"I do!" declared Bunky.

"And do you Melvina Michelle Daniels…"

"Melvina?" Bunky looked perplexed.

"Bunky, I told you I was named after my daddy! Go on, Reverend," insisted Mitzi.

"… take this man to be your lawfully wedded husband to have and to hold from this day forward?"

"I do," declared Mitzi.

"By the power vested in me, by way of the state of New York, I FINALLY, pronounce you husband and wife. You may kiss your bride!"

They took their time kissing.

After a few moments of watching them lock lips, we cheered to their union. "Now that Stanley and Melvina officially know each other's names," announced Mrs. Spears, "Let's all go to the dining room!"

While everyone ate, Josiah got some of the boys in the band to help Jude and George gather the folding chairs to make space for a dance floor after dinner. Thanks to

George and Jude bringing home extra meat from the
Gansevoort Market, Mrs. Spears did it once again, and it
was delicious! We feasted on roast beef, mashed potatoes,
asparagus, and croissant rolls. Dessert was obviously
wedding cake. After toasting the bride and groom,
everyone headed back to the parlor to dance off that filling
meal. It was a grand, good time that none of us would ever
forget!

Chapter 24

I hadn't seen Aunt Flow wearing her red dress in a good long time. I waited. While I waited my back hurt, my breasts swelled, I had to pee. I was thirsty, but I had to pee. I was hungry, and I had to pee. Common smells, like when the city took too long to haul the garbage away, made my stomach feel like I was on a ride at Coney Island, and of course, I had to pee. Could this really be happening? "Nostalgia, it's 10:00! Are you going to sleep all day?" Mrs. Spears knocked on my door. I told Josiah I was tired and came home early last night considering, and I still slept that late!

Oh dear God! What was I going to do? Josiah leaves in a few days for Europe with the orchestra. I have new dances to learn with the new girls at the club. I put on one pound and Esther will have a fit! I don't have any money… This is the worst possible time for me to be in this condition.

* * * *

"Nostalgia! Do you hear me talking to you? It's step ball change right, step ball change left, fan kick, arms up, arms down, shimmy."

I was not in the mood to learn any new choreography today either. My mind was wherever my body was not. I had no control over my emotions, my body, or my thoughts. I'd seen Josiah only a few times since Mitzi's and Bunky's wedding because he was getting some last minute things done before he left for France.

They were all going without me. I had no idea how much I depended on Mitzi and Tessie. We practiced dances at home so when I had trouble picking anything up all I had to do was ask them. Now I was really on my own!

We hadn't seen Drusilla in a while either, so that was weighing on me too. The last time I saw her, she was outside on the fire escape behind the stage. She was deep in thought while smoking a cigarette. Now that I think about it she had been out there smoking a lot, like she was searching for something but just couldn't find it. It's funny how we act when we're looking for something internal. We either go to food, drugs, sex, or God. I had never realized that until I lived here. Maybe I had to get out of Spivey's Grove to notice.

Well, I was about to really be alone now that Josiah, Bunky, and Mitzi would all be in Europe. Tessie and Peter were already there. The house was gonna be so quiet soon. The married couples would still be there, but Mrs. Spears had stopped taking boarders a long time ago because of The Depression. If she couldn't feed her boarders like she wanted to, she wouldn't take them in. Not to mention she didn't want to have to worry about anybody new stealing her silverware. It was either take in less people, or raise the rent so she could buy food. Few could hardly afford $5 a week right now anyway.

The more I thought about it I didn't see myself telling Mrs. Spears I had a baby on the way. My word. Would she ever be disappointed in me. I'm sure she knew Josiah and I had been having relations, heck she couldn't say too much considering her relationship with Mr. Greer, but there was a certain amount of care a woman was supposed to take if she was unmarried and engaging in such activities.

Lily must have had it down to a science. That girl amazed me with her wit. She may have been the youngest, but God certainly saved the best for last in regards to her. I missed my sister so much. She was the one I should be telling about this if anybody. Tessie was gone, Mitzi was fixing to go, and Josiah… the last thing he would want to have to deal with was a baby. He was so excited about going to France.

My mind kept going back to Drusilla on the fire escape. I couldn't remember the last time I had seen her smile before that. I also remembered she had auditioned in the next group after me and she was older than me too, so she was more than likely 21.

All these years I took for granted the companionships and friendships I had formed with being a Cotton Club Girl. When they all go to Europe who was gonna hail me a cab or take me home? Suddenly I felt naked, stripped of all manner of protection, at the whim of whatever element forthcoming, be it man, storm, or circumstance. Alone. Where would a baby fit into all of this?

"Take five!"

I grabbed a cup of ice water from the cooler and began thinking how do I get rid of a baby. I sat outside on the fire escape where I used to see Drusilla smoking, and I began to think. I couldn't go to anyone I knew to ask them that question because they would know immediately I was in circumstances. They'd probably even go back and tell

Josiah. He couldn't ever know about this! Who would know how to get rid of a baby?

Just then Constance and Loretta came out, gossiping like they always do, "… and I still don't see why she would want anything to do with that tomcat no way," said Loretta. They glanced at me before she continued, "Every time I turn around I hear he's out on 110th Street getting a jelly roll from one of those hoochi coochers."

And just like that, I knew who would be able to answer my question.

* * * *

110th Street by no means had the charm or dignity of Striver's Row or Sugar Hill, certainly not the cleanliness, but all the riffraff of Harlem had to go somewhere during the day so that it may crawl out at night. I waited for everyone in the house to go to bed before I snuck out the front door. I had the nerve to use the forbidden back staircase to tiptoe to every bedroom door in the brownstone to make sure I heard snoring, and I did.

After leaving the brownstone, I walked down to 125th street to hail myself a cab. When I told the driver 110th street, he turned and looked at me as if I didn't know what I wanted. I assured him that I was very much sane. "Miss did you want me to wait for you?"

"No sir, I'll be fine," I said as I paid my fare. I thought I would lose the dinner Mrs. Spears made for us as soon as I stepped out. Do they ever pick up the garbage in this part of town?

I smelled spoiled food, spoiled people, dead rodents, and reefer. I witnessed two junkies fighting over a needle and a silver spoon. I felt a pimp, complete with gold tooth and tacky zoot suit, sidle up to me, asking if I was looking for work or company. I heard a slap in the face and the proverbial "Fool, I know you didn't just hit me," as a response. I tasted dryness on my tongue from being so nervous. Yes, someone around here would know where I could do away with a child, but who would I ask?

"Bitch don't chu dare stop on my corner! Find ya own spot!" I turned around to put a face with the voice. The first thing I saw was a scar stretching from the corner of her right eye to the right corner of her lip.

All I could think was Mae West wanted her wig back, but instead I asked, "I'm not looking for a john. I need to... get rid of a..."

I couldn't bring myself to say it aloud, but she already knew, "Oh, you knocked?"

"Yes."

"Well you need to go see Madame Isis," she said. She smelled of cheap perfume and stale beer. The dress was too old, too tight, and too short. The only thing fresh about her were the needle tracks in her arms.

"Can you tell me where she is?"

"Yeah. For $1! Oh, nothin' ain't free round here for you or nobody else, Doll Face," she sneered.

I gave her $1 to suffice her request.

"Big red building on the corner down there. Apt 101. Tell her Sweet Mama sent ya. You might get a discount," she laughed at her own joke while walking away, stuffing the dollar in her cleavage.

I ventured in the direction she pointed, and just as she said, the building was big, red, and on the corner. Men were sitting on the stoop smoking, drinking, shooting craps. I stood there and waited, breathing deeply the foul air the whole time, trying to look confident. I fingered the straight razor in my pocket I had stolen from the bathroom Mrs. Spears shared with Mr. Greer, wondering for the millionth time why those two didn't just go on ahead and get married. Josiah had told me if I was ever confronted by anyone on the street to think the most mundane thought possible to prevent looking scared. He must have been right. They parted the way for me, whistled, catcalled, but no one laid a hand on me.

I walked up the stairs, entering the building's sorry excuse for a foyer. Just as I suspected the second door's lock was broken so, anyone could enter. I walked down the hall and knocked on apartment 101.

"Who is it?" It sounded like the person inside expected my knock.

"A client," I said. I heard rustling, then footsteps. The door opened to reveal a tiny little woman with brown skin, hazel eyes, and the strangest head of hair I had ever seen. It looked like Medusa's snakes sprouting from her scalp. Now the accent was some sort of Caribbean, I think. It sounded like some of George and Cicely's people from Brooklyn, which sounded like Geechie to me.

She looked me up and down moving so that I may enter. I saw bead curtains separating the rooms instead of doors. Lots of plants I didn't recognize, lots of statues I did not recognize either, lots of candles to add to the mysterious ambience of secret knowledge. The odors of sage, curry, and something else I couldn't place muscled their way up my nose with no apologies.

She looked at me closer, and I had a feeling she would know why I was there. "You're with child."

I nodded.

For some strange reason, I refused to let this woman hear my voice. She walked through one of the sets of beaded curtains and returned with a small black bottle that had a cork stuck in the opening. "You came just in time, so you won't need the knife." I didn't want to know how she knew that.

"Do not eat for the next two days. Take this sometime during the third day, while your stomach is still empty. Swallow all of it! You will throw up immediately. Two hours later you will begin to bleed for the next two days after that. Once you are done bleeding it will be gone. Any questions?"

I shook my head no.

"$.50, please."

I gave her the money and left without looking back.

* * * *

That cab driver was persistent! I found him circling the block. When I got in, he said, "I just didn't feel right about leaving you down here."

"Thanks. Can you take me back to 125th?"

"Yes, Ma'am." He drove me in silence all the way there then asked if I wasn't sure he could take me farther. I thanked him, said no, and paid the fare. It would be a long walk, but it might make the process easier.

* * * *

The next few days were some of the longest I would ever know. I was empty to the point of tasting nothing when I burped. A dry saltiness enveloped my lips, the first sign of dehydration. My muscles were weak from themselves and the fetus feeding on them. My teeth hurt from my bones and the fetus stealing whatever calcium I had to offer. I locked myself in my room, pretending I was asleep whenever Mrs. Spears cooked or called me downstairs for a meal.

I missed choreography cues every day, got yelled at several times. I think I caught Arnie O'Neil staring with interest, but making no comments. I performed with a plastic smile on my face every night and matinee, careful not to miss too many steps. Esther noticed the bulge in my midsection. I told her I was going on a diet and it would be gone soon.

When I got back home that Sunday afternoon after the matinee, I told Josiah that I wasn't feeling well and would not be going to The Savoy. He looked disappointed but said I looked tired and understood my wanting to rest. If he only knew.

I went upstairs immediately and opened that bottle of godforsaken contents given to me by Madame Isis to a smell that was more than medicinal, and a taste so bitter it drew my cheeks closer to my teeth. I fell on my knees face first over the toilet retching frothy green liquid, amazed something was inside of me despite my not having eaten for two whole days. My stomach tightened and cramped, tightened and cramped, tightened and cramped countless times. As promised the bleeding started two hours later. Big, clumpy, bloody clots of tissue and plasma exited my body for two more days. By Tuesday at 5:00 pm I was meeting Mitzi for dinner before the 8:00 gig as if nothing of significance had happened.

But something of significance had happened. A part of me was missing and I couldn't get it back. A part of Josiah was missing that he didn't even know about, but I knew… Oh dear God what had I done? I felt physically lighter. The choreographer complimented me on my performance saying every movement had 'virtuosity and depth,' every tap was clean, every kick lengthy. She was so proud.

I felt mentally trapped. There is no escape from yourself, so what do you do when you need to get away from the battles you wage in your head? Harass your friends until they tell you everything's 'gonna be alright?' Ha! They only tell you that to placate you, so your mood doesn't hinder their spirits. How was everything supposed to be alright when I'd ruined two lives and obliterated a third? Wreaking havoc on your own soul was slow death when you were in the land of the living. What was it gonna be like when you're dead?

My morbid imaginings made me ache for Josiah. I decided to ask him to take me to the Seligman Fountain at Morningside Park so we could sit on our bench and just cuddle. It would be one of the last times we did it before he left for France. I couldn't wait to be encircled in his arms tonight. It had been so long since he had touched me.

After the performance, I sat in The Basement watching everyone dance and sing for each other while I waited for

Josiah to put the saxophone to bed for the evening. I still felt tired, but I was more alert than I'd been in weeks. He finally arrived, smiling, saying hello to folks on his way to the table to see me. His smile was so big, then it faded slightly, or was that my imagination?

"Hi," I said.

He looked at me almost as if he had never seen me before, then one corner of his lips raised up, "Hi," he said.

I suggested we take a stroll to the park. He agreed, still looking at me strangely.

When we got outside, he walked slowly, still staring at me at first. Then he quickened his pace as if he were trying to get rid of me. Finally I asked, "Would you slow down?"

"Why, can't you keep up? Seems like you ain't carrying a load no more!" What did he just say? What did he mean by that?

"What are you talking about?" I tried to smile even though I felt my lips quiver.

"I'm talking about last week when I saw you your skin was brighter, your lips were puffier, and your nose was just about to spread." He walked over to me, pointing his finger accusingly into my face, speaking quietly between clenched teeth, "Did you do away with something that belonged to me?" I was frozen, then he shouted, "ANSWER ME!!!"

I swallowed hard, "Josiah I can explain…."

"No… No… No… No… No… No… No! You didn't, Nostalgia, please tell me you DIDN'T!!!!" He was crying. I'd never seen him cry before… and it was all my fault. He sobbed. I put my hand on his shoulder, but he recoiled from my touch like I had a disease. He cried and sobbed with such anguish that I had never heard before coming from him, or any other man for that matter. Then he spoke. "You know what I been doing for the past week?" When I didn't answer he shouted, "DO YOU KNOW WHAT I BEEN DOIN' FOR THE PAST WEEK?"

All I could do was shake my head.

He took a ring box out of his pocket. "I was practicing askin' you to marry me," with tears rolling down his cheeks like they had nothing to lose, he opened it to show me the most perfect solitaire diamond set in gold that I had ever seen! I gasped. When I reached for it he shut the box so fast it squeezed the tip of my middle finger.

"Josiah you about to go to France with the orchestra…" I began.

"And I was gonna ask The Duke if you could go! If he said no I had it all figured out. Lionel Hampton's been playin' downtown at The Stork Club all week. I've been meeting with Lionel Hampton about playing in his orchestra when they open the new Cotton Club in Culver City. If we couldn't go to France, we were going to California. Y'see, I spent this whole week plannin' our future, and you spent this whole week killin' it!" He was breathing so hard his nostrils were flaring. "You remember all them years ago when I told you to promise me you would let me know if anything about us don't feel right to you? Well, you broke that promise!" He began walking away.

I grabbed his arm, and he pushed me away staring at me in disgust, like he didn't know me. Then he walked toward me, reaching his hand out. I heard the lavaliere snap from its clasp as he snatched it from around my neck. I felt the burning, tingling sensation of a welt forming.

He turned from me to the street to hail a cab. One stopped on a dime. He opened the door. I thought he was going to get in it, but instead, he grabbed me by my arm, pulled me around, pushed me inside, slamming the door in one swift swoop. Throwing money at the cabby he said, "Take her the hell away from me." That was the last I saw of Josiah.

* * * *

July 1, 1931, Wednesday

My Dearest Lily,

This will be my last letter to you since I'll be leaving for Europe with The Duke Ellington Orchestra tomorrow morning! My passport came just in time, I have my boarding ticket for the Queen Elizabeth, I'm all packed, and I've said farewell to everyone at the club. I am so excited I could bust! I must admit that I am going to miss Mrs. Spears, Mr. Greer, George and Cicely, and Jude and Mavis. Mavis says that there are lots of hairdressers and cosmetologists in France so Mitzi and I shouldn't have any problem maintaining our looks. Mitzi, Bunky, Josiah and I will be meeting up with Tessie and Peter as soon as we can. It will be so wonderful to see them again after two years. Can you imagine? Tessie seems to love living there. Her dance school is very successful, and so is Peter's pastry business. It will be so good to get some raspberry Danishes again. She told us not to pack too many clothes because we're going to want to shop, so I'm picking out my favorite pieces from my wardrobe and traveling as light as possible.

The Duke says we'll be performing on the ship so those gigs should keep our routines fresh. You know that we'll be on the ocean for a whole two weeks. I just can't imagine being off land for so long, but people have done it for centuries, and I have determined I am not the least bit scared. If I get seasick, I'm sure they have soda crackers and ginger ale on board.

By the time I get back, I trust that you will be all the way away from Noah and married to Henry. Whatever the case may be I will expect to see you if I have to send you and Henry the fare to come up here.

Well, I have to wind this letter up so I can run around and do some last minute errands before I have to board the ship in the morning.

Take good care of yourself until I see you again.

Your Beloved Sister

Nostalgia

PS

Tell Mrs. Barden I said Au Revoir! (She'll know what it means.)

I hated writing my sister a letter filled with lies but I just didn't want to explain to her that I wasn't going, plus if I continued to write to her it would only be a matter of time before I told her that I had gotten rid of Josiah's baby, and he wanted no other parts of me as a result. He didn't call me today, and I knew he wouldn't come by the house or the club before he left. From what I can tell he hasn't told Bunky what happened. Mitzi stayed at the brownstone so that she could pack her things. He came to visit, but out of habit, Bunky still didn't come up the stairs. They seemed so happy. I needed to be happy for them even though I was sad for me.

Mrs. Spears, of course, noticed Josiah hadn't been around the past few days. I told her he was busy doing last minute things. Eventually, I would have to tell her we'd decided to part ways because we couldn't see how we would continue a relationship with an ocean between us. That should satisfy her desire to ask questions, and it was a logical explanation, wasn't it?

"Nostalgia, wake up! We're going down to Pier 72 to see the ship set sail from the dock." Mrs. Spears knocked on my door. I pulled myself out of bed and opened my door.

"Mrs. Spears, I'm not going," I said.

Her brow furrowed. "Not going? Well, why not? Josiah will want to see you before…"

"No, he won't. We decided that it's best that we part ways. There's an ocean between us now…" my voice trailed off involuntarily because my words didn't even sound believable to me.

She and I stood in the doorway just looking at each other because neither one of us knew what to say. Finally, she broke the silence. "I'm sorry to hear it, but I guess I understand it. I'll see you when we return."

I nodded and closed my door gently. I crawled back into bed where I transferred between slumber and tears until it was time for me to get ready to go to the club.

I ate by myself at five o'clock. It felt so strange sitting there alone at that big table where it all began three years ago. It hurt to realize there'd be no more camaraderie or girlish conversation in this dining room in the late afternoon. Mrs. Spears came to check on me several times, looking at me like she wanted to say something.

I was remembering the first time I sat in this room with Tessie and Mitzi all those years ago. Not knowing those two would become my best friends and confidants turned out to be a most pleasant surprise. Sitting there by myself at dinner made me realize something about tonight: I was scared! Before every performance it was always customary to have what performers call green room. It didn't mean we met in a green room per se, it was a time where the performers bonded with each other before they had to share themselves, and each other, with an audience. I realized these dinners at 5:00 before the 8:00 gig served as a green room for me! This was where we bonded before we had to anticipate The Duke's piano riffs, Esther's tantrums when we forgot to hang our costumes in the proper places between numbers, the times when the audience would, or wouldn't, react to what we did on stage.

Tessie, Mitzi, and I were a support system in and of ourselves, and now we were completely disbanded. Even when she went to The Savoy Ballroom, Tessie remained a part of our support system. Now I was about to perform without a support system! What was this going to be like? Well, I would soon find out because no matter what, professionals kept going. No matter what, the show must go on.

Chapter 25

The show went on but I was only there in body. My spirit was somewhere in the past refusing to acknowledge my new reality. Cab Calloway was a much different performer than Duke Ellington. The Duke was a bandleader in that the lead instrument in his compositions was the piano, while the rest of the instruments played underneath. The Duke sat behind the piano all night while his orchestra acquired direction by listening to his riffs.

Cab Calloway, on the other hand, did not play an instrument because he was the instrument! He never sat down, instead he stood on a platform in front of the orchestra waving his baton, dancing, singing, and in most cases, like in the songs *Minnie the Moocher*, or *Edie Was a Lady*, Cab encouraged the band, as well as the crowd, to sing with him. In that sense, Cab made the audience become a part of his orchestra.

Audiences changed every night, ergo the performance was bound to be different every night! The showgirls could rehearse all they wanted to, yet there would be no way of anticipating what would happen on that stage from now on. It frustrated, if not intrigued, me to the point of discombobulation.

I was amazed that one man could persuade an entire room, to literally become a part of his show. The audience had a ball. I didn't. I was distracted the entire night. I constantly lost my footing watching Cab. My sense of direction failed me listening to Cab. I put on the wrong costume for the Jumpin' Jive, because I wasn't digging the beat on the mellow side… Cab, Cab, CAB!!!!

After the last number, I hung my costume up, took off my make-up except for the lips and eyes like Tessie always told me to do, and set my dressing table for the next night's performance. Without thinking I began walking over to The Basement, then suddenly remembered as I was about to cross the street that no one I was interested in talking to would be there.

I looked as Constance, Loretta, and all the new girls were going inside the building, "C'mon Nostalgia," shouted Loretta.

"Not tonight, I'm a little tired. Maybe tomorrow," I shouted back. She shrugged her shoulders and followed the other girls inside. I looked up and down the empty street waiting patiently for a taxi.

"Hello, again." Charles Sherman's voice startled me.

"Hello," I said.

"Are you going to The Basement?"

"Not tonight. I'm a little tired."

"Well, that's too bad. I was hoping we could have some refreshments and get to know each other a little better." His smile was somewhat crooked, but his teeth were so white and straight.

"I'll consider that for another night. Right now I need some rest." I hoped he could see I didn't mean to be rude.

"I'm holding you to that. Let me hail you a ride home. Where are you going?"

"Thank you. 2225, 139 Street," I answered.

Charles put his hand up, and it didn't take long for a taxi to notice. He opened the door for me and gave the driver the fare as I got in, "2225 Striver's Row. Have a good evening, Nostalgia."

I smiled as he shut the door. As the car pulled away from the curb, I watched him cross the street to The Basement.

* * * *

Without seeing Josiah's smile, witnessing Mitzi's and Bunky's charismatic love for each other, and reading Lily's insightful letters, the days blended together into one monstrous heap. Everything from my thoughts to my costumes was heavy, and the best I could do was lug it all around with me everywhere.

That first Sunday evening dinner without Josiah, Mitzi, and Bunky, no one seemed to speak. I hadn't realized before now how much older the married couples were than I was. When folks weren't laughing and gregarious you could see lines, wrinkles, and worries you never noticed before.

Since all we did was eat, dinner moved with turtle-like enthusiasm. Bunky wasn't there to say something inappropriate, likewise, Mitzi wasn't there to reprimand him. I didn't think I would ever get used to not feeling Josiah's hand rubbing my thigh while I ate. Even the food was bland, which was unusual for Mrs. Spears, but I know she missed them too. It just came out in her cooking.

After dinner, I stayed home because I had no escort to The Savoy Ballroom. I probably would have stayed in anyway because I wasn't in the mood to take any sort of company, and I didn't feel like I ever would be again.

They all went to the parlor to listen to a radio show, but I went up to my room. I got out the copy of *World's Best Fairy Tales* by Hans Christian Andersen and tried to read Cinderella, but after being her for the past two years, I found I had outgrown the idea of handsome princes and fairy godmothers.

I went on, flipping through the anthology until I found The Little Mermaid, which I had never read before. I ended up feeling a kindred spirit to the lead character being something she wasn't in order to get the prince. Her efforts did not work in her favor, and in the end, she died. Well, my goodness! I didn't know a fairy tale could have an unhappy ending.

A framed picture Josiah and I had taken on one of our outings to Coney Island sat on my night table. I picked it up and held it tightly to my chest as I cried. Oh, Josiah. When I met you a few years back, I thought you had the most magnificent presence. Now I've found your absence to be just as astounding! "I miss you so much, Josiah," I said it out loud to my own lonely self.

Chapter 26

The obnoxious heat of August served as a precursor into the cooler temperatures of fall. September and October floated on dry, gusty winds with trash and colorful leaf particles hitting us in our eyes if we weren't careful. Constance, Loretta, and all the new girls in the troupe tried to include me in the outings to The Savoy and the frivolous conversations, but there was nothing no one could say to me that would transform me into a social butterfly.

Some of the musicians in Cab's band, especially Charles Sherman, asked me out on various occasions. I know I seemed unsociable, but they accepted my polite decline every time. The boys in the band were so different now. Duke Ellington's men were quiet gentlemen who made sure if they saw one of the dancers leaving they would put her in a taxi, or do whatever needed to be done to see to it that she got home safely. Cab's band members didn't so much as open the door for us! They drank and smoked quite a bit much for me too.

I wondered if Constance and Loretta noticed this. I wanted to inquire, but some of the new members of the troupe were already dating them, and I didn't want to stifle anyone's joy. I can understand having fun. Bunky was a barrel of laughs, but he was never purposefully or outright rude. One of Cab's band members, Johnnie, I think, referred to one of the new girls in the dance troupe as "…dumb as a box of rocks…" The Duke's men would have never said such a thing. Or at least not in a way any of us would have been able to hear it.

The Duke Ellington Orchestra's exit from the Cotton Club marked the end of an era for me. The days of feeling protected at the Cotton Club were over, and it became apparent when I finally decided to accept that my friends and Josiah were all gone.

Despite the early warning signs life and circumstance had a way of shedding light through various situations. I eventually fell victim to the solitude, deciding some company was better than none at all. I needed to try to fit in somewhere. Thanksgiving, Christmas, and my birthday were upon me. On top of everyone being in France there would be no well wishes from Lily, or Mrs. Barden either for that matter. I was so lonely, and as a result, I let my guard down.

I chose not to remember the first night I met Charles Sherman because we had been introduced at The Savoy by Josiah. In a concerted effort to remove Josiah James from all areas of my mind I purposely forgot the way Charles had the audacity to get fresh with me right in front of my date for that evening, or that my date for that evening, Josiah, referred to him as "a piece of work."

I forged ahead like a blind fool and met him at The Basement one Saturday night after the show. He was already there talking and laughing with two of the new showgirls. I watched them for a minute and came to the conclusion he was quite the lady's man. It also came to me that I had never really seen Josiah with any woman other than myself. I ignored that it disturbed me the way Charles was so comfortable talking to two women at one time. When I walked over, making my presence known, he bid them both a cordial good evening. They looked at me with expressions I'd never seen before, certainly not friendly ones. I tried to smile, but they made me nervous, so I walked with Charles to a table in the corner of the room.

"Would you like a drink?" he asked.

"Yes, please," I said. I waited for him to come back, noticing it took a much longer time than I had anticipated. When he came back from glad-handing and getting my drink, I also noticed the orange juice tasted funny. "Something's wrong with my drink," I said.

"Oh, does it not have enough vodka?" he asked.

"Vodka?!"

"Yes. It's a screw driver."

"And this is how it's supposed to taste?"

"Yes. So this is your first drink?"

"Yes."

"Well, I am honored! Just drink it slow, you'll get used to it," he said as he continued to sip his. He had no intention of getting me a plain orange juice.

I was so thirsty I went on ahead and drank it... slowly. I will admit I began to grow accustomed to the bitterness on my taste buds. The warmth going down my insides began to ward off the chill in the air, and I relaxed.

Charles smiled, rubbing my thigh. The last person to rub my thigh was Josiah, and I chose to forget about it by allowing Charles' hand to stay there. "You've finished your drink. Would you like another?"

I nodded. He got up, leaving the table for quite some time again.

Men from the band came by and spoke to me. I smiled, shared small talk, and realized why Josiah never left me for long periods of time: he didn't want any other man talking to me.

When Charles came back with my drink the glass was sweaty, an indication he'd stayed away too long. "How are you feeling?" he asked.

"Okay," I said, and began sipping my second drink. About half way through it, my head began to swim. "My head feels funny. I think I should go home." When I got up, I sat right back down! The room was spinning like I had never seen it do before. I got scared, thinking I might throw up. "Can you please see that I get home?" I said to Charles.

"Why don't you come to my place and try sleeping it off," he insisted.

"No, I want to go home…" I said. He helped me with my coat and led me outside. Our voices sounded funny as if we were talking underwater. He held me up barely because I was so dizzy. I felt heavy and out of control.

"I'm taking you home with me," he said as he held his hand up hailing a cab.

Before I could protest his insistence I go to his place, my stomach did a somersault and all the drinks I had that evening came up on his suit! He was quiet for a moment, before saying, "Maybe you should go home." The cab came finally, and he put me in it.

"Where's she going?" asked the cabby.

Charles gave him money, "She'll tell you." He walked back into The Basement.

* * * *

The cab driver helped me up the stairs to Mrs. Spears' brownstone. "I'll be alright," I told him. He left as my hands fumbled in my purse until I felt my keys. I somehow found the keyhole and opened the door. I began making my way up to my room in the dark when my corneas were suddenly offended by the brightest light imaginable.

Mrs. Spears screamed, "Mason!"

I felt hands on either side of me taking me by the elbows, lifting my feet off the stairs, whisking me to my room.

I was so sick I didn't make it to breakfast or church. I threw up all night long with Mrs. Spears and Mr. Greer taking turns checking on me. I was scared all night, thinking I would never stop throwing up. Every time I got comfortable in my bed I had to get back up to go to the bathroom, sometimes I didn't make it, I'm ashamed to say.

I finally got to sleep as sunrays were showing through my curtains. When I woke up, I raised my torso off the mattress slowly until I was sure the room wouldn't betray me by shifting of its own volition. I set both feet on the floor, got up carefully, tippy-toeing across my room like I might have been on top of a frozen lake. It felt so good to move without my stomach acting like an entity separate from the rest of my being. I opened my door to the scent of pine cleaner punching me in the nose. It permeated the hallway, the bathroom, especially the toilet bowl.

After I had relieved myself, I slept for the rest of the morning until Mrs. Spears woke me in time to go to the club for the 2:00 matinee. As I was leaving, she said, "And I expect you'll be bringing home a guest this evening."

"Yes, Ma'am." Somehow I was not looking forward to dinner.

* * * *

I took my make-up off, except for lips and eyes, of course, at the end of the afternoon. Everyone was asking me how I was doing. Apparently, they had all seen the state I was in last evening. Those that seemed the most concerned, the boys in the band and the new girls in the troupe, made me the most wary. I couldn't help but feel they were feigning concern.

Loretta and Constance asked me one time how I felt and didn't say anything else. I had meant to ask those two how they felt about all the new blood that became a part of the troupe in recent weeks, but I couldn't decide on an appropriate time. They seemed to get along fine with the new girls. I did too I guess, but that didn't mean I trusted them.

As I was stepping outside, I felt a hand on the small of my back and a whisper, "Hello," into my ear.

"Good evening Charles," I smiled.

"Where are you headed?" he asked.

I wanted to say to Heaven if I pray hard enough! Instead, I said, "Home. I was wondering if you would like to join me for a quick bite to eat, and then we head over to The Savoy for the rest of the evening."

He smiled that crooked grin, "That sounds wonderful." He held up his hand for a cab. One stopped, and he opened the door. I got in and slid over, making room for him.

"2225 139th Street, please." We rode silently for a moment.

"I see you fared well once you got home last night. How was your morning after consuming your first glasses of forbidden drink?"

"I slept well." For some strange reason, I didn't want him to know how hard a time I had last night. I felt like he probably would have laughed.

"I'll bet you did." His smile seemed even more crooked now, for some reason.

When we stopped in front of the brownstone he paid the fare, and we got out. While I found my keys, he stood very close to me, which I thought was odd. He was right on my heels as he followed me into the foyer.

When I opened the door to the parlor, he seemed surprised to see Mrs. Spears, Mr. Greer, Jude and Mavis, and George and Cicely, waiting for us. He was so surprised the smile ran from his face as if it had caught fire. "Oh, you don't live alone?" he stammered.

"No sir, she most certainly does not," said Mrs. Spears as Mr. Greer stifled a laugh.

George and Jude were on their feet. "I'm George, that's my wife Cicely," he said making a gesture toward the settee where Cicely sat. He shook hands with George for what seemed like longer than usual. Charles' brow furrowed as he looked in George's stony countenance, and then down at their hands as he struggled to release his.

"I'm Jude. That's my wife, Mavis." Jude's handshake was not as formidable, but he looked Charles in the eye just the same.

"I'm Mr. Greer…"

"And I'm Mrs. Spears, and your name is?"

"Uh, Charles Sherman, Ma'am."

"Well, it is a pleasure meeting you. Dinner's ready. Let's all go to the dining room, shall we?"

* * * *

"And where are your people from, Charles?" asked Mrs. Spears as she sat down at the head of the table.

"Connecticut," answered Charles. I watched him cutting his meat. He seemed very nervous.

"Where do you live?"

"On Lenox, just down the street from the club."

"WHERE just down the street from the club?"

"I don't like just giving out my address."

"Well, I don't like not knowing who is in my home and what kind of neighborhood they reside in." After Mrs. Spears had made herself clear, he was about to protest, then he happened to notice George leaning in slightly, and Jude's look saying "I dare you".

"130th and Lennox, Ma'am," Charles said reluctantly.

"How long have you played in Cab's orchestra?"

"About five years."

"So you've done quite a bit of traveling?"

"Yes, Ma'am."

"Well, we all know what they say about men who travel."

"No, I'm not familiar with what they say about traveling men."

"They say…"

"Is anybody ready for dessert? I know I am!" said Mr. Greer. "Evelyn why don't you come on in the kitchen, and help me cut that pie," he insisted.

"Mason, I'm still…"

"C'mon Evelyn." Against her own judgment, Mrs. Spears followed Mr. Greer into the kitchen to prepare dessert.

While they were cutting up the pie it was quiet at the table except for our silverware hitting the dishes, Charles chewing his food, and George cracking his knuckles. When Mr. Greer and Mrs. Spears came back out with the dessert tray, we were all finished, and they began gathering our plates.

Charles ate his pie so quickly he nearly choked, "You ready?" he asked me.

"Almost," I said.

"Well, I'll be in the foyer waiting for you. Good evening everyone." Before anyone could speak up, he had gotten up from the table and was gone.

We all looked at each other, then burst into laughter!

* * * *

The second phase of the evening was more of the same. We took a silent cab ride to The Savoy and after he had paid he didn't wait for me to get out of the car. I followed him to the door where he paid for my fee to get in, then he saw his fellow band mates and forgot about me.

Luckily I happened to see Constance and Loretta seated at a table having drinks. "Hi! Can I join you ladies?"

"What? Is she out two nights in a row? Girl, have a seat," said Loretta. Constance flagged a waiter for me as I sat down.

"I'll have orange juice with some cherries, please." The waiter smiled and stepped away.

"Did I see you come in with that Charles Sherman character," asked Constance. "I thought after last night you would have gotten enough of his antics."

"Believe me, all we did was come in together. And we won't do anything else 'together' ever again," I declared.

"Good," said Constance. "Cause I've never heard a good word about that man."

"Me neither," said Loretta before continuing, "Even before he came here with Cab's band he's always had a reputation as a lady's man. Girl, you don't want any parts of that," she sipped her drink.

I was taken aback. "Well, why didn't y'all tell me of this before?"

"When do you ever talk to us before now? What would we look like telling you who to talk to if you never really talked to us?" Loretta had a point there.

Then I realized now was the time to ask, "How do you two feel about all the new blood that has filtered into the troupe since The Duke has taken everybody else to Europe?"

They both got quiet, deep in thought, then Loretta said, "They're new, they think they know everything, so I'm going to leave them alone to grow up."

"Me too," said Constance.

I decided that was the best way to handle the novices as well. The waiter brought my drink at that moment. I raised my glass, "To the new girls!"

Constance and Loretta raised theirs too, and said, "To the new girls!" With that we clinked glasses, and sipped our non-alcoholic drinks.

Chapter 27

All the dancers received telegrams Monday morning that we were to be at The Basement promptly at 9:00 Tuesday morning for a very important meeting. We sat in The Basement without make-up yet still looking glamorous in our hats, coats with fur-trimmed collars, leather gloves, good stockings, and high-heeled shoes.

There was coffee, and of all things, Skaagens Danish Pastries served. Without hesitation, I looked until I managed to find two raspberries.

Arnie was present wearing his signature green tie and speaking in that Irish accent that refused to go anywhere. "Thank you, Ladies, for your dedication, and your efforts to arrive on time at such short notice. As you are all well aware, the Ziegfeld Follies are no longer performing at the Ziegfeld Theatre in the theater district due to some difficult times. Therefore the Ziegfeld Follies will begin performing here this week starting Wednesday. They are scheduled until further notice to perform every Wednesday, Thursday, Friday, and Saturday evenings. All of you will be performing every Tuesday evening, Wednesday afternoon, Saturday afternoon, and Sunday afternoon. Is everyone clear thus far?"

None of us spoke because we were all too stunned!

Arnie continued, "Today you need to clean out your spaces in the dressing rooms and move all of your belongings here to The Basement. The Ziegfeld girls will be using the space until further notice."

"And how is this going to affect our wages?" shouted Constance.

"Starting this week your new wages are $15 per week," stated Arnie before continuing, "are there any other questions?" No one spoke. "If there are no further questions, all of you need to start moving your costumes, make-up, and whatever else from across the street."

"I have a question," said Constance. "In order to get to the stage, we have to walk down the street in our dance shoes. Do you know how expensive it is to buy them in the first place and to keep them resoled throughout the year? Wearing them in the street that much will ruin them quicker. And why do they have to come here? They're the world-famous Ziegfeld Follies! Why can't they just go to Europe or somewhere instead of taking our gigs?" Loretta tapped Constance on the back of the hand as she spoke, in an effort to shut her mouth but her tongue would not be bridled. Constance had a talent for saying what was on the collective mind of the troupe. "Furthermore, do you realize how much you just cut our wages, and on short notice at that?"

"Constance, stop…" begged Loretta.

However, Constance's mouth ran like a pair of cheap stockings in the winter. "And another thing…"

I suddenly remembered something Tessie said years ago when we were talking about Geraldine Crocker: people with big mouths had a way of disappearing too. "CONSTANCE! That's enough," I said.

Arnie kept smoking his stinking cigar as we managed to calm her down. "Do the rest of you feel the way she does?" No one answered. "Okay. Thanks to Constance your wages are now $20. Constance you clean out your space and take your stuff home. Good luck finding another gig in this town," and with that Arnie was about to leave.

As he walked past her, Constance threw her coffee in his face! Loretta let out a cry. The rest of us looked on wide-eyed, just as surprised as Arnie. He walked toward her as if he were about to strangle her. I was so scared he was going to grab her, but Loretta got in the middle just in time.

"She didn't mean it, Arnie. I'll help her clear her stuff out!" Loretta had a pleading look in her eye, begging him not to do what he wanted to do.

He and Constance eyeballed at each other long and hard, before he backed away, laughing, taking a green handkerchief from the breast pocket of his suit jacket to wipe the coffee off of his face and tie. "Hurry up, clear out of the dressing rooms across the street. The Ziegfeld girls will be moving in tonight."

I realized then even though the theater district down on Broadway suffered from a lack of patronage due to The Depression, entertainment venues in Harlem had not suffered half as much. Downtown patrons still came uptown to see live, burlesque, variety type shows. Live shows downtown, however, were being replaced by talking, moving picture shows. Theatre owners realized there were no live performers to pay in addition to the rent and property tax on the buildings, which is what happened to the old Ziegfeld Theater. They were bought out by the

Loews, and would soon begin showing moving picture
shows too, therefore the girls needed someplace to perform.

Truth be told the 'Tall, Tan and Terrific' Cotton Club
Showgirls were patterned after the Ziegfeld Girls, and at a
time when we were doing better than them, it was only
natural Florenz Ziegfeld and his Follies would expect what
they thought was their due, I just wished it didn't cost us so
much. It never dawned on me how lucky we were that we
had continued making $30 a week in spite of The
Depression, while most performers downtown were really
feeling the pinch.

That was also why The Duke took his show out of the
United States, because he didn't want to have to suffer. The
less money you made, the more power Arnie O'Neil, Dutch
Schultz, or whatever gangster who owned the speakeasy
you performed in, had over your life. The Duke knew it,
and he got out just in time.

Apparently, Arnie was doing a bit of babysitting as
well. In addition to forsaking the lack of patronage at the
theater, Florenz Ziegfeld had been sick for some time. As a
result, he and his wife, Billie Burke, had gone to California
in hopes his health would improve, while she went to work
with Samuel Goldwyn in an effort that they too could cash
in on the thriving moving picture business.

They sold the theater to settle some of his debts and
pay medical bills. While Florenz was recuperating, and
Billie was starring on the big screen, Arnie would be giving
the Ziegfeld Girls a place to perform. I could understand
doing favors to help other people out, but not at the expense
of your own responsibilities.

* * * *

"So how is Constance," I asked Loretta as she sat down next to me at our new dressing room in The Basement.

"I don't know. I found a note on the kitchen table saying she was going to Chicago. I looked around the apartment, and all of her stuff was gone." Loretta didn't seem shaken or surprised as she put the remnants of burnt matches on her eyebrows to make them appear darker.

I, however, was stupefied! "What do you mean she went to Chicago?"

"I mean she went to the Windy City. She said she'd send me a telegram once she got settled."

"Don't you think it was a bit sudden?"

"Not really. She'd been talking about getting out of New York for a while actually. I guess getting fired from here was the push she needed."

"How did she end up here in the first place? I mean one day Helen was here and then the next day Helen was gone, and there was Constance."

"Well, I had told Big Richie about Constance because I knew Helen would be turning 21."

This was news to me! "You did? Well, how do you know Constance?"

"She and I both studied at The Denishawn School of Dance and Related Arts in Hollywood, California," explained Loretta. "As usual, they would take colored students, but would not allow them to dance in the troupe. So when we graduated, Ted Shawn told us he could get us an audition for the Chocolate Kiddies over in Denmark."

Wow! The Chocolate Kiddies were a colored dance troupe, much like the Cotton Club Showgirls, however, they were based in Denmark, and traveled all over Europe.

Loretta continued, "I didn't want to go so I came here to New York. Constance went, and got the gig. After they had broken up, she came here, found me, and asked if maybe I could get her an audition. Arnie was in Sing Sing at the time. So Big Richie asked him, and since it would be a headache to hold auditions just to fill one spot, Arnie gave him the okay to replace Helen with Constance. What did you think happened?" Loretta asked with a furrow in her brow.

"Oh, nothing," I said, trying to sound nonchalant.

"Anyway," Loretta continued, "I'm auditioning for Martha Graham, and Jose Limon next week. I don't know if they take colored dancers, but I will soon find out. Hey, why don't you come with me? Y'know, once I leave you'll be the only one of the old troupe left."

"Yeah, I've been thinking about that. Maybe I will." Of course I wasn't going with her to those auditions! I'd had no formal training, this was the only place I'd ever danced, and I wasn't quite ready to leave it just yet. In fact, our conversation reminded me I needed to let Arnie know I'd lied about my age at my audition, and I wasn't turning 21 any time soon. Maybe he would let me stay longer.

The next day I arrived at the club a little early. Big Richie, Arnie's right-hand man and bullhorn whenever he was hiding out at Sing Sing, was on his way out of Arnie's office looking pensive.

"What are you doing here," he asked.

I smiled politely, "I needed to speak to Mr. O'Neil real quick. May I see him?"

"Who's out there, Richie?" Arnie called.

Big Richie stuck his head back inside the door, "It's Nostalgia, Sir."

"Well, let her in," he ordered.

I gave Big Richie a smile of thanks, as he gave me a curt nod in return. The malodorous air in the messy little office threatened to stifle my breathing and soak into my clothes, reeking of cigar smoke, cold coffee, and stale whiskey. His disheveled desk was overloaded with papers, receipts, and documents.

I made it a point to look straight ahead, wondering why Mrs. Spears and Mr. Greer wouldn't get married, as Josiah had taught me. I figured thinking a mundane thought would keep my head from looking down and finding something on that desk I was not supposed to see. I decided the less I, or anyone else for that matter, knew about Arnie and his business activities, the better off I would be.

I noticed the trash can in the corner overflowed with crumbled paper as I waited for him to speak. I felt his eyes looking through me instead of at me. He reminded me of a dragon spouting smoky breath from his lips as he placed his cigar in the ashtray, "Well," he asked in expectation.

"I have a confession to make, Sir," I began like a new swimmer treading deep water.

He leaned back in his chair with a small smile on his lips to let me know I had captured his undivided attention.

"When I auditioned back in 1928 I lied about my age…" I began.

He raised his hand, cutting me off, "I know. How old are you really, Nostalgia?"

I was so shocked I didn't speak right away. Arnie had known all along I wasn't 18 when I auditioned and had never uttered a word to me about it!

"I turned 19 this past January, Sir. Are you mad?"

"Mad about what? You lied about your age, but you auditioned fair and square, and earned the spot. No harm was done. You can stay for two more years if that's what you want." He shrugged his broad shoulders as if he wasn't surprised by the conversation we were having. Obviously, he'd had it several times before. I, on the other hand, could barely contain myself, I was so nervous! Then I figured out something to say.

"Thank you so much, Mr. O'Neil."

"You're welcome," he said as I left his office, feeling as if I had just unloaded an elephant off my back!

Chapter 28

What used to be my favorite time of year, the Holiday Season, and then my birthday soon after that, left me feeling cold and tainted as a sink full of stagnant dishwater. I didn't know what to do with myself or my time. I wasn't needed as much at the club thanks to the Ziegfeld Girls, and because I allowed her to think I was in Europe, I never heard from Lily. To make matters worse there was no one to fill the voids of my friends or Josiah. The Depression across the country and my personal doldrums made it hard to get out of bed every day.

The weather was so cold, and the big brownstone was so drafty. We only had heat in our bedrooms during the evening hours, and in our bathrooms when we took baths. The cold was an ever present, dreaded companion that taunted us. It was annoying to step inside the house only to feel no real difference in the temperature from outside.

To earn a little bit of honest money in addition to what Mr. Greer won playing the numbers, Mrs. Spears and I began making hobo pies in the kitchen. Sometimes they might be filled with fruit, but most times they were made with meat George and Jude continued to filch from the Gansevoort Market. Most of the time we baked them in the oven, but on those rare occasions when Mr. Greer could get his hands on some lard, we would pan fry them. Mrs. Spears and I had both gotten into the habit of not asking Mr. Greer where he got his hands on things. He would gaze back at anyone who gave him an incredulous look and say, "Just be grateful, and don't ask me no questions."

* * * *

Letters and postcards came from Europe on a weekly basis. Sometimes they came to the house, other times they came to the club, but they never came from Josiah. One day Arabelle, one of the new girls, was reading a letter out loud from Sally:

December 10, 1931

Ladies,

Last night we had the most wonderful show! Bill Bo Jangles Robinson was in town, so he performed on stage with us. It almost felt like we were in New York. As usual, he almost took the stage from us but didn't quite succeed. His legs weren't the ones the French audiences were interested in. Guess who else we performed with last night: Josephine Baker! That Banana Dance is seductive! No man in the room could keep his eyes off her, especially not J…

And just like that, Arabelle stopped reading aloud. She took several moments to continue reading silently with the rest of us wondering why she stopped. Without turning her head, Arabelle cautiously shifted her eyeballs in my direction, as if she were afraid she might trample my feelings. From the expression on her face I knew… I… just… knew.

I made up some lame excuse to go to the bathroom so they could finish reading the letter out loud. I stayed outside in the cold with tears running down my cheeks until I thought I had given them sufficient time to finish. However, when I stepped back inside the building to put matte powder on my make-up, I heard the last of it:

… Josephine and Josiah have been quite the item since we got here to France. We had only heard about it from Bunky, but after last night's performance they showed up together at this after-hours club called The Rouge, and they were very much together! I suppose he has forgotten all about Nostalgia…

The dread stemming from the depths of my stomach made my lungs feel entitled to a full deep, inhalation. I knew what I was going to get when I reentered that room. Sure enough, Arabelle clumsily put the letter away while the other girls looked at me with a variety of expressions ranging from pity to smirks of satisfaction, to flustered nervousness. However, no one spoke a word. I knew they wouldn't.

I realized then why neither Mitzi nor Tessie had said a word about Josiah in their letters or postcards, staying mum, I suppose, to protect my feelings. I should have expected to hear that he had moved on sooner or later. I was here, he was there, and the ocean between us had no intention of drying up. Even if it did that would be no guarantee he would come back this way.

I found myself with a new mission on my hands: I was going to forget about Josiah James. He was just as dead to me as I was to him. His name would continue to stay banned from my tongue, as I would attempt to disconnect his memory from my thoughts. He was no longer mine, and I would find some way to get over the guilt of it being my fault he was gone.

I had gotten along fine for 16 years before I had ever laid an eyeball on Josiah James! What would three years of my life amount to if I took the time to think about all the living I wanted to do before dying? He was gone, and life had never stopped moving since he left, so I had the obligation to move along with it. And that is exactly what I would do.

I met Loretta at the Savoy Ballroom the following Sunday evening just to get out on the town to celebrate her good fortune at making the cut for the Jose Limon Dance Company. The evening for her was bitter as well as sweet because she missed not being able to share the news in person with her best friend, Constance. Apparently, Constance had sent a letter stating the usual things such as all was well and that she had found a gig at a club somewhere on Lake Michigan Avenue in Chicago. She seemed happy, but most importantly, Constance was away from New York of her own accord.

In addition to adjusting to life without Constance, Loretta also had to get used to the idea that she would be leaving for Argentina on tour with Jose Limon's company at the beginning of January. Watching her wait for her passport to come, packing, learning a new language, and running around the city doing last minute errands reminded me of watching Josiah, Bunky, and Mitzi get ready for France.

Facing the jealousy for the second time made it no easier to cope with, but I managed to smile at her blessing in the face of my own disappointment. If I had gone with her to the audition as she suggested, I might be getting ready for the big adventure too. I decided to take full responsibility for not trying. It would have been the least I could do in an attempt to get away from the city and experience something that had nothing to do with Josiah or the Cotton Club for that matter.

It would have been proof to myself that I was more than "Tall, Tan, and Terrific!" It would have been evidence I had grown from being a performer in a jazz club, to being a world class dancer on an international stage. I supposed I wasn't ready for such a challenge right now.

When the waiter set our plates in front of us, I was famished. Sunday dinners at the brownstone were no longer big and elaborate to save money, not to mention there were no guests arriving to entertain. Avery and his wife stopped coming soon after the Skaagens family relieved him of his chauffeuring duties due to lack of funds. The food at Mrs. Spears Sunday dinner table was the same as it was every other night of the week.

Since The Depression hadn't shown any signs of letting up enough for Mrs. Spears to cook as much as she used to on Sunday evenings, I began eating dinner at the Savoy, and though it wasn't Mrs. Spears' cooking, the food wasn't bad. Especially since it took my mind off of how things used to be. These days I gravitated toward just about anything that took my mind off of how things used to be.

Instead of reminiscing about Josiah and all the fun we had during the Christmases of 1928-1930, I spent the holidays in Mrs. Spears' kitchen making hobo pies for the homeless and less fortunate folks in Harlem. I learned how to keep them from coming apart by using what Mrs. Spears called an egg wash around the edges before pressing them together using the prongs of a fork.

Every time Mr. Greer got his hands on peaches, pears, or other types of fruit, not to mention jar containers, we preserved them in the pantry to use for fruit hobo pies. Jude and George's treasures from the Gansevoort Market enabled Mrs. Spears and me to continue making beef and chicken hobo pies. The butter, flour, sugar, and eggs Mr. Greer acquired were rarely used to create traditional breakfasts anymore but instead needed to make the pastries we bartered, sold, or gave to our struggling neighbors.

Despite doing some ungodly deeds to keep from starving and getting kicked out into the street, we thanked God for every little victory. One more day with a roof over our heads, heat in our bedrooms, hot water for our baths, and the like, made us more fortunate than most battling The Depression in the winter of 1931. We entered into the year 1932 hoping restoration and gentrification would finally come to us!

Chapter 29
1932

Once all the girls were done getting out of costume and taking off their make-up, the band members and other performers would come across the street to The Basement to laugh and joke about the evening's performance, and to entertain each other like they always did in the past.

These days, with Loretta and Constance having moved on to greener pastures, I was officially the only one left of the Duke Ellington era. The paradigm shift amazed me all the time! I stayed in the same place while everything around me moved. Like a skit from a Charlie Chaplin or Buster Keaton movie, my feet moved without taking me anywhere, while the scenery glided on a horizontal plain.

Though I was roughly the same age as all the other girls physically, in my mind I felt more mature. They laughed and giggled at stupid stuff. Their heads were always turning, constantly distracted by the antics of the band or each other. The boys in Cab's band were just that: boys. They were slick, smooth-talking, and less than gentlemen. In fact, they reminded me of snakes.

There was a rumor that Charles had taken up with Marnie Beckford, one of the Ziegfeld Girls. The other dancers rolled their eyes in disgust at the very suggestion that he was jelly rolling a white girl, whereas I could have cared less! I knew first hand Charles Sherman was a heel who wasn't worth the trouble of getting worked up over.

Talking about him just enforced for me that the conversations between the girls were gossipy, unsubstantial vignettes serving as a recreation from one number to the next. As far as I was concerned nothing worthy of remembrance came out of their mouths. They talked terribly about each other as well, whenever someone stepped away to go the bathroom, or just happened to be out of earshot for whatever reason.

I ignored them, figuring I must have been the talk of the town. If they felt I thought I was better than them, then I most certainly was! My life had become a cycle of performing four times a week, going home immediately, making hobo pies for the less fortunate folks in the neighborhood, and going to church on Sundays. I was fine with it for now. It was simple, glum, but under my control, at least.

These were the thoughts I was thinking as I crossed the street that Tuesday evening in January after a performance. There was no one on the street to help me hail a cab, not that anyone would have anyway since the boys in the band were more interested in chasing any skirt they thought they could get under.

Thinking it was a taxi, I raised my hand when I saw some headlights coming around the corner. As the car stopped in front of me, I heard the footsteps coming from the alley behind me. Whoever it was covered my head with a thick black hood while pushing me into the car! I struggled, but someone else who had apparently been waiting for me in the back seat grabbed my hands and began to tie them. I kicked as hard as I could to prevent another person from tying my feet! I had heard four sets of laughter before someone said in an Irish accent much like

Arnie's. "She's a tough one, ain't she?" They all laughed as I expended my energy in trying to breathe, trying to get loose, trying to scream. The material that bound my hands and feet began cutting into my flesh after a few minutes, it was so tight.

I couldn't tell how long the ride was, but it wasn't short. I heard snippets of conversation from masculine voices in Irish and Italian accents. I smelled whiskey and cigarettes. I was scared, so I stayed quiet. I had no idea who these men were, or what they wanted with me. I wondered if I would ever see Mrs. Spears or Lily again.

At one point I heard a window being rolled down and felt the cold night air rush into the back seat of the car. Too afraid to ask these men where they were taking me I sat silently, listening to a comment about the Lenox Lounge here, a wisecrack about how bad Dutch Schultz's breath stank there, and speculations that Madame Stephanie and Bumpy Johnson were sleeping together everywhere in between. If the situation had not been so foreign and frightening it would have been humorous to hear grown men, wise guys and thugs at that, exchanging scuttlebutt about the underworld elite. I prayed to God one day I would find it funny. At this particular moment, however, I was shaking at the thought of what might happen to me next!

When the car finally stopped I knew I had been taken well away from Harlem. The air was colder, moist, and smelled strange, like sludge from underneath a rock had surfaced after millions of years.

I was shoved out the car then grabbed on either side at my elbows. They walked so fast I lost my footing, and they began dragging me. I felt mud and gravel staining my shoes, ripping my stockings. I cried. My nose itched, but they had such a tight grip on my elbows that I could not even brush my hands across my face, which was still covered in that constraining hood. I guess what frightened me most was I couldn't see who I was dealing with or where they were taking me. I had no choice but to hope I wasn't going to be butchered and gutted like a slaughtered pig.

We were suddenly inside a building. It was still cold and the air was still damp, but it wasn't moving. I heard metal chinking on metal, heavy doors opening and closing. Where was this place? I heard a door creaking open while the men led me up several flights of stairs. I heard another door creak open. Then metal sliding on metal again. I heard keys rattling, unlocking yet another door. A hand had laid on the small of my back before it pushed me violently inside a room. Once I felt my elbows finally free, I snatched the hood off my head to find myself looking at Arnie O'Neil!

Chapter 30

Swallowing hard, taking a moment to survey the new surroundings, I noticed a cot pushed next to the cement wall where pictures of showgirls and newspaper clippings hung. There was a table in the center of the room with more newspapers scattered all over it. In the corner of the room, there was a sink with a mirror above it and a toilet next to it. Against the opposing wall stood a tall skinny chest of drawers with a RCA Victor on top playing *Minnie the Moocher*. That song would never be the same for me again. I concluded I was in Arnie's cell at Sing Sing.

I tried to sound normal but my voice cracked anyway, "May I ask you why I'm here?"

A crooked smile oozed across his lips like melted sewer sludge. "I wanted some entertainment for the evening, and since I did you the favor of allowing you to stay with the company after lying about your age, I figured you owed me," he sauntered over to me as if he really expected me to put up with this!

Telling him no may very well cost me my life, my dignity even, but I did not see myself giving him my body, let alone the satisfaction of using me.

"I don't owe you nothing! I dance at your club, and you pay me for it. That's the extent of any relations I will ever have with you."

"You talk to me like you have options," he laughed.

"Is that what you told Ida, Drusilla, Helen, Abigail? I'm not scared of you, and I ain't no junkie like Geraldine Crocker." What possessed me to say that? The smug look on his face held on to his countenance until I mentioned Geraldine Crocker. The smile then dissipated like vapor shooting out of Mrs. Spears' tea kettle.

He walked over to me with the same expression he had when Constance threw coffee on him, but this time there was no one there to stop his open palm from slapping me across my cheek bone! He slung me onto the bed, laughing as he began unbuckling his pants. I knew what he was about to do so I looked around the room for something, anything solid. I saw a baseball beside the RCA Victor! I struggled to get off the cot, pushed past him, and ran toward the corner of the room to the dresser, grabbing the baseball.

We ran around the table like the monkey chasing the weasel, with him slinging the buckle end of the belt at me. I couldn't tell if his aim was bad or I was a fast runner, but one thing was for sure: that buckle would have done some serious damage to me had I stopped moving. I kept the baseball tucked solidly in my fist until I found an opening.

One thing Daddy taught Lily and me to do was throw and catch a baseball. The three of us used to take our mitts and go outside in the yard to throw the balls around in diamond formation two at a time. Daddy said I could throw better than Lily. I hoped he was right because I was determined to find out in a few seconds. I didn't know how many times we went around that table, but I was never going to be able to hit him where I wanted to if we continued to go around in circles.

I got bold, gathered a bunch of the newspapers on the table, and slung them in his face! When he snatched them away, he noticed I had moved closer to the side of the table, so he followed suit like I knew he would. I threw the baseball, nailing him square between his legs! He grabbed himself, his thighs and knees came together in an effort to support his aching manhood. His crumbling knees hit the floor followed by his torso, then his face.

My eyes scanned the floor desperately for the whereabouts of the baseball. I found it next to a chair leg. Picking it up I noticed Babe Ruth's chicken scratch signature scrawled on it. I made the mistake of stepping directly over Arnie, attempting to run, but he grabbed me by my ankle, pulled me down to the floor, got on top of me, our faces nose to nose with his putrid breath making me sick. "You want to know what happened to that junkie whore, Geraldine? She came here one night telling me she was pregnant and the baby was mine," he laughed incredulously, "as if I would really claim it and take care of her! I offered her $500 to get lost, but she wouldn't take it. So I had my guys help her get rid of the kid with a few kicks to the gut until she couldn't stop throwing up!" I couldn't see the humor he found in this. Maybe he was impressed with himself for having gotten away with it all these years. "After that I had them drop her off at home, literally." He continued, "you live in her old tenement house with the old couple don't you?" I said nothing.

He punched me in the nose. When I tasted my blood trickling from my nostrils, I hit him across his jawline with my hand that still held the baseball. I continued holding it as though it was glued to my palm, with a challenge in my eyes if he wanted to insist on hitting me again. Once he got off me, I used my elbows, the backs of my knees and thighs, and my heels to scoot backward on the cement floor toward the cot. I noticed droplets of my blood on the floor and staining the front of my blouse and coat.

He went to the door and called someone to come to his cell. I heard footfalls coming down the hall. It was a cop. "Jimmy, talk to the operator so I can use the phone." Jimmy unlocked the door, entering, strolling to the left corner of the room. I hadn't even noticed there was a phone in the cell!

Jimmy spoke with another person on the line, obviously granting permission to connect to an outside line. Giving the receiver to Arnie he left the cell without so much as a glance in my direction.

"Yeah, it's me. You remember that Crocker girl that used to visit me back in 1925? Yeah, the dark-skinned one with the green eyes. You remember where you dropped her off that night? Good! Torch it!"

"NO!" I shouted as I ran over to Arnie. He grabbed me by the face, pushing me back down onto the floor. I yelped, hitting the cement tailbone first.

He then went over to the door and called out, "Somebody, come get her. I'm done." He paid no more attention to me for that moment. Instead, he got a bottle of whiskey and a shot glass from somewhere and had a drink.

When the goons came to get me, I still had the baseball in my grip. I threw it at Arnie one last time, shattering the shot glass as he drank from it. With a split lip quivering over blood-stained teeth, he smiled, "Don't kill her. Take the scenic route back to Harlem. That'll give the house time to burn." Then looking at me he continued, "I want you to live with the knowledge that you could have prevented the deaths of everybody in that brownstone had you given me the jelly roll tonight!"

They threw the black hood over my head again, dragging me out of the cell.

Chapter 31

When Arnie's goons dumped me off a block away from the house, I could see the flames in the distance, but I did not have the energy to run in the direction of them. My body ached all over from the pummeling and kicking I had endured all night. My brain pounded as the sounds of screaming people running past me toward the blaze stuck in my ears. I had a feeling that nothing would prepare me for what I was about to see when I finally reached Mrs. Spears' brownstone.

It seemed like the whole world was on its way to 2225 139th Street! The fire should be out any minute because there was a hydrant right in front of the residence. It should be going out any minute. My journey to the house was long and labored, but the flames didn't seem to be dying out at all. If anything they were gaining more power. When I got there the fire department still had not arrived, so our neighbors had formed a bucket chain on both sides of the dwelling. Men and women were coming from their houses with buckets and tubs full of water trying to douse the flames, unfortunately their diligent efforts were no match for the formidable heat-thirsty tongues lapping away at my home!

I saw Mr. Greer coming from the house carrying Mrs. Spears out in his arms. She was unconscious! Why was there blood all over her face? He laid her down gently as a bevy of women from the neighborhood rushed over to her, putting cold compresses on her face and trying to bring her back to consciousness. He turned right around and ran back into the house. I heard myself scream, "NO!" but he was gone. I saw no one else, not George or Cicely, or Jude or Mavis. They all lived on the third floor. I looked at the house going deeper into the blaze. If they weren't out by this time, there was no way for them to escape! The whole house was engulfed by this point.

The fire department sirens had finally sounded. In the distance, I saw the trucks lumbering from the direction of The Bronx, because the closest fire station happened to be on Tremont Avenue. The firemen exited the truck with all the urgency of wet noodles. They hooked the hose up to the hydrant, but the water did not come out!

Two of the male neighbors came over to the sidewalk carrying Mr. Greer's severely burned body. He was screaming in pain and agony, "I couldn't get them out! I couldn't get them out! Where is Evelyn… EVELYN!!!!" He was so frantic he scared everyone. Dr. Gaddison arrived with his doctor's bag. Thank God there was at least one emergency professional who actually cared about us.

By the time the fire was put out the foundation was all that was left, otherwise, the residence was unrecognizable. Nothing was salvageable.

* * * *

Mrs. Spears never regained consciousness. The doctor examined her and came to the conclusion that she had hit her head on something while trying to escape. The combination of her age, the smoke inhalation, and a probable concussion were the culprits to her demise. They gave me all of the belongings she had on her person, which was only the nightgown she had worn to bed that evening, and the extra house key she always wore around her neck. Her nightgown, which had dried specks of blood on the collar, smelled of smoke mingled with Van Cleef & Arpel's.

I stared at the extra house key as it lay in my hand. There was nothing for it to open now. Why should I keep it? I suddenly got so angry at the entire situation I almost threw it on the other side of the ward. Before I could lift my arm to sling it as far away from me as I could, something told me to not only keep it, but guard it with my life. I took a deep breath, looking at it as tears distorted my vision. I unclasped it and put it around my neck. I lay down on the bed and cried, trying to regain my composure before going to check on Mr. Greer.

* * * *

The smell of burned flesh almost made me gag as I sat in the ward at Harlem Hospital watching Mr. Greer sleep. He was wrapped in bandages all over his body, and the nurses told me to expect he would be in pain when he woke… if he woke. I hoped he would because I didn't know what to do with myself. I had never been alone before in my life. If he dies, I would be completely alone. I really couldn't go back home now because I'd lied to Lily about having gone with Duke Ellington to France. Why didn't I just tell her the truth? Why didn't I just tell her I made myself lose Josiah's baby and now he hates me? Why couldn't I have just decided to go on back home?

I could have married Bernard Jackson… no… I couldn't be happy living down there again after the first year I lived here. I couldn't have gone backward. I had to stick it out and hope that those beautiful days would come back in spite of the Stock Market Crash, the bank run, and the Great Depression. I wanted to believe the Ziegfeld Follies would leave and the Cotton Club Girls would again be the primary dancers. I wanted to believe the good times would come back. That everybody would come back from Europe, that time would heal Josiah's heart, and he would love me again…

Mr. Greer coughed. He coughed. He was awake! "Do you remember me?" I said meekly. He smiled, trying to sit up until he remembered he was in pain. Wincing he lowered himself back down to the pillow. I called the nurse who came by to check his vitals. She looked grim as she wrote on the clipboard, then left us alone.

I took Mr. Greer's fragile hand in mine but did not squeeze it because I was afraid I might hurt him. His hand was cold. "Evelyn?" he said weakly.

Oh God, I knew this was coming. "Mr. Greer, she died…"

"No, she didn't die… I got her out!" He coughed, trying to sit up again but the pain forced him back onto the pillow. He started crying from the physical agony of the burns plus the mental anguish of losing everyone who was in the house that night, especially Mrs. Spears. With no words to comfort him, all I could do was sit there and watch him cry. It disturbed me that I could not touch him because of his delicate flesh. I could tell he needed a hug.

In my mind, I saw it all over again. He carried her out, set her down on the sidewalk, then turned around to go back to the house to try to save George and Cicely, and

Jude and Mavis, but the flames had lapped their way up to the second floor, making the third level of the house impossible to reach.

The firemen couldn't get to the water in the hydrant. Ha! All those hot summer days when I watched every child in the neighborhood jump around playing as it spilled water into the street, let me know Arnie O'Neil had the fire department on his payroll to sabotage select hydrants around the city. That's the only way a house that had a fire hydrant sitting in front of it could burn!

A nurse came over and told me I should go for now so they could calm him down. "Make sure you come back, Nostalgia," he said through tears. I promised him I would.

* * * *

I managed to get back that evening before visiting hours ended. He was sitting up in bed while a nurse helped him finish his dinner. He looked so beaten by life and circumstances. I refused to let him see me cry. However, my efforts to smile weren't working.

"Don't plan to stay too long. He needs his rest," the nurse whispered to me before leaving.

I tried to make conversation, "How was your meal?"

"It wasn't Evelyn's cooking…" was all he could say about the bland repast.

Looking at him reminded me that everybody was gone. Dead or in France… gone. I was scared. I had no money, and I didn't know how long I would be allowed to stay at a shelter after I was released from the hospital, not that I wanted to.

The house might have been cold after the stock market crashed, and we lost all of our money to the failed banks, but at least I still had my feather bed and three hot meals a day. Now, I didn't even have that. After being propositioned at Sing Sing, spurning his advances, not to mention telling him I knew all about Geraldine Crocker, and suspected he might have facilitated the disappearances of other girls in the troupe, Arnie would kill me if I showed up at the Cotton Club. My goodness… I didn't even have a job anymore.

I took for granted how easily everything came to me in the beginning when I got here that I never prepared for days like this. That's the bad thing about everything coming so quickly and just the way you want it: it never occurs to you that hard times are bound to come too. When I started working for Mrs. Barden back in 1924, I was only 12 years old. Listening to those radio broadcasts made me want to be here to experience Harlem.

The problem with my life was that I never thought about what I would do with my life once my time at the Cotton Club ended! It never occurred to me my body would get tired, or younger girls who were better dancers than me would be up to the challenge and would want it just as much as me. That's the funny thing about age, when you're young, you never think you'll be too old or too tired for anything. That's how you ended up being thrown to chance, change, or whichever way the wind happened to blow.

"Nostalgia?" His voice was so weak.

"Yes, Mr. Greer?"

"Can you hold my hand?" I took his frail hand in mine. We were quiet for a few moments.

"How do you know Mrs. Spears," I asked.

He gave me a brittle smile. "We used to pick tobacco on an old plantation in Raleigh. She was beautiful even back then. She had these long silky black braids on both sides of her head. When the sun hit her skin, she turned copper. Brown with these pinkish undertones. She was five, and I was ten when we said we were going to get married someday. But when she turned sixteen Daniel Spears saw her, and it was over for me. Her father told her she was going to marry him." Wow. There's a lot of that going around, I thought.

"What made him more special than you?"

"We were all ex-slaves and sharecroppers," said Mr. Greer. "The Spears family weren't ever slaves, let alone sharecroppers. Her father saw marrying Daniel as the only way to break the sharecropping curse. The Spears' came from Africa and worked as indentured servants for white folks that were actually fair people. The name Spears was a reference to their West African ancestors who were warriors. They were, and had always been, freedmen. They were wise with their money, and bought a lot of land and farmed it themselves. Daniel didn't want to be no farmer, so he got a job on the railroad, and moved her up here."

"How did he die?"

Mr. Greer smiled and shook his head at my question.

"Daniel Spears ain't dead. Daniel Spears is very much alive!"

Chapter 32

I heard Mr. Greer laugh for the first time since he had been in the ward. "Evelyn had everybody fooled with that mess." I guess the surprise on my face must have been comical. Weak as it was, it was good to hear him laugh.

"What do you mean he's still alive?"

"I mean what I said."

"But how can that be? I used to go with her down to The Empire Savings and Loan of New York once a month to deposit the pension check!"

"That ain't no pension check. That's the settlement money from the accidental death and dismemberment insurance." Mr. Greer caught his breath a moment before continuing, "Y'see, he was in a railroad accident and lost an arm. So she rushes to the hospital to see him, and there is another woman sitting next to his bed. Come to find out the woman was the mother of his four children! If a man works on the railroad, he either has a woman in every town where the train stops, or he has a woman somewhere on the line. Can you imagine finding out your husband has four children with another woman after telling you the whole time you were married he didn't won't any chaps at all?" He was quiet again, trying to catch his breath, then he continued, "Evelyn wrote a letter to his mama saying she was going to divorce him. Well, his mama wasn't about to allow that kind of disgrace to the good name of the Spears family, so she told him to come back to North Carolina, and let Evelyn keep the house and receive the settlement check, and the pension check if he had died first. The railroad and the insurance company don't even know he ain't in New York."

"So he's in Raleigh?"

"No, he ain't in Raleigh. They also own land in Woodsdale N.C. A Little place called Hagars Mountain. His mama made him take the woman and the four chaps to Woodsdale to farm that land. Yeah, Woodsdale ain't too far from Virgilina, where Jude and Mavis…" at the mention of Jude and Mavis tears formed in his eyes.

We were both quiet again. Then he broke the silence, "Evelyn decided she didn't want to stay at the place on 145th and St. Nicholas. She sold it, bought the brownstone on Striver's Row and once she got settled she asked me to come live with her." He smiled, "she didn't have to ask me twice." We were both quiet again after that. Mr. Greer was probably thinking about Mrs. Spears, the house, and everybody in it.

I couldn't keep my mind off of what he had just told me! A lot of things made sense after I heard the story. Now I understood why she and Mr. Greer never married. But even after Daniel betrayed her, she and Mr. Greer still managed to have a big house with a bunch of children. Tessie, Mitzi, me, and everyone else that lived in the upstairs of the house were the sons and daughters Daniel never gave her.

This also explained why she preferred riding the bus to the train when she traveled down south, not to mention that heated exchange she had with Charles Sherman about "men who travel". Would I ever be able to tell Josiah why Mrs. Spears and Mr. Greer never married?

Then something occurred to me! "Should we tell Mr. Spears about the fire?"

Mr. Greer thought a minute, a fresh set of tears formed in his eyes. Sure enough, he voiced what I knew he was thinking, "What would Evelyn do?" he sighed.

Then his eyes lit up as if she'd spoken to him, "Do you remember her account number?"

Actually, I did, "Yes, sir."

"Good. The first of the month go down to the post office, get that last check, and deposit it into Evelyn's account. Wait a few days, go back to the bank. Take all of her money out. Every last cent! Then call the railroad company and tell them that he's dead and to stop sending checks…"

"But…"

"No! Let Evelyn have the last laugh after the way that man treated her. Send a telegram to her family and tell them what happened. Trust me, Raleigh might be big, but it's still small enough for news to travel fast. They'll tell my family and his that she's gone. By the time he finds out and tries to come up here to see if she left anything, or to get the checks coming to Woodsdale, it'll be too late."

"But Mr. Greer the railroad company is going to want a death certificate. How do I get that?"

"Nostalgia, everything got destroyed in the fire… including my identification. Tell the railroad company both of them died, and tell these nurses I'm Daniel Spears. That way she and I can get buried next to each other, you get whatever is left over from the burial insurance, what she left in the bank, and whatever's in the safety deposit box at the post office."

"Safety deposit box?"

"Yeah. Did they give you all of her belongings when they told you she was…"

He couldn't bring himself to say it so I continued, "Yes."

"Did they give you that key she used to wear around her neck?"

"Yes, but she said that was an extra house key!"

"Ha! That's my Evelyn. She can hide an elephant in plain sight. That's the key to the box. Evelyn was bound and determined to never keep money in the house in case of fire or burglars, and after that mess happened on October 29, she got the box at the post office. If there was ever a bank run again she was going to be ready! When I'm gone, you know what to do." We just looked at each other.

"Mr. Greer… you're going to be fine…"

"Nostalgia, I'm old, and the doctor says 80% of my body got burned in that fire. It's only a matter of time. Send telegrams to everyone's family and to France. Tell them everything was destroyed in the fire including the bodies and that you'll be sending the death certificates in a few weeks. Write my brother a letter letting him know I'm gone." Before I could ask he said, "Don't even worry about no death certificate for me. I was born in 1862 by a mid-wife, so I don't even have a birth certificate. He'll know what to do."

All that talk about death certificates must have put a pitiful look on my face because he said, as if to try to cheer me a little, "Evelyn says you seemed to be hurtin' about what happened to your sister after you disobeyed your father when he was about to make you marry that man. Lily's young and her husband is old. He'll be dead soon enough for her to do some living. And judging from the way Daniel Spears treated Evelyn, I'm sure she would tell you fathers don't always know what's best for their daughters." He started coughing again, the hacking kind that hurts your chest. The nurses ran over to us and told me to go back to my ward.

* * * *

When I came back to see Mr. Greer the next day the bed was empty. I felt an anchor tugging on my heart, sinking it into vast depths. I turned to go find a nurse, hoping they had moved him to another ward as opposed to… but the nurse had walked up behind me treading as lightly as an angel. She shook her head, and I knew he was gone.

She led me to a little room with two chairs and a desk, "I'll leave you alone for a few minutes then I'll come back." She gave me a handkerchief before she left.

This was really it. I was all by myself. The only company I had was my own thoughts, and they were so morbid I didn't want them. However, they were a part of me, so I was stuck with thinking about all I had to do, all the people that were lost, whether they were actually dead, or in France.

The nurse came back with a clip board, "Are you ready?"

"No, I'm not, but I have to start somewhere and at some point so it might as well be now," I said.

She gave me a wry smile, nodding her head. She seemed to understand. "I need to ask you a few questions about the deceased." It amazed me how clinical nurses could be no matter what. "What was his name?" She looked at me pointedly.

I stared back, stating evenly, "Daniel Spears."

* * * *

I was released the next day from the hospital and told to go to a shelter on 116th Street. Being in that godforsaken place gave me all the gumption needed to do what Mr. Greer instructed me to do. The first thing I did was the hardest thing: report all the deaths to the city so they could begin the process of preparing the death certificates. After that, I contacted Brooklyn, Virgilina, and France. I decided to wait until the certificates were printed to contact Raleigh. The first of the month happened to be a few days after my release from the hospital, so I got the last settlement check from the post office and took it to The Empire Savings and Loan of New York to be deposited into Mrs. Spears' checking account. I hoped desperately it wouldn't bounce. It felt strange running that errand without her.

While I waited another week before liquidating the account, I stayed cold and hungry as I wandered the streets, rode the subway during the day, and slept in the shelter with one eye open while my body tossed and turned on a lumpy mattress with a thin blanket at night.

I constantly asked God to forgive me for taking my blessings for granted. Mrs. Spears' big warm house and good cooking, my friends, my surrogate family, Josiah, The Cotton Club, all of it had escaped my grasp because it never dawned on me nothing lasts forever.

My first clue life was a fragile, priceless flower was when I was forced to leave Spivey's Grove the way I did, and I ignored it then. I had thought for years I wanted to leave, even saved for it, but it didn't become a reality until I was faced with the threat of living the obvious second phase of a life I wanted to change.

I thought about this while sitting on a crowded bench with the other women in the dining area of the shelter. The oatmeal was bland, runny. I tried to pretend it was Mrs. Spears' oatmeal, hot, thick, smooth, sweetened with brown sugar, and spiced up with cinnamon, nutmeg, and lime shavings. Who but Mrs. Spears would ever think to put lime shavings in oatmeal?

I thought about Mrs. Spears again later that morning as I sat by myself in the sanctuary of Abyssinian Baptist Church. I'd gotten into the habit of going there when the cold blistered through Mrs. Barden's old coat. From out of nowhere, the 23rd Psalm was faithfully rolling off my lips as if it had been waiting for me to speak. As I allowed the mantra to warm my flesh, and settle my mind, I could have sworn I heard Mrs. Spears say, "What are you doing here? You don't have to stay here." The key!

I got up from the pew, hurried into the aisle, excusing myself as I accidently hit another woman in my haste to leave. I knew better than to run in church, but I didn't care! My toes, my fingertips, my spirit had been imprisoned by a consistent world of glacial air since I had left Harlem

Hospital. There was something waiting for me at the post office in a forgotten safety deposit box that could end this phase of my misery.

Chapter 33

I arrived at the post office right at 8:00 and there was already a long line. It was cold, but I was warm from the run from the bus stop as well as from the hope that there was enough money to get a decent room for the evening at least, and maybe even a hot meal.

The postmaster opened the door to let us in, and I continued to wait patiently.

"Next," someone shouted from a window. I figured out which one and walked toward it promptly. "Yes, ma'am?"

"I need to check my mother's safety deposit box, please."

"Do you have the key?"

"Yes, sir," I said as I fished it out from inside the collar of my coat.

He looked at it, recognized it, and then asked, "What is the box number?"

"I don't know, but my mother's name is Evelyn Spears."

"One moment please," the postal worker went to the back. I waited some more. When he returned, he had a small rolodex. "The name again please?"

"Evelyn Spears, her address is... was 2225 139th Street."

"I have it right here. Your name again, please?"

"Nostalgia Richardson, I'm her daughter."

"Do you have identification?"

"Yes sir," I said as I took it out of my purse. One thing Mrs. Spears always said was to have identification on your person because you never knew when you'd have to prove who you were.

The clerk looked at it, then compared it to the information he saw on the rolodex card, and seemed satisfied. "Come with me please." He opened the big heavy door allowing me to come to the back. I followed him down a long hallway that reminded me of a morgue, or a prison, or any place that was public, private, personal, and impersonal all at the same time. The walls were gray, the floor was brown, the air was old.

He stopped in front of a big steel door, then fumbled with a ring of keys, trying this one and that one before coming to the right one. I screamed inside my head the entire time, "Open says ME!!!" Finally, it opened. We walked inside.

Embedded into the walls, there were metal boxes on top of metal boxes, and a long table in the center of the room. I stood there between the entrance and the table not knowing what else to do, so I waited while he looked for a particular row of boxes. When he found the row, his eyes scanned it, then stopped on one specifically. He struggled to slide it out of its space, straining laboriously to set the metal box on the table in front of me.

"The box number is 1019, Miss Richardson. I'll leave you alone. Take all the time you need." He was gone.

I was nervous as I unclasped the necklace, taking a minute to hold the key in my hand and look at it, marveling at the silver-toned heaviness of it. It was warm from having lain on my chest for the past two weeks. I decided whatever I found in the box, I would be grateful for. No matter how big or how small I would be grateful for whatever was in that box, even if I could only get a hot meal, I would sleep on the street if I had to, but I would be grateful at all costs for the contents of it! I took a deep breath. I unlocked it. I lifted the lid.

I had never seen so much money in all my life! There were no coins, only greenbacks, crisp, sweet-smelling greenbacks wrapped in neat packs. I took one of them out of the box slowly as though they might dissolve if I were not careful. The money felt cool in my hand. I took the liberty of sniffing it. I know that sounds peculiar, but money does have a distinct smell, and I just wanted to make sure it was not my imagination, that my senses of sight and smell were in agreement!

I carefully undid one of the packs. It was all 20 dollar bills. Thirty-five 20 dollar bills were in the pack. That's $700! I counted nine other identical packs inside the box, making it a total of $7000 in all! I also found a note in Mrs. Spears' meticulous handwriting:

To Whom It May Concern:

If you are reading this note, it means that I am deceased and you have the key to this safety deposit box. The contents of this box, no matter how much money is in here, are to be used ONLY to pay the property tax on the brownstone at 2225 139th Street in Harlem, New York. If the property no longer exists, please for all intents and purposes be wise with these funds. They are not to go into any banking institution or to be used on the Stock Market. They are to be divided among the current residents of the

home at said address. I beseech that this money be used
sparingly and with much care.

Sincerely,

Mrs. Evelyn Spears

I took my time rereading specific lines of the letter: if
the property no longer exists… these funds… are to be
divided among the current residents of the home at said
address. The property no longer existed, and I was the only
surviving resident. Dear God. I had just come into $7000!

My emotions didn't know where to go! One minute I
was ecstatic about my good fortune, the next minute I felt
that I should be sharing this wealth with George and
Cicely, and Jude and Mavis. The next minute I was excited
about being able to afford an apartment, suddenly I
remembered I needed to bury Mrs. Spears and Mr. Greer.

I took another look inside the box and found some life
insurance papers. Mrs. Spears had thought of everything.
The names on the policies were, of course, Mr. and Mrs.
Daniel Spears. The burials were for $3500 each to be paid
by The New York Life Insurance Company upon receiving
the death certificates. Whatever was left over, if there was
anything, would also go to the current residents of 2225
139th Street in Harlem NY.

I took one of the $700 packs out of the box, and the
insurance papers, and put them in the breast pocket of my
coat. I placed the lid securely on top of the box, locking it.
Placing the necklace back around my neck, I exited the
room, walked back up the hallway to tell the clerk that I
was done with the box.

"Alright Miss Richardson, thank you for your business, and I'm sure I will see you again."

I smiled politely, leaving the post office. I had much to do for the next few days.

* * * *

I got a copy of the Amsterdam News as soon as I got back to Harlem to begin my search for an apartment. I wanted no parts of Lenox Avenue, Morningside Heights, Sugar Hill, or Striver's Row. I had long since put in my mind that I would have to leave my old life behind, but now that I had a chance to find a new apartment, I would at least have a legitimate address for Tessie and Mitzi to use to keep in touch with me.

I found an ad for a furnished, four-room flat on the corner of Riverside Drive and 125th street. It was a part of Harlem of which I knew nothing about, thus making it the perfect place to create a new beginning. If the need to track down death certificates and establish communications with the Reading Railroad and the New York Life Insurance Company in regards to the funerals had not been eating at the back of my mind, the thought of moving to a four room private residence would have been invigorating to my spirit. Maybe one day it would be, it just wasn't going to be today.

I had spent the morning walking around the neighborhood, getting the nerve to meet the potential new landlord, wondering how I would answer such questions as to why do I have no clothes other than what was on my back, where was my family, why was I not married, why would I need so much space if I planned on living alone? I readily decided if the landlord was a Jew, I would merely show him two month's rent in advance, and hope in God's mercy.

The structure at 98 Riverside Dr. was a six-story building made of brownish-red brick. The gargoyles on either side of the roof of the building looked like they were standing guard of all who entered and exited the residence. I looked on the bell panel for the landlord's apartment. Apartment 1-A belonged to G. Aronowitz. If this Aronowitz person wasn't the landlord, he could certainly tell me where I could find the gentleman.

"Who is it," answered a grainy voice through the microphone system.

"Hello, I'm looking for the landlord, and I figured you would know where I might find him."

There was a pause, then "I'm coming."

Wow. That was easy. It was obvious by the voice this Mr. Aronowitz was an older, heavy smoker. I thought he would be coming to meet me with a slip of paper that had the landlord's contact information.

When the door opened a little woman with a mountain of wrinkles, horribly dyed red hair, and a big hook nose appeared. She was holding a cigarette between her lips and a little lap dog in her arms. The dog, which was well-groomed, sniffed in my direction, lolled its tongue out and showed his teeth as if he might have been smiling.

"I'm sorry to bother you Ma'am, but I just wanted some information as to how I might get in touch with the landlord about the ad for the four-room apartment," I said.

She smiled, "There is no landlord. I'm the landlady, Mrs. Aronowitz. Dusty here seems to like you. Come with me to my apartment and let's talk." I followed her into the building.

The foyer was nowhere near as big as the one in the brownstone. The first floor was a long corridor with mailboxes on the right, and apartments on the left. At the end of the hallway was a flight of stairs. Mrs. Aronowitz showed me into the first apartment on the left. As she walked in front of me, Dusty went out of his way to look over her shoulder at me, still smiling. I thought he might jump over her shoulder and into my arms! His tan fur was clean, neatly trimmed, while his brown eyes were clear, dancing with happiness and energy. I realized he was the happiest creature I had seen in a long time.

Mrs. Aronowitz's apartment smelled heavily of smoke, otherwise it was quite cozy. The furniture paid ode to Queen Anne fashion with a high-backed burgundy sofa, matching Queen Anne chair, obviously her throne, and a dark oak coffee table. Green velvet curtains were held open with gold ropes, while the radiator sputtered moist heat. A George Gershwin record played on the RCA Victor.

"Have a seat," she said placing the dog on the Queen Anne chair. "I'll be in the kitchen making tea." As soon as she stepped into the kitchen, Dusty leaped out of the chair to join me on the sofa. I couldn't remember the last time any creature had given me so much attention. I was surprised at myself for being so responsive to his affection.

She came out of the kitchen with a china tea set, reminding me so much of that first tea party with Mrs.

Spears all those years ago. I was determined not to shed a tear, or at least wait until I was somewhere private.

There were no tea bags or sugar cubes. Instead, Mrs. Aronowitz poured the tea straight from the kettle. I tasted lemon, orange, and cinnamon. Delicious. "I see you like Russian Tea. It's my mother's recipe. Please enjoy it."

She was quiet a minute, observing me, satisfied that I'd gained Dusty's seal of approval. "Ever since my husband died Dusty has been my companion. He's a great judge of character. So you saw the ad for the apartment. Will you be living alone?"

Here it comes, I thought to myself. "Yes, Ma'am."

She nodded her head before asking more questions. "Where will you be moving from?"

"Striver's Row. I lived in a brownstone that was destroyed in a fire. All of my belongings were there."

"I see," she said slowly. "Do you have a job," she continued.

"No Ma'am. I was a dancer at the Cotton Club for the past three years, but it was time for me to move on from that job. I do have money saved, though," I added quickly.

She nodded again with her face showing no emotion, making it impossible to determine if I stood a chance or not.

"So what were you looking for in an apartment?" Well, that was a strange question for her to ask, I thought.

"A lot has happened to me in these past few months, and I need a place to recuperate, quite frankly. I've lost everyone and everything that was important to me, so I am starting over." After I had said this, she looked at me, then stood up.

I thought she was about to tell me I had to leave when she said, "Let me show you the apartment."

Mrs. Aronowitz put out her cigarette and walked toward the door. I don't know what got into me, but I picked Dusty up off the couch, expecting he would be joining us. "Oh, no! This time he stays here," she said to him more so than to me. He made a small sound voicing his disappointment, but ran over to the Queen Anne chair and hopped in it after I'd put him down. I had never seen an animal so sociable!

We went out into the hallway and walked to the staircase at the end of it. "The apartment is on the third floor," she said. "It is fully furnished, but you will need your own bed linens, and dishes. You see where you pick up your mail here on the bottom floor. For outgoing mail, every floor has a mail chute beside the staircase."

We ventured up the stairs, making our way to the third floor. The staircase was merciful thanks to the many stairwell breaks between the floors.

We stopped in front of a heavy door that had a number three on it. She opened it letting me go in first. The hallway was long with polished wooden floors. There were eight red doors, four on each side of the hallway. Letters A, C, E, and G were on the right side of the hall, while letters B, D, F, and H were on the left.

She stopped in front of 3- H. Mrs. Aronowitz unlocked the door to reveal a small foyer with a little door on the right. She opened the door to show me a spacious coat closet. We stepped over a threshold into a big sitting room. The furniture was plain and brown, with a decent couch, love seat, easy chair, and coffee table. Even though the style was somewhat dated, I didn't smell any dust or mold. A big picture window offered a beautiful view of the Hudson River with little glaciers floating downstream toward Battery Park City, or Brooklyn. There were no shades or curtains, just as she had said.

"Let's take a look at the kitchen," Mrs. Aronowitz suggested. We stepped over another threshold leading the way to a spacious kitchen with a gas stove, a single deep sink, pantry, refrigerator with an ice box, and lots of cupboards I would need to fill. There was also a laundry machine with a wringer on the side so I could wash my clothes… when I could get some anyway. The kitchen table was a good size with only two chairs, which at this time was way more than I needed.

About the only thing, I didn't like so far was that the sink was facing a wall in the room. The kitchen sink in my parent's home, as well as in Mrs. Spears' brownstone, had a window over it giving you a view of the outdoors, which actually made dishwashing somewhat pleasant. Oh, well, looking at a wall while doing dishes was certainly not the first new idea I've had to get used to, especially not here lately.

"Are you ready to see the bedroom and the bathroom?" she asked. I nodded my head. We walked out of the kitchen, crossing the sitting room to yet another threshold. This time there was a miniature hallway with two doors facing each other. She opened the door on the left to a big bedroom with a four-poster bed that, of course, was devoid of linens. However, there was a night stand on the left of the bed, while a dressing table and a wardrobe with mirrored French doors stood across from the foot. The dressing table and stool reminded me of my room at Mrs. Spears' brownstone.

With as much stoicism as I could muster, I continued to tell myself I would not shed a tear until I was alone. What really caught my eye in this room was yet another picture window looking out over the Hudson. Well, I knew what I would be seeing every morning should I decide to stay here! The last room Mrs. Aronowitz showed was the bathroom, which had a lion's foot tub surrounded by a pink shower curtain, a toilet bowl of course, a sink, and lastly a towel cabinet with glass doors. The tile on the floor looked as though it had never been walked on. I realized it would take me a while to get settled into this place, considering the details I had to take care of for the deaths. However, I had the same feeling I did years ago when Mrs. Spears invited me to the brownstone. It was exciting to see a new place that would be mine if I wanted it.

I decided it was time to talk about the rent, "How much?" I asked.

"$65 to be paid the first of every month. I know that's a little expensive in the way of rent, but you must consider there are two picture windows overlooking the Hudson, as well as an intercom system. Today I will need the first two months in advance."

I nodded my head, took another look around at each room before giving Mrs. Aronowitz $130.

Satisfied, she gave me the keys to the foyer, the apartment, and the mailbox. She said I looked tired and that we could sign the lease agreement later on in the week. I was grateful for that. I looked around the apartment, my new apartment, once she left. I then took a seat on the couch facing the picture window overlooking the Hudson River, and I cried.

Chapter 34

"Now what do you call this dish again," I asked Mrs. Aronowitz. Everything was changing for me, including the food, which actually wasn't a bad thing, just… different.

"Beef Stroganoff. Do you like it," she asked.

"Yes," I said. When I first looked at the milky texture of the beef with the noodles, I didn't think it looked the least bit appetizing. However, it smelled delicious, so I braced my taste buds and forged ahead. It was not nearly as hard to swallow as I thought it would be, in fact, it had this mix of tangy and spicy that was unique! I'd never experienced Russian cuisine.

"Would you like some more Russian tea," she asked. I nodded my head then she filled my cup, before taking a seat across the table from me. She watched me closely like she wanted to ask me a personal question. I waited, listening to Dusty chew on a doggie bone as he lay under my feet. A sigh escaped her lips, then the question, "How long have you been alone?"

"Going on a couple of weeks, I guess. To tell you the truth I lost track of time when I lost everything and everybody else. I walked out of the Cotton Club, and just before I could hail myself a cab to go home…" my voice trailed off involuntarily turning into teary-eyed hesitations.

I couldn't bring myself to speak on what happened at Sing Sing that night, or how it led to the deaths of everyone in the household. Arnie in all his nastiness was right: living with the survivors guilt was the worst type of torture. With bodily injury, a doctor could give you a time frame as to when you'd be healed. However, mental torture had to run its course, that's if it ever ran its course. Was there ever really a way of getting over the pain? Memories could be triggered by sights, smells, sounds, not to mention emotions, from as far back as childhood. Stigmata could not be controlled!

I forged ahead with a shortened version of the truth, "I got fired from the Cotton Club that night. When I went home, the brownstone was in flames. The tenants who lived on the third floor couldn't get out. The landlady and her husband died a few days later in the hospital as a result of burns and smoke inhalation. I was released from the hospital and stayed in a shelter for a few days before going to get money from my safe deposit box and coming here."

By the time I finished saying that much my cheeks were wet, a thick film of mucus covered my top lip, my head ached from dredging up images and memories I wanted to keep buried for the rest of my life. I should have known I would have to deal with them at some time or another before life would let me move pass the pain if it ever did.

Thankfully Mrs. Aronowitz didn't expect any great detail. She excused herself briefly then came back into the room, giving me a handkerchief, while Dusty hopped into my lap as if he knew I was no longer hungry. They let me sit there at the table as if they could sense I was looking for myself, still wandering aimlessly through the daze and haze of that night at Sing Sing, which lead to the smoky pyre that robbed me of all my possessions, not to mention the people who loved me.

It suddenly seemed strange to me that she let me have a place to stay despite knowing I had no job to speak of! She didn't know me, and there was no one who could vouch for the story I told her. Why would she allow me to stay here? "Ma'am, why are you giving me permission to stay here," I asked. "I mean, you don't know if I'm telling you the truth about my circumstances."

"Well," she said, "I happen to remember reading about the fire in the Amsterdam News, plus you've given me no reason not to trust you. You obviously need a place to stay. You said you had funds saved, and when I asked for first and second month's rent in advance you gave it to me with no qualms." She looked at me as if she expected me to say something before she continued, "For tonight why don't you sleep on my couch? Then tomorrow we'll go to Macy's to find you at least two new outfits so you can change your clothes," she suggested.

"Thank you," was all I could say.

* * * *

The trip to Macy's was more work than pleasure because I was in no mood to shop. However, Mrs. Aronowitz was right. I had to get some decent clothes in order to be taken seriously when I went to get the death certificates to redeem to The New York Life Insurance Company, and The Reading Railroad.

I wanted to get the shopping trip over with as quickly as possible, so I picked out one plain flowered dress with a slim belt cinching the waist, one dark suit to wear to the funeral, and finally, a new coat. Mrs. Aronowitz brought it to my attention that my constant companion, the coat Mrs.

Barden gave to me just before I left Spivey's Grove, was alas showing signs of age and wear, not to mention it still had the crusty bloodstains leftover from my meeting with Arnie O'Neil and his thugs.

"And don't you think you need a new purse and some shoes," Mrs. Aronowitz suggested. I thanked God she was there because I would have picked out any old thing just to get out of there in less than thirty minutes. Mrs. Aronowitz made sure I chose a purse complimenting the two pairs of shoes, and that the shoes went well with the dresses.

We went downstairs to purchase a few dishes: a cup, a saucer, a bowl, a plate, and a dinner plate, as well as a fork, a spoon, a knife, and a soup spoon, to start my cupboard. Once we left Macy's, she insisted we go to the hardware store to get four shades for my windows. She said she would loan me a set of bed linens and a blanket until I felt up to going back to Macy's and getting my own.

All in all, I spent about $200 that day. Between the rent and the shopping I had spent $330 of the $700 I had taken with me from the safety deposit box, and I still hadn't bought food, pots, pans, toiletries, or towels! I had so much to do, and all I felt like doing was crawling into a bed, falling asleep in hopes this whole ordeal would be over somehow once I opened my eyes. But I knew it wouldn't be.

There were times in your life when you had to be awake to experience every moment of the trauma, otherwise you risk never escaping it. Every wound would have to be felt without the luxury of anesthesia, or you would end up covering it only for it to be felt at a later time, and then it would be worse because you waited until it was impacted by yet another event forcing you to face it.

After eight months I was still knuckling under the pain of Josiah leaving me and taking up with Josephine Baker. Lying to Lily about going to France with the Duke Ellington Orchestra did nothing to ease the torment. In fact, it gave me more to endure at the time. Now the sting of losing The Cotton Club, and everybody in the house dying so tragically, shed all the layers of my skin as if I might have been the only onion left in the world. Would this ever end?

* * * *

In the coming days I asked Mrs. Aronowitz to accompany me to City Hall to get the death certificates, The New York Life Insurance Company to retrieve the checks to finance the burials, the funeral home to make the final arrangements, the post office to mail the death certificates, the memorial services for George and Cicely, and finally, the double funeral and interment for "Mr." and Mrs. Spears. No one came from North Carolina because there was nothing that could have been salvaged from the fire, aside from not having the money to make the trip.

While dealing with the New York Life Insurance Company, the Reading Railroad, and the funeral home, I had to constantly remember to keep my story straight so Mr. Greer could be buried next to Mrs. Spears in place of the real Mr. Spears!

Through it all, I got into the habit of sitting in front of the picture window watching the little glaciers swim downstream. Sometimes the sun was shining through an industrial haze in an effort to create a reflection on the water, other times sleet or snow settled down onto the streets quietly from a cottony heaven. I allowed myself to shed as many tears as possible in my new apartment so I wouldn't cry in front of anyone I didn't know when I got out into the street. To the world, I somehow presented myself as a woman who was about the business of moving on with her life while life had stopped for others. I seemed calm and in control at all costs.

When I was at a loss for how something should be handled, such as what information should go into the obituaries for the Amsterdam News, or making sure the funeral home wasn't over charging for services rendered, Mrs. Aronowitz covered every detail I'd overlooked or forgotten. In dealing with her husband's death arrangements, she knew to ask questions and see to business I would never have fathomed. Her expertise was more than appreciated.

In the early part of the spring while the air was still freezing during the morning hours, but somewhat warmer in the afternoons, I looked in the mailbox and found a $1000 refund check from the funeral home for the funds not needed for the funerals! Mrs. Aronowitz was adamant that I was to use the money to take care of myself. According to her, I was to take that money to finish getting what I needed for the apartment, and buy some clothing and accessories.

I cashed the check at the Empire Savings and Loan of New York, where fortunately it did not bounce. I put $800 in the safety deposit box at the post office and took the rest to Macy's where I bought pots and pans, bed linens and towels, toiletries, as well as several more articles of clothing, accessories, and shoes.

When Mrs. Aronowitz suggested I splurge on a radio or an RCA Victor and some records, I told her no. I decided my own thoughts, without distraction, were what I needed to listen to so I could get to know this new woman I was becoming due to unexpected life experiences. I was ready to deal with how I had changed from being the idealistic little girl who moved here in 1928, became a Cotton Club Showgirl, and had fallen in love with Josiah James. All of that was gone now. It was time to prepare myself for a new experience. I had no idea where my new life would lead me, but whatever happened I was determined to be thoroughly groomed!

Chapter 35

"Nostalgia, open the door!" Mrs. Aronowitz's frantic knocking reminded me of the morning when Mrs. Spears, me, and Mitzi panicked because the banks lost our money! The last thing I needed was an unwelcome surprise, especially when life was just beginning to conform into a routine. I was getting used to living by myself, the apartment was gradually turning into my cozy abode, a few of the neighbors were getting used to seeing me, and as a result would give me salutations. I'd even gone back to the Abyssinian Baptist Church for Sunday services on a regular basis. What unwelcome comeuppance could be in store for me this morning?

When I opened the door, Mrs. Aronowitz was holding a copy of the Daily News in one hand while Dusty with his ever present doggy smile sat nuzzled in the crook of her arm. She looked excited, which sparked my curiosity. "Well, good morning," I said, "what brings you here so early?"

"I know you were sleeping, but I couldn't let this wait. Look what I found in the paper!" She had circled an ad stating The Martha Graham School of Contemporary Dance was auditioning potential new students! I felt a small flutter in my stomach, but I came to my senses. "Mrs. Aronowitz, that isn't the kind of dancing I do…"

"Dear, you said yourself your old life was gone! If this isn't the type of dancing you do then maybe it's something you need to try in order to continue reinventing yourself. You told me you wanted to indulge in things that had nothing to do with your old life on Striver's Row, or your work at The Cotton Club. Set yourself apart from your old life, but find a new way to dance."

I could not help but agree that her suggestion made sense, but how would I get started? Then it dawned on me: how did I get started the first time? Minus Tessie and Mitzi, how would I get started this time? From out of nowhere, I knew what I needed to do!

Later that morning I found myself on 42nd Street in the theater district buying modern dance slippers, tights, leotards, and records. This time the records were not big band jazz, but the music the clerks insisted the modern dancers performed to.

I was actually curious as to what I would hear when I put them on the Victrola… that's when I remembered I didn't have anything to play them on, so I made a trip to Macy's to purchase a Victrola, after all!

I was so tired from carrying all of my wares by myself that I took a taxi back to the apartment to drop everything off. I got a quick bite to eat before venturing out again to find a beauty parlor. Before leaving my apartment, I realized I hadn't had my hair or make-up done since before Mavis and Cicely died.

Taking a few moments to look at myself in the mirror, I took my hair out of the bun to finger my tresses. It wasn't quite as long as it was when I first moved to Harlem, but it was still an impressive head of hair! It fell to the middle of my back in long, bouncy waves like my mother's. Before I knew it, I wondered if my mother's hair was still as black as mine… Shaking my head, I decided the excitement of the morning and the afternoon wouldn't be tainted with regrets from years before. I pulled my hair back in a ponytail, splashed my face with cold water, especially around my eyes, determined to come back with a new look.

* * * *

"Well, I'd always heard a woman's life is about to change when she cuts her hair," said Mrs. Aronowitz. "You have certainly evolved from the person who stood on my doorstep asking to see the apartment all those months ago."

I felt different too!

I had found a salon at 125th and Broadway, and asked the receptionist to give me the best hairstylist on the premises. Barbara was everything my head was asking for! She told me the flapper style look was no longer fashionable, so instead of replicating the earlobe length bob Mavis created for my first coif, the cut would only be past my shoulders and, at my suggestion, she gave me no bangs. Josiah loved bangs. Barbara parted the front of my hair down the middle, then straightened the roots until they were tapered close to my scalp. Afterward, she curled the ends in an upward flip until they landed softly just above my shoulders. I looked like Hedy Lamarr!

When my hair was done, I asked if there was a make-up artist on duty. Linda came recommended in high regard, shading my eyelids lavender, my cheeks pink, and my lips light mauve. Fortunately, I was able to purchase the hair products and make-up at the salon instead of having to run back downtown to the theater district.

When I walked out into the street, several men tipped their hats, but I pretended not to notice. Truth be told, I was thrilled! I don't recall receiving any male attention at all in recent months, and I reveled in it. Between the new clothes, the stylish cut, and the fresh spring make-up colors I felt reborn. I felt ready to tackle any new challenge, including an audition for The Martha Graham School of Contemporary Dance!

After telling her about my day over what had become our nightly spot of Russian Tea, I left Mrs. Aronowitz's apartment to go up to mine, to listen to the new records on my new Victrola.

I learned from Tessie and Mitzi that a dancer should always sit still to listen to the music before attempting to move or dance to it. Meditating on the name of the song, exploring how it made you feel, then allowing those feelings to soak into your muscles and bones was the best way to develop a relationship with unfamiliar music. They'd also advised me it would more than likely take several turns of the Victrola for the mind and body to become accustomed to the mood, the riffs, the highs, and the lows of the songs.

A part of me looked forward to what I'd hear once I turned on the Victrola, yet another part of me felt anxious. What if I didn't like what I heard, or what if my interpretation was nothing Martha Graham deemed dramatic enough to train as one of her students?

Everyone had a starting point, a place where nothing was known, never experienced. But I told myself I'd been at starting points before, just not on my own. I convinced myself everyone at some point in their lives had to go somewhere by themselves for the sake of learning their own strength, becoming familiar with who they were in times of happiness or trouble. I reminded myself I'd survived worse things than an audition for a dance company of an unexplored genre. "I can do this… I will do this, and I am starting now," I said aloud. I picked up the first record, placed it on the Victrola, closing my eyes I listened with all the purpose and intensity of a sponge soaking up a thick, sweet liquid.

Chapter 36

I knocked on Mrs. Aronowitz's door the next afternoon with a heart sailing on a summer breeze! That morning the audition room was hot, muggy, oppressed with the sweat and stench of every dancer who'd had the opportunity of training with the remarkable Martha Graham before me.

That previous evening after listening to the music I closed my eyes, remembering how Martha Graham looked in the little vignettes I'd seen between movies at the picture shows. Her make-up, especially around the eyes, was always theatrical, and her hair was always pulled back in a tight bun at the base of her neck. I wore four layers of blotted red lipstick, false eyelashes with ten coats of mascara, eyebrows shaped with charcoal, dark pink rouge on my cheeks, and a tight bun in my hair to the audition.

I didn't know what color to wear for a leotard, so I chose a purple one with black tights because it was my favorite color. Sure enough, everyone else wore the typical black leotard and white tights, thus making me easier to spot than a red robin among blue jays. And I danced.

Something inside me propelled me to the front row, right behind the choreographer where I listened as carefully to her instruction as a panther hunting a deer, watched her every move like a thief awaiting a potential victim, letting it all marinate into my brain, and trickle into my muscles, sinews, and bones.

I couldn't wait to tell Mrs. Aronowitz that despite my anxious jitters I'd made the cut! Immediately after the audition, I went to the post office to get money from the safety deposit box to pay for my tuition.

By the time I got back with the funds, they had a schedule ready for me. I was to start training at The Martha Graham School of Contemporary Dance the following Monday morning at 8:00 am. There were still things I needed to buy for my classes, so the rest of the week and the weekend would be filled with much vigor. I embraced the excitement because it renewed my energy. I hadn't felt like this since the morning I was told I'd made The Cotton Club dance troupe. But this time it was different because I'd graduated to something more taxing mentally as well as physically. I was on the brink of becoming a conservatory trained dancer.

I didn't sneak in from behind, or lie about my age this time either: I was myself! I even revealed my true level of education, and I thanked God I'd never stopped reading after finishing sixth grade. I looked at my new schedule and found that in addition to Technique I and Analysis of Human Movement, my classes included Dance History, Anatomy and Nutrition, and Dance Theory, which meant I'd have to purchase at least three textbooks.

Furthermore, I went to this audition by myself. I was deemed proficient enough upon MY OWN talents, experience, and merits to train to be a professional dancer. All I had to do was never give up, show up every day, take what I'd learned from one level to the next, to earn my certification. It wouldn't be easy, but it would definitely be worth it.

Mrs. Aronowitz opened the door holding Dusty. Both of them smiling. "I can tell by your knock you made the cut." She hugged me before I stepped over the threshold as Dusty licked my cheek.

* * * *

Upon entry into The Martha Graham School of Contemporary Dance, the years 1933 and 1934 proved nothing short of successful for me. I graduated from the school acquiring my certification in the genre of Contemporary Dance. Mrs. Aronowitz was so proud she bought a beautiful black and gold frame to hang the document on the wall in my living room. I saw it every day as a constant reminder that nothing was impossible.

* * * *

The former burlesque house at 253-125th Street was purchased by a Jewish gentleman by the name of Sidney Cohen. Through his partnership with Morris Sussman, the building was reopened on January 16, 1934, as an all colored review called the Apollo Theater. Best of all, the venue catered to a predominantly colored audience. I auditioned to be a chorus girl with all the brashness of a conquistador, confident my experience as a Cotton Club Showgirl and my training from The Martha Graham School of Contemporary Dance were sufficient battlements. I was correct in my presupposition because mine was the first name called in making the cut.

I was performing eight shows a week at a salary of $35 with no threats of Arnie O'Neil, my age, or the Ziegfeld Follies taking it away from me. The only factors in getting and keeping this new gig were my talent and my fortitude.

The year 1933 also marked the end of the prohibition of alcohol as per the 21st Amendment to the United States Constitution. It was now legal to drink alcohol, liquor, hooch, or whatever anyone preferred to call it, in the clubs. There was no longer any reason to "speak easy" in Harlem, or anywhere else in the United States anymore. As a result, gangsters such as Dutch Schulz, Lucky Luciano, and Vito Genovese moved uptown to invade Madame Stephanie St. Claire's policy bank, as well as to demand payment for "protection services" from various Harlem merchants.

When the NYPD ignored her complaints about the activities of the ofay mob bosses, Madame Stephanie announced in newspapers all over New York that the NYPD was corrupt because they had accepted kickbacks from her in the past and refused to honor those agreements under the new circumstances. Her claims resulted in the termination of at least 10 officers from the police force. This however didn't stop the violent beatings and killings of numbers operators who refused to work with Dutch Schultz. After having Harlem as her turf for so long, the Madame was not willing to let it go so easily, no matter what offer, or threat, Dutch made.

Mitzi and Tessie continued to write me letters from Europe. Mitzi let me know The Duke Ellington Orchestra had run its course in France and would be moving to England to perform. Tessie's dance school and Peter's pastry business were both continuing to thrive, so they had no intentions of leaving France.

Neither of them mentioned Josiah which was fine with me. My life had moved in places and directions I'd never anticipated. Had I gone to France, or California for that matter, I never would have learned how to live on my own or been able to call myself a conservatory trained dancer. The best part was I no longer felt guilty about how Josiah and I ended, how all the other residents of the brownstone died, or how I left Lily in a lurch by leaving Spivey's Grove, or lying about going to France and ceasing to write her letters. When the time was right, I'd get back in touch with Lily, and hopefully she and Henry would be married and maybe have a few kiddies.

I'd finally gotten over the memories, the nightmares, and the bad feelings about mistakes I'd made in the past, whether I facilitated them or not. The best thing I could have done for myself was to stay as far away from East Harlem as possible. Miraculously I'd gotten so caught up in decorating my new apartment, going to school, attending church, being co-dance captain for the Apollo Theater Dance Troupe, and living my life, that I barely missed life before the fire. However, I soon learned right when you've found yourself unencumbered by your past, it always bullied its way back into your beautiful new existence.

Chapter 37
1935

March 19, 1935 started as any other day for me. I had
gotten up that morning to stretch my muscles, breathe
deeply, and feast on a breakfast of brown sugar sweetened
banana oatmeal. We would be performing this week with
Bill Bo Jangles Robinson at the Apollo, so I had to be
prepared. I briefly remembered how he'd take the stage
away from the Cotton Club Showgirls, and I refused to be
totally upstaged by his long legs and hoofing.

Everything in the street was normal when I went to the
theater for rehearsal at 10:00. I'd even taken a moment to
step into the Kress Five and Dime Store for an extra banana
to take with me to my dressing room in case my legs began
to cramp.

By about 2:30 that afternoon we heard something in
the street. Loud voices we couldn't make out, police sirens,
maybe even a gunshot! Mr. Sussman ran down the main
aisle of the theater telling us practice was over for the day.

"So should we be back at 6:00 for the 8:00 show?"
Ethel asked. Mr. Sussman looked like he was hunting in a
trunk for the words to answer her, but he just couldn't find
them.

Finally, he threw at us, "If the streets don't clear out by
6:00, then don't plan on coming back tonight. Now hurry
up and leave!" With that he turned around, running up the
aisle to the entrance of the theater.

Rather than linger, I ran downstairs to gather my stuff
because I could have sworn I heard glass breaking in the

direction of the theater's box office! I had already survived a bank run, so I knew what the street sounded like when trouble was nearby. I'd come from that row unscathed, and I was bound and determined to have a repeat of the same this afternoon.

The first thing I thought about once I got downstairs was to get all of my belongings because God Himself only knew when we'd be able to come back to this place. Once I'd placed everything in my bag, I began to scheme how I would get back home. On a regular day, I'd just walk home, but nothing sounded regular outside. Shots were firing, glass was breaking, and people were vociferating statements that were inaudible, thus making it impossible to determine what the trouble was about.

What was really scary was I was in it alone. I'd no sense of direction as to how to get home. I didn't know if a cab would even be brave enough to stop for anyone. I needed to have the faith that some cabby would take pity on a woman all alone out in the street and give her a ride.

Something told me not to go to the main entrance of the theater, but to duck out the back door behind the stage. I opened it carefully. Thankfully all was quiet in the alley, but I heard anger in the street. I ventured toward 125th walking on imaginary eggshells, saving my strength until I had no choice but to expend it by breaking into a run. I prayed there would somehow be a cab, if not an opening, that would lead back to my apartment building.

I got to the top of the street where I noticed the majority of the activity was around the Kress Five and Dime. All the storefront windows had been broken out! The shouting was in English and Spanish, which explained why I couldn't discern exactly what was being said.

It looked like every black person in the world was against every white person, especially if those white people were cops. Utter chaos ruled everything around me to the point the surrealism reminded me of October 29, 1929.

A scream infiltrated my eardrums from a woman sitting in the street holding a handkerchief soaked in blood over the face of a felled man, probably her husband. I ducked when I felt a glass bottle zoom past my ear, over my shoulder, into the window of another business.

I began to run away from the direction of my home when I heard, "Nostalgia!" I turned around in the direction of my name to find Mrs. Aronowitz sitting in a cab waiting for me. Her timing pleasantly astounded me.

I ran across the street as she slid over to make room for me. I opened the door, hopped into the taxi, and as my instincts told me, the cabby continued driving in the opposite direction of the apartment building. We continued toward East Harlem where some of the brawling seemed to be not so bad.

"What is this all about?" I finally asked.

"A copper told me a Puerto Rican boy had stolen something from the Kress Five and Dime, and everyone seems to think he'd been fatally shot," volunteered the driver.

"Well was he?" I asked.

"We don't know, Dear, but if he was, I could understand why everyone is so angry about it. He's only 16," Mrs. Aronowitz replied, wide-eyed.

I looked out the window thankful some of the ruckus had seemed to die down. Then I noticed we were approaching Striver's Row. I'd not been to this part of Harlem since the funerals of Mr. Greer and Mrs. Spears. Oh, dear. How would I feel about seeing the space where the brownstone once stood? When we were about to pass my former residence, it suddenly didn't matter!

I saw a group of young black men beating a white man who looked like Peter Scoggins when he came back from the jail all those years ago!

"Stop," I shouted at the cabby, who obeyed my order by slamming on breaks.

"Why are we stopping," asked Mrs. Aronowitz. I had to ignore her question for the moment.

"I need to stop those men from beating him! Please help me," I begged the driver.

"I have a gun, but do you know how to use it," he asked.

"I'm from South Carolina! Of course, I do," I said, grabbing the pistol from him, knowing right well I only knew what Lily had written to me about guns in her letters when Noah taught her how to shoot.

I got out demanding the men stop. They continued to beat and kick Kroyer Skaagens as if they had no other purpose in life but to make a defenseless white man miserable. I lost patience, raising the pistol in the air, firing three shots as if I'd come out of my mother's womb holding a Smith and Wesson. They stopped, in fact, everything ceased to move. Lily was right. Holding a weapon did make you feel like you could conquer the world! However, I didn't have time to wallow in my new found prowess. "Bring that man over to the cab and help him inside," I demanded.

They looked at me as if I'd asked them to lick the bottom of my shoe. One, who obviously deemed himself the ringleader, spoke on everyone's behalf, "What do you want with this ofay?"

I pointed the gun directly at him, "You ask that question as if it has anything to do with you." The click from my transferring another bullet into the chamber was loud, and I imagine scary when you were on the wrong side of the barrel. His whole body shook, but he ordered the rest of his comrades to help Kroyer into the cab.

They weren't careful as they dragged him from the sidewalk to the street to load him into the back of the car. The ringleader made it a point to kick him in the small of the back once they'd gotten him part of the way inside. I maneuvered the barrel around in my palm, hitting him across the face with the handle. Ignoring the bloody gash now gracing his cheek, I stood tall, daring anyone else in his little posse to challenge me. With that, I got into the cab, and told the driver to get us back to 125th and Riverside by any means necessary!

Chapter 38

Our apartment building was far enough from Broadway and the bulk of the fighting that the driver had enough time to leave his taxi to help us get Kroyer up the steps and into the foyer. I gave him extra for his trouble, and he thanked us, wishing us good luck as he ran back into the street. Mrs. Aronowitz didn't know what to think, but she helped me help Kroyer into her apartment and onto the couch. She looked at him, shaking her head with pity in her eyes. Dusty ran around us looking on with excitement and curiosity. "I know exactly what he needs," Mrs. Aronowitz said as she made her way to the kitchen. Now is not the time for tea, I thought as I looked at Kroyer.

I'd have to wait until everything calmed down outside before I would be able to go out and find Dr. Gaddison, that is if he would be willing to venture to this side of town. There was no telling when it would be safe enough for him, or anyone else for that matter, to go out into the street, not to mention we wouldn't be the only ones in need of his services. It could be days before we could get him here to check on Kroyer.

The gash on the side of his head where those thugs repeatedly kicked him spouted purple blood. We had to keep him from falling asleep for a while at least, or he might not wake up. I had to keep him talking. "Kroyer, do you remember me?" I said.

He smiled wearily, "You're the one with the funny name who was staying with Mrs. Spears when I went to see my brother." I decided it was a good start.

"Yes. My name is Nostalgia. Do you see how many fingers I'm holding up?" I asked as I held up three on my right hand.

"Looks like three," he said.

"Yes, that's right." I tried to smile, but it was hard.

He looked bad from the beating, and he smelled horrible from living out in the street. I wasn't sure, but I could have sworn I saw little bugs crawling in the hairs of his beard. I hoped Mrs. Aronowitz had kept some of her deceased husband's shaving materials. That beard could not stay on his face too much longer before its miniscule residents decided to tour the apartment. Worst case scenario I would have to ask one of the gentlemen who resided in the building for a straight razor, a cup of shaving foam, and a brush.

What was Kroyer doing here in Harlem, anyway? Before I could begin asking more questions, Mrs. Aronowitz was back with something other than the tea set I expected to see. She ambled in struggling with a tub of hot water, a bottle of a clear liquid, a towel, and a wooden stick. She sat it all on the table while Dusty took the liberty of hopping into Kroyer's lap, licking his face and the wound on his head. She exited the room again. Everything she brought in looked strange, but I continued to speak to Kroyer.

"Can you tell me the name of your oldest brother," I asked.

"His name is Peder. I think we have established that I'm coherent. Will you be able to take me to a hospital?" he asked.

"Not for some time," I said. Then I couldn't hold my curiosity any longer, "what were you doing at the brownstone?" He had a beaten, broken look in his eyes I hadn't seen since Peter came back from jail. The resemblance brought back so much that I had worked so hard to forget.

Mrs. Aronowitz came back with bandages and her sewing kit. Sewing kit? Why would she… then it dawned on me what she was about to do! But before she could get started mending Kroyer's head, a deafening sound startled us all followed by shattered glass littering the living room floor! The brick landed next to the coffee table. The turmoil had followed us back home.

A low growl started in the depths of Dusty's throat as a hand we did not recognize groped through the hole in the window, not even stopping when the forearm got cut on random jagged pieces of glass. When the assailant found the latch, he undid it and raised the window all the way up, pulling himself into the sitting room! Mrs. Aronowitz screamed. Dusty wriggled out of Kroyer's arms charging toward the unwelcomed guest, barking, growling, baring his fangs. In response the culprit swatted the poor little dog across the nose.

I picked up the heavy tin tub of hot water, and slung it right in his face! He yelled curses at me as I began beating him over the head with the tub until he climbed back out of the window. I heard him shout to someone outside in the street, "Stay out of there, she crazy!"

I ran over to the window, shouting "Yeah, you better run!"

I heard someone else shout, "Leave that building alone. Coloreds live there." That's when I got an idea!

"Mrs. Aronowitz, take Kroyer to my apartment," I said giving her my keys.

"But…" however, I gave her no time to protest.

"I'll be there shortly, go on ahead of me," I did my best to reassure her.

Reluctantly she gathered Kroyer off the couch, placing his arm over her shoulder, heading out to the hallway with Dusty following close on their heels. I ran around her apartment looking for paper and something to write with. When I found what I needed I made several crude signs stating in large letters, "DON'T LOOT! COLOREDS LIVE IN THIS BUILDING," hoping it was enough to keep the damage from becoming too great, I hung the signs in front of what used to be Mrs. Aronowitz's windows, as well as on the building's front doors.

I then picked up the tin tub that once held the hot water and placed the bottle of clear liquid, the bandages, the towels, the wooden stick, and the sewing kit inside before heading upstairs to my apartment. When I arrived, Kroyer was prostrate across my sofa with Dusty sitting on his chest. Mrs. Aronowitz was coming out of my kitchen with a glass of water and a look of sheer distress. "I haven't seen anything like this since I was a young girl in Russia during the Turkish War!" It was a bit of cold comfort to realize I wasn't the only one reminded of something tumultuous thanks to these startling events.

Finally, I told her pointedly, "I figured out how you're planning to use all that stuff, and since I have no way of getting him to the hospital, I hope you know what you're doing!"

She gave me a wry smile, "My dear, I've had to do this several times. Don't be scared. The worst part will be the screams of agony. While I do it, I need you to let him scream, make sure the stick is between his teeth, and allow him to squeeze your hand as hard as he needs to. Now you keep him occupied while I get more hot water and thread the needle." She gave me the glass of water to give to Kroyer, and took the tub and the sewing kit to the kitchen.

He drank as we exchanged small talk. I tried not to make him laugh too much because I didn't know how badly all the kicking he endured had affected his ribs.

When Mrs. Aronowitz came back with a new tub of hot water, she let me know she was ready by taking one of the towels, pouring the clear liquid on it, and then laying it on the side of his head. He yelped at the sting. Then Kroyer noticed the needle, threaded and momentarily pinned to the upper bodice of her dress, waiting to be used. He looked at me then back at her, horrified. "Is it really that bad? Can't this wait until you can get me to the hospital?"

"No, it can't. We don't know when the streets will clear," I reasoned.

"And we don't know how soon you'll be seen once we get you there," Mrs. Aronowitz added, pouring more of the clear liquid into the glass, handing it to Kroyer. Her steady gaze demanded he drink it. Taking the glass, he knocked it back in one shot, furrowing his brow, curling his lips in disgust. "That, young man, is pure Russian Vodka! Not the watered down trash you get in these American clubs," she declared before placing the bite stick between his teeth. She unpinned the threaded needle from her dress. "Apologies," she stated, with the flatness of a hot Royal Crown Cola as she gathered together the bloody flaps of skin hanging from his head to begin her excruciating embroidery.

Kroyer whimpered like an abused pup as he chomped down on the stick, holding tightly to my hand.

* * * *

The three of us and Dusty remained holed up for two days in my apartment with me sneaking down periodically to Mrs. Aronowitz's place to get ingredients for Russian Tea, Borscht, Stroganoff, or whatever Russian fare she thought would be crucial to Kroyer getting his strength back.

She applied lemongrass compresses, and sage balms to his head and ribs, for those two days as well, while we held a collective breath. If he could move after two days, the ribs were bruised, but if he couldn't, then they were broken, and we'd have to take him to the hospital. Kroyer turned out to be very lucky. He still had to move gingerly and apply salve every four hours until they were healed, but at least he could remain in my apartment.

Even after he bathed his odor permeated throughout my little flat those first few days as I prayed Mrs. Aronowitz and I wouldn't choke on the stench. At least we were on the third floor, making us high enough that we didn't have to worry about anyone trying to crawl through the windows when we opened them. I borrowed a straight razor and other toiletries from a male tenant. After Kroyer had bathed, he left a ring in my tub so dark I thought I would never be able to get rid of it! I shaved him, cut his hair, cleaned behind his ears, and under his nails.

When the streets were cleared, and her windows were boarded up until they could be fixed properly, Mrs. Aronowitz and Dusty went back downstairs to their apartment where she found some of her husband's old clothes she had yet to take to the Salvation Army. Kroyer was grateful for a clean change in garments. They were a little loose, but he didn't care because it had been ages since he'd worn anything fresh. He was grateful for the couch too.

I told Mrs. Aronowitz he would have to stay with me because apparently, he had no other place to go. She told me unlike a tenement house, an apartment was a private residence. As long as I continued to pay the rent on time, it was none of her business who stayed with me.

I had to get used to living with someone once again after being on my own for so long. It astonished me that I was taking care of someone, as opposed to being taken care of! I'd never had anyone dependent on me to cook his meals, expected me to sew buttons on his clothes, or needed me to listen to him talk.

While the Apollo was temporarily closed for renovations due to the riot, I managed to find a gig dancing as a showgirl at The Pink Easy, a night club in mid-town.

That first night we were alone, and I'd come home from performing, I found Kroyer wide awake, looking for me. It was late, and I was tired, but I realized he'd been by himself most of the day. Mrs. Aronowitz told me she would make him dinner so I wouldn't have to worry about cooking for him before I went to the club that evening.

"Hello," I said as I entered.

"Hello. Do you always come home so late from work," he said. It annoyed me that he felt I had to answer to him as to when I arrived home, but I kept my tongue.

"Actually, yes I do. Unlike your brother, I see you're not familiar with the hours of a night club performer."

"No, I can't say that I am," I noticed his eyes looked glassy while he spoke.

I went to the kitchen to warm up the tea kettle and get the tea set. When I came back, I placed the tray on the coffee table and sat down in the easy chair while he remained on the couch. I could feel he wanted to talk but did not know how or where to begin. I, on the other hand, knew the perfect segue, "how long have you been in Harlem?"

He closed his eyes as though he were searching for the answer somewhere behind his lids, "I don't know. It might have been the fall of 1934. I guess I lost track of time living out on the street." Well, I could certainly relate. After living in that flophouse when I was released from the hospital, the days and nights blended together in a mishmash that was impossible to sort out and process.

"Why were you at the brownstone," I asked pointedly. He started crying. I didn't know what to do except watch. The last time a man cried like this in front of me it was Josiah… Goodness, was I ever more surprised at all the memories, having this man in my presence, conjured to the forefront of my brain!

I found a handkerchief, gave it to him, waited until he managed to regain his composure. He wiped his eyes, sobbed, sniffled before he began to talk. "I had a… Chinese girl, I used to visit in Chinatown, down around Mott Street…" he started crying again.

I remembered him and Peter exchanging words about her years ago in Mrs. Spears' parlor, but I pretended it was the first I'd heard about it. He continued, with a smile on his lips, reminiscing, "I used to have Avery drive me there several evenings a week. She'd sneak down the fire escape of her building, get into the car, and Avery would drive us to Washington Square Park. We'd sit there on our bench, talking, kissing, holding each other, sometimes until as late as when the sky would turn orange in the east. We always looked toward the east because she said it brought her closer to her ancestors and family from her homeland." His voice cracked with emotion, but he continued, "We did this for close to two years until one night she didn't come down to me. Instead, a young man came out, may have been her oldest brother. He strode toward the car as if he wanted my blood," he stopped to breathe momentarily, his eyes damp. "He told me Mai Ling was sent back to China, and I'd never see her again. He added that if I attempted to come back, he and the rest of her brothers would love to meet me! To enforce the threat, he took some metal, star-shaped weapon from the sleeve of his shirt, and flung it at the car. It shattered the glass on the passenger side and scared Avery and me to death. I got in the car like a coward. Thank God the street was empty. Avery almost destroyed the rubber on the tires getting me home."

I didn't speak right away because I knew there had to be more to the story, "so you ended up in Harlem because your China Doll's brother threatened you?"

He shook his head, "No, but that incident started a domino effect. I was a mess after that. I couldn't eat. I'd sleep all day and sit up all night. My parents were angry with me for refusing at the last minute to take Doris Merrill to some stupid debutante ball; and I refused to escort anyone else to those frivolous parties after that. Had they known about Mai Ling they would have disowned me too.

"One night they had a dinner party and invited some silly girl of wealthy parentage, expecting me to entertain her. I not only told them I wasn't interested, I told them I was better off finding a wife on my own than settling for the incompetent, soft-headed dames they'd brought to the house to meet me." He rolled his eyes, biting into a tea biscuit.

I shook my head in disbelief because I couldn't imagine having the temerity to speak to my parents in such a tone, then I took a sip of my tea to keep from laughing outright. "What did they do after you … voiced your opinion?"

"I don't know," he laughed at himself before going on, "I ran up to my room, threw a few of my things in a satchel. Avery was no longer working for my family by this time. That evening I took a cab up to the brownstone. I got out of the car and was in for a heart-sinking surprise. When did it burn down?"

I felt my own eyes getting misty. "Back in January of 1932."

"The neighbors told me you were the only one who lived," he said. I nodded my head, and before I could stop my face crumbled, tears rolling down my cheeks.

It was his turn to get me one of his handkerchiefs. We sat across from each other, crying over the same things and different things. It was awkward, but comforting too. I don't know how long we sat there before I went to my bedroom for the evening.

* * * *

The next morning I fixed him a breakfast of eggs, beef sausage, and biscuits. "What are those things," he asked, looking at the biscuits with curiosity. I smiled, "They're called biscuits, and your brother loves them, I might add!" I put a little bit of butter and jelly on half of one as he looked on. I set it on his plate. "Try it," I said.

He looked at it with a raised brow. When he bit into it, his eyes lit up, "Mmm… Peder used to eat these?"

"Well, they tasted better when Mrs. Spears baked them," I smiled at the fond memory.

"This is better than a Danish pastry," he was about to pick up the second half.

"Whoa! Put that down and eat the eggs and sausage next," I laughed. I poured each of us a cup of coffee, and we ate in silence for a while.

He leaned back in his chair, looking at me, before asking, "What were the circumstances?"

"I beg your pardon," I didn't know what he was referring to.

"The 'circumstances beyond' your 'control' that were preventing you from seeing your sister." He took a sip of his coffee before continuing, "I was almost sorry when Peder came into the parlor and interrupted you that evening. Remember?" I nodded my head, surprised he recalled such an isolated incident. "Well? If it's a long story, I've got time," he said in expectation.

I thought about it for another minute, deciding whether or not tell him. Coming to the conclusion that the distance from our siblings would cause both of us to need some sort of therapy, I began, "The reason I left my hometown of Spivey's Grove, South Carolina is because had I stayed my parents would have made me marry a bootlegger. I was 16 at the time. My younger sister told me their intentions one night when the man was at our house for dinner. I'd been planning to come here anyway, so I just decided to make the move a little sooner than I anticipated. I sent Lily, my sister, a letter telling her I'd arrived here. She wrote me back, letting me know the man paid our father for me, so Daddy, refusing to give the money back, made Lily marry him in my stead. She was 14 at the time, and the bootlegger was 49."

When I finished, Kroyer was staring at me with his mouth open. "So, am I the most horrible person you've ever met?"

He shook his head in answer to my question, then said, "I'll do you one better." He closed his eyes a moment, as though summoning the strength to speak, then opened them before going further, "That night Peder took Tessie to Perth Amboy for dinner, I told our father. He called the restaurant. That's how the owner knew Tessie was colored."

I shook my head, speechless, upon hearing this revelation! However, I was in no position to judge Kroyer. His decision to tell their father about the dinner cost Peter six months of jail time and prompted him to leave the country, while my decision to flee to New York put my sister in a frightful marriage. Either way, due to our selfish choices, we were both miles away from our siblings, and hurting over it. There was no need to fuss at him.

I asked, "Have you spoken to Peter?" When he shook his head, I could tell he was on the verge of tears. "Well, I've heard from Tessie several times since they left for France."

Kroyer's blue eyes brightened, "How are they?"

"He changed the spelling, not the pronunciation, of his name to P-e-t-e-r S-c-o-g-g-i-n-s."

One corner of Kroyer's lips curled slightly, showing his approval, "What else?" He sounded excited, encouraging me to continue.

"After that he found your family in Denmark. He and Tessie got married…"

"They're married now?"

"Yes, and apparently a bunch of your long lost cousins from the Netherlands attended the wedding. He has a pastry business, and she owns a dance school." I hadn't seen Kroyer smile before today. "Why didn't you keep in touch with Peter after he left?"

"I fell on hard times, lost the post office box, and my money," he looked depressed again before asking, "Do you know how your sister's doing?"

"No, I don't. But I'll get back in touch with her when the time is right."

"What's stopping you now?"

"That I can't go into, but I'll see about her soon." I could tell he wanted to ask more questions but thought he should stop while he was ahead.

I changed the subject, "I know how you ended up in front of the brownstone, but what made you stay there?"

He scratched his head where Mrs. Aronowitz stitched his wounds, then said, "That first night, after I got out of the cab, I slept on the steps. When I woke up, I found my satchel had been stolen. What little money I had was in it," he shook his head at his carelessness before continuing. "My brother loved it there. He said Mrs. Spears' brownstone was the warmest house he'd ever experienced. According to Peter, there was true and genuine love in that place, which is why he visited so much. This was before he went to jail, of course.

"I felt what he was talking about the night I came to see him, despite you and Mrs. Spears seeing me as the enemy. It made me jealous he'd found a place of refuge whenever life in Washington Square got superficial. Peter loved everyone in that house.

"After my altercation with my parents, I went there planning to beg Mrs. Spears' permission to stay. When I found just the foundation, the neighbors told me only you survived. They must have gotten used to seeing me sitting there because one morning I woke and found a coat thrown over me. Another time I found a blanket. Sometimes they gave me these little pies that had meat or fruit baked inside of them. I think they called them…" and we said in unison, "Hobo pies!" We both laughed a little. It was nice to know someone in the neighborhood continued to give those out after Mrs. Spears and I were gone.

Kroyer continued his story, "There were times when I managed to find a penny or two on the street, and I'd go to a soup kitchen or a bread line. Anyone else would have gone back to Washington Square, begging forgiveness, but I'd no desire to be back there, no matter the cost. I know it sounds foolish, but I stayed hoping you would somehow come back for whatever reason. Peter was right about that place. Where there is true and genuine love, there is also safety. That day, you came just in time to save my life." His voice never cracked, but there were tears streaming down his cheeks.

By the time he was done, I had my mind made up, "And I'm going to save your life again! I'm sending Peter and Tessie a telegram to let them know you're here."

* * * *

I sent Tessie and Peter the telegram in regards to my perils with Kroyer later in the day. I heard from them within two days instructing me to get Kroyer a passport while he was recovering from his injuries. Peter further advised as soon as Kroyer was well enough to travel, to let him know so he could send a boarding ticket for the Queen Elizabeth in a timely fashion. The tone of the telegram, despite all the 'stops' was one of excitement! It felt like Peter had been praying for years he would hear from his brother.

Sometime during the middle of May, a doctor friend of Mrs. Aronowitz made a house call. With the black eyes gone, and the bruised ribs healed, he determined Kroyer was well enough to travel. He even commended Mrs. Aronowitz on her skill at stitching Kroyer's head, saying "this couldn't have been a more effective job had I done it myself."

I sent Peter another telegram informing him of Kroyer's clean bill of health and the arrival of his passport. Just as he said, Peter sent a boarding pass for the Queen Elizabeth within a week. Kroyer was scheduled to leave the following week from Pier 72.

On his departure day, Mrs. Aronowitz and I escorted Kroyer downtown with mixed feelings of joy and melancholy. While we were happy he was going to be reunited with his older brother, we were sad to see him go. However, we understood there was nothing for him here in New York. He had absolved his relationship with the Skaagens family of his own volition, and all he knew was the pastry business. Once he arrived in France, he would be going into business with Peter, changing the spelling of his last name, more than likely, and getting to know his long-lost relatives in Denmark, as well as Tessie.

It was a triumphant occasion watching him board the ship. We waved to him from the dock with tears of joy in our eyes. It did wonders for my heart to be the catalyst for helping others, especially a pair of siblings, reconnect after an involuntary estrangement. It felt like atonement, forgiveness, for the mistakes I made with Lily would come shortly.

Chapter 39

The year 1935 also marked the time when crime boss
Dutch Schultz, as well as other members of the underworld
elite, was tried for tax evasion by federal prosecutor
Thomas Dewey, which facilitated a botched assassination
attempt on Dewey's life. Apparently, the national crime
syndicate was none too happy with Schultz for authorizing
the failed hit without their consent! As a result, on October
23, 1935, in Newark, New Jersey, while dining at the
Palace Chophouse, Dutch Schultz, along with three of his
henchman, was shot by members of the infamous Murder,
Inc.

But the talk of Harlem was how Madame St. Claire
sent Schultz a telegram to his hospital deathbed stating, "As
ye sow, so shall ye reap," on behalf of herself and all the
uptown numbers runners. Her right-hand man, Bumpy
Johnson, ended up negotiating with Lucky Luciano that
proceeds from the Harlem policy rackets would remain
with the numbers runners as long as the taxes were paid.
The deal made Bumpy Johnson the King of the Harlem
Underworld, and the Italian crime families made up for
profits lost due to the end of prohibition.

* * * *

"Nostalgia, a telegram came for you this morning,"
said Mrs. Aronowitz as I was coming back into the building
from running some early morning errands. The thing I
hated most about receiving unannounced telegrams was
they were bound to be enclosed with bad news. My
stomach did a somersault sending the rest of my insides

crash landing to bottomless depths as I took the envelope from her.

Noticing my wariness, she offered to let me sit down in her apartment while she made me a spot of tea. I decided to take advantage of her kindness. As soon as I entered, taking a seat on the couch, Dusty hopped into my lap, smiling like he always did. I looked at the outside of the envelope before I opened it. It looked to be sent from right here in town! The last thing I needed was for Arnie to know I was here. What would I do if this was one of his threats after I'd done all I could to stay as far away from Lenox Avenue as possible? I took a deep breath, reasoning with myself that I hadn't played any numbers, drank any hooch, or communicated with anyone from the club since that vile night the brownstone was burned. He really had no way of knowing I was still in New York, not that he would have cared anyway, as long as I kept a low profile. Deciding it was best to get it over with, I tore into the telegram with no regard to keeping the envelope neat. It was from Mitzi!

Nostalgia stop

I just wanted to let you know that The Duke Ellington Orchestra will be performing this weekend at The Stork Club Stop

Would you like to meet Bunky and me afterward Stop

It would be wonderful to see you again Stop

Mitzi Stop

I smiled, relieved it wasn't from Arnie, and ecstatic to hear my best friend was in town! Mrs. Aronowitz came into the sitting room with the tea set just in time to see me jump up to run down to Western Union. "It's good news, Mrs.

Aronowitz, but I have to respond right away. I'll be back before the tea gets cold!" I promised. I made a speedy exit, leaving a pleasantly surprised Mrs. Aronowitz with a slight smile on her lips.

I wrote Mitzi back saying I would love to see her, but I'd no intention of meeting her where I might run into Josiah. I asked her to meet me Sunday afternoon at my apartment for dinner instead. I also suggested she call me because continuing to send telegrams was bound to get expensive. "Hello," hoping it was Mitzi, I answered on the first ring.

"Well, hello, Lady! What you know good?" Hearing her voice after all those years gave me amnesia for all the nightmarish experiences I'd gone through since I'd seen her last! I started crying, tears of joy.

"I know I need to see you soon! Can you come for dinner tomorrow evening after the matinee? I know it won't be Mrs. Spears' cooking, but it will just have to do."

At the mention of her name we were both silent before Mitzi said, "I'm looking forward to seeing you, Nostalgia. I'm sure whatever you make tomorrow will be fine. Should I bring Bunky, or did you want it to be just us girls?"

"Thanks for asking. I want it to be just us. How long will you be in town?"

"For about a month. The Duke is cutting a record, so they'll be in the recording studio for rehearsal before actually making the final cuts. You know The Duke is ever the perfectionist."

"Yes, I remember. Well, I have to go get ready for The Apollo. I'll see you tomorrow night. Tell Bunky, hello and I'll see him later."

"Okay. Nostalgia, how did you…" Mitzi suddenly stopped.

"How did I what?"

"Oh, never mind. I'll talk to you tomorrow."

"I look forward to it." I said, still wondering what she wanted to ask me. Whatever it was, I figured she thought it best to wait until we were face to face.

* * * *

Sunday afternoon, as soon as the matinee wrapped up at The Apollo, I rushed home to put the finishing touches on the chicken I left slow-roasting in the oven that morning. In addition to the bird, I baked biscuits, steamed red potatoes and string beans, and for dessert: carrot cake.

I glanced around the apartment one last time before letting Mitzi in. I opened the door, and we screamed, hugged, cried! She looked even more beautiful than the last time I'd seen her. I could tell by the bun at the nape of her neck her hair had grown quite a bit. Her skin was golden-caramel, flawless. Her brows were plucked into catlike arches, emphasizing the height of her cheekbones, making her eyes look bigger, especially since the lashes were graced with several coats of mascara. Her suit was a long blue jacket cinched at the waist complimented by a pair of wide-legged pants. Leave it to Coco Chanel to make a woman look feminine despite wearing trousers! I felt as though my slim, mid-calf length skirt and frilly blouse looked dowdy and old-fashioned by comparison. "You look beautiful," I said.

"As do you!" She hugged me again before looking around the apartment. "Look at this place! You've been here ever since the …" she stopped, not wanting to talk about the fire.

I picked up quickly, "Yes."

She nodded, smiling through the mist glazing her eyeballs. She looked relieved to find something else to talk about when she saw my certificate from The Martha Graham School of Contemporary Dance hanging on the wall. "Look at that frame! I am so proud of you!"

"It wasn't easy, I'll tell you that. I happened to remember everything you and Tessie made me do to prepare for The Cotton Club audition, and I took it from there." We stood looking at each other for a few more moments. "Are you hungry?" I asked.

"Famished," she said, as we made our way to the kitchen.

Over dinner, Mitzi told me all about Europe. The elaborate architecture, the rich food, and the glamorous fashions made France the epitome of decadence, while England, on the other hand, was stodgy, ancient, and gray. The one thing both countries did have in common was that coloreds weren't treated as second class citizens, making the return to the states especially difficult.

Our memories of Mrs. Spears, Mr. Greer, and the married couples ricocheted between knee-slapping laughter and heart-wrenching tears. Those dinners on Sunday and

Monday evenings would always be nestled fondly in our hearts.

Finally, Mitzi asked me, "How did you end up leaving The Cotton Club?" I knew it was coming, but it was hard to answer nonetheless. There was no other way to deal with the question but head on.

"I walked out of The Basement one evening to hail myself a cab. A black car stopped for me. Someone came from behind, put a hood over my head, and pushed me into the back seat. They took me for a long drive." Mitzi sat hypnotized while I spoke. I breathed deeply, finding the strength to continue, "When they finally took the hood off my head, I found myself in Arnie's cell at Sing Sing." Mitzi let out a small cry. "He didn't rape me, but he beat me up when I refused to give him what he wanted. He owned up to what happened to Geraldine Crocker…"

"He what?"

"Yeah, he admitted to beating her. He'd gotten her pregnant, and when she refused to disappear, he…"

"Stop! I don't need to hear it anymore! You got out..."

"Yeah, I got out alright, in time to see the brownstone in flames when his goons took me back to Harlem," I sobbed.

Mitzi looked puzzled until understanding widened her eyes, "Arnie had the brownstone set on fire?"

I nodded as the tears streamed down my face, leaving droplets on my blouse. I didn't try to stop them. Mitzi found a handkerchief for me and held me while I cried.

* * * *

The month Mitzi and Bunky came to town was one of utter joy! The three of us had dinner in my apartment on Sunday and Monday evenings. It was so good to have company once again. During the week in the mornings and afternoons, while Bunky was in the recording studio with The Duke, and if the dance troupe wasn't practicing in a rented space downtown, Mitzi and I would go out for lunch, or shopping to get my wardrobe more up to date.

The first time she picked out a pair of pants for me to try on I was skeptical, but once I slid them over my thighs and hips, I was captivated at how they enhanced my figure by making my hips appear straighter, while the cinch in the jacket added emphasis to my waistline. I was so excited I bought four pant suits! When I walked down the street, I couldn't help but strut. They were so comfortable, too. I was convinced, that Coco Chanel was a genius!

One day after coming home from meeting Mitzi for a stroll in one of the parks overlooking the Hudson, a scent I hadn't smelled in years wafted into my nostrils upon opening the door to the building. I found myself remembering the first time I smelled Knize Ten Cologne. Surely it was a coincidence, I thought until Mrs. Aronowitz intercepted me in the hallway.

"I thought that was you," she smiled, "you have a visitor!"

I followed her into her apartment to find myself facing Josiah James.

Chapter 40

He didn't even wait for Dusty to hop out of his lap before he stood to his feet. All we could do was stare at each other. His skin was still black, accentuating the whiteness of his teeth. However, he'd grown a mustache that was very becoming. His gray flannel suit and purple tie made him look distinguished. It was no mistake life in Europe had agreed with him. Mrs. Aronowitz cleared her throat, breaking the awkward silence, "It seems you two have some talking to do. Dusty and I will be in the kitchen making tea." She picked up the ever-smiling Dusty and headed toward the kitchen.

"Nice pants," he said.

"Nice mustache," I replied. Part of me wanted to be intertwined in his arms, while another part of me wished he were still in Europe, or anywhere else I wasn't. "So Mitzi told you how to find me?"

"No, Bunky did the honors."

"Same difference. Why are you here?" I'd worked so hard to get over him I found myself resenting his presence.

"I know you went through a lot after we left. I wanted to see if you were alright, but you seem angry I came by."

"Quite frankly, I am. I heard about you and Josephine Baker…"

"That was nothing but a bit of messin' around!"

"Well, that 'bit of messin' around' was enough to make me get over you!"

"Is that what you call Charles Sherman? As if he could make you forget about me! I heard you weren't even at his funeral."

"His what? Charles Sherman is dead?"

"Yeah. Back in February of 1932, maybe? They found him in the alley behind The Basement beaten to death."

"What? Did he owe anybody money?"

"I don't think so. I heard he was jelly rolling one of the Ziegfeld Girls. Arnie found out about it and put a hit on him," Josiah observed my reaction to hearing the news.

It obviously happened after they took me to Sing Sing. On the way back to Harlem after that dreadful episode in Arnie's cell, I vaguely recalled a conversation about him wanting to "teach Cab's band members a lesson" about sucking up to the Ziegfeld Girls! Apparently, they'd created an example using Charles Sherman. I found myself even more curious, "What happened to Marnie?"

"Who?" Josiah gave me a blank stare.

"The Ziegfeld Girl Charles was…"

"Oh! She lost the gig. Word is she's now a cigarette girl in one of the clubs around Atlantic City."

"A cigarette girl? In New Jersey? Goodness, that's a fall from grace."

Josiah nodded, agreeing with me. We silently looked at each other again before he said, "You are so beautiful."

"I've also moved on with my life!"

"I heard. The Martha Graham School of Contemporary Dance, The Apollo, the apartment. You've done well for yourself."

"Well, I'm glad you know! Now whatever you came to say, say it and get out, because I've gotta keep livin'." Josiah looked surprised, but I couldn't help but be blunt. He was interrupting my existence, and I had no time for distractions.

"Say what I want and go?"

"Yes, please," I shouted, "and get the he…" but before I could finish he grabbed me, placing his mouth over mine. I tried to push him away, but the part of me that missed him wouldn't grant strength to the part of me that desired to resist him. When he loosened his grip from around my waist, I escaped to the other side of the room.

"I wanted you to know I'm not planning to go back to England after the record is cut. Lionel Hampton is still the house band for The Cotton Club in Culver City. This time I'm going." He took the ring box out of his pocket, the same one from the last night we were at the Seligman Fountain! "You have some thinking to do," he said, placing it on the coffee table, and just like that he was gone.

Mrs. Aronowitz came out of the kitchen with the tea set. Looking around perplexed, she asked, "Where is the gentleman?"

"He had to leave abruptly," was all I could muster.

"What is this," she asked, taking the ring box off the coffee table. She opened it, gasping, "He asked you to marry him? Well, what did you say?" Mrs. Aronowitz seemed more excited than I was.

"He didn't ask me to marry him. He told me I had some thinking to do." Now I was confused. I could have sworn I was over Josiah James! I had planned to never have anything to do with another man. As for my career, my next endeavor was to audition for a dance company that would be performing outside of the United States.

As selfish as it may sound, I enjoyed taking care of me. I realized it the night Kroyer had gotten snippy with me about coming home late from The Pink Easy. I enjoyed relaxing in my quiet abode after a night of entertaining. It suited me just fine to leave dishes in the sink for a few days before I was ready to wash them. On a hot night in the summer after leaving the theater, it did wonders for my spirit to get out of the tub to walk around naked, drip-drying to cool off.

"Think about what," Mrs. Aronowitz advocated for Josiah. "Did you get a look at this ring?"

"Yes, Ma'am, I've seen it," I insisted.

When she realized I was annoyed she looked at me, shaking her head, "I can see you two have a history, but if I were you I wouldn't let it reduce my chances of having a future. You've got plenty of time to live by yourself in an apartment. After a long happy marriage, and he's made you a widow! Trust me, I know from experience." Mrs. Aronowitz sat down on the sofa to pour us each a spot of tea.

* * * *

Three days later my phone rang, and I don't know how, but I knew it was Josiah before I touched the receiver. "Hello?" I tried to sound calm, but my voice cracked involuntarily.

"Are you done thinking? The Duke finished in the recording studio today. The band is going back to England in a couple of days, and I'm going to Culver City as soon as I buy a car and a copy of *The Negro Motorist's Green Book*," he couldn't have been more abrupt!

"Slow down. May I ask you a question?"

"Okay."

"Have you forgiven me for not telling you I was pregnant, and killing your baby?"

"I wouldn't have come to see you if I hadn't. Every time I decided I was going to throw that ring away I couldn't do it. I missed you so much over the years. I'm not going to lie to you and say that Josephine Baker was the only one, because she wasn't. I've had my women, I've had my fun, and you're the only one I remember."

"So I don't have to worry about you bringing that up the next time we have a fight? If we're going to get married you know we're going to fight every now and then." I was bound and determined not to be my spineless mother if I ever married.

"I'll never bring it up again. You were young then. You didn't know how I would react because you knew I wanted to go to Europe. Just promise me you'll never do it again."

"I promise."

"Good! You and I need to go downtown to get the marriage license tomorrow morning. I'll be there to get you at seven!"

"Alright," I was on cloud nine.

"I love you, Nostalgia!"

"I love you too, Josiah." After I had hung up the phone, I took the ring out of the box, and placed it on my finger!

* * * *

The following evening Mitzi spent the night with me, so she and Mrs. Aronowitz could escort me the next morning to the municipal building downtown where we met Bunky and Josiah.

We knew Mrs. Spears would not have approved of Josiah and me marrying in front of a judge, but we had no time for anything elaborate. Bunky and Mitzi were going back to England with The Duke in another day, plus Josiah wasn't sure how long it would take us to get to California.

In addition to Mrs. Aronowitz serving as a witness, the boys in the band, as well as the Cotton Club Showgirls, were also there. Bunky and Mitzi served as best man and matron of honor respectively. The ceremony only lasted fifteen minutes, but that was all Josiah and I needed after being separated four years.

After the nuptials, we took a car back to Harlem for a chicken and waffles brunch at one of the restaurants on 125th and Broadway. The boys in the band, the showgirls, and Mrs. Aronowitz had crowded the establishment to the extent that anyone who wasn't celebrating our wedding was not allowed to enter. We gladly paid extra for the privilege.

When Josiah and I got back to my apartment we received a telegram of congratulations from the Scoggins family of Paris, France, wishing they could have attended.

After seeing Bunky, Mitzi, and the rest of The Duke's entourage off the next morning, Josiah took me to the post office to clean out Mrs. Spears' safety deposit box, then back to the apartment to help me pack. California here we come!

I will admit I was a little melancholy about having to leave the apartment at Riverside Drive, and the Apollo Dance Troupe, but Mrs. Aronowitz was right, I couldn't let Josiah get away again.

The car he bought was a 1931 Packard for the long drive out west. However, he insisted before we head toward the Pacific Coast, I tie some loose ends. We ventured down south to Spivey's Grove to see my family! I was scared, but I knew he was right.

Before we departed New York, I called Mrs. Barden to let her know I was on my way back for a visit. She was anxious to inform me Lily no longer worked for her because she'd married Henry, and they owned TWO mercantile establishments! One was outside the city limits, while the other, formally owned by Mr. Chavis, was in the middle of town. My little sister was a proprietor!

Mrs. Barden went on to say Noah Holdtstaff had gone to prison years ago, but died thereafter of a mysterious illness. She wrapped up our conversation by saying, "You see! I told you you'd be glad you kept in touch with Lily."

It wasn't Lily I was worried about. What would I say to my parents? Would they even be interested in seeing me after the way I left? It was a question I would soon see answered, I thought as we traveled south on the US 1 Highway. I marveled at the difference in travel mode this time: no crowded buses, no stops I wasn't interested in making, and no Mrs. Spears. This time it was me in the comfort of a plush vehicle, sporting a Coco Chanel pantsuit and a fur coat, with my husband's hand on my thigh. My, how it had all changed!

I wasn't a little girl running away from a life I would never be able to control. I was a woman who'd lived on her own, performed with some of the most talented people in the world, found true love, lost it because of foolish choices, and found it once again. I'd survived a bank run in the financial district in New York City, stood toe-to-toe with a hardened criminal and lived to tell about it, buried people who thought the world of me, nursed someone back to health after a race riot, swore up and down by my own standards I was defeated, and found I still had much living and giving to do as a woman and an artist.

No, I decided, there was no reason for me to be ashamed of who I'd become when I looked my father and mother in the eye for the first time in eight years. I was a woman who'd chosen to live her life on her own terms, and I'd won!

When I saw them, I'd be neither haughty nor embarrassed. I'd be respectful of them giving me life, and raising me for 16 years. But if they were adamant about not wanting to see me, or persisted in continuing to see me as a daughter they'd lost, then I could live with that. I still had Lily, Josiah, Tessie, and Mitzi. I'd been a dancer at the world famous Cotton Club as well as The Apollo Theater. I'd earned a certificate from The Martha Graham School of Contemporary Dance. I had the credentials and the means to establish my own dance school once I got to California. I was also married to a man of my choice, whom I loved dearly. This time when I traveled to a place I knew nothing about I would not be alone, and I would also have a plan. I felt prepared to face whatever I encountered in Spivey's Grove, South Carolina, as well as in Culver City, California.

THE END

Afterword

Cotton Club Princess is a work of fiction that was on my heart for nearly two decades before I began putting it on the page. Using the Harlem Renaissance and the Great Depression as backdrops, *Cotton Club Princess* spans the years 1928-1935. As the author, I feel the need to make clear what is fact, and what is purely my imagination.

The town of Spivey's Grove, South Carolina, for example, came to fruition when I found out about another novel set in my hometown of Roxboro, North Carolina during the 1920s, that was published three years before I started writing. Spivey comes from Spivey's Corner, North Carolina, famous for the National Hollerin' Contest, while Grove pays homage to Walnut Grove, the hamlet in which The Little House on the Prairie series by Laura Ingalls Wilder is set.

Also in the novel, The Empire Savings and Loan of New York is positioned at 48 Wall Street where the first branch of the Bank of New York still stands to this day. The fundamental difference between the fictional Empire Savings and Loan of New York, and the real Bank of New York is that in the novel the financial institution succumbs to the Stock Market Crash of 1929, otherwise known as Black Tuesday. As a result, the bank closes in the wake of a bank run, and remains out of operation for months while the characters scrape by on winnings from the Harlem numbers rackets, manipulating the gas and water flow under the nose of The New York Edison Company, and bartering goods and services from their neighbors on Striver's Row.

The real Bank of New York, however, is one of the few banks in US history to have remained open in spite of the dire events surrounding October 29, 1929, and to this day has never closed! While a frantic crowd did gather in the Wall Street area upon the crash, which happened that morning at the opening bell, I could not find documentation that any type of violent confrontation ensued between the crowd and the police, like in the novel, and certainly not anywhere near 48 Wall Street.

Another product of my imagination is the events that took place at The Basement. As written in the novel and in real life, the basement was across the street from the Cotton Club at 646 Lenox Ave. I know the basement served as a place for the performers to get a bite to eat between sets. As far as serving as a place where the performers fraternized, or held get-togethers after performing has not been confirmed. In the novel, The Basement serves as the main gathering place where members of the Duke Ellington Orchestra, and later Cab Calloway's band, meet and socialize with the Cotton Club Showgirls, as well as other well-known colored performers who were barred from fraternizing with the white patrons. Furthermore, in the novel, The Basement later serves as a dressing room for the Cotton Club Showgirls when club owner, Arnie O'Neil, agrees to give performance dates to the girls of the Ziegfeld Follies. While there is documentation that Duke Ellington performed with the Ziegfeld Follies at the Ziegfeld Theater in Manhattan's Theater District, I found none that the

Follies ever performed at the Cotton Club, or in any other venue uptown.

The relationship between Cotton Club Girl Tessie Jefferson, and wealthy white socialite Peder Skaagens, is for the sake of the novel, in that I could find no documentation that any Cotton Club Showgirl ever dated a club patron.

I could find no documentation that Lionel Hampton ever served as bandleader at the Cotton Club in Culver City, California. He did, however, perform there as a drummer for the Les Hite Orchestra, before organizing his own band in 1934. While they may have performed at the Cotton Club in Culver City as a guest act, I can find no documentation stating that they were at any time the house band.

The Negro Motorist's Green Book, a book mentioned by Josiah in the last chapter of the novel, was first published in 1936 to assist colored people when traveling across the country to keep them safe from towns hostile to non-white members of society. I took dramatic license in mentioning the book because in the novel, when Josiah and Nostalgia begin the journey to Spivey's Grove, it is December of 1935.

Finally, the character Arnie O'Neil is based on the actual owner of The Cotton Club, Owney Madden. While Big Richie is based on Madden's main henchman, Big Frenchie. The reason I changed these name is because they are the only historical figures in the novel who exchange words with the heroine. While Duke Ellington, Cab Calloway, Langston Hughes, Josephine Baker, and the like are all mentioned by the main characters, they never engage in conversations with them.

Arnie O'Neil and Big Richie, on the other hand, not only acknowledge Nostalgia, the main character, but are suspected of facilitating a series of mysterious disappearances of several Cotton Club dancers. The Cotton Club did close shortly during the year 1925 for selling liquor, and not because a showgirl went missing, or was murdered, as was indicated in the novel. I feel the need to stress that to my knowledge no Cotton Club Showgirl has ever disappeared under questionable circumstances, and most certainly not at the authorization of Owney Madden, or at the hand of Big Frenchie, as this too is another figment of my imagination that I had the pleasure of including in this, my first novel.

KMD

January 8, 2016

Acknowledgments

First giving all honor and all glory to God Almighty, the original author and finisher of every book, novel, and story ever written. Without you, Lord, the discipline, creativity, eloquence, and plot needed to be a writer could not have been attained, ergo I "write, for these words are faithful and true"! (Revelation 21:5) God, you are truly great!

To my wonderful husband, Taylor Kipling Diggs, who encouraged me continually to never stop writing.

To Joan Daniel Whitlock, I appreciate you believing in this project upon hearing about it years before the first word hit the page.

To my cousin, author and playwright, Calvin Ramsey: Thank you for making me aware that *The Negro Motorist's Green Book* existed.

To my cousin Sharlene Falls, thanks for your creative insight, and one day we will work together.

Thank you so much, Barbara Terry, Danielle Vann, Carol McCrow, Elisabeth Pennella, and the rest of the staff at Waldorf Publishing: you guys rock!

Thank you, Janifer Wilson, owner and proprietor of Sisters Uptown Bookstore in Harlem, for giving a debut author a chance to shine.

To all the research assistants who helped me acquire a taste, a feel, and a smell for the Harlem of the 1920s and 30s, I truly appreciate you.

Finally, to Pastor James McCarroll of First Baptist Church, Castle Street, in Murfreesboro TN for the word that confirmed that this novel be written: It takes tenacity and audacity to see the promise!

About the Author

Gifted with a unique voice and free spirit, Karla Mitchell Diggs entered the world stage in 1971 in the city of Roxboro, N.C. where she was educated in the public schools of Person County.

After a high school career that included extensive participation in the Person Senior High School Drama Department, Karla took her talents to Meredith College in Raleigh, N.C. While there, she became the first African-American to pursue and earn a Bachelor of Arts in Theater. Karla furthered her education by attending the American Musical and Dramatic Academy in New York City, where she acquired a Certificate of Completion of the Integrated Program.

She has since performed in theatrical productions in New York City, Pennsylvania, Ohio, Virginia, and North Carolina.

Karla currently resides in Murfreesboro, Tennessee with her husband and two daughters where she continues to write. *Cotton Club Princess* is Karla's first novel.